I0574525

DOVES IN A TEMPEST

THE VALLEY OF HORROR

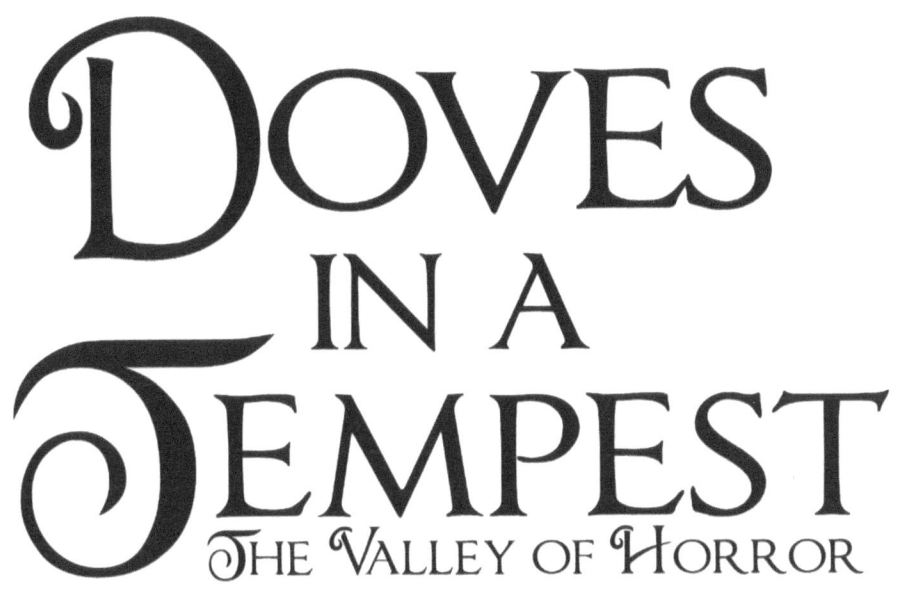

BILL SCHWEITZER

Black Rose Writing | Texas

©2023 by Bill Schweitzer
All rights reserved. No part of this book may be reproduced, stored in a retrieval system or transmitted in any form or by any means without the prior written permission of the publishers, except by a reviewer who may quote brief passages in a review to be printed in a newspaper, magazine or journal.

The author grants the final approval for this literary material.

First printing

This is a work of fiction. Names, characters, businesses, places, events, and incidents are either the products of the author's imagination or used in a fictitious manner. Any resemblance to actual persons, living or dead, or actual events is purely coincidental.

ISBN: 978-1-68513-160-9 (Paperback); 978-1-68513-261-3 (Hardcover)
PUBLISHED BY BLACK ROSE WRITING
www.blackrosewriting.com

Printed in the United States of America
Suggested Retail Price (SRP) $22.95 (Paperback); $27.95 (Hardcover)

Doves in a Tempest is printed in Calluna

*As a planet-friendly publisher, Black Rose Writing does its best to eliminate unnecessary waste to reduce paper usage and energy costs, while never compromising the reading experience. As a result, the final word count vs. page count may not meet common expectations.

PRAISE FOR
DOVES IN A TEMPEST

"...both a charming coming-of-age story, and a page-turning mystery."
                    –Carolyn Geduld, author of *The Struggle*

"*Doves in a Tempest* is an addicting and thoughtful novel. Equally a coming-of-age story and an irresistible mystery, the story provides a cast of characters who are, in a word, real. You'll be attached to each one as they adventure into an experience of immense magnitude.

Is it science-fiction? Is it a sinister government-fueled cabal? Schweitzer opens up all possibilities and will keep you engaged throughout. It's Schweitzer's unique voice that really shines though, as he eschews the halcyon days of nostalgia and replaces them with compassionate ruminations."
                    –Ryan Morgan Miller, author of *The Vain Curse*

"Move over, Stephen King!

In his novel "*Doves in a Tempest*" author Bill Schweitzer weaves a spooky psychological tale that begins on a summer night in the year 1958 in the Hill Country outside of Austin, Texas when five young friends on the restless verge of adolescence hike into the woods in search of an adventure. What befalls them that night is the first link in a chain of strange, frightening and inexplicable events, including odd, surreptitious activity in and around the labs of a chemical engineering company and a troubling number of hallucination cases arriving in the emergency room of a local hospital.

The story unfolds in a combination of narration and journal entries and has a "*Twilight Zone*" vibe that keeps the suspense high and the pages turning. And though the book is close to 300 pages long, when you (quickly) reach the last page you'll wish the story went on. But happily, a sequel to "*Doves in a Tempest*" is on the way!"
                    –Patti Liszkay, author of *Tropical Depression*

Into the tempest the wild doves flew,
unwitting and innocent, how little they knew.
As into that maelstrom of grief they spun,
ripped apart, rent asunder, no longer as one.
Storm-flung to where only eagles dare wing,
Too frail for such altitudes,
Too new for such things.
Life's harsh travails were unveiled to them there,
as unguided, untethered, they whirled thru that air.
Riding a squall's such a cruel way to fly,
and secrets uncovered there make dim third eyes cry.
Uncharted perils awaited them then,
Laid bare and in focus now, but not knowing when,
they'd unknot those mysteries outside their ken.

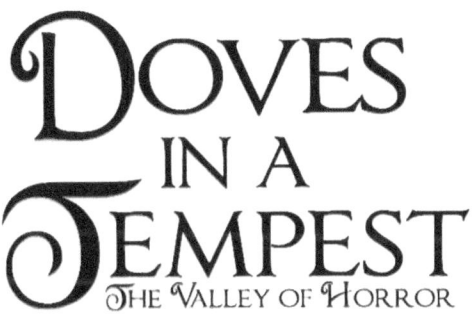

To Maggie, who puts up with me and goes above and beyond to care for me. Every one of the female heroes in this story has a strong dose of Maggie.

PROLOGUE

Those sweet summer days seemed to linger forever. You remember. In that time before cell phones, electronic games, and helicopter parenting, a garden hose was your water fountain, a bicycle your limousine, and you had to invent your own fun, using your own imagination. The books you checked out from the local library were printed on paper, with pages you actually had to turn, and smelled of musty adventure.

School was out, and thoughts of homework, tests, and boring classes were but faded images in a dust-moted album. Looking back, they wasted so much time during those endless summers. Or did they? Were they, in fact, hard at work; plowing new furrows into their fertile minds, nurturing the neurons that maintain such a fragile hold on our long-term recollections, and stirring sleepy synapses to sow new memories—of the feel of summer sun on bare shoulders, of those delicate feathers of icy cirrus clouds, spun out and crystallized across a pale June sky, of the crisp, acrid perfume of a new-mown lawn, and of the sounds of children's unrestrained laughter, with their sloppy grins and tousled hair? Most memories dim over time, but some, those most disturbing, will haunt the dreams of a certain five for the rest of their lives.

An unlikely group found one another that fated year. In that ephemeral moment, they were graced with a childlike innocence that brought with it fragile vulnerability, yet shielded them with an armor of naivety that made them game to confront life's most perilous unknowns. There would be many that summer—the unexplored provinces of selfhood laid bare; and those as yet unimagined ventures that would menace their very lives and sanity. That summer the fundament shifted beneath them and slipped away with a tectonic rumble. When they found that damn valley.

Chapter 1
By Way of Introduction

Sometimes shyness is simply reluctance to be bothered by the mundane.

June 6, 1958

We were feral children in those days. They called it the Baby Boom—when World War II G.I.'s returned home to the happy task of impregnating their wives and sweethearts, with all the youthful enthusiasm that long separation warranted. Little thought was given to child molesters, or other dangers, real or imagined, that haunt the dreams of modern parents. We <u>were</u> loved; and those dangers <u>did</u> exist, but they weren't reported with the ferocity and breathless fervor they provoke on today's twenty-four-hour news cycle. The boundaries of conduct our parents imposed were both lax and fluid. We ranged far and joyful, with little attention to time or distance, to explore whatever regions and activities were not limited by our legs and imaginations. This is a story of such children; the year is 1958...

Mrs. Dorothy Ashton, a tall, slender woman who smiled through horn-rimmed glasses, had shepherded the sixth graders that year, including Anna Belle Cook and James Hatcher, who occupied front row seats in her class. Jealous classmates whispered that acid-tongued Anna Belle was the teacher's pet; and truth be told, she was. Her essays were exceptional, if a bit rambling.

Dorothy Ashton looked forward to reading them, and discussing possible improvements with Anna Belle, who soaked up her suggestions like a little sponge, except for the one to cut back on the sarcasm and come more directly to the point. Serious James was too quiet and shy to attract much notice. His work, like Anna's, was remarkably error free, but his hand was rarely raised, even though he always knew the answers when Mrs. Ashton called on him.

In the room next door, the fifth graders answered to Miss Lillian Strawn, a pleasant-looking woman who seemed destined to go through life without a serious suitor—blissfully unaware that her lonely existence was due to breath that would melt the paint off the walls. Her students were of two inclinations, those who (behind her back, of course) called her "Fart Mouth," and those who chose the less audacious "Miss Stinky." It seemed there was no agreement whether fart was a curse word, and hence the dissension among her charges. The larger faction, of which "Little" Betty Lou Dupree (a mere soupçon of a girl) was a member, held the firm conviction that it was a cuss word; after all, it had four letters. The opposing group, numbering in the minority, were equally convinced that it was not. Oh, Stevie Lindquist, with his pale blue eyes magnified to absurd proportion by the thick lenses in his glasses, was willing to admit it might be a "semi-cussword," but that was <u>IT</u>.

One day when Miss Strawn made a short trip to the office to pick up some mimeographed test papers, Levi "Shrimp" Stieglitz took the opportunity to sneak a roll of Clorets breath mints onto her desk, hoping she would get the hint. The class members giggled; Levi was considered to be the class clown, and often used humor as a foil to compensate for his small stature. Little Betty, who thought Levi was just about the dreamiest thing ever, gasped in fear that he would get caught, while Levi's friend Stevie smirked and patted his back.

Sadly, Miss Strawn did not take the hint. She held up the roll of breath mints and asked who lost them. No one spoke. She asked again, growing a bit testy. Little Betty, terrified that this would somehow come back on Levi, raised her hand. "I found them on the playground Miss Strawn. You can just take them to the office for the lost and found the next time you go."

This last day of school, these five friends huddle at the back of the green-tiled lunchroom. "Puke green," they always say. When you barf up the cafeteria lunch, it blends in. Here in the back, they are away from the louder, roughhousing sorts. They are the ones chosen last for dodgeball, the ones who are teased, ridiculed or, at best, ignored. Before coming together, each of them preferred their own solitary company to that of others—their own rich mindscapes to the petty pursuits of the average child. Their ages ranged from nine to eleven, and they had little in common—except their social and physical awkwardness. They struggled to fit in, to make and keep friends.

Anna Belle sits in the middle, unconsciously taking the dominant seat. She's the freckled tomboy—clearly uncomfortable in her thrift-shop dress—the one with long careless braids in her ginger hair, wearing tattered sneakers on nervous feet. She exhibits exceptional toughness, both mental and physical, for a mere girl of eleven. A mishmash of adult seriousness, brash daring, and self-doubt, Anna perches precariously alight the threshold of adolescence. She does not suffer fools gladly. No, she cuts them no slack whatsoever. Glowing crimson undertones layer those remarkable eyes, and flame like a vermillion sunset when she glowers—in Little Betty's direction (most often), or toward anyone who pisses her off (a regrettably easy thing to do.)

Let's glance forward and sneak a peek in her journal, at the entry she made on the final day of that star-crossed summer:

Anna's Journal
Log Entry, August 31, 1958

I can't believe next week is already the start of school. And at Lamar Junior High! There were plenty of times I didn't think we'd survive it—the summer, that is. I'm still not sure we'll survive all this stuff— oh I know our parents think it's over, but we know better now. And James and I going to Junior High will split up the gang.

James—he reminds me of Ichabod Crane from "The Legend of Sleepy Hollow." He's tall and skinny and his bones stick out the way I imagine Ichabod Crane's must have. He IS kinda cute though, with those black-rimmed glasses always sliding down his nose so he wrinkles it all up. And the way he wears his hair in a big wave makes him look a little like Buddy Holly. I guess I wouldn't mind <u>too</u> much if he was my boyfriend, but I can tell he has a major crush on Little Betty. Who needs a boyfriend anyway?

Little Betty—we call her that because she's so tiny, what they call "petite." She makes me furious sometimes, she was so naive and spoiled in the beginning, before all that stuff with her father, but other times I just feel sorry for her and want to hug her. She's cute—really pretty, the way all girls (except ME!) wish they were, with her blond ponytail, turned up nose, and those blue-green eyes the color of the sea over the coral reef in that picture in the library. One time when I took a ride through the country with Mom, I saw a field of ripe wheat lit up in the sun and it reminded me of Betty's hair. At least she finally quit wearing pink all the time and so many frilly clothes. I can tell she isn't interested in James but she IS crazy (in the truest sense of the word – HA!) about Levi.

Levi—he's even shorter than Little Betty. We call him Shrimp, which is mean I guess, but he pretends not to mind it. I can tell he does though, so I have to remember to just call him Levi. Uncle Abe and Aunt Sophie are trying to figure out if they can do something about it with some kind of new hormone treatment. I hope it works for the little guy. He's Jewish, but not the kind that won't eat pork and wears a funny beanie. I know Betty thinks he's cute with his curly black hair and how neat he always keeps himself. I swear you could use his part as a straight-edge. He turned out to be really brave for such a shorty—he may have saved my life! I suppose when you're that small you have to make up for it somehow.

The last official member of the gang is Stevie Lindquist. He's the youngest because he skipped the third grade, and I guess that's why he's so childish sometimes. The poor kid is chubby and clumsy, and has such a wild imagination (although I will never accuse him of that again after this summer!) and has those thick glasses he has to wear. I think it's cause he's always reading, although I read a lot too and I don't need glasses. Mark is his big brother (I think Mark is fifteen) and is completely different from Stevie. Mark is tall and athletic and super handsome, but as dumb as he is good looking. They both have blue eyes cause Lindquist is Norwegian or Swedish—Scandinavian anyway—but Stevie's are real pale and washed-out looking, like somebody took regular blue eyes and added water, (and always magnified by his glasses) and Mark's are this deep blue you can't help drooling over, especially when he flirts with you like he does with me sometimes (he really does!!) That's *why he gets so many girls, but I don't care cause like I said he's so dumb and is <u>WAY</u> too old for me anyway.*

Georgie Woods is an honorary member of the gang. We made him that because he went through so much with us. He's such a sweet little boy. His mother works with Mom. They are Negroes and he was the first Negro I ever really met (besides his mother.) I wish he could go to school with us where he could get the advanced classes he needs—he is SO smart! We all are, and that's why he fits in, even if he is only 8 and a Negro. (A Negro is NOT a very good thing to be here in Texas.)

Anyway, next week it will be over (summer vacation, not all the bad stuff) - what I will always call The Summer from <u>HELL</u>. And it was my fault. Oh, if you ask Betty or James, they would say Stevie started it all, but I was the one who dared them. We could have just ignored Stevie and maybe we could have avoided it, and just enjoyed a normal summer. That's just wishful thinking though, I did, and summer was like a bad nightmare, and we haven't awakened yet. But you know, in a strange way I wouldn't have missed it for anything.

Anna signing out, log entry for August 31, 1958

This group may seem a rather odd assortment of friends, but two things bind them together. One, they are ostracized by the other children, but they don't care, they share few interests with the average student. There's that second thing as well—they are uncannily smart. And now there's a third. One that will connect them forever—the events of that summer.

CHAPTER 2
SCHOOL IS OUT

First, A Glimpse Ahead

"The future ain't what it used to be."
–Yogi Berra

Tuesday afternoon, June 10, 1958

And so, the tales were told. The tellers stared at one another—even Mark sat in silence. Despite the Texas heat, a chill settled over the room, and Stevie shivered visibly. Finally, Anna spoke up.

"So, you're telling me—we all went to the same place at the same time, that DAMN valley—but something different happened to each of us. Awful things that scared the BeeJeebus out of us. And we weren't dreaming because we could feel, and smell, and hear. So, if we weren't dreaming, what the HELL was it? And what do we do now? What if it's still there? What if it—all the its—come after us? What the GAWRD DUMP FLACKIN' HULL do we do now?"

Stevie blinked at her with empty eyes. "They ARE coming. Those voices are still in my head. I still hear them. They're coming. I don't know how and I don't know when, and I don't even know how I know, but they're coming."

James nodded. "I still feel it. It's still there, inside me. Not as bad or as painful, but it's there. It happened, and I dreamed it again. I feel it. I can feel it's coming. I've never been this sure of anything in my life."

Betty started to wail. Between racking sobs, she said she dreamed it too, dreamed the horrid thing is coming back. Levi spoke as calmly as Betty did loudly. Yeah, he felt it as well. It was coming for sure.

The scarlet undertones disappeared from Anna's eyes, and her voice was the barest of whispers.

"Abso-flackin'-lutely."

Back to June 6, 1958 – In the Cafeteria
Leaning across the table, they crowd around a wrinkled piece of paper Anna has attempted to smooth out. Levi's brow furrows. "So, the chart goes to the bottom of page ten, and that represents five hundred words a minute. That's five hundred words a page. Dumb test scale didn't allow for any faster times, but I can calculate them. Start with Stevie—he made it to page fifteen, the end of paragraph four, about half the page, or two hundred and fifty words, that's seven hundred and twenty-five words a minute—not bad Stevie."

Betty frowned. "Are you sure that's right? How do you do the calculations so fast?"

"I just do them in my head—they're right. Okay, James, you finished through page sixteen. That's easy. Sixteen times five hundred is eight thousand words, eight hundred words a minute. And you both had 100% comprehension, right? We all did, right? So—no adjustment for errors. Honkin' on there, James! Little Betty—finished fourteen pages—seven hundred words a minute. Not bad, Betty, more than twice as the fast as the other kids. Anna, twenty pages—really? That's an even thousand words a minute. Smokin' hot Anna! And finally—drum roll please—me. I finished twenty-one and a half pages—one thousand seventy-five words a minute—we have a winnah!"

"DAMN you, Levi! I'll beat you next year!"

Levi smirked, "Next year you'll be up at Lamar, Anna, so we'll never know."

Yes, these are the kids who ranked at the top in the annual aptitude test—by a wide margin—the competition that first brought them together. Gathered around the cluttered cork board, they watched their scores tick upward after each test phase, and it became a friendly competition as they quickly outpaced the rest of the students.

They are the ones who skate through their classes, always turn their flawless homework in on time, and are off the scale in the test for reading speed. Those kids. Don't tell anyone, because they wouldn't want this secret to get out, but they've dubbed themselves "The HI-Q Gang."

Betty's Diary

"If you read someone else's diary, you get what you deserve."
–David Sedaris

Friday June 6, 1958
Dear Diary,

Today was the last day of school!!! Of course I made straight A's again, so I have a perfect record through the 5th grade. Mommy says I can get a special gift whatever I want but what I really want is to be 2 inches taller and you can't buy that. I'd have her get me a record player but she says rock and roll is evil so there's no use having one. Maybe I'll ask for one of those little radios so I can listen to KNOW (K-NOW!!!) when she isn't snooping around which is almost always.

I guess it doesn't matter much. The best thing about being out of school is no more dance lessons!!

I can just sleep in and play with my friends!!! She lets me play with Anna Cook even though she says they are poor and I should try to find some friends who come from our church. In another week I have to start Vacation Bible School and go there 3 days a week for a whole month. All she ever wants to do is go to church!!! All the kids in my Sunday School are stupid. I'm sorry Dear Diary, I know that's not a Christian thing to say but it's true. That's why I like my new friends, they are smart like me. Today at lunch we agreed we will call ourselves the HI-Q gang. It means high IQ. Isn't that neat?

- Betty Lou Dupree

P.S. I think Levi is cute!!!

P.P.S. If Mommy knew I like a Jewash boy she would be mad cause she says the Jewash killed Jesus and will all go to hell. I don't think Levi should have to go to hell because he didn't have anything to do with the Jewash who killed Jesus 2 thousand years ago!!

~ ~ ~

Saturday, June 7

Dear Diary,

I went to Anna's this afternoon and the whole HI-Q gang was there!!! We go there a lot because her mother works a lot so we are all alone with no grownups to bug us. We agreed to get together every day this summer!! I like Anna even if she is kind of mean sometimes and sourcastic. It's just her way of kidding though (I think) so I try not to let my feelings get hurt. Even when she's mean and sourcastic she takes care of me like a big sister. James doesn't let anyone pick on me too much either. I'll tell you a secret Dear Diary, I think he likes me. <u>LIKE</u> likes. He's nice and all but I still like Levi. <u>LIKE</u> like like like!!!! (Mrs. Levi Stieglitz!!!) When we were outside playing Statue, Bobby Randall came running up crying. A bunch of mean boys were making fun of him and chasing him. Boy did Anna let them have it!!! She told them she was gonna beat their A-double-letter-after-Rs. That's how Anna says it. Sometimes she says "Word after Jack that means donkey." And SOMETIMES, Dear Diary, if she's real mad she just says the word!!! Levi said Bobby's mother says he was just born wrong. His Aunt Sophie told him it means Bobby had a birth deefect because he didn't get enough Oxigen to the brain, and his mother is just a poor ignarant woman with no one to help her. Mommy says its because Satan went inside his mother's tummy before he came out and made him stupid. I told her I thought Christians were supposed to take care of the weak and boy did she ever get mad!!! She said someday I'll understand how Satan gets into women and does bad things. She said Bobby is a child of Satan not a child of God and I should shut up and quit talking about things I don't understand. I don't dare tell Mommy about the Oxigen then she would really get mad. That's all for today Dear Diary. Tomorrow is Sunday so I have to rest and not write in you. I go to Sunday School (with all these stupid kids) before church then to church service. Then we usually go home for Sunday dinner but tomorrow we get to eat at the Chicken Shack with people from church. I love going there even if it is with those stupid kids from Sunday School. They have the BEST fried chicken and they have these little packets of honey. The honey is for the biskits (also the BEST) but I always put some on my chicken to make it even better!!! And they have *this beautiful painting that's on the wall. The word is mural, I just looked it up. Anyway the last time we were there the waiter said it's Lake Travis at sunset and it's just a little ways out of town. Now I want to go there so bad!!!*

That's all.

P.S. Mrs. Levi Stieglitz!!!!

P.P..S. I always snap the lock shut and lock you up when I'm done writing. Then I hide you and hide the key I tape it to the bottom of my desk lamp. I hide you behind some of the books on my bookshelf—I can pull them forward and turn you sideways in back. They are short ones so they still line up in front with the big books. I'm extra careful because if Mommy ever reads you I'll be in so much trouble!!! If Daddy does I'll just be DEAD!!!

Anna's Journal

What is it about young girls and diaries? Even Anna the tough tomboy kept one, though of course she never labeled it a diary. She called hers a "journal," and she remained quite firm on this point.

Anna's Journal
Log entry Friday, June 6, 1958
School is out today. That's good, I guess, but I don't really mind it like some kids, except I do get bored a lot. Mrs. Ashton had to go really slow because of all the dumb Cedar Whackers in our class. I don't think they are all really Cedar Whackers, but that's what I call anybody who's a stupid redneck. James says there are real Cedar Choppers (what he calls them) living out along 2222. Chopper/Whacker—TomAto/ToMAHto. His dad got called out there for a fire the dumb A-double-letter-after-R's had set burning their own damn

wood. Then when the firetrucks got there the Cedar Whackers came out with guns and tried to chase them away, but the cops came with the firemen and made the stupid Cedar Whackers let them put it out before the woods caught on fire. And I swear some of their stupid kids go to our school. I mean, in the last test I was reading on a college level, and some of those idiots can barely read Dick and Jane books. At least I have some smart friends now. The "HI-Q Gang." What a dumb name, but they think it's cool so I go along. At least I can TALK to them and they understand what I'm saying. Not like when I asked that Joanie Pritchett girl if she had always lived in Texas, and she said no, she used to live in Dallas. How can anybody that FLACKING stupid make it through basic potty training? And as if the stupid kids aren't bad enough, there are all those conformists—the ones who just care about being popular. I call them conformists because I am a NON-conformist. I don't care about what I wear or who likes me. We couldn't afford fancy dresses even if I did care, so that's a good thing.

Anyway, my friends are ok. James is kind of cute, even if he's skinny, and he's pretty smart too. Levi is the smartest, he's a year behind me but still beat me in the school achievement testing. I would have been first if it wasn't for him. And Stevie, he's only 9 but he already skipped a grade and he came in right behind me. I think Little Betty tied with James in last place, but actually there were only a few points difference in any of our scores. Mom is really happy I have some friends now. I don't have much patience for dumb kids so I never had many friends till this year. I guess this summer won't be so bad.

Anna signing off—end log entry June 6, 1958

Chapter 3
What Stevie Saw

"Even if the aliens are short, dour, and sexually obsessed— if they're here, I want to know about them."
-Carl Sagan, *The Demon-Haunted World: Science as a Candle in the Dark*

June 8, 1958
It happened in a life beat. If he had blinked, he would have missed it, and their lives would have been so very, very different.

But he didn't.

~ ~ ~

The early June night descended softly here on the edge of town. The veil of stars still visible in those days gilded the sky, and the hum of insects beat rhythm to the songs of tree frogs and night birds. Back then the northern suburbs dwindled away with no defined boundaries—a crazy quilt of new developments, old farms, and clusters of cheap, cracker-box houses financed by the VA in the rush to the burgeoning suburbs after World War II. From the new Lindquist home, Stevie had an unobstructed view of Hitching Post Lane for the two undeveloped blocks it stretched straight north, bordered by even rows of 65' x 120' rectangles.

Far too soon, those rectangles would sport concrete slabs, followed by the skeletons of the ugly "ranchers" Big Pete Peterson (your friendly neighborhood builder) would throw together, to be snapped up by families eager for the exciting lifestyle he promised here in Lone Star Ranchettes.

In his ads on late-night television, Big Pete sounded like he just stepped off a West Texas oil rig, but maybe he actually hailed from New Jersey, and maybe, just maybe, he affected that corny accent— but it sold down here in Austin, Texas, U.S. of A., sitting, as it did, on the threshold of the Texas frontier, the place where the West begins. Lone Star Ranchettes was among the northernmost of the new suburban developments sprawled out on the desirable north side of town. It was carefully placed here, far north of the river, and well west of the east Austin shanties, where white skin was found only on someone slumming or hopelessly lost.

The Lindquist house was one of those Pete Peterson ranchers. Their new home faced Hitching Post Lane, with a cement driveway flanking the left side of a plush green lawn, and leading to a double car garage with a single overhead door, one that opened on little rollers set into aluminum tracks. Enter the house from the garage and look straight down the hall to discover the entrance to "Stevie's Place." (According to the scribbled sign taped to the door.) Inside Stevie's Place, a bunk bed nestles against one wall, there's a small closet with a sliding door on the other, and a squadron of model airplanes hangs from the ceiling—proud testimony to Stevie's proficiency at assembling those plastic models sold by Reveille. Straight ahead, a single window faces north, towards the end of the block, with a boy-sized desk tucked in under the sill. Stevie sits at this desk, staring out the window toward the horizon. The Venetian blinds that serve as the window cover are raised, providing a panoramic view of the undeveloped land to the north.

In this picturesque corner of paradise, straggly oak and cedar struggled to gain a foothold in the thin limestone and clay soils here on the edge of the Edwards Plateau and the Texas Hill

Country. This ecosystem rolled on for miles, up and down craggy, forested hills, pockmarked by weedy fields full of cactus and mesquite, and watered by as yet unpolluted springs, creeks, and ponds—a dream come true for Stevie and his new friends, and ample fuel for his fertile imagination.

That fertile imagination made Stevie the brunt of many a joke and the target of considerable derision. Nor did it help that, when excited, his voice soared toward registers only audible to beagles and bloodhounds. So, you're excused if, like his friends, you regard his story with a hulking dollop of skepticism.

With school out for the summer, Stevie was allowed to stay up late, fiddling with the crystal radio set he made with the help of his father. Hal Lindquist worked as an engineer at Alpen Labs, the new engineering firm bringing in smart, educated talent from around the country, so he was more than up to the task of helping his nine (and a HALF thankyouverymuch) year-old son construct a working radio from one of those RadioShack hobby kits .

Tonight, Stevie managed to tune into a show called "Theater of the Universe—Where the Impossible is Possible and the Improbable is Commonplace." Cue the scary music. He listened with shallow breath to "The Ship from the Dark Side of Mars"—the tale of how a shiny disk full of tiny green creatures had been spotted over rural Kansas, spreading sheer terror among the citizens of a small town. A beam of light from the disk abducted the beautiful (and virtuous) Lucy Love, local preacher's daughter and object of the secret affections of one Dash Danger, handsome and daring pilot, and owner of a struggling crop-dusting business. Upon witnessing Lucy's capture, the ever-alert Dash dashed (yup, they actually said that) straight to the airstrip where Barnstormin' Bertha, his intrepid crop duster, sat ready for action. By a lucky (read farther for discussion of luck vis-à-vis Dash) coincidence, the industrious Dash had been experimenting with an ingenious new fuel additive to give old Bertha a little more oomph. It had not been tested, but this was an emergency, so he dumped a little from the gallon container straight into Bertha's tank, scowled at it, set his heroic jaw, and dumped in the rest.

Dash was the image of valor as he donned his WWI flight helmet and leaped into the cockpit. As Bertha roared into action, he felt himself slammed back into his seat when she shot up into the night sky, boosted by her new diet of super fuel. Luckily (Dash enjoyed all manner of good luck that night), the moon had waned, so the gleaming alien craft stood out against the black canvas above. As the supercharged Bertha soared up above the flying saucer (well, what did YOU think it was?), he eased the yoke forward, but left the throttle wide open. Bertha surged ahead as Dash formulated a desperate plan. He knew he needed to act fast, because who knew what dastardly horrors those soulless green creatures had in store for poor, innocent Lucy? High over the saucer, with Bertha's old engine screaming in agony, Dash shoved the yoke forward, and plunged toward the unsuspecting aliens. Just as the ancient plane was about to crash into the shining saucer, Dash yanked back on the yoke with every sinew in his bulging arms (descriptions of those sinews formed a major part of the narrative, but this is the abridged version), and old Bertha strained and leveled out, a hair's breadth from making contact. The dive provided extra momentum, and as the plucky crop duster crept ahead, Dash pulled another lever—one that dumped a full load of pesticide right in front of the saucer. This caused the blinded aliens to lose control and come skidding down on a handy wheat field (reference previously alluded to luck), with Bertha and Dash right behind.

The rest was, well, predictable. Heroic Dash subdues aliens, blushing Lucy falls into his arms, and at this point an embarrassed, but thoroughly wrought, Stevie quit listening and stared longingly out the window at the starlit horizon.

He was about to shut the radio off when the voice changed. Static scrambled the broadcast, although he detected faint speech in the background. Stevie twisted the dial, but got the same result all across the band and returned to looking out the window.

He said he saw something come down. Said a bright flash of light flared over the distant hills and woods, and then—nothing. That's what he told them the next day.

CHAPTER 4
PLAYDATE

"Sweet childish days, that were as long,
As twenty days are now."
William Wordsworth

June 9, 1958

The old basketball, its surface worn slick and thin from years of play, careened off the garage door beneath the basketball goal. Stevie stood alone at the first position in 'Round the World, and this latest attempt wouldn't change that. From the third position, Anna shook her head at him and scampered after the ball. She managed a one-handed catch right at the end of the driveway, swiveled, and "chunked" it over to Levi Stieglitz at position two. The force almost knocked the little guy over, but he swallowed the pain (swallowed it deep in his gut, put it out of his head, the way he always did; you had to when you were ten, still only a couple inches north of four feet tall, and weighed in at a lousy fifty-two pounds.) He turned and lunged forward with a two-handed set shot, sending the basketball wobbling toward the basket, where it bounced against the backboard and began circling the rim like water around a drain, before teetering, hanging for an impossible few seconds, and dropping through.

"Nuthin' but net!" crowed Levi, drawing an exaggerated eye roll from Anna.

"Was NOT!" shrilled an indignant Stevie, as Levi skipped over to position three with Anna, stopping along the way to bend over, waggle his butt in Stevie's direction, and expel a remarkably raucous and prolonged cloud of flatulence. Levi compensated for his Lilliputian stature with his apparent ability to fart at will. Possibly a side effect of his mixed-up metabolism—the same metabolism that lent him exceptional quickness—when one of the other children shouted "Fart, Shrimp," he never failed to deliver.

The basket consisted of a sagging ring and torn net bolted to a warped plywood square. It hung precariously off the roof above the rickety single-car garage, whose only window had long since donated its glass to an errant baseball. The garage adjoined an equally sad little house, with chipped and faded clapboard siding, and topped by thin, weather-worn shingles well past their most optimistic life span. Welcome to the Cook household, home of Anna Belle Cook and her mother, Carrie Cook, RN—still attractive, despite the faint worry wrinkles beginning to appear around the corners of her eyes. The gang preferred this gathering place since Nurse Carrie was rarely around to supervise, and, eager to atone for her irregular working hours, possessed a resigned tolerance of youthful tom foolery.

"Good shot, Levi." Betty's smile was shy, her eyes down-turned, and her cheeks wore just a tad more color than normal.

James scowled at her. "Come on, Betty, pay attention. I stuck the knife way over there; you'll never reach it."

Mollified, Betty glanced at the knife. She pressed her lips together and executed a graceful split that ended with a black and white saddle shoe resting daintily on top of the pocketknife, and her hands splayed out to the side. "Dance lessons, Mr. Smarty."

James gulped down the lump that formed in his throat at the sight of those pink short shorts stretched high and tight against slender legs—a confusing departure from his recent view of girls as objects to be scorned and only reluctantly tolerated. "Yeah, but try to throw from that position now."

They were playing a game called Splits. The two players alternated trying to stick a pocketknife in the ground, as far from the opposing player as possible. If it stuck, that player tried to reach it with one hand or foot. It was like an amalgamation of Mumblety-peg and Twister. The rules allowed Betty to lift one hand from the ground and take her turn with the knife. Her attempt to stick the knife from the new position was awkward—the feeble throw only propelled it against one of James' legs.

"Ow! You lose—can't hit the other person," pronounced a gleeful James.

"Oh, who cares! Anyway, it's hot out here. Can we go in now?"

This produced a cacophony of responses, with indignant Levi and James wanting to stay outside, Stevie more than ready to go inside (nothing to do with escaping a humiliating loss, I'm sure), and Anna grudgingly casting the deciding vote.

"Oh, what the HELL (Anna was scandalous in that way, the others wouldn't have dared use such language), Little Betty is just gonna 'cwwwy' and heaven forbid she should actually sweat! Y'all come in. You can each have ONE coke, but only if you put a nickel in Mom's grocery jar." In Texas in those days, all soft drinks were cokes. Only Yankees drank pop or soda pop.

As they tailed into the little house, Anna fetched the old basketball and James pocketed his folding knife after swiping it across his cut-off jeans to remove any dirt or mud. In the 1950s, no self-respecting Texas boy would be caught dead without a pocket knife—the bigger the better.

It was the kind of home real estate agents list as a "doll house," to make a small, cramped house seem more appealing. The interior featured yellowing linoleum tiles and peeling Formica countertops in the kitchen/dinette combination, and cheap, threadbare carpeting in the tiny living room. Two claustrophobic bedrooms shared a single bath adorned with chipped tile, where green-black mold crept inexorably across the grout. The house sat on the east side of The Old Laredo Trail, a four-lane thoroughfare strewn with strip centers and small businesses, that provided subtle separation of the immaculate new suburbs on the west side from these drab postwar bungalows to the east. A community of white (we're still in Texas, Bubba) blue-collar workers lived here, those who could scrape together the minimal down payments necessary to qualify for thirty-year VA and FHA loans at low interest rates. Here they pursued their pathetic little slice of the Great American Dream—modest shingle or pine board clad two and three-bedroom homes set on shaky pier and beam foundations; with peeling paint, patched roofs, and open carports or decrepit detached garages, shoe horned onto wee little lots. It was a place where grubby children ran red-faced across unkempt yards, unrestrained by their defeated, hollow-eyed mothers, whose only hope of a better future played out each afternoon on *Queen for a Day*, or on the never-ending string of game shows, where lucky, smiling women in starched dresses won wonderful prizes and escaped the drudgery of their mundane lives.

Anna's father did not maintain his residence here. The eminent surgeon ditched the pretty little nurse when she tearfully announced her pregnancy, and scurried back to his wife and family. One secret payment, and a surreptitious word in the ear of an influential patient, enabled the desperate nurse to make an inordinately large down payment, secure a mortgage loan (unheard of for a single woman in those days), and buy her silence; so, when Anna popped her sweet ginger head from between Carrie's legs, she had a disgraced mother and an unsightly little house to come home to, if no daddy.

The little entourage gathered around a small table next to the kitchen, where Anna handed out the soft drinks and collected grimy nickels, painfully aware of how hard Carrie Cook struggled to make ends meet. The faded old clock hanging on the kitchen wall indicated four-fifteen, and Carrie worked the three to midnight shift at the Brackenridge Hospital emergency room, trusting Anna to behave in her absence—not that she had any choice. She rotated between this and the midnight-to-eight shift. Although these shifts were grimly referred to as the "meat grinders," they paid a small bonus she could ill afford to do without.

The beverage choices included Dr Pepper, Big Red, RC Cola, and Hire's Root Beer. Carrie would restock them during Saturday shopping if enough nickels were piled up in the mason jar next to the undersized refrigerator. Levi noticed Anna holding back. He opened a cabinet, pulled out one of the Welch's Jelly Jars that served as glasses, poured in half of his root beer, and handed it to Anna.

"Courtesy of Stieglitz Drugs," he whispered, referring to his Uncle Abe's drug store. For this, she rewarded Levi, now sporting burning red ears, with a small, embarrassed smile, a quiet "Thanks, Shrimp," and a "frog" on the arm so he didn't get any wrong ideas (for my younger readers, a "frog" in 1958 was a poke in the deltoid with the center finger pushed forward from the fist so that its knuckle made the initial contact. Executed properly, a frog can raise a small, satisfyingly painful lump.)

Stieglitz Drugs was a favorite hangout for local kids, where a soda fountain with a sparkling Formica countertop gleamed behind the magazine and comic book racks, next to two isles of miscellaneous over-the-counter remedies and heath aids. The druggist's counter hid discretely in the back, out of view of the hormone-saturated teens seated at the four booths, where five cent jukeboxes blared out the latest rock 'n' roll hits. Old man Stieglitz was hip—he knew what cooked. The rotating stools at the counter were, by silent agreement, reserved for the younger kids. You could order phosphates, fountain cokes, root beer, thick malts, and three flavors of ice cream. The menu included almost anything that could be grilled or fried. These offerings were enough to satisfy the sophisticated dining requirements of even the most demanding Austin customers back in 1958, when Tex-Mex staples such as El

Patio and Mat's Famous El Rancho provided about the only exotic alternatives to steaks, barbecue, burgers and fried chicken.

Abe Stieglitz was Levi's uncle, Aunt Sophie, the glowering pharmacist who endured Abe's shenanigans as the price of keeping peace in the family. They adopted Levi as a baby when an overloaded gravel truck t-boned Abe's younger brother Daniel and wife Kris in their new Buick, as it careened through their intersection with shrieking brakes and a thick wake of sand and rock. The happy couple, on the way home from the hospital following the birth of their first son, hurtled through the front windshield and landed on the asphalt pavement, where Kris lay in an oddly tiny, crumpled ball. The white paper bag she'd been holding in her lap now rested in the direct gaze of her sightless eyes as they contemplated the festive label on the front.

It read "Free Gifts for New Mommies."

Both parents were DOA, but Levi remained at St. David's hospital in an incubator for preemies. Abe and Sophie were "Uncle" Abe and "Aunt" Sophie to all the gang. They were the only parents Levi had ever known.

The group eventually settled down, having made the requisite bathroom visits, whispered (Betty to Levi) about the black mold spreading maliciously in the grout among the bathroom tiles, exchanged the latest knock-knock jokes, and argued whether the thermometer reading of ninety-four degrees made this the hottest day of the summer.

Stevie interrupted the brief silence in that register only he, dog whistles, and chalk scraped across a blackboard could reach, "Wait 'till I tell you what I saw last night! Just wait!"

"Oh, I'm sure we're all perfectly happy to wait," shot back Levi.

"It was real late, maybe eleven-thirty or even midnight, cuz 'Theater of the Universe' was over," babbled an unperturbed Stevie.

"Whatever the HELL that is," muttered Anna.

"I saw a humongous flash out in the hills. I think something came down. It must have been a flying saucer. There wasn't any noise like with lightening, and besides there weren't even any clouds. I mean, the whole sky lit up over the hills. It HAD to be a flying saucer—maybe it crashed or sumpthin'. It could have little green guys in it; they might come here. We gotta go check, we gotta!"

Betty was indignant. "Stevie Lindquist, if you think I'm about to go out in those woods in this heat, you've got another think coming. In fact, a whole bunch of thinks. There's bugs, an' snakes, an' poison ivy, an' who knows what? Anna wouldn't want to go there either," she finished, her lips drawn tight and smug in the assurance that, like her, Anna would never consider such an unsavory venture.

Anna, about to refer to Stevie in especially derogatory terms, rose to that irresistible bait. "Oh, I don't know, just cuz Little Betty is such a DAMN (on a roll now, using all her favorite words) wimp, doesn't mean I won't go. In fact, I think we should ALL go—tonight after dark, so we can prove to Stevie there's no FLACKIN' (so deliciously close to that other F-word, this was Anna's invention, and one that never failed to elicit a shocked gasp from Betty) flying saucer, and no little green men. I DARE you, ALL of you. Mom won't be back tonight 'till about 12:30. If we meet here at 7:30, we'll have plenty of time. Are you wimps in or not?" The gauntlet was cast.

"I'm in!" said Levi, perhaps a bit too eager to agree with the girl who slurped down half of his root beer.

"All RIGHT!" Stevie yelled, "I'll show ya, we're gonna find that saucer!"

Betty's lower lip quivered, and those bright sea-green eyes took on a little extra shine. "Ya—ya—y'all are MEAN! ALLA' Y'ALL!" When her language devolved into that Texas twang she worked so hard to hide, it was a safe bet the waterworks were not far behind.

James spoke up in what he imagined as a gruff, manly tone. "It's okay Betty, us guys will be there. It won't be so hot at night, and we'll watch out. Everybody should bring a flashlight. 7:30 it is."

Snuffling now, Betty succumbed to the peer pressure. "Oh, all RIGHT! I'll come if everybody comes, but I'll be here if I MUST." If drama queen had been a term back then, it would undoubtedly have applied to Little Betty.

Their decision made, the group dispersed, setting out for home and supper on bicycles of various vintages and sizes. Nothing too fancy in those days—with their heavy frames and fat tires, riding those bikes definitely helped develop strong legs. Some sported racks, others exhibited baskets up front and in the case of Little Betty, her new twenty-four-inch model glistened shiny and pink, and featured both, plus a bell, a headlight, plastic streamers in the rubber hand grips (also pink), an artificial (pink) tank on the down tube, and one of those oversized seats with springs to cradle Betty's spoiled little bottom. Schwinn came out with a new model that year, called the Corvette, that boasted a lighter frame and thin tires. That baby could fly—but this unfortunate group could only dream of such wonders. They set off, their heads swimming with the excuses they would offer their parents that night when they came home late and grubby.

~ ~ ~

June 9, 1958
Dear Diary,

I am writing today's entry early because we are going to the woods tonight to show stupid Stevie there's no (Anna bad word) flying saucer. I didn't want to go (I still don't!!!) but they made me feel bad if I wouldn't. And Stevie and I got in an argument about what is cussing. He says some words are just semi-cusswords. I don't believe that. Here is how I think it goes.

1.) *Taking the Lord's name in vein. The worst and if you say it you will go straight to hades when you die.*

2.) *The F-word. If you accept Jesus Christ as your lord and savior you can be forgiven for using it but you still shouldn't.*

3.) *The S-word that means doodoo.*

4.) *The D-word that means go to hades and the H-word that means hades. Anna uses them all the time. Stevie says they are cusses but not too bad. I think they are but are even worse if you say D-word you or go to H-word because then you're telling someone to go to hades.*

5.) *The F-word that means pass gas. Stevie calls this a "semi-cussword." I still think it's a cussword.*

6.) *The words Anna makes up like the one that's like the F-word. Stevie says these are semi-cusswords and are funny. I think it's kind of like cussing and anyway it's what she really means so that makes it cussing.*

–Betty who doesn't want to go to the woods tonight but has to.

CHAPTER 5
WE ALL WENT DOWN TO THE WOODS TODAY

The green-gold evening light filtering through that first copse of wood provoked a strange quieting effect on the boisterous assemblage. Only moments earlier, as they pedaled furiously past the last few houses, their shouts of bravado pierced the twilight stillness of those final outposts of North Austin civilization. Tired families, gathered in front of black and white images flickering across glowing screens, scarcely registered the outside noise as they sat entranced, glued to their prime-time favorites. At this hour you found *Maverick* families, *Jack Benny* aficionados, and *Steve Allen* devotees staring in wonder at the tiny performers. Mix them, and the conversation would become awkward as they groped for something—anything—to discuss. This was the epitome of the "togetherness" prescribed as the panacea for the ills plaguing fast-paced modern society. Families chuckled in unison at smarmy jokes, on cue with the laugh tracks that accompanied the narrative. Pavlov's viewers, now conditioned to laugh on command, they soon became equally conditioned to buy, buy, buy—all the amazing products advertised there, the effluvia of the superheated postwar economy, all that stuff they hadn't realized they couldn't live without. Not until the commercials convinced them—convinced them and gave them permission to join the burgeoning "consumer economy." It wasn't greed, it was progress; and progress was desirable so long as it meant easier living, modern homes filled with all the latest appliances, and bigger, faster cars.

Anna cut the corner at the end of Hitching Post Lane, oblivious to any threat of oncoming traffic, to inch past Levi as the group swung left on Palomino Pathway with its steep drop to Creekside. They threw their hands in the air and whooped with uninhibited joy as they sped down the long hill.

Never again would they be this young and carefree. Not after tonight.

With yowling brakes, they turned right on Creekside, once again heading north. Levi approached the turn with wild abandon, sliding his rear tire as he leaned hard into the turn, and whooped again as he shot back into the lead. Creekside continued on for several more blocks, ending where a yellow wooden footbridge traversed Shoal Creek to the new streets on the west side.

Levi crossed first, jumped off his bike, and shouted, "Tightrope challenge!" He hopped up on the four-inch handrail and walked back across the creek with his arms stretched out to his sides for balance. Jumping down again, he said, "I choose Stevie." According to the rules, if you successfully crossed the bridge on the handrail, whomever you selected had to cross next.

"There's no time for this," Stevie whined.

Levi began to chant, "Ste-vie, Ste-vie, Ste-vie." The others joined in and helped shove Stevie toward the bridge.

The narrow handrail arched twelve feet above a shallow creek where clear water burbled over menacing-looking rocks. Stevie worked himself into a near panic as he struggled up onto the handrail, fighting for balance. He wobbled from side to side and shuffled his feet awkwardly, with shortened, insecure steps. Tears clouded his vision, and upon reaching the apex of the bridge, his right foot missed its target and slid down the creek side of the railing. He grabbed for the rail and managed to hook it with his left arm. In the meantime, his left foot slid down the other side, leaving him hanging by one arm and one leg, slipping fast and screaming in distress, hitting the octave that exists about a foot or two beyond the right side of a standard piano keyboard.

The others began laughing so hard their reactions were delayed. Betty, not seeing the humor in this, responded first. She leaped forward, grabbed the back of his pants, and pulled as hard as her diminutive size allowed. This had the effect of yanking the pants down over a chubby pink bottom. The sight so horrified Betty that she let go, and what little progress she'd made toward lifting him back up reversed into downward momentum that resulted in him slipping even farther. Stevie dangled by a single hand and foot, with that charming little bottom reflecting the rays of the setting sun. As his weakening grip let go, Anna and James regained their wits and ran forward to pull him back onto the bridge, where he flopped around, struggling to pull up his pants. Betty reddened and turned completely away, Levi collapsed into gales of riotous laughter, Anna covered her mouth with both hands in an unsuccessful attempt not to giggle, while James sputtered and choked in his own effort not to laugh. It took several minutes for them to recover their composure. Betty kept reassuring Stevie that she didn't see anything—really, she didn't—but it did not help that each time she repeated this, Levi said HE sure did, honking with laughter the whole time.

As she wiped away a tear, Anna admonished the group that they needed to get going. Now, close to the place with the best trails into the Hill Country woods, they started off and arrived without further incident.

The light had faded, and the gathering twilight cast a somber blanket over their fervor. Even Stevie appeared subdued by the intermingling of gloom, bird calls, and the drone of insects, as the day grudgingly retreated before the relentless incursion of velvet shadows. Early June evenings were long, with fading remnants of daylight lingering until eight or eight-thirty. That time was upon them; their departure from Anna's house was delayed because Betty's mother insisted on checking her story with Anna's mother, who, of course, knew nothing about this plan and had begun her evening shift at the Breckenridge emergency room. However, Anna did a bang-up impression of her mother, so when Betty's mom called, the voice she heard detailed all the safe, indoor activities planned for the girls' evening—they were going to have a taffy pull, play with a Ouija board (something Betty's fundamentalist mother would have been appalled to learn if she had a clue what it was), and maybe catch a little TV—Dinah Shore would be on later.

"That was STEW-PEN-DUS Anna," Levi had gushed.

"Yeah, real good," murmured Betty, as she saw her last glimmer of hope to avoid this little adventure snuffed out.

Now, stashing her little pink bicycle behind a thick bush, she could hear the others' hushed whispers as they found suitable hiding places for their bikes, about half a block into the woods to ensure no older kids would happen along and apply what Old Man Stieglitz called "the five-finger discount."

Their precious bicycles concealed, they started down the trail with Stevie in the lead. The darkening gloom rendered the path—obvious in daylight—confusing and disconcerting. With its thorns and stickers, underbrush in the Texas Hill Country can bite, and those young legs were soon covered with scratches, the seeping blood providing a feast for the early evening mosquitoes, gnats, and tiny biting flies. Betty, ever on the verge of tears, slapped futilely and pouted. The older kids were too proud to admit to any discomfort, and Stevie, oblivious, was in the groove now, determined to quiet the condescending mockery he'd suffered since blurting out his tale that afternoon.

Here at the threshold to the Edward's Plateau, the trees, rather larger than those farther west, were dominated by the Ashe juniper the locals called cedar, along with a mixture of oak varieties—escarpment live oak, the white and red oak families and the ubiquitous post oak—along with a mixed assortment of trash trees such as hackberry and persimmon. Their unshorn branches tangled overhead in a fearsome web, and the forbidding underbrush was laced with thorns and pockmarked with prickly pear, the pervasive barbed menace that thrives in the brutal heat and karst soils of the area. As the last vestiges of light drained from the sky, the flashlights clicked into life. Their meager beams only added to the sense of foreboding as the little gang trudged along, immersed in their own silence. Sleepwalking along the narrow pathway, they ventured ever deeper into the forest.

Darkness enveloped them in a phlegmy embrace, as though they were slogging through dense, viscid muck that distorted time and place, and forced their steps to be halting and uncertain. Rotting branches littered the ground, the inevitable consequence of trees packed too tightly together, engaged in a desperate struggle to reach the sunlight above the forest canopy. Their putrid odor permeated the thick, humid air, and the surviving branches twisted around overhead in a perversely wraithlike tangle—a Danse Macabre obscuring the view of the sky.

Betty kept hurrying, sometimes almost running, to keep up, but every time she blinked or let her gaze wander, she found herself far behind again. James struggled to reconcile the familiar forest map in his mind with the crepuscular silhouettes swimming around them. The yellow beam from his flashlight bathed a knotted old oak in its dissipated luminescence, transmuting the familiar form into spectral absurdity. He *knew* that tree—knew its coarse bark, knew the protuberant knots he'd so often used to pull himself up into its welcoming branches.

That tree should have been left in the distance; yet here it stood, a silent sentry guarding the entrance to the deeper woods, as though they had barely started.

After what seemed an interminable time, they topped a rise, and the trees parted, exposing a broad swath of horizon and sky, but the dusting of stars across the dense inkiness of the moonless night provided scant illumination. Back in those days, little of the light pollution that now obscures the Austin area star-scape spoiled the view. Today, even in far West Texas at the McDonald observatory, the scientists bemoan the growing incursion of light from the rapid growth of such surrounding communities as Marfa, Ft. Stockton, and Alpine. But on this night, the Milky Way arched overhead, lending its muted luminescence to the otherwise opaque vistas.

They huddled together there in silence, feeling the fog lifting from their minds. Secretly relieved to have some idea of where they were, being closer together brought comfort. James figured they had been walking for at least an hour, maybe two—time seemed, well, fuzzy.

Stevie pointed to the next hill, "I think it went down over there, on the other side of that mountain."

"Do you THINK or do you KNOW?" demanded Levi. "Cuz this is getting REAL old!"

"GWARD DHARM FLACKING OLD!" said Anna, coining yet another near curse.

Stevie stared ahead. "Know," he mouthed quietly, and started off again.

The path ahead reverted to a snarl of ghostly trees and treacherous underbrush. They continued for about another hour—but that couldn't be right. The hill Stevie pointed out looked so close. Betty crowded next to Levi, whispering "Do you think we're losted?" *Did I say LOSTED? NO! What is WRONG with me?*

But the answer came from the introspective James, who often made solo forays into these woods to ponder the unfathomable mysteries of eleven-year-old life with an overworked single father and his disturbingly alluring girlfriend. "No, I come here a lot. It is harder to tell at night, but I recognize stuff. I just don't understand why we're taking so long."

"Hey," Anna interrupted, "shut the FLACK up for a minute. Can y'all tell how quiet it is? No birds, no insects, no noise from cars up on The Trail (the local shorthand for The Old Laredo Trail.)"

"Yu-yeah, but n-no, do y'all hear a humming noise?"

"I don't hear anything, Stevie, no, wait, yeah, it's like, like..." and Levi trailed off, unable to describe the faint pulsing thrum that filled his ears and echoed through his brain, almost as if it were trying to form words. One by one, the others nodded agreement. The sound resonated softly, at once both mechanical and organic—

alien—yet teasingly familiar, discordant, and hauntingly persistent. It somehow drew them on, an invisible Pied Piper gently guiding them into the night.

Stevie's plump face shone with a faint layer of perspiration brought on by the humid Texas night as he grimly set his jaw and started forward again. Anna frowned, expunging her lungs of air in an exasperated sigh, and started along behind him. Like automatons, the others followed suit, retreating into their own strange and lonely thoughts, fighting the overwhelming sense of detachment.

Time dragged. In normal circumstances, a group of nine, ten, and eleven-year-old children would suffer the boredom so characteristic of their species. Observe these creatures in one of their natural habitats, a schoolroom for instance, and they would fidget, wiggle, make faces and whisper among themselves unless suitably entertained, distracted or threatened.

But they continued trancelike through the night. Were they dreaming? What went on between those little ears that was so damned interesting? After what felt like hours, Stevie stopped short as the path split. To the right, the path descended, to the left, it rose. You and I, Dear Reader, are now thinking of Robert Frost, but for these young-un's, poetry was the last thing on their minds.

Anna's scowl registered her impatience, "Which way now, Dummy? We'd better take the left fork to the top."

"No, go right, the path goes down, crosses a creek, then goes up the hill. We go right, we're almost there.

Anna folded her arms tightly across her chest, right across that embarrassing training bra her mother started making her wear when she began developing what Mom called her 'little bee stings.' The one the boy who sat behind her in homeroom kept leaning forward and snapping. Until the time Mrs. Ashton left the room to deliver some papers to the office—when Anna turned around and slapped him silly. The one damp with sweat from the stifling heat. "Are you sure, Jimmy boy (how he hated that)? Seems to me up is up, and down is down, but who am I to question the obvious?

James scowled and shined his flashlight at a bush on the right. "I'm sure. Look, there's a cactus behind that bush. I know, it got me good once." And sure enough, through the branches of a little dewberry bush, the flat, thorny paddles of a nasty prickly pear were barely visible, proof positive James knew exactly where they were. Or did he? Those pesky little cacti were all over the place. But sometimes all it takes to convince others is enough bluster and certainty. It seems to work for about 35% of the U.S adult population, according to the latest polling.

"Okay, Jimmy boy. You win. Let's point Stevie in the right direction and get this the HELL over with." She grasped Stevie by the shoulders and shoved him down the righthand path.

Now the sense of time reversed. They flew down the path, though, with effort, they could tell they walked at the same careful pace as before. Was the universe trying to make up for the gag it played all night, that distorted deceleration of time? Who can say what caused the distortion? Time is such a subjective thing—oh, not that we can't precisely measure it, not that we can't calibrate our instruments to the steady rhythm of radioactive decay. No, we can do all that—but how we EXPERIENCE the passing of time is another big ball of candle wax. Well-seasoned folks learn that the older you get, the faster time passes, perhaps life's cruelest surprise. Just as so few remain, the days fly by, and before you know it, you're lying on silken sheets, with people filing past, saying what a good job the undertaker did of making you "look natural." For these fledglings, however, the pages of their lives stretched out ahead, in an endless series of chapters still waiting to be penned.

As James predicted, a tributary of Shoal Creek trickled across the path at the bottom, and the narrow trail rose on the other side. Stevie splashed across, almost as if he didn't even notice the tiny stream. One by one, the others crossed, stepping from stone to stone, but occasionally slipping off into shallow water that barely covered the soles of their sneakers. Betty went last, starting out trepidatiously. James reached out a helpful hand; she took it with a quick glance in Levi's direction, and allowed James to help her across without getting water spots on the black and white saddle shoes she had been unwilling to exchange for sneakers. Levi remained oblivious to what Betty clearly regarded as a duty that should have been his, and Anna turned her eyes away to avoid being caught glaring in their direction. "THAAANK you, James," Betty crooned, "I'm glad there is one gentleman here."

"Wu, welcome," sputtered James, feeling an unwelcome fullness in the front of his tightie-whities. He quickly changed the subject, "What now, Stevie?"

"It will be right over this hill," came the unusually confident assurance. "That's exactly where it landed." So now it had become a landing; what had started out as possibly having seen something come down had morphed into an actual landing in Stevie's fevered imagination. In his mind he pictured a shining silver disk, like the one in the "Theater of the Universe" story—he HAD seen it—but had he? *Oh yes, seeeen it—looks like this.* The image swam in his head, coming into sharper and sharper focus, as though it were being burned into his brain, drawing him onward. *I'll be the hero, this is the part where I walk up and say 'welcome to planet Earth, I come in peace.' Me, Stevie Lindquist, I'll show 'em, I'll show 'em all.* His pent-up excitement had somehow changed to quiet determination. "Let's go, we'll see it when we get to the top."

As the group slogged on up the hill, they each imagined they saw a faint glow on the horizon, pulsing and glimmering in rhythm to the thrumming in their ears. Stevie perceived the same vivid yellow as the flash he saw last night. To the others it varied, soft mauve to Betty, misty red to James, an ever-changing rainbow of alternating waves to Anna, and a light gray glow to Levi. They fell back into silence. Time ticked along at a normal pace, and despite the three switchbacks and steep incline, they soon reached the summit.

None of them were prepared for what happened there.

Chapter 6
Just Another Day at the Office

"The mass of men live lives of quiet desperation"
–Henry David Thoreau

Monday Morning

Hal Lindquist slammed a heavy hand down on the raucous alarm clock that kept insisting 6:15 was the correct time. An hour later, having meticulously dressed, downed coffee and choked down a few bites of blackened toast and half-cooked eggs, he pecked Carol on the cheek and headed out to the garage. As he switched on the light, Hal took a moment to admire his grandest acquisition—a shiny new Edsel Corsair. Although Ford marketed the color that gleamed in the garage light's glow as "Snow White," it more closely resembled what an infant might deposit on a burp towel after having downed a bottle of bad milk. The inset rear quarter panels were a contrasting baby blue, along with the roof. It was an impressive eighteen and a quarter-feet of ugly, so laden with chrome it was a wonder it moved.

Hal beamed with pride.

He pulled a white handkerchief from his coat pocket to wipe an imaginary spot off the massive vertical grille, whose stylish shape evoked the mouth in Edvard Munch's famous painting, *The Scream*. The letters E D S E L ran rakishly from top to bottom of this chrome-encrusted atrocity. It was an announcement to the world that the brilliant marketers at Ford, unable to agree on one of several names that tested well, swallowed what little pride they may have had, and branded the future hope of the Ford Motor Company after Henry Ford's unfortunately named son, Edsel. Hal walked along the passenger's side to open the garage door, fussing with the handkerchief at various points along the way. Once the garage door swung open, the full glory of the Edsel caught the morning sun. Captivated by the ostentatious wing-like taillights that adorned the trunk, Hal smiled his satisfaction and gave these the hanky treatment as well.

Once he determined that no more spots required his attention, Hal slid behind the giant steering wheel, inserted the key, and lit up the massive 410 cubic inch flathead V8 that powered the behemoth. His smile broadened as the impressive array of chrome rimmed instruments blinked to life. He checked the gauges, then eased the 2.2 short tons of rolling design contradictions out onto the driveway.

Hal continued contentedly on his way to The Trail, where he turned north until he swung into Billy Evans' Texaco. He ordered the obsequious attendant to check "everything" and fill the car with 21.9 cent premium, before walking inside the station and popping a nickel in the vending machine for a Baby Ruth candy bar to mask the taste of Carol's lousy breakfast. As he exited the building, the simpering attendant had finished washing the sparkling windows and was holding his door open. "Everything was in tip-top condition, Mr. Lindquist."

Hal grunted, pulled out, and continued north along The Trail until he turned west on highway 183, then onto a series of winding side roads that led into the undeveloped wilderness southwest of the highway. The powerful V8 purred along, and Hal couldn't resist goosing the gas from time to time, causing the gearbox to lurch into second and propel the rolling living room forward in a most satisfying manner. Never mind the wind noise where the windows failed to meet, a common flaw in pillarless roofs, but intensified by the lax Edsel quality control.

Too soon, he reached a private gated drive flanked by guardhouses on both sides, and presented his identification card to a stern-featured guard who glared at the little picture with contempt and suspicion, then held it up while he squinted at Hal, before extending a grudging finger to press the prominent red button that opened the gate. "Good morning, Mr. Lindquist."

Hal sighed and said, "Good morning, Harry." This little drama played out every day.

The smoothly paved drive wound through dense woods for more than a mile before reaching the entrances to five parking lots labeled "Visitors, Agricultural Engineering, Chemical Engineering, Electrical Engineering, and Administration." Hal swung into the Electrical Engineering lot and selected a space promising to provide shade against the heat of the afternoon. Taking one last self-satisfied look at his new Corsair, he walked down the sidewalk to a sprawling glass-clad building that formed a huge V, with the entrance at the point. The glass paneled exterior reflected the surrounding woodlands, rendering the building virtually invisible in certain conditions. Inside the entrance, the only marque in evidence bore the words "Alpen Labs," etched over a long guard desk that dominated the center of the atrium. Austin locals, with their penchant for nicknames, had shortened it to "the lab." Once again, Hal handed his ID to a guard, who glanced at it and motioned him on. He then hung the badge around his neck and proceeded on around a set of elevators to enter the spacious company cafeteria where three doorways led to broad halls at the back. Guard stations with small gates sectioned off each corridor. Hal took the leftmost, again flashing his badge at the guard, who looked at the four blue bars before opening the gate and waving him through. This hallway led to the electrical engineering offices, design rooms, and labs for fabrication and testing. Hal bypassed the doors leading to the secretarial and administrative pool, and management offices. At the main design room, he took a card from a rack and clocked in. Hal had arrived five minutes early that morning.

The other two hallways led to the Chemical, and Agricultural Engineering Divisions. Chemical Engineering workers wore dark orange bars on their badges and the Agricultural Engineering Workers, or "Farmers" in company vernacular, had green bars. In all cases, the number of bars, from one to five, designated a worker's status. As a senior level engineer, Hal's badge flaunted four bars, the highest before attaining management status. Five bars made you a manager with your own private office, and anything above five meant an office "Upstairs" in the second-floor executive area and a discrete, pure black background on your ID. The labs for each section were located toward the ends of the corridors, with heavy bolted doors blocking entry.

In the early days at Alpen Labs, the EE's reigned supreme, as competition with other government contractors heated up in the race to produce the first viable integrated circuits (ICs.) More recently, they conceded the contest to Texas Instruments and Fairchild Laboratories, settling in to pursue a second-generation design. The Chemical Engineers, nicknamed Labbies, had been a small group working on various substrate wafers, the semiconductor material used in integrated circuit fabrication. The Labbie wing ran between the much longer EE and Ag wings. Two years ago, when management concluded that Alpen Labs would not be the first to cross the IC finish line, they converted the Agricultural Engineering Wing where the Farmers worked from its prior use as a storage facility. Now the Chemical Engineers launched new, highly secret projects, and rumors spread that these somehow involved the Farmers as well. These days the executives Upstairs directed their attention on the Labbies, along with the bulk of the funding.

The morning was winding down when Jerry Peterson stopped by Hal's desk. Jerry, a loquacious sort, was an unlikely friend for the more somber Hal. Nevertheless, they formed a close relationship since they were both relative newcomers, a rarity in the EE division.

"Hal, grab something quick at lunch. I want to show you something outside—we'll need all the time we can squeeze in." Jerry's eyes gleamed with mystery, and his grin promised secrets to be investigated.

Hal had been looking forward to a hot lunch that would be a gourmet feast compared to whatever culinary abomination Carol would concoct for dinner, but acquiesced and grabbed a sandwich, iced tea to go, and a bag of potato chips. Jerry hovered at his elbow, urging him on to tempt gastric distress, so he forced down the limp egg salad on white bread and allowed Jerry to lead him outside.

The building nestled in the center of a rambling wooded campus where no scrub brush remained and nary a single invasive cedar or trash tree had survived the enthusiastic assault of the chain saw brigade. This left a picturesque park ornamented by majestic old-growth oak and pecan, with a few graceful sycamore and venerable red cypress scattered about. The plantings combined low flowering bushes with a sprinkling of small specimen trees that bloomed in the late spring and early June, while elegant waves of bougainvilleas flowed over sculpted trellises around the borders of the gardens, creating a dazzling gala of color. Crushed granite and flagstone pathways invited exploration as they wound through the two hundred acres surrounding the front and two sides of the building, with benches placed to take advantage of the most appealing views. Fish ponds dotted the property, watered by rippling, spring-fed creeks, and set off by delightful meadows where multitudes of bluebonnets, Indian blankets, and Black-Foot daisies blossomed in the spring.

Jerry's hurried excursion, however, didn't leave Hal any time to stop and smell the flowers.

He set out around the right side of the complex. The winding path meandered towards the rear parking lot until it led them to a tall chain-link fence with menacing-looking razor wire along the top. The single access road to the lot disappeared into the woods. Hal couldn't tell where supply trucks entered, but could imagine that this road, like every other entrance into the expansive one thousand plus acre estate, led to a heavily guarded gate. A yellow school bus was pulling up as they arrived at the fence.

Jerry's eyes twinkled. "Now take a gander at who gets out of this bus."

The bus pulled into the parking lot, stopping short of where the Farmers and EE wings fanned out. Roughly thirty young men and women in their late teens to early twenties got out and followed a sidewalk toward the building. Obviously not employees, they dressed as one might expect of university students enjoying their summer break—the girls wore Capri pants or shorts, some quite short—what Jerry called "ass ticklers"—and airy sleeveless blouses; the boys wore jeans and colored knit shirts. Chatting and laughing, they strolled down the sidewalk toward the back of the building and disappeared from view.

"Look at those little cuties!" Jerry gushed. "I'd skip lunch for one of them any old day."

As usual, Jerry's lecherousness annoyed Hal, but something else about this nagged at him. "Where are they going? I didn't think there were any back entrances except the loading docks."

"Exactly the right question," came a voice from behind them.

One of the Labbies was out for a quick smoke—not allowed in the building. The single orange stripe on her ID below the name Jenny Weber designated her Chemical Laboratory Assistant status.

"I've worked here since they opened the Labbie wing and never heard of any other entrances. I wonder where it leads."

"Jerry Peterson, and this is Hal Lindquist," said Jerry, stretching out his hand. Not one to miss the chance of an introduction to an attractive female, this was what he typically referred to as a "nicely wrapped package." She appeared to be in her late twenties. A short bob of raven hair framed a heart-shaped face, and her friendly smile, accentuated by flaming red lipstick, stood out in vivid contrast to her black hair and honied-cinnamon skin.

"Jenny Weber, Lab Rodent."

Hal looked puzzled. "Rodent?"

"Gopher, to be precise—Jenny go for this, Jenny go for that. That's what they call us Lab Assistants. If you sneak back here at five, you'll see those kids load back into the bus and take off. Different ones on different days, but this has been going on for over a month. Sometimes they aren't kids at all, but poor-looking Negroes and Mexicans. Those guys always dress like they're going to church. Something's going on, many secrets are being whispered about these days in the dark depths of the lab."

This tweaked Hal's curiosity. "I wonder what this is about? You guys and the Farmers have been sucking up all the big grant money. Those kids aren't old enough to make any meaningful contribution, and they don't act like the brightest bulbs in the package—not my idea of what summer interns look like—they would never allow interns to dress that way."

"Nope, interns come in through the front like everybody else, they automatically award those little nerds two stripes—sure tells me where my place is. Besides, we never, NEVER, offer internships to women. Think about it, have you ever seen a woman with more than one stripe working here? Even the gals who work Upstairs wear the single stripe of infamy."

Hal frowned at his watch. "We need to get back, but tell you what Jenny, let's meet here after work and talk about this some more. You've aroused my curiosity."

"Deal, but I won't be able to stay long, I have a date tonight with a hot fireman who needs a little cooling off."

"Makes me want to put on a uniform," smirked Jerry, to Hal's obvious embarrassment.

"Bye, GENTLEMEN, see you at five." Unfazed, she placed just the right emphasis on the word.

That afternoon, as promised, the students emerged from the building, loaded into the bus, and departed. This time they were quieter and more reserved. Several guards accompanied them, guided them onto the bus, and stood watch in rigid silence until it disappeared from sight.

The headline in the next morning's paper stood out in bold black letters:

"UT COED DIES AFTER JUMPING FROM TOWER."

A gruesome picture of a pretty young girl accompanied the article. She was sprawled out on the mall beneath the famous University of Texas Tower with what looked like blood pooled beneath her head. Hal frowned at the grainy photo—did he recognize her from somewhere?

CHAPTER 7
BETTY'S STORY

"... Real fairytales end in blood or tears."
Luna Lindsey, *Emerald City Dreamer*

As she crested the top, Betty realized she was alone again. Had she somehow dropped behind? Coming up the hill, she dogged Levi's heels, trying to keep up, but now he and the others were nowhere in sight. Logically, she should have been terrified in this situation, but logic fled some time earlier and she now wore an uncharacteristically mature expression of bemusement.

Maturity in children is a funny thing; it doesn't follow a bright straight line through their lives, but zigs and zags—leap frogs, hides and reappears, sneaks in and out. It isn't one simplistic thing, but a conglomeration of different traits, talents, and hormones—blending and clashing, pushing and pulling, at once working together and at twice and thrice in conflict and confusion. In some ways, Betty was precocious. She rose before school each morning to attend gymnastics and missed playtime to attend ballet and tap; practicing, in the words of her proud mother, "religiously." In other ways she acted like a small tot, still sleeping with a night light, surrounded by an incongruous assortment of stuffed animals and dollies. Her mother often assured her she was "cute as a bug," yet she remained riddled with insecurities. She strove desperately for acceptance, but, like poor unfortunate Bobby, suffered her own considerable share of mockery.

"Now Betty, you know they only tease the ones they like."

Still, somewhere, in the dark eddies of her mind, that place where platitudes never intrude, Betty knew better.

But now, out of the silent shadows, a preternatural calmness settled over her. The fog lifted from her thoughts and she gazed down the hill and across the rift in the surrounding area. In the Appalachian backwoods, they would have called this a "holler," but here in Central Texas it was nothing more than a rugged and nameless valley, a wrinkle in the Hill Country fabric where the Balcones Fault stretched, shattered and displaced the underlying layers of clay, limestone, and granite.

There are two major types of faults, strike-slip faults where tectonic plates slide and displace vast portions of the earth's crust laterally, and dip-slip faults where sections are displaced vertically as one is thrust over the other. The Balcones Fault is the latter type, and this displacement can best be seen as an exposed uplift at the southwest corner of Lamar Boulevard and Barton Springs Road in Austin. Back in 1958, geology professors from the University of Texas would bring their classes to this site to study the fossil-rich limestone layers so conveniently on display. The Balcones Fault zone runs roughly from Dallas to Del Rio, but it is at this intersection we find the very schism where the West begins. Across Lamar to the east, the land begins a gradual transition from the Edwards Plateau to the Blackland Prairies, a flat to gently rolling region of thick muddy soil the locals called "gumbo," where cotton farms dominated in those days. Climb the outcropping on the southwest corner, and you enter a region of sparse top soils, better suited to the cattle or goat ranching of the West than serious farming. Betty stood on a rise in the easternmost section of this region.

Her vantage point afforded an unobstructed view. The mauve glow colored the very air now, it shimmered with bright pink highlights Betty savored as she inhaled. She breathed in clouds of pink cotton candy with all their sugary goodness, and she exhaled pink, spun-sugar swirls. How very wonderful, like a Candyland Wonderland—the words sang in her head. Tiny lights danced across the gorge, winking and sparkling; she laughed out loud and clapped her hands as, far down in the valley, one of them started towards her, growing as it approached.

She looked around for the others. How she wanted them to see, especially Levi! He would like her if she could show this to him. They would hold hands and skip through the pink sweetness, chasing and being chased by the glittering lights.

But Little Betty remained alone.

The realization caused her chest to constrict. She found her voice and called out— "Levi, Anna, Stevie, James, where ARE y'all? Come HERE, y'all gotta see this, hurry, where ARE you?" The only answer, plaintive and distant, was carried on the waves of mauve mist. A single word, her name, "Behhttteeeeeee oh, Beehhtttteee," drawn out, long and melodious—floated up and caressed her waiting ears. Had she ever heard anything so lovely, so perfect in pitch and tone, with such depth of feeling? It called out to her in a strange and wonderful way, a symphony for her soul. A long breath whistled out, and she relaxed, the tightness gone.

The speck of light continued to grow as it approached, bobbing—now up, now down, floating on unseen currents, glittering and pulsing, first dim, then bright, a bright pink light— too bright to make out any detail. It floated higher as it neared, rising far above her, far above the hummock on which she stood entranced, so high it grew small once again—tiny but undimmed, so high now she craned her neck to follow its journey, as it became virtually indistinguishable from the blanket of glimmering stars overhead. It would have been except for that persistent pinkness. It hung there for the briefest of moments, suspended, another minuscule droplet in the Milky Way. Then, as abruptly as it had risen, it began dropping, growing as it approached, at first flaring like a meteorite, what Betty would later describe as a "falling star," then slowing, expanding, and fluttering around the edges. The brightness all but blinded her. Her heart hammered—she blinked repeatedly, trying to focus as it stopped and hovered a few feet in front of her.

The brightness gradually subsided, and a winged form came into focus. Why, it was a beautiful fairy—a fairy princess, clad in silken clouds of diaphanous pink! The fluttering of the translucent wings slowed slightly, but caused the pale pink glow surrounding the fairy to pulsate in rhythm, and kept her suspended a few feet off the ground. A lovely smile revealed teeth of the purest white, and spread across a face the color of fresh cream, with glowing turquoise eyes set well apart, beneath a head adorned by luxuriant layers of long blond curls. She looked like Tinker Bell all grown up. Betty drank in a lungful of sugar-flavored air. She imagined being swept up and carried away to an enchanted land inhabited by fairies and sprites, with pixies that looked like Levi, waiting to welcome her to a wonderful new life where you didn't need lessons to dance like a prima ballerina, with nothing to do but play all day and eat every delicious kind of sweetie imaginable—where no one called you "Little" Betty, and no one teased or belittled anyone else. It would be Neverland and Disneyland wrapped into a single utopia for children; oh, she couldn't wait!

"Hello Betty, wouldn't you like to come with me? We'll go to Fairy Land and see the Enchanted Forest, and you can eat all the candy you want. Fairy Land has the very best candies, waiting just for you." The invitation lingered, along with a perfect, outstretched hand on the end of a flawless arm. The long, delicate fingernails glistened with something like liquid gold swirled with powdered diamonds, and the voice was melodious and soothing.

Betty reached out eagerly, magical images spinning through her head—but—something was wrong. Instead of a soft hand gently taking hers, cruel fingers seized her wrist in a raw grasp. It hurt.

As tears formed and blurred her vision, her stomach spasmed into a hard ball and she felt the sensation of being wrenched up into the air. She blinked through welling wetness to clear her eyes, as the fairy princess began to waver and change, mutating bit by bit into a hideous old crone—a harpy ripped from the pages of ancient Greek mythology. Betty wretched and bile erupted in her throat. The green eyes darkened and yellowed, the pupils narrowed into vertical slits like the gateways to hell; those flowing blond tresses turned to gray, and frizzed into a vile, tangled mass. That buttermilk skin took on the appearance of corroded metal, swathed with hairy warts oozing stinking yellow pus. The nose grew long and disfigured, with enormous mucus-packed nostrils, and the translucent wings morphed into those of a mammoth bat—crenelated wings that beat faster and faster as the grip on Betty's wrist only tightened, and they rose to a terrifying height, through air now starless, thick, and dank, and reeking of primordial putrefaction.

Betty screamed, but the night swallowed the sound, rendering it feeble and distant, even to her own ears. The world below was the size of a play village—they must be miles up in this rancid air. She cried out now, begging to be taken down—crying in vain for her mommy, her daddy to save her. "Put me DOWN—put me down NOW. Please, NO please, I don't want to go, put me DOWN!"

The apparition stared at her and spoke, its hollow, tortured voice like the closing of a rusted gate:

"Pretty Girl, come up and play.

Pretty Face will fade away.

Pretty Eyes that sparkle bright, will dim, and turn as dark as night.

Pretty Hair with wave and curl, won't last long on Pretty Girl.

Pretty Teeth and Pretty Smile, lost forever in a while.

Pretty Face and Pretty Head, soon will wither and be dead.

Pretty Girl shall live this spell, and can this fortune never quell.

Pretty Girl, you've seen your fate, you've seen it now, but much too late.

Pretty Girl, you've seen in me, the future waiting now for thee.

Pretty Girl, back down with you, but don't forget this fortune true."

The words invoked a new terror; Betty imagined herself changing, growing as old and deformed as this thing that held her. The vision rendered her airless.

Then the iron grip relaxed, and Betty's terrified gaze focused on the yellowed fingernails as the gnarled fingers opened. For an endless moment she hung suspended, one of those cartoon characters that runs off a cliff. In that instant, her mind filled with horror. A fall from this height, now inevitable, meant certain death. Time had frozen and her brain burned with fear—fear that only grew and grew.

How much terror can the mind endure before it shatters? How far can credulity stretch before the mind snaps? How long can one await the approach of inevitable death without having their tenuous hold on sanity fractured forever? In that instant, Little Betty became a mad thing; terror clutched her throat and squeezed it closed. Fear clouded her vision and left her sightless. Icy tendrils gripped her stomach, and she descended into a realm of formless dread.

Then, as suddenly as the horror began, it ended. She stood back in the same place, the ground firm under her feet, miraculously unharmed. Now she ran—back down the path, splashing across the creek with no thought to her shoes. She heaved chest-wracking sobs that robbed her of oxygen and made her gasp for air—then sprinted up the next hill, and down the back. She felt no distortion of time now. Fear and a wailing behind her drove her faster. Then her feet slid out from under her. The thin leather soles of her dainty shoes lost their grip and sent her tumbling into thorny bushes that ripped at her legs. As she lay there wheezing and bleeding, hands grabbed at both of her arms and yanked her up. She shrieked as wild-eyed horror came flooding back, fighting to free herself, when Anna screamed in her face— "we've got you, RUN." Anna dragged her along on one side and James on the other, as she found her footing and started to run. The others ran along with them until they burst out of the woods, where they stood on trembling legs in the pale glow of the single street lamp. Their chests swelled with labored palpitations as they gulped for air, each face streaked with tears as they fought to contain their sobs.

Anna was the first to gain some measure of control, "Where were you little fuckers?" (No pretend curses now, her mouth had outrun her filters.) "Did you guys see it? Where the hell were you?"

"Where were YOU?" A chorus now, a garbled cacophony of accusations. Finally, they calmed enough to understand that, yes, they all saw it, and had each been alone when they did. No one wanted to believe the others didn't abandon them.

"Enough! My house, tomorrow at three, every damn one of you—and no one says a fu—FLACKING word to anyone else. We're gonna figure this out, but now it must be late, our parents will kill us."

As they slowly nodded, Betty thought to look at her watch. She wore a Tinker Bell watch, and the sight of the cartoon fairy, holding a lantern for the hour hand, with her wings forming the minute and second hands, made her shake all over again. The hands read 9:30, little more than an hour had passed. "No way! It's only about 9:30, can that be right?" Those with watches confirmed the time.

Then Stevie's eyes bulged, "Betty PEED herself! Look at the BABY! Betty peed all over herself!"

It was only then Betty felt the dampness spread to her sodden shorts, and noticed the trickle of urine down her leg to her socks. She started bawling again.

"Shut up Stevie," shouted a suddenly furious James, "leave her alone. She couldn't help it."

Anna's eyes flashed, "Yeah Twerp, keep your flacking mouth shut and leave her the HELL alone." She walked over to Betty and, fighting back her own tears, put her arm around the frightened girl. "It's okay, Sweetie, we were all scared. We'll go to my house. You can take a bath while I wash and dry your clothes. I'll call your mom and make up a story. It'll be okay."

"We'd better head home," said Levi as he headed reluctantly back down the path to fetch his bike. The others followed, wasting no time finding their hidden bikes and getting back out to the street.

"Three tomorrow, my house. Come on Betty, come with me." Anna started the procession, each one turning to their own house, first Stevie, then Levi.

James lived across The Trail in Anna's neighborhood, so he turned off last, waved goodbye and summoned enough false bravado to say, "Don't you worry, Betty, if any of them says anything I'll feed 'em their teeth."

Betty, still snuffling, trembled and burned with embarrassment when they got to Anna's house. Anna took her hand, led her inside, and down the hall to the bathroom. She turned on the water to the tub and grabbed a washcloth from the linen closet shoehorned into the room. She showed Betty a bottle of shampoo and handed her a bar of soap, "When you take off your clothes, hand them out to me and I'll start the wash. Better give me your shoes too. I'll figure out what I can do with them. It will be fine Betty, we're back, and we're safe now. Pretty soon you'll be headed home with clean clothes." Her reassurance indicated a confidence she didn't feel as she stepped into the hall to wait.

Shivering, Betty pulled off her wet clothes, then wrapped them in her blouse, which remained dry. She opened the bathroom door and stood there holding out the little bundle, "Here Anna."

Shock registered on Anna's face—she was unprepared to be confronted with a totally naked Betty. But this was no big deal, was it? No different from changing into swimsuits in the dressing room at the pool, they were both girls, after all. She tried to suppress the involuntary gasp, tried, unsuccessfully, not to stare, and to ignore the sudden heat flushing her cheeks as she grabbed the bundle and almost slammed the door. "T-take your time, it will take a while for these to wash and dry."

Betty moved as if in a trance. She stepped into the tub and began soaping herself. At home, she would have a bubble bath with some rubber floating toys, but tonight she didn't notice the difference.

Anna began the ordeal of washing the urine-soaked clothing. She rolled the old washing machine from the garage into the kitchen, connected the water from the faucet and ran the drain hose into the sink. It had one of those old-fashioned wringers and loaded from the top, an outdated model Carrie Cook purchased from Willie Kocheck's EZ Appliance down on Red River. Willie ran ads on late-night television promising free delivery and EZ terms ("This is Willie Kocheck telling you to come on in for EZ down, EZ pay...") He specialized in selling refurbished appliances to low-income households and had the reputation of honest dealings among the Black and Hispanic communities in East Austin. A nurse's aide Carrie befriended made the recommendation. The Kocheck return policy, more than generous for the time, offered low down payments, free delivery and a 30-day guarantee with every purchase. Unable to afford the five hundred dollars for a new washer/dryer, Carrie chose a 10-year-old washer, and a dryer of similar vintage for $10 dollars down and $5 dollars a month until she paid off the $50 price. At least three other used appliance dealers sold absolute junk at inflated prices within a two-block radius of Kocheck's, but he was an honest man who genuinely cared for his customers and always ensured the refurbished models he sold were in top shape. Anna had become so proficient at setting up the outdated model that she completed the task within a few minutes, and the rugged old washer slogged away. The dryer stayed in the garage, with the vent hose attached to a woman's stocking, since the garage had no outside venting.

Once the washing started, Anna picked up the phone and dialed Betty's mother, "Oh hi, Penelope, Carrie Cook here—I just wanted to tell you that Betty may be a little late getting home—those silly girls got taffy all over themselves, so I'm popping Betty into the tub to clean up before I send her on home. Oh no, don't worry, I'll follow her and make sure she gets there safely."

Anna was good. FLACKING good.

Down the hall, Betty sat in the tub soaping away. She stared straight ahead at the black mold creeping along the grout between the discolored tiles, her gaze focused far away. Her movements were robotic, and she hovered on the edge of consciousness. The incessant rubbing with the thin washcloth had turned her skin a raw shade of red, but she took no notice, moving with disturbing repetition. She ignored the knocking at the door and seemed not to recognize her name.

Heaving a sigh, Anna turned the knob and entered the bathroom. Betty sat upright, methodically soaping every part of her body, as though unaware of Anna's presence. Anna shook her by the shoulders, and the distant eyes blinked and turned to Anna, then looked at the washcloth and soap in confusion, not understanding when Anna told her to rinse off and get out. Anna grabbed the cloth and helped Betty rinse herself, reached down to pull the rubber stopper, and hauled her to her feet and out of the tub. Betty emitted a little moan as her confusion cleared. She began to whimper, throwing her arms around Anna and sobbing incessantly. A horrified Anna, now dripping herself, awkwardly patted the wet back and struggled to reach for a towel. When Betty paused to draw in air, Anna pried herself loose, and shoved the towel into uncooperative hands "Here, now dry off and I'll find you a robe."

Anna fought to hold it together herself. It helped a little having to deal with the feckless Betty. She was nearly paralyzed with fear from the night's images, but years of watching her mother's financial struggles had trained her to compartmentalize the bad stuff and focus on the here and now. Carrie would often transfer a few of the monthly bills into a special file to defer until the following month. She would then sneak into her bedroom for what she thought was a private cry, but the walls in the old homestead were thin, and Anna's little ears were sharp. And there were the times they would be checking out at Big Bear, when Carrie would glance at the checkbook balance, and quietly ask the cashier to return a few items. She held her head high when she did this, but Anna would want to disappear, to melt through the floor. Especially that time the checker was Stevie's brother Mark. She hadn't really known him, but had seen him hanging around Stevie's house, so they had at least a nodding acquaintance. It was those times that chip on her shoulder grew just the tiniest bit heavier.

Anna rummaged through her closet for an old robe and took it to a waiting Betty, who had dropped her wet towel on the floor and stood blubbering in the hall by the bathroom. Anna handed it to her with a terse "Put this on, the laundry won't be ready for a while."

Letting the robe gape open, Betty stuck her arms through the sleeves, grabbed Anna in a bear hug and sobbed into her chest. "Did you see it; did you see it, Anna?"

"Yeah, I saw it, now get ahold of yourself and CLOSE THE GWARD DAMN ROBE!" Shouting now, overwhelmed with confusing emotions.

Betty stepped back fearfully and snuffled loudly. She rubbed red eyes as mucus poured from her nose.

"Oh, for... here's a tissue, wipe your nose, I'm gonna put your clothes in the dryer." Anna figured the clothes had washed long enough, so she grabbed the dripping wad, transferred it into the dryer in the garage and started it up on high. Betty sat on the tattered couch, sobbing softly, leaning forward and clutching her elbows.

"Lie down," more softly now, "those will take a while, I'll see what I can do with your shoes."

Most of the urine had soaked into the white bobby socks, so Anna soaped the shoes lightly with an old rag, rinsed it and wiped off the soap. Another old rag did a sufficient job of drying them— they might feel a little damp, but tough beans. She was not Betty's mother.

Betty fell asleep, still whimpering and groaning. Anna sat in a big, overstuffed chair, the only other furnishing in the modest living room, and, suddenly overtaken with exhaustion, let her head fall between her legs. She soon dropped off as well, with troubling images muddling her dreams. She awoke with a start when Betty screamed, "Let GO, let me GO!"

Shaking the slender shoulders gently, Anna murmured, "Wake up Sweetie, you're just dreaming." Betty's eyes flew open with confusion and fear as she groggily began separating her dream images from the reality before her. Anna glanced at the clock. "That should be long enough, put on your clothes and you can head home." She fetched the clothes, still slightly damp, from the dryer, and herded Betty into her bedroom.

"Stay with me Anna, I'm scared." She was still whimpering and shivering.

A reluctant Anna followed her in, but kept her eyes averted until Betty had, not without complaining, put on the damp clothes. While Betty put her shoes and socks back on, Anna grabbed the robe, wet towel, and washcloths, and started them going in the dryer—she would dry them for now and worry about washing them tomorrow.

"All right Twerp, when you get home don't say a DAMN word about tonight. We'll talk about it tomorrow. And for God's sake don't yell and talk in your sleep."

"Okay, Anna. But Anna, I'm scared to go home alone." And, as if on cue, the waterworks started up again.

"JEEZ-RUS CRISCO what a BABY! All right, I'll ride over with you—tell your mother my mom followed you home in the car. Can you remember to do that? And not a FLACKING word. Nobody's gonna believe us, anyway."

That night they fell into bed drained and exhausted. The horrors of the evening haunted their dreams, and they awakened late the next day. Anna's dreams were a tangled mix of what she had seen in the woods, and of Betty standing naked in front of her, grabbing her in a hug. Then somehow Betty became James, but with Betty's body.

When Anna awoke, the hands of her alarm clock pointed straight up, and she was touching herself.

Chapter 8
Down the Rabbit Hole

Did you ever wonder how Alice got down that rabbit hole? She wasn't small 'till she ate the mushroom she found at the bottom.

Stevie's Tuesday Morning

"Stevie, what is wrong with you today? First you sleep until noon and now you're hardly touching your lunch."

Stevie stared at the sandwich and chips with blank eyes. His mother had made his favorite—peanut butter, honey, and banana on toasted white bread, with a liberal side of Fritos and a cold Dr Pepper to wash it down.

"Just when we thought the little lard bucket couldn't get any weirder, he out-weirds himself again."

"Marcus Allen Lindquist—apologize to your brother!"

"Soooorrreeee, Steeevieee."

Normally at this point Stevie would smirk broadly at his older brother, but the exchange didn't even register. He took a few bites of the sandwich, ate some Fritos and took a swig of Dr Pepper. "Mom, may I be excused now?"

"Stevie, are you ill?" his mother asked in a worried voice, stepping over and feeling his forehead.

"No, Mom, just a little tired. Can I go now?"

Returning to his room, he sat at his desk and stared dully out the window. A few minutes later his door opened and Mark barged in without knocking—a surefire way to set off a wail of protest in normal times. "OK, Lard Ass, what's wrong? Something's up with you—come on, spill."

At fifteen, Mark was everything his younger brother could only hope to be—handsome, athletic, and popular. Stevie's only advantage was his exceptional intelligence; already having skipped a grade, he coasted through his classes, whereas Mark struggled to maintain average grades. Mark was relentless in his teasing at home, but was otherwise protective of his little brother, and his concern now was real.

"Nuthin'," Stevie muttered, determined to stick to his promise not to say a FLACKING thing to anyone.

"Bull HOCKEY," Mark retorted. "I know you and your little moods. You can fool Mom every day and twice on Sunday, but you ain't foolin' me. Something's up—spill."

"I SAID nothing's up. Now go away and leave me alone."

And on it went, back and forth, Mark growing angrier and louder, and Stevie weakening, until he rationalized that Anna had been talking about adults, and Mark was anything but adult.

"OK, but you gotta promise not to tell, and not make fun of me, even if you don't believe me, and you won't, but give it a chance, I swear this is all true." Then, as an incredulous Mark listened, it came pouring out.

Breakfast with the Stieglitz Family

Levi arrived home drained and exhausted. Barely able to don pajamas, he mumbled a quiet goodnight to his aunt and uncle before collapsing into bed. He slept hard; his dreams tormented by visions of what he'd experienced. He did not awaken until 11:30 the next morning, with his bedclothes twisted into a wad from tossing and turning. Abe and Sophie were long gone to the drugstore, but he found a note on the kitchen table: "LAZYBONES—if you ever decide to get up, come on down to the store and Abe will feed you something better than cereal. Love, Aunt Sophie."

He gagged at the thought of food, but sometimes you had to "go along to get along." If he admitted it, Levi didn't want to be alone with his thoughts, so he dressed hurriedly and headed to Stieglitz Drugs.

Abe waved Levi over to the soda fountain counter as he stepped through the door, but he stopped briefly at the comic book rack and grabbed the newest Superman—*"The Super-Key to Fort Superman."* Abe had a fried egg and two strips of bacon bubbling on the grill, and poured a frothing glass of milk from a blue dispenser with *Superior Dairies* spelled out in glossy chrome letters (What is an old Jew doing serving bacon? The Stieglitz's were Reform Jews with strong atheistic leanings, and although Abe had great respect for Jewish tradition, he did not believe in the need to keep Kosher.)

"Where have you been, Buddy? Did you plan to stay in bed all day and sleep straight through to tomorrow?" Abe grinned, he used this line any time Levi stayed in bed past ten, and never failed to chuckle at his own joke. But behind the jovial smile, Abe felt something was off with Levi, he had come in a little late the night before, and acted distracted, almost dazed. When he checked on Levi this morning, the boy moaned and squirmed in his sleep. Abe thought about waking him up but decided the late night must have been too much for the little fellow and let him be. Sophie and Abe worried about Levi's growth, more than merely small for his age, he hovered just below the bottom of the normal range. Sophie was talking about a new therapy called Human Growth Hormone, or HGH.

HGH was extracted from the pituitary glands of cadavers, what could possibly go wrong? A brand-new treatment in 1958, Sophie had been researching it obsessively. Abe was skeptical, he loved

Levi as if he were his own son and didn't like the thought of experimenting with his health. Being so small had to be tough. Abe was proud of the way Levi stood up for himself and compensated for his diminutive stature with his exceptional speed and agility, as though nature had taken one thing but replaced it with another. Abe's Christian friends might have said "When God closes a door, he opens a little window," but Abe's on-again, off-again relationship with the Big Guy didn't allow for that kind of comforting platitude. The conversations continued with no decision, but Sophie could be pigheaded once she had her mind set. Like freshly poured concrete, it firmed up more by the day.

Sitting on his favorite stool, drinking cold milk, reading about the Fortress of Solitude, and listening to his smiling uncle cracking wise made Levi feel a little better. He would be safe here, reading comics and listening to his uncle's dumb jokes and crazy stories until time to head out to Anna's house.

Firehouse Rules at the Hatcher Place

Rod Hatcher was a guy's guy. Carla had died delivering James, whose middle name, Carl, was what Rod had imagined the masculine form of Carla would be, and Rod as a single dad had struggled with raising the boy. His sometimes, well, most of the time, girlfriend helped during those long shifts at the fire station, but she had a job too. It helped, and didn't help, that she was ensconced in the efficiency apartment atop the garage, the mere width of the small backyard away, that she leased from Rod on fairly generous terms. This arrangement caused an undue amount of whispering by the neighbors in 1958 Austin, and considerable confusion on James' part, especially during those times Rod visited her in the little apartment to do various "maintenance projects." Things in that place were always breaking down.

Garage apartments, referred to locally as "Granny Flats" were common in Austin. While frequently Granny did live there, the owners often rented them to college students or young singles who couldn't afford apartment rent. The Hatcher abode was another of those small cheap homes in Bentwood Acres, a few blocks from Anna's house. A single-car garage in the rear of the oversized corner lot had its attic space converted into a small apartment with the kitchen running along the back. The central room was a combination living/dining/bedroom, made possible by the Murphy bed Rod had built into one wall; humble accommodations to be sure, but Rod's girl Jenny was grateful for it, having lived crammed into a small apartment with three other girls for several years. The Granny Flat was a major step up from that arrangement. Besides, Rod was easy on the eyes, and a lot of fun when she convinced him to relax. That could be difficult, his job as Assistant Fire Captain came with heavy responsibilities, on top of the ongoing mysteries of child rearing. Nevertheless, a girl could try.

James slept the sleep of the dead until "noon-thirty," as Rod would have called it. Like the others, his dreams had been fitful and troubled, a gruesome replay of what he experienced the night before, interrupted by flashing images of Betty falling into the brambles as he ran, demented, out of the woods, of her crying in urine-soaked shorts; then, perhaps the most disturbing, a smiling Jenny, wearing only a long T-shirt, replaced Betty's image. Lately she seemed to think it perfectly acceptable to show up in the morning, especially on weekends, barefoot and clad in the T-shirt she wore to bed the night before. She'd traipse across the backyard, come in the kitchen door, and stand on tiptoe to give Rod a quick smack on the lips. When she did this, the tee would ride up in back, sometimes exposing the bottom of white cotton panties. Then she would come over to where James sat, give him a peck on the cheek, ruffle his hair and say something like "Morning Handsome, your daddy better watch out—you're gonna give him some competition one of these days."

James would flush and mumble an embarrassed reply. Even worse, in recent weeks, he would sprout one of his first erections, standing at attention like a little soldier. He'd attempt to hide it with his napkin, trying to think of something, anything, to make it go away. Rod and Jenny seemed oblivious. He would dream of Jenny and those T-shirts, and wake up with those unwelcome erections. This morning he had a humdinger.

When he stumbled out to the kitchen, he found a brief note on the table—Good Morning Cutie, your dad had to go into the fire station, and I'm off to work. You're on your own for breakfast and lunch, but I'll pick up something for supper and stop by before your dad and I go out, Your BEST Girl, Jenny

The unmistakable impression of a pair of lips, emblazoned directly below this salutation in scarlet lipstick, had a little arrow pointing to it and the words *One of these days, Big Boy! (Ha, ha.)*

As James stared at the bright red image, his little soldier sprang back to attention, and he was left alone until time to join the others at Anna's house. He was usually happy, even elated, when Rod went on shift. Although a great dad in most ways, playing baseball, basketball, and football with James, teaching him how to shoot, clean and load Rod's 30-06 hunting rifle, and introducing James to Friday night fights, Texas Longhorn football, and a host of other "guy" things, Rod could also be harsh, as he sought to navigate the unfamiliar waters of parenthood.

Now James faced the impending hours of alone time with a sense of dread. The terror he had experienced crept back into his consciousness. He poured himself a bowl of sugary cereal, doused it with milk, and turned on the television in the living room. It was one of those in a large wooden cabinet that included a radio and a pair of speakers, but the screen itself was an eye-straining fourteen inches. Only the overly dramatic soap operas popular with the housewives of the postwar era came on, but even watching one of these beat sitting there reliving the events of the previous evening. He selected "As the World Turns," and tried to concentrate on the slow-moving story involving a doctor and the implied affair his wife was having with their lawyer. Big time boring, but he left it on for the noise before walking back to his bedroom to shuffle through the pile of comic books for what seemed like the hundredth time.

James eventually chose one with Betty and Veronica on the cover, wearing short shorts and blowing kisses to Archie as he pitched a baseball to a waiting Reggie. Paging through the accompanying story, he was overcome with sleep. In his dreams this time, comic book Betty became real-life Betty, and Veronica became Jenny. Archie was Levi, and James the hapless Jughead, watching from the sidelines. The two girls swooned over Levi/Archie, and James felt a surge of red anger rising uncontrollably in his chest. The feeling was not unfamiliar, he experienced something similar with growing frequency, something feral and elemental, beyond his conscious control. In the dream, he grabbed a bat and headed toward Levi with murderous intent. He awoke with a start—he not only had an erection but was rubbing it up and down, shuddering with a sudden thrill of ecstasy that whispered the first delicious promise of early adolescence. He rubbed harder. It felt even better, but after a while made him shiver with weakness. Unable to complete the premature journey he had begun, having come to the periphery of something he did not understand, he stopped, panting and standing on trembling legs. This was new and confusing. He knew a little about the birds and bees, but his knowledge was a jumble of half-understood rumors circulated among his equally clueless classmates, and Rod's off-color jokes. Standing there by the side of his bed, breathing deeply to catch his breath, he glanced at his watch. Two-thirty; close enough—he could not bear to be alone with this confusion and fear for another moment. He ran out to his bike and set off for Anna's.

She jerked back her hand, overcome by a flash of shame. Her fingers felt wet and a little sticky. She was a lefty, and apparently her wrong-handedness carried over into this. Holding the hand away from her body, she threw off the covers with her right hand, used it to open the bathroom door and scrubbed the offending fingers with a vengeance.

"Is that you Anna Belle?" Her mother always said it with strong emphasis on the "Belle, so that it came out as two syllables, 'BEH-ELL.'" Carrie had chosen to spell it as two words rather than the more common Annabelle, thinking it lent her daughter an air of uniqueness. Anna didn't like it much, but she had always been Anna Belle to her mom. She was registered at school with both names, and was Anna Belle to her teachers and classmates. She decided that when she matriculated to Junior High, the Belle would be long gone. For now, only the small group of close friends had agreed to drop it, on threat of bodily harm—ironic given the level of verbal abuse she regularly heaped on them.

"Coming Mom," she gave her fingers a perfunctory sniff. They smelled like Ivory Soap. She thought of that commercial—99 and 44/100% pure. She wondered about that other 66/100%.

"I thought you were going to sleep all day—this isn't like you Anna Belle. What did you do to make yourself so tired?"

"I dunno. I guess I read 'til pretty late—I think I even heard you come in after your shift. Was it an especially rough one?" She blurted out the question, hoping it sounded reasonable and would change the subject.

"Pure chaos. Besides the usual drunks, truck wrecks, and hypochondriacs, we've been having a rash of UT students and also a few minorities who are high on something that makes them next to impossible to control. They experience hallucinations that give them weird reactions. Sometimes we have to pump them full of drugs to make them calm down. They fall off to sleep and start yelling in their sleep; some even get up and sleepwalk. We had to call in extra LVN's and orderlies tonight to maintain even a shred of control. I just got up myself—I was absolutely exhausted. We don't know what they're taking or where they're getting it, but we'll have to send some of them to other hospitals if it keeps up. But honestly, some people. I had to call one coed's mother to tell her about her daughter, and she went off on how Rock' n' Roll is the devil's music, and Elvis Presley, Little Richard, and a few others are all agents of the devil. I don't understand what's wrong with some people Anna Belle. I'm going in early today, and may not be home on time. I worry about you here all alone, Honey, but I'm glad you have such nice friends now; they're welcome here any time. That mother reminded me of little Betty Dupree's mom, Penelope. She's extremely religious like that. Now I'm not saying there's anything wrong with being religious, but those holy roller types, I just don't know..."

"Oh Mom, let me make breakfast, you sit down and drink your coffee. I'll scramble up some eggs, make some toast and check if there's any sausage or bacon. How does that sound?" This offer deftly circumvented any need to talk about her night or dreams. Yeah, Anna was good.

After breakfast, Anna insisted her mother lie down on the couch and close her eyes for an hour, which she gratefully agreed to do. Anna set an alarm, sat down, and closed her eyes until time for Carrie to dress for work.

Once Carrie pulled out of the driveway, preoccupied by happy thoughts of what a considerate little girl she had, Anna flew into action. She did the breakfast dishes, then started a proper wash for the robe and towels from the night before. This done, she dressed and tried to keep her mind off the previous night, her disturbing dreams, or whatever the HELL she was doing when she woke up.

Shortly after Carrie left, respite came with James' early arrival.

"Is it okay to be here now? Your mom's gone, right? Dad went to work, and I couldn't stand being alone any longer."

"Yeah, come on in. I'm going nuts myself. Having to act normal around Mom this morning, trying not to think about last night, CRAZY. How did you sleep? I had awful dreams."

"Me too. Hey, did you get Betty home?" He was unable to disguise the concern in his voice.

"Yeah, finally. What a pain in the A double letter after R she is. I practically had to bathe her myself, had to wash and dry her DAMN clothes, and she just whined and cried. She fell asleep while her clothes dried, but woke up yelling. I even had to follow her home because she was SCARED."

James gulped at the mental image of Betty naked in the bath. "She's still a kid, Anna. We need to cut her some slack."

Anna glared; this was exactly what she'd expect James to say. "Forget Betty, did you see her, him, whatever the HELL that was last night?"

James looked confused. "What do you mean—her, him? I would have said IT or them."

"I guess, maybe. Anyway, no talking about it until everyone's here." If asked why she imposed this rule, she would have been hard-pressed to answer, but it seemed important. "You can talk about today," she decided. "Did you sleep in real late? I didn't wake up 'till about noon. I was SO tired."

"Twelve-thirty for me. We were gone less than two hours last night, but it felt like all night. I was as tired as if it was. This morning was... weird... is all I'm gonna say. I came early because being alone was getting to me."

"What about Daddy's GIRLFRIEND? I'll bet you wouldn't mind being alone with HER."

James went red, and then felt himself going red inside, the red mist rising into his chest and working its way to his head. His hands quivered with anger as he fought to control himself. "That, that," he couldn't come up with a word. "I don't care nuthin' about her. I guess she's okay, but she's a renter, she's NOT his girlfriend. Anyway, she's at work too."

"Ummm hmmm, whatever you say Jimmy Boy."

The red mist overflowed, out his ears now, coming out his mouth and nose and about to burst through the top of his head. "DON'T YOU EVER CALL ME THAT AGAIN—ANNA <u>BELLE</u>." He was shouting now, right up in her face.

She stared back and spoke in a quietly intimidating voice, in complete contrast to his yelling, "No Anna Belle, No Jimmy Boy. Deal? Or you and I are gonna do more than FLACKIN' talk about it."

The red mist came whistling out, like air from a leaking balloon. Calm now, "Deal. Sorry for yelling. Honest Anna, I don't understand what gets into me, and it's been worse since last night."

"Or me. Sometimes I just like to push your buttons. It's stupid and mean. I'm sorry too."

They were interrupted as the others began to arrive. Now the stories could be told.

CHAPTER 9
HE SAID, SHE SAID

"There are things known and there are things unknown, and in between are the doors of perception."
–Aldous Huxley

When Anna opened the door, Levi stood there, and Little Betty was pulling into the drive, followed by an ancient gray Studebaker that appeared to be held together with Bondo, belching black smoke and rattling. DAMN Stevie—the little twerp brought his big brother, after she had specifically told them not to tell another soul. The Studie's doors protested with loud rusty groans as Stevie and Mark forced them open. They piled out and started up the walk.

Boiling with indignation, Anna dashed out to confront them, "Stevie, didn't I tell you not to tell anyone? Why is he here?"

"Easy Cutie, I'm not gonna tell anyone about your little secrets." Mark smiled disarmingly, and Anna melted—just a little. At fifteen, Mark already had the broad shoulders and deep chest characteristic of his Scandinavian ancestry. He wore his light brown hair in a "flat-top with fenders," a popular style among the hipper of his teenage friends. He looked guilelessly down at Anna with deep blue eyes. After all, what would it hurt to let him in? And had he called her CUTIE? Yeah, what would it hurt?

"He's not a grown-up Anna, and he promised to keep it secret."

Recovering a little— "Oh, okay, it's too late now anyway, come on in."

Mark took the overstuffed chair as if it was his due, and the others scattered about on the couch and floor. "All right kiddies, Stevie told me the most ridiculous story I ever heard. Who wants to tell me what actually went on last night?"

They started in like the bursting of a dam. The volume increased as they tried to talk over one another. Out of the chaos, Mark could tell these stories differed. They were similar until they reached the final hilltop. From that point the only thing in common was their insistence that the others had disappeared.

"TIME OUT, we're gonna do this one at a time, and anyone who interrupts is gonna have a conversation with Mr. Iron and Mr. Steel." He held up clenched fists. Mark got the idea for those names from the Tennessee Ernie Ford song, "16 Tons." He thought it awfully clever.

"You're the hostess, Red, you go first."

Anna's Adventure

Anna started at the beginning, with Stevie telling them about seeing the object coming down from the sky. Mark interrupted, telling her to start with the part where they went to the woods. So, she fast forwarded, and began her story at the point where they started the trek into the woods. She related the first part of the journey accurately. She had taken particular pains to hide her bicycle, knowing if it was stolen her mother would be hard-pressed to replace it. Carrie found the refurbished model at a second-hand shop and went to great lengths to store it at a friend's house as a Christmas surprise. That had been over a year ago. When Anna saw the gift sitting under their modest Christmas tree, she burst into tears of joy; it instantly became her most prized possession. She never let it drop to the ground the way some of the others did, and never failed to store it inside the garage at night. She was the last to find a secure enough hiding place, behind a dense bush.

Anna remembered those woods having been a very different place at night; the dim old flashlight she found in a drawer kept flickering. She had to bang on it to get it to light up the many times it winked out. Even when it worked, the feeble yellow light was only visible for a few feet, and turned the trees into grotesque apparitions bearing scant similarity to their daytime appearance. She was soon lost, and had to trust James. Progress seemed impossibly slow, and she found it difficult to concentrate, almost as though she was dreaming. She had no recollection of the humming noise they'd heard. She recalled reaching the place where the trail split. When James wanted to take the trail to the right, it seemed wrong. They were headed for the highest hill in the area, and he took the downhill branch. They'd been walking for what seemed like hours. She was ready to insist on turning around, when they reached the creek crossing and started back up.

Once the trail rose again, her head cleared, and her time sense returned to normal. Up to this point, all the heads nodded in agreement with her story.

When she told about reaching the top of the final hill, her story diverged. She was suddenly alone. It was disconcerting. She looked around in near panic as her little flashlight flickered out. The only light on this moonless night was the marginal illumination from the collection of gas globes thousands of light years away. She blinked frantically, trying to adjust her eyes to the near blackness. An unusual little girl for her tender age, Anna had watched her mother go through some hard times, more than once teetering on the verge of losing their shabby little home. She'd learned to interpret her mother's moods with precocious insight, and to shoulder more than her reasonable share of the burdens. This toughened her beyond her years, and made her resilient to those daily anxieties. But this was different; she felt a growing sense of dread as she received no response. Then, suddenly, her terror subsided, as though some external source controlled her autonomic responses. Her racing heart rate slowed, and her harsh, ragged breathing slackened. As she stood there, a pale glow began to shimmer deep in the gorge. It steadily brightened, and flowed up the sides of the valley like a rising tide until the faint illumination surrounded her.

The path ahead came into view as it snaked down the hill and deep into the forest. For a few moments she stood there in eerie silence, rooted in place. Her memory of this interval was vague. She was unsure how long it lasted—she thought only a few minutes.

Her gaze shifted down the path, and she could pick out a bit more detail. Some distance ahead the trail disappeared, melting into the forest. Eventually, she noticed a shape emerging from the forest at the limit of her vision. The group shook their heads. Stevie squealed, "NO, that's wrong," in a register that would have been the envy of any Soprano Acuto Sfogato. One could imagine dogs howling for blocks around.

Mark got up, walked over, grabbed Stevie's underpants in back and yanked the Fruit of the Loom patch up between his shoulder blades, "I SAID shut up and let her finish."

Stevie made a noise like a kitten with her little kitty tail caught in a blender.

This momentarily broke the tension and the entire group began to giggle, fighting to stifle their nervous guffaws under Mark's menacing glare.

"That little brown stripe in the back is stylish!" Levi was consumed with laughter. Stevie, not so much.

Anna regained a modicum of control, snorted one last time, and resumed her account.

The shape zigzagged back across the path, disappearing into the forest each time, then reappearing closer. Fog obscured the details as it approached. She could only tell it resembled a human, an adult. As it emerged for the last time, now as close as the room was wide, the fog lifted. A beautiful woman appeared, gliding, almost floating, across the path. Her profile and bearing were regal. Anna remembered the lady had long red hair cascading down across her shoulder. She wore a graceful, flowing green gown that swept the ground but was pinched in to reveal a slender waist. She walked in dreamlike silence, floating to the left side of the path, where she turned back. Anna gasped in disbelief, her breath lying soft on her tongue with the warmth of the summer night. In this profile she was looking at a man. His chiseled features were as handsome as the woman had been beautiful, with the same red hair, but cut short, leaving the scent of hair tonic gentle on the breeze. Anna described the tuxedo he wore as a "fancy suit."

Slowly the apparition crossed the path, back and forth, Anna didn't remember exactly how many times. Each crossing brought the change from female to male and back again. Anna was not afraid, but experienced an all-embracing sense of confusion. Still silent, the eerie performance was making Anna's head spin.

Anna tried to speak, but her mind had forgotten how to make her lips obey. At last the thing stopped and turned toward her. From this perspective, it was strange to behold, half woman, half man—both beautiful and handsome, the features on each side mirroring the other, yet different, one side feminine and the other masculine. It stood rooted, but began to tremble, quivering faster and faster, until it became a blur of vibration. The features distorted, then gradually merged into one unholy composite of the two.

Carrie Cook was in the habit of yelling at their television whenever poor grammar was used, or words were misused. One of her pet peeves was the use of the word mixture to mean blend, or vice versa. She had taken plenty of chemistry classes to earn her nursing degree, and had it drilled into her that in chemistry, there is a distinction between a mixture and a blend. In a mixture, the molecules of each component remain distinct and unchanged; in a blend, the molecules join to make new molecules that cannot be separated back into those original parts. Anna had listened to these rants often enough to realize that what started out as a mixture of male and female, was now a blend of the two, but in a most distressing way. Now it was dreadfully wrong—a vile distortion, grotesque in its chaotic combination of feminine and masculine.

A Wrong Thing.

As our understanding of genetics, psychology, and brain science has progressed, attitudes toward individual gender identities have evolved. We now realize one's place on the male/female continuum—gender identity—is a matter of genetics, one's own perception, and the choice to be who you are; but this was a different time.

The creature now facing Anna lay somewhere off that line, somewhere on another axis, in another reality, a dimension with a separate set of vibrating strings. This cat was neither alive NOR dead, Baby—a cat but not cat, you dig? —a thing from beyond her ken, horrifying to behold and impossible for Anna to describe.

Wrong.

The Wrong Thing was clearly in pain. A plaintive sound echoed from its mouth, and it reached out to Anna with a pleading, submissive gesture. The sound sent a chill down her spine; not a word, it was a keening, animalistic attempt at a word.

Wrong.

Anna said her mind snapped. She said it broke; the world broke for her, and still feels broken. Said it splintered, said she was cloven in half—a sophisticated expression, but Anna was a precocious little brat. She tried to scream, but the gurgling sound that came out only fed her panic. The Wrong Thing slouched toward her, mewling, stinking of desperation, with its arms outstretched, looking like a toddler's failed attempt to draw Mommy or Daddy. But this Picasso-esque drawing did not belong on the refrigerator door. Oh no—only in a house of horrors. Anna wrenched back her tortured psyche, turned, and fled.

She couldn't remember ever having run so fast, ever having been able to run that fast. The dim light from the valley was fading now. She banged the little flashlight against her pumping legs until at last it flickered on, sending out a pathetically insufficient beam, but better than nothing as the glow from the valley dissipated. Anna mounted the last hill like flat ground, and started down, through the twisting and turning switchbacks. Then she saw Betty snarled in brambles and stopped to help her, when James appeared from nowhere. They hoisted Betty up to start her running again, as Stevie huffed by and Levi sprinted far ahead.

When she noticed Betty staring at her with tearful, pleading eyes, Anna didn't relate Betty's accident. She omitted the detour to her house, and simply said she followed Betty home to make sure she arrived safely. James narrowed his eyes, but didn't contradict her. Anna said she had horrible nightmares that replayed the evening, leaving out the parts with Betty and James, and not mentioning the next morning, only saying she overslept.

Mark frowned, "That's sure not the same story my punk brother told me. Parts were the same, but not the BS about what you saw. I don't know which story was dumber. Say, are you little brats setting me up? Is that what this is? Hilarious, HA HA. Well, I ain't buyin' it. Not your half-man, half-woman, and not Stevie's flying saucer with little green men."

The cacophony started up again, each one protesting, swearing, their story was real, wait and see. Swear and hope to die, hope to make my mother cry. Betty would swear on the Bible— a whole stack of Bibles! Levi kept crossing his heart. Only Stevie sat silent, still aching from the wedgie he received, burning with embarrassment.

Mark shut them up again with repeated threats. The group was adamant; they had gone to the woods, followed the trail to the top of the highest hill, and something horrific happened. The endings were consistent; they all ran away, starting out alone, and didn't see the others until they reached the spot where Betty fell into the bushes. He squinted at them suspiciously. If they were putting him on, it was a damn convincing job. He had to think, had to find a way to poke holes in their stories.

"All right for now. Tell ya what we're gonna do—same as before, each of you gets a turn to tell what happened. Since you all agree on what happened until you got to the top of the last hill, leave that part out. Okay? James, you look like you have better sense than these other yahoos, why don't you go next?"

James

He agreed with trepidation, fearing his story would be met with the same disbelief and derision. Yes, it was as Anna had described up to when they reached the last summit.

Yeah, when he reached the top, he was suddenly alone. Yeah, he'd called out and received no response. He had the best flashlight of the bunch, a professional model his dad kept at home for emergencies. It was held five double-D batteries and provided decent illumination for fifteen to twenty feet. Rod always kept it loaded with fresh batteries, so James could make a thorough sweep of the area. The others were nowhere in sight.

Like Anna, he panicked momentarily, but then felt a comforting sense of calm. James felt he'd gone into a trance, his thoughts drifting—for what? Five minutes maybe? He blinked and found himself gazing down into the valley, where a mist crawled up the hillsides. It was a glowing fog, red as the fire engines at the station, but not so thick as to obscure the distant hills, only a translucent crimson haze. As much as he could see it, he could FEEL it. The blood red mist was now rising in him. He felt it first in his feet, and it rose along with the mist coming up from the valley. The feeling was impossible to describe. KIND of a tingling sensation, KIND of a warm feeling, no, DEFINITELY warm, almost hot as it crept up his legs and into his torso (he was NOT gonna mention how it felt when it reached his ding-dong, didn't have the words to describe THAT anyway.) Once it reached his chest, it seemed to fill his lungs with heat and make it difficult to breathe; he had to gasp for air, his breath turned hot and seared his insides. His throat burned, and his face heated up. It hit his brain in a frenzy of blistering rage, and his thoughts seethed with uncontrollable anger.

While these thoughts occupied his mind, the crimson mist reached his level and rose high above the hilltop. It swirled, formed eddies, and the eddies formed images, the way puffy cumulus clouds form kitties and bunnies.

But these were no bunnies.

They were angry, menacing things that disappeared soon after they formed, but kept relentlessly at it. They rose, fell, spun, and swept across the sky. Eyes glowed and glowered, ragged arms stretched out with disfigured talons, and dreadful mouths opened to reveal endless black chasms. A demonic symphony issued from them. It was Night on Bald Mountain; it was Die Valkyrie; it was the crescendo of a thousand massive pipe organs, screaming out in a wavering, thundering discordance of minor chords. He could feel the sound, feel it penetrate his gut and furrow through him.

The phantasms rose higher and swept closer, reaching out with hungry arms, lashing the air with serpentine tongues and wailing their profane hymns. James wanted to run, but his legs refused to cooperate. He stood frozen in place, unable to move or look away. They formed over him and dove, crushing him in a fiery embrace that threatened to turn his insides to blackened embers and suck out his last fragment of emotional control. A ragged, filthy tongue snaked out and licked James across the face. There was a dark hole where the mouth belonged. It stank of shit and piss, and took him back to a day etched deeply into his memory.

Let's rewind a few years and accompany James and his dad on a brief detour out Farm to Market Road 79 northeast of Austin, as it wends its way through a series of nondescript farming towns— little more than wide spots in the road in the 1950s. Taylor is the first burgh we reach of any real size, where the bucolic town square hosts a quaint old church, fashioned from stained, timeworn stones, in the charming greensward at its center. FM 79 leads by the square and then on out of town, past fields thick with cotton, to the even smaller hamlet of Thorndale. Turn right there, cross the railroad tracks and head down a broad main street, where you can appreciate the design influence of the iconic German Haupstrasse, a gift of the German immigrants who settled the area. This is quintessential rural Texas. A sign with blue lettering reading "Rosie's" hangs over the small café where the local farmers gather for morning coffee and bring their families for a special lunch after church on Sunday. Next door is the hardware store and farther down is Krause's Butcher Shop. The Haupstrasse flavor is evident in the parking row down the middle of the walkable street.

As tempting as it may be to investigate the charming shops, we'll roll slowly on out of town, past a block or two of neat wood-frame houses with high windows and broad, shaded verandas. Then we'll continue out into the countryside and pass a few more cotton fields and a picturesque dairy, where black and white Holstein cattle graze on green fields of Coastal Bermuda, before we encounter the undeveloped woodlands that hint at what this area looked like before the German, Austrian, and Czech settlers began clearing the land in the late 1800s. As we motor along, we pass the remaining stands of post oak and cedar. Some areas are partially cleared, in others the trees are untouched. A mile or so after we've entered this area, we encounter a rusty metal gate to our right, flanked by sagging barbed wire fencing supported by cedar posts. Through this gate, a roughly graded dirt and gravel road takes us up a gentle rise, past cleared fields, a small tank (Texan for pond), and up to a wooded section with an old wooden building nestled there. It would be a wild exaggeration to call the dilapidated building a house. Once a modest two-bedroom farmhouse, a more accurate appellation now is "shack." The firehouse owners thought of it this way, having named it Fire Shack 1, or simply "The Shack."

It served as a weekend getaway for North Austin firemen, Rod Hatcher's colleagues, and here, in 1955, eight-year-old James had his first encounter with an outhouse.

The indoor plumbing at Fire Shack 1 was by then an artifact of ancient history, and anyone wishing to do their business is directed to the shabby old outhouse next to The Shack. Like cats, eight-year-old boys are curious creatures, so when it came time for James to visit the outhouse, he bent down for a close look at where his issue would land. The stench of raw sewage assaulted his nasal cavities with a vengeance. He wretched and lost his lunch down the small hole, where it splashed merrily and released a fresh largesse of olfactory abuse. The sequence repeated itself twice, resulting in one utterly nauseous, nasally traumatized little boy.

This memory was vividly invoked by the odor issuing from the not-mouth as the apparition licked James' face.

The tongue was rough and left a bloody trail. It forced his mouth open, and probed deep down his throat, carrying the repellent stench with it. He felt his air supply being cut off. The combination of something being thrust down his throat and the rancid smell caused him to gag violently, over and over, until he vomited the foul thing out in a shower of sputum and blood.

Suddenly he could yell. That was the word he used, but truth be told (and he wasn't about to), he screamed like a little girl, and the ghoulish fiend dissolved back into the scarlet mist. James wrenched himself backwards, turned, and fled down the hill, across the creek and up the next rise. He ran like one possessed, down the next hill with all the twists and turns in the path, pumping hard, sucking in air and blasting it back out, blowing away the stench, letting it cool the fire in his lungs and clear the burning anger from his brain, as the macabre orchestra faded behind him and the red mist dissipated. Then he saw Betty tangled in a nest of nasty brambles. His heart leapt into his throat, although he didn't QUITE describe it that way. As our young heroes relate their stories, we shall learn they all kept certain little secrets to themselves. In his version, he lifted Little Betty from the brush before Anna showed up, but remembered Anna helping him hoist Betty to her feet and help her run, catching up to the others as they cleared the fringe of the woods. Like Anna, he omitted the detour Betty made to Anna's house.

Eight eyes bulged from their sockets when he finished; Betty looked ill, and Mark pursed his lips and furrowed his brow. For a moment, no one spoke. Then Levi broke the silence, "Okay, okay, but that's NOT what happened."

"TOLD you," Stevie shrilled. The neighbor's dog howled and fell over dead; he was found the next morning, with a small pool of dried blood where it had trickled from his ears.

CHAPTER 10
MEANWHILE, BACK AT THE LAB

Day 2

"Miss Weber, would you mind stepping into the conference room for a moment?" George Richards wore an unpleasant scowl. It was unheard of for a five-striper like him to interact directly with a lowly single-striper like Jenny.

She looked up from the table where she prepared equipment setups for the chemists. These trays held a basic set of laboratory equipment—racks of test tubes, beakers, microscopes and slides, flasks, Bunsen Burners, and a host of other things, a design unique to Alpen Labs. A thick rubber mat in each tray had a cutout for every piece of equipment, with small labels to designate what went there. Each chemist had a tray with his name, customized to his needs. Jenny could prepare them with her eyes closed. She knew where the components were stored, and the cutouts made loading the trays error-proof. "Yes, sir, right away." She beckoned the lab assistant working next to her, "Lucy, can you take over for me for a minute? Thanks."

She followed Richards down the hall to where he held the conference room door open. A long table dominated the room. It appeared to be carved from a single piece of dark wood, polished to a deep glow that highlighted the exquisite grain. Jenny estimated its value would exceed her annual salary. The far wall featured floor to ceiling windows along its length. Chalk boards on rollers flanked the ends of the room, and one end, presumably the front, included a pull-down projection screen and a rolling cart weighed down with the biggest television set Jenny had ever seen. That monster had at least a 25-inch display. A stern-looking man sat at the table. He wore a severe brown suit with a white shirt and dark blue tie. His badge had a solid black background. Jenny squinted; she'd never interacted one-on-one with an Upstairs executive.

Richards pulled out a chair for her—then his eyes flew open as he spotted a chalkboard at the front. A kind of title in bold lettering read "Project Mind Warp." He hurried to the front, turned the board around and pushed it up against the wall. Too late, Jenny looked down, trying to pretend she didn't notice. The man seated across from her glared at George Richards, but didn't speak. Richards, visibly nervous now, sat back down next to Jenny.

"Mr. Arndt, this is Jenny Weber. Jenny, Mr. Arndt is our head of security here at Alpen Labs. He is the one responsible for everything from our guard stations down to the keypads to access all the offices." He delivered this last part condescendingly, as if explaining security to a child.

Yeah, DUH, asshole, Jenny thought. *What the hell is Project Mind Warp?*

"Hello Miss Weber," Arndt said. "This will not take long; we have just few questions for you." Jenny couldn't place the heavy accent. "Can you tell to me what were you doing at the back fence yesterday at lunch?" His voice was honey, nothing to fear here little fly.

Oh shit! Oh well, I was looking for a job when I found this one. Out loud, "I had gone out for a smoke and some air."

"And who were those gentlemen with you?"

"I didn't even know them, sir. I think their names were Landlist—something like that, and, oh, Jerry or maybe Johnny something, I'm sorry I really don't remember." *How the hell did you know this stuff?*

"Um, and so why did you meet them there again in the afternoon?" There was no honey now, I've got you little fly.

Jenny's mind spun. What innocent explanation could she offer? She fought for control; it was as if this creep was peering into her soul. "Oh, they, uh, those guys thought the bus was bringing in intern candidates. I told them I didn't think so, we would never allow our interns to dress the way they were. Real casual, you know? More like for going out to a bar than coming to work. We agreed to meet back there to see if they had changed or something." Playing the innocent young thing now. Eyes wide open, she fluttered her eyelashes, but not too much. *Oh, poor stupid me, I'm only a dumb girl, after all.*

Arndt smiled thinly. "I see. Thank you, Miss Weber. Before you go, I must to remind you of security agreement you signed at your hiring. As you must be knowing, it is very comprehensive. I hope you realize it cover this meeting and what you seen here; for instance, the chalkboard Mr. Richards turned around when you came in." Now his voice had become flat and expressionless, his eyes locked on hers.

"Oh, NO Sir! I mean YES Sir! I don't understand all that gobbledey goop, anyway."

"Nevertheless, formality only, but I do need remind to you of our agreement. I'm afraid the penalties for violating it would be quite severe." He shrugged, not MY fault, little fly. "Thank to you for so forthcoming Miss Weber, you may go now. Mr. Richards, please to stay with me for few minutes."

Jenny's heart pounded as she returned to the lab. Man, could she use a smoke right now, she'd picked a lousy day to try to quit. She detoured into an area where test results were documented, grabbed a paper and pen, and started writing.

At noon, Hal and Jerry sat at their usual table, when an envelope slid onto Hal's tray. Startled, he looked up to see the black hair bobbing up and down on the back of Jenny's neck as she hurried away. He opened the envelope and pulled out a handwritten note— "DESTROY this after you read it. Seriously, tear it up into little pieces. Richards pulled me into the conference room this morning, with the head of security, a guy named Arndt. He knew about our being by the fence yesterday. Knew you guys were there and knew we went back in the afternoon. He reminded me of the infamous security agreement—all but threatened me. What the hell—do they have cameras or spies or something? Has anyone talked to you about it? I don't think we should discuss anything here, not even by phone. There's something else too, can we discuss it somewhere tonight after work? This has me spooked. Do you guys know where The Frisco is? Can we meet there between 5:30 and 6, straight after work? I'm watching you read this, if you agree, stand up and go refill your drink or something, and that will be my signal to meet you there. And please tear this up, really. – J"

Hal handed the note to Jerry, who read it with his mouth dropping open, he nodded, and Hal slowly tore up the note, got up and threw it in the trash, wrapped in a soiled napkin. He glanced around for Jenny. She was on the other side of the room and nodded briefly.

By 5:20 Jenny sat at a booth in a back corner of The Frisco. The two men joined her before long.

Once they slid into the booth, a motherly waitress came to the table, smiled at Hal and said, "Hi there Sugar, what can I bring y'all today?" (For some reason, Texas waitresses habitually confuse their customers with a sucrose-based condiment.)

The two men ordered coffee and Jenny ordered a chocolate malt and a piece of The Frisco's famous chocolate ice box pie—a chocolate fix would be just the thing. She puffed away on a much-needed Winston; Jerry bummed one and lit up, while Hal fiddled with his pipe. "Did you guys hear anything?"

"No," Jerry answered, "I'm guessing they figure they got the message to us through you."

"Are there cameras watching the grounds?"

"Probably," Hal said, "They have all the latest security goodies, they take it very seriously."

"They're obsessed with that shit," Jerry added.

"One more thing—have either of you heard of Project Mind Warp? It was written a on a chalkboard at the front of the room, along with a mess of other stuff. Richards went white when he realized it showed, he turned the board around so I couldn't see it. If he had simply ignored it, I probably wouldn't have thought anything about it."

"Mind Warp, huh? Sounds like some government deal, they're always coming up with weird names. Man, I wish I knew what that's about." Jerry loved this sort of intrigue. In today's world, he would have a room in his basement plastered with articles about Area 51, the Kennedy Assassination, the Deep State, and Clorox injections or horse suppositories as a cure for various viral illnesses.

Jenny furrowed her brow. "Hey, there might be a way. I'm friendly with one of the secretaries from Upstairs. She's tight-lipped about company stuff, but if I'm," she changed into a quavering falsetto, "going to lose my job! You just HAVE to help me.'" She grinned and returned to her normal voice, "I might persuade her to tell me something."

Jerry launched into his best conspiratorial mode, whispering so Hal and Jenny had to lean in to hear, "Alright Agent J, you have your assignment. The question is, how do we communicate without getting caught?"

"Aren't you Agent J?"

"Ladies first, I'm J2. I guess we can keep coming here, do you live nearby?"

They both nodded.

"Perfect, we just need a signal for any time we need to meet."

After a whispered discussion, they agreed that if Jenny wanted to meet, she would wear a red scarf at lunch. Hal and Jerry would sit at a different table from their norm if either of them wanted to meet. The men finished their coffee and left. Jenny continued savoring her pie, which Hal had gallantly paid for as he left. Jenny signaled to the waitress, Millie by the name tag on her blouse, "Did

I see some of those famous brownies in the display case? Can you wrap one up to go for me?"

Returning to the table, Millie handed her a white paper bag with an oversized slice of gooey chocolate brownie. She clucked sympathetically, "This is on the house, Hon, I can recognize when someone is self-medicating with chocolate. But take it from an old lady, Sweetie, those guys aren't the answer. You're a beautiful young lady with your life ahead of you. So what if some jerk dumped you? Those married guys can smell your pain, but you don't want to go down that dead end. I been through it all, and here I am at my age, pouring coffee in a café."

Jenny threw back her head and laughed, "Oh, I'm sorry," she choked, "I'm not laughing at you, what is it, Millie? I'm Jenny, by the way. I work with those guys, and trust me, they do NOT have a shot at this gal. I have a boyfriend I'm leading toward the altar, step by baby step, and so far, everything is working according to plan. My problems are work-related, and I was commiserating with a couple of coworkers. But you're spot on about the chocolate, if I don't resolve this mess soon, I'll be as big as a barn."

"Oh, I'm so happy to hear that, cute little Jenny! Forgive a nosey old woman, sometimes I can't help myself."

"Don't worry about it, Millie, I think it's sweet of you to be concerned. I'm gonna make sure I sit at your table the next time I come in."

This exchange may seem odd, but in the small-town atmosphere of 1950s Austin, such familiarity was typical. Fifty years later, some of Millie's younger colleagues still worked at The Frisco, serving the same steady customers the same menu offerings as the day it opened in 1956, and the chocolate icebox pie was still to die for.

When she left, Jenny didn't notice the black Buick in the corner of the parking lot. The driver watched her pull away, then got out and entered The Frisco.

The next two days passed uneventfully, but Friday Jenny wore a red scarf, and the afternoon found them back at The Frisco. She had talked to her friend; Barb said Project Mind Warp was indeed a government project, and it also involved The University of Texas Psychology Department. Barb figured those students came from UT, but she couldn't say about the Negroes and Mexicans. She had no clue what they were up to. That much Jenny had learned the first time she approached Barb. She convinced Barb to do some digging, ostensibly to find out if she was about to be fired. Barb found nothing mentioning Jenny, but found something much more interesting. Project Mind Warp also involved The Farm. They seemed to be experimenting with those kids; she didn't know where. Like Jenny and the men, she had always assumed there was nothing on the back of the building other than loading docks. And one other thing, on the day they had their first meeting at The Frisco, Barb saw an unusual amount of activity in the Upstairs "War Room," an enormous conference room that made the ones downstairs look like slums. Something was going on, something that demanded the full attention of the board of directors. Then Jenny had another surprise. She reached into a voluminous purse and pulled out a heavy, loosely bound book.

"Ever hear of a Key Map? Real estate agents use them to find their way around—they show every, and I mean EVERY road in whatever area they cover." She opened the book, "Here's the page with the lab, you can see the entrance road here. But look up here where you should see the road coming in the back—nothing! I'm telling you, these maps have every little country road, every suburban street, every highway, everything. Somebody, somebody high up, doesn't want anyone to know how to get there. These maps are critical, they're used by real estate agents, the police, ambulance drivers, and the fire department. My boyfriend is the Assistant Captain at the North Austin fire station, and he swears by them."

The two men squinted at the map. "Yeah, this looks like the entrance road, I should see a road up here that looks like an extension of it with a break in the middle for the building. You're a pretty smart cookie, Jenny. What do you think Jerry?"

"Methinks a road trip is called for. Tomorrow's Saturday, let's meet here for breakfast, then take a little drive and look for the missing road."

They huddled together and decided to meet there at 9 Saturday morning. A smiling Millie offered them a refill from the coffee station next to their booth, where she had been fiddling with the pots and brewing a fresh batch. Hal and Jerry demurred, but Jenny smiled and accepted a refill.

After the men left, Millie plopped down in the seat across from Jenny. "Do you mind if I take a load off for a minute, Honey? I been here since early this morning and my feet are killing me."

Jenny smiled, "Not at all. Does your shift last much longer?"

"Another hour unless someone doesn't show for the next shift. I'm getting too old for this, but a lady's gotta eat. My daughter Clarissa lives up in Dallas, but she's got problems of her own with three brats and a worthless husband." She babbled on as though they were old friends, offering intimate details of her private life. "How about you Sweetie, are you all alone here in Austin?"

"More or less, my folks live in San Antonio, so it isn't too far, and I have my boyfriend and his eleven-year-old son, a really sweet kid, super smart. I moved here a few years ago to attend UT, but took a job at the Lab when I ran out of money. I'd only been working there for about six months when I found a nice Granny Flat I can afford without roommates. My landlord became my boyfriend, and I make a few extra bucks watching his boy when Rod is on shift at the fire station."

"Oh, very convenient," said Millie with a broad wink, "you know Honey, people will tell you no one will buy a cow if they're getting the milk for free, but I've found it doesn't hurt to give 'em a little taste of cream to whet their appetite."

Jenny blushed. My goodness things had gotten personal in a hurry. This kind old woman was so easy to talk to, in a way she could never have talked with her own mother. She turned the conversation to more mundane subjects, excusing herself about ten minutes later. As she left, Millie came up and wrapped her in a hug.

"My customers are my friends, Jenny; if you ever need to talk, just come see Millie."

As Jenny pulled away, the man in the black Buick smiled and walked into the little café.

CHAPTER 11
THE REST OF THE STORIES

"And now you know...the rest of the story."
–Paul Harvey tagline, *The Rest of the Story*

Betty went next. Her clear recollection of what she experienced matched the other tales up to the time she reached the summit. Although her narrative reflected her tender age, she related the story with most of the key points. She broke down a few times, but the others, the older children in particular, encouraged her with a surprising amount of patience. She recalled slipping and falling into the sticker bush, how it hurt and how it sliced up her bare legs. At that point, Mark interrupted.

"I only see minor scratches on your legs, how do you explain that?"

Please excuse Mark, he didn't know Betty very well, so he was unprepared for the torrent of tears the simple question evoked. Once they got her calmed down again, she insisted her legs had been badly scratched, and both James and Anna confirmed they had seen the cuts. In fact, they all had suffered scrapes and abrasions to some extent, only to find the worst of them disappeared once they exited the woods.

"Y'all ain't helpin' your case any here," Mark grumbled. "But I can't believe alla y'all are this good at acting. Levi, let's hear what you've got to say."

Levi

Levi described the journey to the valley much as the others. He remembered Betty asking if they were "losted." And like the others, when he reached the top, he was alone, and terrified, but soon entered a brief fugue state. When he came out of the fugue, there was a spectral grayish light he described as similar to dawn or twilight, that allowed him to see a figure coming up the road toward him. At first it appeared to be growing, but when Levi looked at his surroundings, he could see that he was shrinking, down to the size of an ant.

As the figure approached, he recognized it as being similar to the golem, or mud monster, of Jewish mythology, but more human in appearance. He tried to run, but the creature stepped on him. It was wearing heavy-soled hiking boots with a deep tread pattern, and he was trapped within a tread. His flashlight provided a few feet of yellowish illumination, and the effect was that of being imprisoned in a cave. He began running around, seeking a way out, but was caught in the labyrinth. He'd hit one wall, then turn and run in another direction, only to find himself blocked again. He was crashing into the blockages, it was painful, but his fear drove him on. The air was foul, as though the golem had stepped in animal excrement. Levi wheezed and choked with the stench. Finally, he saw a faint spot of gray light and ran toward it. There was a narrow opening, mostly blocked by mud and rubble. Digging desperately, he piled rubble behind him or tossed it out when he could. He was able to create a small depression to crawl into as he continued working, turning his hands raw and bruised. Finally, a single bulky rock remained, frustrating his exit. He cried out his frustration, but attracted unwanted attention in the process.

~ ~ ~

"Then I heard a noise, like something coming, like a whole bunch of footsteps. I shined my light down the cutout, and saw this enormous thing coming. I think it was an ant, but you gotta remember I was as little as an ant, or even smaller. It made a screeching noise, like this, eeeeeee, eeeeeee."

Levi made a noise like a bird of prey, a hawk or eagle perhaps. The others jumped. Round-eyed, Stevie jerked backwards.

"It looked right at me and, you know that thing ants have in front, like a big claw, only it's their mouth? That thing was opening and closing. I thought I was a goner. I tried to scrunch into the hole where I was sitting, and push the rock out of my way, but it wouldn't budge. The ant opened the claw thing and lifted his head to get me, I swear it was right there." Levi held up his hands on either side of his face, with his fingers bent into claws. "But then his head hit the top and it made mud fall down and block him. He started screeching then, and throwing his head around, and that knocked down more stuff, so it trapped me, with a giant rock on one side and dirt and stuff on the other. The ant was thrashing around, and stuff kept falling down. It made a massive pile behind me, so I leaned back against it and pushed on the rock with my feet with everything I had. It started to move and kind of teetered there for a second. Then the pile I was leaning against crumbled, and the ceiling started cratering, but the rock in front of me fell out, and I could escape. I crawled out fast, and then I nearly fell. I was standing on the edge of the hill where it was like a cliff, not straight down, just really, really steep and I almost fell down. Then the giant looked down and saw me, I guess he did, I still couldn't see his face, but he reached down to squash me with his thumb. It was as big as a bus, maybe bigger. So, I jumped and started sliding down the side of the hill. I couldn't stop myself; I kept sliding down, faster and faster, like I was falling. I dug in my heels trying to slow down, and then I hit a tree—hard. It hurt bad, I thought I broke a leg, but I managed to get up and walk around a little. There was a narrow trail there that led back down the hill. I somehow held on to my flashlight, so I had a little light. I was way down the hill then. I looked back but couldn't see anything. I was still scared and wanted out of there. I started running down the path until it came to the creek. But I was still tiny, so it looked like a river and was rushing like rapids. I went up and down looking for somewhere to cross, and I saw where a tree had fallen. But it was huge, so I had to climb up on it. And then I had to find my way across, even the bark was like massive, and that made it hard. But when I got about halfway across, boom, I was big again, standing on this tiny little branch. I almost fell in the creek."

Stevie interrupted, "You're still not big, Levi." The others giggled nervously.

Levi glared at him, "I was as big as I am now. And I was close to the path we came on, so I headed over there and ran back. I didn't see you guys until I was out of the woods, but I heard you right before I got there."

"What about this morning?" Anna asked. "And last night, did you dream about it? Did you sleep in real late? How about scratches and stuff, did they go away?"

"Yeah," he answered, "To all of it. The scratches went away, at least the bad ones, and I got scratched up real bad falling down the hill, and my dreams were awful, like it was still happening, but they didn't wake me up, I slept 'till noon."

The group fell silent for a few moments, exchanging puzzled looks and a few whispers. Anna sat to one side of the old couch. James sat next to her, with Betty on the other end. Stevie and Levi had flopped down on the floor next to Mark.

Mark looked at his little brother. "Okay Squirt, your turn, but make it quick, can you possibly do that? Start when you got up to the top."

Stevie

"Okay, Mark, get off my back. I was in front, right, cuz I was showing the way. So, I got to the top first, and figured you guys were right behind me, so I didn't worry for a minute, but when I turned around to look, nobody was there." Like the others, he said he experienced a moment of panic, then went into a kind of trance. He described it as feeling the way he imagined sleep walking would feel.

When he snapped out of the trance, the world around him had changed. Colored lights rose from below, like pictures he had seen of the Aurora Borealis, but coming from below him instead of from the sky. It was light as day, in every color of the rainbow. The light painted his surroundings with vivid colors, sharply defined edges, and extreme contrasts. Distant objects swam and danced in the waves of light. Engrossing and spectacular, it distorted his young mind as it bent to absorb this new reality. He watched, entranced, for what seemed a very long time. The glow emanated from the floor of the valley below. Shimmering walls of color rose above the rim of the valley and high into the ebony night, then flared and dissolved into a billion fractals, gleaming with color and light, that drifted down to the valley floor, before starting the cycle over. Stevie described it as glitter, saying the Aurora turned into a million pieces of glitter that floated back to earth like flakes in a snow globe.

With each repetition of the cycle, the light grew more intense and pulsed, a metronome born of light and color. It became so glaringly bright that Stevie had to shield his eyes, fragmented, and fell a final time. The valley floor had come alive with glowing radiance, when a rift appeared and split the valley in two, forming a chasm stretching the length of the valley, widening out as it grew. The gash sucked at the fractals of brilliance, drinking them in until all the remaining light emanated from deep within its blackness, as a tiny dot of intense brightness. Now it swelled, a luminescent tumor of light itself, expanding and rising until it became fully visible, suspended above the valley floor. Below the glowing object, the rift closed as abruptly as it had appeared. The thing floated there, its brilliance moderating until Stevie could perceive the shape—the classic "cigar-shaped object" of UFO parlance. Still awash in vibrant luster, it oozed light, a kaleidoscope of light that sparkled, danced, swam, pulsated and flowed across its surface.

Stevie stood transfixed. He had been transported to the stuff of his imaginings. It was there; it was real; it was the most beautiful thing he had ever seen. Breaking out of his revere, he set out down the hill. A broad path he had not noticed before led straight down toward the glowing object, where it hung suspended. He scampered down, not the gait of the chubby, clumsy boy he had always been, but an effortless gallop with his feet scarcely touching the ground, unconstrained by gravity. He ran this way until he reached a plateau immediately above the level of the craft, where he pulled to a stop. Stevie heard something now, but not in the usual way. The sounds originated from inside his head, directly within the auditory cortex of his brain, unblemished by the external mechanisms associated with hearing—an indistinct chattering, mixed with a kind of music—pure tonality and incredibly beautiful, the soul of all music. One perfect note, at once seductive and hypnotic—pervaded his consciousness. He walked forward mesmerized, almost mechanically, drawn by the captivating sound.

Stevie had taped a drawing to the wall of his bedroom—his vision of a flying saucer based on the stories on those late-night radio programs. It mirrored what he was seeing now. The shape was identical, but in Stevie's drawing a ramp led down, with several little green men exiting the craft.

~ ~ ~

Light flares in the bottom section of the craft, a ramp extends to the ground in a fluid, organic motion.

Little green guys, identical to those in Stevie's picture, exit and progress down the ramp. They are slightly cartoonish in appearance, but appear friendly and, at least for now, non-threatening.

The chattering in Stevie's head increases in volume and intensity. It sounds like English, but as though dozens of voices are speaking in unison.

When the vast majority of people think, they are conducting what psychologists call an "inner monolog." Simply put, they think in words and sentences. There are exceptions to this, some people think visually, there are instances of pure emotional thought, and very young children are less likely to use internal vocalization. Imagine what it would be like if this internal monologue originated from an external source. Stevie experiences the chatter and the music in this manner. That is how those suffering from schizophrenia describe the auditory hallucinations they endure.

Meanwhile, back in Stevie's head, the voices grow louder and more discordant. He desperately wants to say something, but his mouth is frozen. He wants to welcome these new visitors. He will be the emissary from the Planet Earth. History will record this momentous meeting, and how he ensured the peace and prosperity these friendly aliens brought with them. He senses they can read the thoughts he directs to them— *Welcome to Planet Earth! I greet you in peace. Your visit honors us. I am human Stevie Lindquist. Who are you, and where do you come from?*

With this, the chattering only increases, drowning out the beautiful music. The volume of chatter keeps increasing, faster and louder, until it hurts, like a massive flock of birds squawking inside Stevie's head. *Stop, please stop, too loud, you're hurting me, please, Please STOP!*

They reach out, smiling and nodding, gesturing for Stevie to enter the ship, but he is experiencing the mother of all migraines. The chatter becomes a chorus of jack hammers pounding away at his brain, and the glow from the ship intensifies to an excruciating glare that pierces his eyes and feels like a knife being thrust into his head. The more they smile, the closer they come, the more unbearable the agony. He finds his mouth, screams, and runs.

Runs back the way he came, back out of the valley, down the hill, across the creek, up the next hill and down again. The crescendo of mind-splitting chattering stays with him, although at a diminished volume. For the rest of his life, those voices will never completely leave him. They lurk in some remote corner of his mind, shoved away where he can ignore them for long periods, but in some quiet time, when he least suspects it, the faint murmurings will begin. Like a worm it comes. Crawling out among the neurons, insinuating its presence into his consciousness. Bringing back the horror of the pain, if not the pain itself, scraping raw the memories he seeks to erase. No amount of booze, no combination of drugs, no meditation, no activity, no music, however loud, will ever erase the voices completely.

He sees Betty lying in the thorn bushes as he pants by. No more the graceful runner whose feet never touch the ground, he is back to being fat little out-of-shape Stevie, and he's not stopping for anyone or anything.

~ ~ ~

That night he dreamed the sound, dreamed the blinding brilliance, dreamed the pain, dreamed the dread that this would be with him forever.

~ ~ ~

Thursday, June 12
Dear Diary, (this is all super secret—don't tell anyone!!!)
I'm sorry I haven't been writing, but something terrible happened and was afraid to write about it.

Stevie said he saw something (he said a flying saucer) come down in the woods Sunday night so Monday night we went out to see what it was. We waited until after supper cause Anna's mom worked that night. Of course Mommy was all worried about me going over there at night and had to talk to Anna's mom, so that was a problem. But Anna called Mommy and pretended to be her mother. She can sound just like her! So anyways we went and Stevie knew where to go—him and James (James goes to the woods a lot.) It was so scary Dear Diary. But the scary part is what happened. It's too much to write it all this is just the most important stuff.

It sounds so stupid. I saw this fairy princess but when I reached out to take her hand, she grabbed me and turned into like a witch or something. It was like she got old and ugly and scary, then, oh she had like bat wings and could fly, and she took me way up in the air and I screamed and screamed. I have never ever been so scared. Crazy scared. Then she said something funny like she was putting a curse on me to get ugly and not be pretty any more. I think that was the worst thing. Every time I go by a mirror I stop and look to see if I'm changing. This morning I stood in front of the bathroom mirror for an hour, just looking and looking, and remembering what that thing said.

And she just dropped me but I didn't fall. I was just down on the ground again and not hurt. And then I just ran and ran. Oh and I was all alone when this happened I couldn't see anybody else. And then I fell into sticker bushes that cut my legs up and hurt like anything. And I couldn't get up, but Anna and James came along and kind of lifted me up and got me to running again. Then when we got out of the woods everybody was back and we were all scared and crying. Finally we kind of realized we were ok. But then that stupid Stevie pointed at me and said I peed and called me a baby. And Dear Diary, I had pee-peed. I had pee-pee running down my legs and my panties and shorts were all wet. I didn't even know it till then and I was so embareased I started crying again but Anna and James told Stevie to shut up (Anna said a bad word at him.) Then she took me home with her so I could take a bath and she washed my clothes and put some stuff on my cuts and a band aid on a bad one. I barely remember that part cause it was like a dream almost. I just know she took care of me and I was crying a lot.

I've been having awful dreams ever since. I always see the fairy princess turn into a witch and it's like it all happens again. Even during the day sometimes I just get so scared. I don't know what to think. It really happened but it's like it was a dream. I so want it to just be a dream but it happened to everybody and they all remember but they all remember something different. How can that be if it was real? Stevie says a flying saucer came down and they can control our brains and make us hear and see stuff that's not there. Anna says he's full of (bad word.) I can't tell Mommy and Daddy they would get so mad at me for going they would say Satan is punishing me or something. Anyways we're gonna go back in the daytime Saturday. I'm really scared to go back but I'm kinda scared not to.

I'm sorry this was so long Dear Diary, but thank you for listening.

CHAPTER 12
ROAD TRIP

"Do not follow where the path may lead.
Go instead where there is no path and leave a trail."
–Ralph Waldo Emerson

Saturday morning agents J, J2, and Hal, who preferred to ignore that agent nonsense, slipped into their favorite booth at The Frisco. Breakfasts were a specialty here, with all the sweet, gooey and greasy goodness anyone could desire. Pancakes, waffles, biscuits 'n' gravy, eggs every way imaginable, all graced the menu—including their signature *Eggs Decorated*—scrambled eggs with cheese, topped with spiced pinto beans and salsa, with a big order of crispy hash browns on the side—an order of which was sliding down Agent J's lovely neck. Jerry's plate was adorned with two fluffy biscuits split open and topped with redeye gravy, flanked with four strips of crisp bacon and two slices of buttered toast. Ever the engineer, Hal had ordered `a la carte—a Denver Omelet, sausage patties, a double order of wheat toast with jam, and hash browns with gravy, hopefully enough to last him through another day of Carol's cooking adventures.

Millie hovered over their booth like a mother hen, making sure their coffee cups were full, and they had plenty of butter and jelly for their toast. She treated Jenny like an old friend, called the men "boys," chirped brightly about what a beautiful day it was, and said she hoped the rain would hold off one more day. As they finished up, she hustled away the dirty dishes, wiped up some imaginary spills, and asked for at least the third time if she could bring them anything else.

With the dishes gone, Jenny spread out the Key Map. The route they would take spanned six pages, so they had to keep turning back and forth to plan their journey. They eventually found a road that led toward the back side of the lab. The map showed it ending abruptly, a few miles before the back entrance. "This looks like our best shot," said Hal, and the two nodded their agreement.

"What is THAT thing?" Millie called out from the coffee station. "Is that thing a map? My heavens, I never seen a map like that. Are y'all taking a trip? This sure is a nice day for a little drive. Do you mind my asking where you're headed? Gotta keep tabs on my girl!"

Jenny laughed, "It's called a Key Map, Millie. The kind real estate agents use to find houses when all they have is an address. We're going to visit a friend from the office who's been at home sick. Hey, how about I take her a piece of chocolate pie?"

Millie glanced at the page they had open, "My, my, I didn't realize they were building houses over in that area. When will they ever stop? Before you know it, two hundred thousand people will live here." She shook her head as she went to fetch the pie and the check.

As Hal pulled the shining Edsel onto the Old Laredo Trail, the man in the black Buick entered The Frisco and sat in the booth they had occupied. Millie came right over, and he ordered a cup of coffee, which she brought him before nervously exchanging a few words with him. He took a few sips before walking to the pay phone at the front.

They continued heading north on The Old Laredo Trail for several miles before turning west on FM road 183, or Research Boulevard, as it became known in later years. Jerry peered at the map, flipping the pages back and forth, searching in vain for the exit. Hal, losing patience with his navigator, was about to pull over to check the map himself, when Jenny interrupted from the back seat, "About five more miles to the light at Whitetail Crossing, take a left there."

She had memorized the route, not trusting Jerry's navigational skills. Being male, he was assigned the responsibility of providing directions, and had done a splendid job for those first two turns. Sitting demurely in the rear seat, her little white bag with the boxed pie in her lap, Jenny took over, as Jerry, by now lost, continued flipping uselessly through the map.

Agent J led them down a series of obscure country roads that wound their way into the hill country. They passed a few goat farms and miles of undeveloped woodlands, before coming to the road that appeared to lead to the back of the lab. This was where the bus and delivery vehicles must have entered and exited the rear parking lot. The faded sign identifying the narrow road as Farm Road 19 was easy to miss, but at the last turn Jenny cautioned Hal to watch the odometer, so he slowed as the remaining 1.4 miles clicked over on the dashboard display. Hal smiled ruefully and muttered, "Like I said, Jenny, you are one smart cookie."

"Okay," she said, "according to the map, this road ends after another two miles, right Jerry? Let's see if it actually does."

Jerry grunted his agreement, as if he had a clue where they were. The road was smooth for about the first mile, but became increasingly rough as they proceeded. The heavy Edsel did a decent job of soaking up most of the bumps, but clunked as the single axle rear suspension bottomed out and jolted the passenger cabin on the worst. They jounced along this way for another mile, where a line of sawhorses painted yellow with black stripes blocked their progress. Three plain black Ford sedans parked behind them further blocked the way. As Hal stopped to investigate, two men wearing hard hats and yellow jumpsuits walked toward him. The one who appeared to be the supervisor waved at Hal, "Sorry pal, road is out down there, afraid we can't let you go any farther."

"It is? Looks fine from here—in fact it looks like it smooths out. Say where does it go? We're kind of lost."

"Where are you going, maybe we can help," the man continued, ignoring Hal's question.

"Oh, uh," Hal's mind spun, trying to come up with a reasonable answer.

Jenny came to his rescue. "Spicewood Springs Road, do y'all know where that is?"

The man smiled. "Well shoot, y'all <u>are</u> lost. You need to turn around and head back to 183. Turn right there, then go about five miles and you'll see it."

"Really? I would have sworn we could cut across. Say, how much of this road is out? I think it must connect somewhere." Jenny fluttered her eyes and smiled demurely.

"Nope. Road is out, probably won't be fixed for weeks, state doesn't care much about maintaining these rural roads; we're here to assess the damage and keep people from getting into trouble. You don't want to go down there in your nice new car."

"Okaaaay," she sighed, "I guess we'll go <u>aalll</u> the way back to 183. Sure wish you'd let us try it."

"Can't do that. Y'all have a nice day now." This conversation was over.

Hal began the slow process of backing to a spot where they could turn around, then drove until they were safely out of sight. "Some coincidence. Those guys may have dressed like road repairmen, but their cars sure didn't look like the kind they'd be driving. And they were a little too slick. Let's look at the map and see if any other roads go in that general direction."

They got out and spread the Key Map book on the hood. Jenny commandeered the map and explored potential routes until she found one that paralleled the direction they had been going. "Let me find this one, then we'll follow it down here, see? It won't take us all the way, but we might be close enough to see something."

She folded the book open to the page showing the new road and deftly outflanked Jerry to slide into the front seat.

With Jenny spitting out directions along the way, they turned on the new road within fifteen minutes, having made every turn correctly.

The new route was better suited to the pickup trucks favored by the area farmers than the sleek new Edsel. The air conditioning worked though, so they kept the windows rolled up against the dust that swirled up off the dirt roads. They rocked and bounced along until they progressed far beyond where they'd been so unceremoniously stopped. When they were as close as possible, Jenny told Hal to pull over.

"We need to hoof it from here, gentlemen. According to the map, we should see the back of the lab if we walk in about a mile." She pointed into the dense thicket beside the car.

They had expected something like this, so they had worn old clothes and shoes. Jerry came the best prepared, wearing a pair of rough-out boots along with heavy khaki pants and matching shirt. Jenny wore sneakers, worn jeans and one of Rod's old work shirts. Hal looked like he was dressed for the office, with scarcely worn slacks, some minor fraying of his shirt collar, and a slightly scuffed pair of Florsheims. Following Jenny's lead, they picked their way through the thick underbrush until they found a deer trail that made walking easier. After they had gone about a half mile, a barbed wire fence blocked their path. It bore a yellow sign with harsh red letters reading *Private Property—Keep Out. This means YOU!* Similar signs hung at various spots along the fence, as far as they could see in the dense woods. Jenny frowned, then stepped on the bottom wire and lifted the one above it— "In for a dime, in for a dollar, crawl through boys."

As Hal opened his mouth to protest, Jerry bent and struggled through, slightly ripping the back of his shirt. No sooner had he straightened up than an old man emerged from behind some trees. "Guess y'all ol' boys cain't read can ya'? Sign says keep out; sign means keep out. This here's private property and I aim ta keep it that way, with the he'p of my girlfriend here," he patted the shotgun resting casually in the crook of his arm. "She's loaded with buckshot, and unless y'all 'er hankerin' fer a pant load, you'll go on back the way you come."

Jerry's eyes bulged. "Oh, so sorry sir, we didn't mean any harm," said Jenny, "we're bird watchers, and we thought we saw a paisano—a road runner—come in here. You didn't see one, did you? My friend only needs one sighting to fill his quota for today."

"You don't look like no bird watchers I ever seen. The boss over there ain't exactly dressed fer it," he said, pointing at Hal.

"See a lot of bird watchers, do you?" Jenny replied coolly, "Don't worry sir, we'll be on our way, we wouldn't want to argue with your girlfriend there." She smiled and lifted the wire for Jerry to escape.

The old man didn't reply; he stood cradling his shotgun and watched them make their way back down the trail.

Once they were out of sight, Jenny stopped and looked around. "There's more than one way to skin an old geezer." She began to climb a sizable oak tree—its trunk bent enough to make climbing possible, and she scurried up as though she had been climbing trees all her life.

"You're full of surprises, aren't you?" said an amazed Hal.

"Little San Antonio girls grow up climbing trees, BOSS." She smiled and scrambled up until she had a clear view toward the lab.

What she saw astonished her. Beyond the point where the old man had emerged from the trees, she spotted several men. They wore identical gray uniforms, almost military in appearance, and though she wasn't sure at this distance, it looked like they wore sidearms. In the distance, the parking area behind the lab was a beehive of activity. This far away she couldn't see anything clearly, and couldn't tell where the bus had been delivering those students. As she strained her eyes, one of the uniformed men stared back at her through a pair of binoculars with baseball-sized lenses. She waved at him brazenly, but scrambled back down.

"Time to go," she hurried down the path, not even looking to see if the men were following. "Let's get the hell out of here." When they arrived at the car, she related what she'd seen as they drove off. They hadn't gone far when she noticed a black Ford following in the distance. "Those fuckers are following us! Sorry for my French, but I mean, what is going on?"

When they returned to the paved section, Hal coaxed the Edsel's massive V8 into action, driving as fast as the narrow, twisting roads would allow. The gap between the two cars remained unchanged, however. The black Ford maintained the same distance, a menacing escort all the way to the intersection with 183. As Hal executed the right turn at 183, the Ford closed the gap.

The 1958 Edsel Corsair was powered by a 410 cubic inch, 345 SAE gross horsepower V8 engine with a 4-barrel carb. Despite its considerable heft, the Corsair is estimated to have been able to achieve a very respectable 0—60 time of 7.4 seconds, and cover a quarter mile from a standing start in 16.1 seconds. The top speed was over 120 mph. This was impressive performance for a large passenger vehicle. In normal driving the brute sucked down a gallon of cheap 1958 premium gasoline for every 9.8 miles it covered, but Hal had filled the tank that morning in his usual obsessive anticipation of a long trip, and most of the twenty gallons remained in the tank.

So, when Hal mashed the accelerator pedal, with FM183 stretching straight and clear in front of them, the powerful V8 roared into action. The Corsair squatted on its iron haunches and leapt forward, as the innovative floating speedometer swung like a drunken carousel. He expected to pull smartly away from the mundane Ford Fairlane sedan, so it startled him when the bargain-basement sedan not only maintained the same distance as before, but gained on the speeding Edsel. After coming within a few car lengths, the Ford backed off again, silently mocking its larger cousin. That thing had something special under the hood.

The next light was the Spicewood Springs Road intersection. Traffic this far out in the country on a Saturday afternoon was virtually nonexistent, so Hal, desperate to lose the persistent shadow, decided he would check for any slow-moving cross traffic and blow through the light if it was red. It was, but an old tractor chugging along with a hay baler in tow, had started through the intersection. Hal swerved into the empty oncoming lane, missing the front of the tractor by inches and sliding onto the gravel shoulder where the Edsel fishtailed wildly before finding enough traction to shoot forward again. Behind them, the black Ford stopped at the light, turned right when it changed (no right on red in those days), and pulled into a nearby Gulf station with its bright orange logo. The driver, now sans the hard hat he had been wearing before, got out, walked over to the pay phone outside the station, and began dialing.

Jenny's eyes had grown wide as she saw the approach of the old red tractor's heavy iron grill. In the back seat, Jerry yelped when the back tires slid off the edge of the road. "Can we go home now? I think I crapped my pants."

After Hal pulled back into The Frisco parking lot, he rolled down the power windows and turned off the engine.

For a moment, they stared at each other in silence. The ride home, post Spicewood Springs Road, had been quiet, with each member of the group lost in thought. Jenny was the first to speak, "Wow, some day. I'll take any bet you want to make those guys work for the lab, for that Arndt guy who heads up security. I would have paid good money for a pair of binoculars when I was up in the tree. I could see the parking lot, and tell it was full of activity, but that was about all. At that angle, most of the back of the building was hidden, so it's still a mystery where those people on the busses were entering."

Hal grimaced, "As curious as I am, I think we should drop this. They obviously don't welcome our interference, and I would hate to lose my job over this. In fact, I'm dreading Monday morning already."

"They can't afford to lose you, Kemosabe," Jerry interjected, "they might welcome seeing the back of my pants at the door, but you're a stud my friend. If Alpen has any chance of winning the bid for the gen two chipset, it will be because of your prototype. All we need to do is pick up some books on Texas birds and leave them on our desks, so our lame story is a little more credible."

"Don't sell yourself short Jerry, you contribute immeasurably, you have a definite knack for finding flaws in my designs, as irritating as that can be. No, I'm thinking EE is becoming expendable. Look how little of the funding we receive these days. All the emphasis is on the Labbies and Farmers. They'll ditch us long before they fire any single stripe Chem Lab assistants like Jenny."

"Thanks for the backASSward complement, 'BOSS.' Listen, you guys have families to think about, I don't blame you for wanting to stop. If I lose my job, it will hurt, yes, but it won't be the end of the world for me. I can always join Millie rustling coffee at some place like The Frisco and take some classes at UT. I only need a couple more semesters to complete my degree in chemistry. I'm told if you're a gal with an undergraduate degree in chemistry, the world is your oyster."

"What are you saying Agent J?" asked Jerry. "Do you mean you're going to stay in the game?"

She twinkled, "Oh, I might do a little clandestine digging. I'll be more careful, but as they say, Watson, the game's afoot."

CHAPTER 13
IN THE LIGHT OF DAY

"We can easily forgive a child who is afraid of the dark; the real tragedy of life is when men are afraid of the light."
–Plato

Tuesday Afternoon, continued

Finally, Mark spoke up. "Y'all are for sure, aren't you? You really believe this crap. You went for a walk in the woods at night, but different things happened to each of you. It was all bad—really, really, bad, but no two of you remember it the same."

The heads all nodded. Anna's expression was defiant, the rubber band securing one of her braids had popped and the braid was rapidly becoming undone, as the ends frayed out in an untamed ginger tangle, "You heard us. Do you really think we could invent something like this?"

The little redheaded chick has spunk. Come see me in a couple years, Sweetcakes. "Okay, tell you what we're gonna do. I work at the Big Bear all week, but I have Saturday off. We'll meet somewhere and see what it looks like in daylight. Can we meet back here again, Red?"

"My name is Anna, and you know it. Anyway, Mom doesn't have her weekend schedule yet, we shouldn't count on it."

"Come to my place." said James, "My dad will be on a seventy-two-hour shift, and I overhead our renter say she won't be around. Wait till about ten, so we can be sure they're both gone."

They agreed, Mark would squeeze them into the old Studebaker and drive them.

Return to the Scene

Saturday morning found five bicycles stored in the Hatcher garage, and the rusty old Studie parked in the drive. Rod was at the fire station and Jenny was at The Frisco with Hal and Jerry.

Mark began calling out orders, "Levi, you and Betty up front, you're the smallest. The rest of you in back."

"Shotgun!" yelled Stevie, right before Anna grabbed him and shoved him into the middle seat.

Mark grinned. *Yeah Red, you come see ol' Mark in a few years.*

Starting the old Studie was always a delicate undertaking. It required the right amount of priming for the ancient carburetor to start, but not flood. Then enough grinding the starter for the engine to cough, sputter and turn over without killing the battery. Mark usually accompanied this by pounding the dash and shouting encouragement to the old girl he'd named Maybellene. Eventually, she rumbled into action, running on at least four of her six cylinders. Mark pushed the clutch to the floor and shoved the gear lever into reverse as the gear wheels squealed in protest. It was a safe bet this symphony would play out each time he changed gears, feathering the gas and double clutching to get the faltering clutch to work one more time. Mark preferred to leave the gear in second to avoid the downshift from third to slow down for corners. The muffler, hanging low, frequently scraped the ground over bumps, and roared in fitting accompaniment to the black smoke billowing out the exhaust. Mark had learned that if he hit the gas, then backed off, she would backfire in a most satisfying manner. BAM!

Betty jumped when this happened and grabbed Levi's hand, which he snatched back in embarrassment.

Maybellene was a nineteen fifty Studebaker Starlight Coupe. This meant the occupants of the rear seats had to fold the front seats forward to climb into rather tight rear accommodations. She made eighty-five horsepower on a good day, but her good days were long behind her and the acceleration she managed was leisurely at best.

In 1958, if a Texas youngster took Driver's Education Theory, followed by Behind the Wheel, they could obtain a valid license as young as fourteen. Mark passed both courses at Mirabeau B. Lamar Junior High, along with the written and driving tests at the Department of Motor Vehicles, where they awarded him with a small cardboard square bearing his picture and the words "Texas Automobile Driver's License" on the front, along with his name and address. Mark had it laminated, and next to the old Studie, it was his most prized possession. When he started the first Driver's Ed course, he struck a deal with Hal—if he managed to raise the money to buy a car, Hal would allow him to drive it and would cover the insurance. Hal figured that would be years away, but a determined Mark landed an after-school job as sacker at the neighborhood Big Bear grocery store, and started saving his earnings. On weekends, he pestered neighbors for lawn mowing jobs at a buck a yard, including trimming. He collected a few paltry tips along the way and hoarded the birthday checks he received when his personal odometer turned to fifteen. Once his bank account totaled seventy-five dollars, he began his search for something, anything, with four wheels and an engine that would start and stay lit. A buddy pointed him to an East Austin used car dealer who held court down the road from Kocheck's Appliances, and there Mark found the girl of his dreams, who he christened Maybellene, after the Chuck Berry song of the same name, before the ink dried on the title. You might have recognized her as a pile of junk ready for the scrap heap, but she had just enough life left in her to make it back to Mark's driveway. Mark wheedled an unenthusiastic Hal into rebuilding the carburetor, replacing the brake pads, changing out the sludge at the bottom of the engine, adding a new filter, and topping off the fluids. This got her running fairly reliably, and they took on other minor restoration projects whenever Mark's bank account permitted. It was enough that with her quarter tank of gas and weekly half pint of oil, she was able to chug along and deliver the HI-Q Gang to the trail into the woods. When Mark turned off the key, the old Studie dieseled on for a while, shuddered, then stopped with a soft protesting backfire. Mark ordered his young passengers out; their exit was reluctant, as memories of their last trip swam into their consciousness.

It was very different in the daylight. The trees, so ghostly in the gloom of night, appeared perfectly normal, and their thick overhead canopy provided welcome relief from the hot June sun. The prickly pears that seemed so threatening at night were adorned with red and yellow cactus flowers, serving as a smorgasbord to a host of hungry honey bees. Time ticked by at a normal pace, and the air smelled sweet and clear. The group, still nervous, huddled together and let Mark take the lead, speaking only to give him directions.

After they had walked a few blocks, Mark stopped, cocked his head, and shoved a bush beside the trail to one side. A small Black boy hid there, trying to stifle his sobs as he cried softly. He started to run, but Mark grabbed his collar and pulled him out onto the path. The boy's face was a mask of terror; blood from his nose had been running down on his shirt, his lower lip was split and one eye had swollen partially closed. "What are you doing here, Boy?" Mark said, his accusatory tone dripping with an implication of guilt born of centuries of white privilege.

In 1928, the city of Austin adopted a new master plan aimed at the "beautification" of the city. This plan codified zoning ordinances that served little purpose other than as a Jim Crow era blueprint for redlining and segregation, and established a "Negro district" in East Austin. In those days, Black settlements were scattered around the city, although many were centered in the former plantation lands of East Austin. The plan exacerbated the segregation of these communities, and Blacks living in more westerly areas were "relocated" to the east side of East Avenue—what today is Interregional Highway 35. As a result, the foundation was laid for decades of institutionalized discrimination. Segregation was deeply ingrained by the 1950s, and the Black population had long since been forced back into this area. Over the years, the Black community developed their own enterprises and institutions, including over fifteen Black-owned businesses, and a significant number of churches, as well as Tillotson College and Samuel Huston College, today combined as Huston-Tillotson University. By the 1940s, the Black population had declined as a percent of Austin's population, although their overall numbers had continued to increase. Hispanics, who represented a slightly smaller population, were similarly segregated into the barrio south of East Eleventh Street. They developed their own businesses as well, introducing the delicious Tex-Mex cuisine that flourished across Austin by 1958. 1954 had seen the Brown vs The Board of Education Supreme Court ruling ostensibly reverse all state laws permitting segregation in schools, but little changed in Texas, and it was many years before Austin schools were effectively desegregated. Although it was technically possible for Black children to attend any school, white schools were physically distant, no bus or other transportation service was provided, and Black children were not welcomed. As a result, only 13 Black teens attended an integrated high school by 1956, a single Black girl attended an integrated Junior High for the first time in 1958, and elementary school desegregation lagged even farther behind.

Only 3 years earlier, a young Black boy in Mississippi was brutally murdered for a trumped-up story of his having abused a 21-year-old white woman. The local white community accepted without question her accusation that the 14-year-old boy, by the name of Emmett Till, had accosted and made sexual advances towards her.

What actually happened is unclear to this day. One of the more likely explanations is that Emmett, who had a severe speech impediment, entered the store to buy bubble gum. He found B's difficult to pronounce, and had been taught to whistle softly to overcome his stutter. This may have somehow been taken as a wolf whistle. It was reported to the authorities as an unwelcome physical attack, and Emmett was later kidnapped and viciously murdered by the woman's husband and accomplices. An all-white male jury acquitted the murderers in record time. A year later, protected by laws against double jeopardy, the killers admitted their guilt, and in her old age the woman confessed she had made it up. This was far too late for poor Emmett, who had been dragged from his great-uncle's home, beaten, mutilated and dumped lifeless in the Tallahatchie River by the woman's husband and friends. Due to this and scores of similar instances, young Black men of 1958 knew that a single misstep around a white person could end their lives. That fear has persisted and is a part of life for Black men to this day. White children growing up in Austin in those days rarely encountered Black children, and their only interactions with Black adults were with those performing lower skilled jobs such as housekeeping, custodial services, and lawn care work.

For a young Black boy, senselessly beaten only moments earlier, this confrontation by a sneering Mark only compounded his terror.

CHAPTER 14
TAKE YOUR SON TO WORK DAY

Lay down, body
Lay down a little while
Lay down, body
I know you're tired
Lay down, body
You is tired
Lay down a little while
Lay down a little while
Soul needs restin'
Lay down a little while
–Lay Down Body - traditional, in the style of a Field Holler

An hour earlier, 8-year-old Georgie Woods accompanied his mother to her Saturday job as housekeeper for a white family who lived in one of the custom homes in a neighborhood to the west of Creekside. In Austin, west is best, and this area was a bit more upscale than Pete Peterson's Lone Star development on the east side of the creek. On most weekends Georgie stayed home with his aunt watching him, but today she had been called in for last-minute overtime at her own job as one of the custodial staff at the University of Texas, where a crazed coed had trashed her room and the common area at Kinsolving Dormitory. This left Rose Woods with no option other than to bring Georgie along. She made him take a bath, even though he had bathed the night before, and dressed him in the slacks he wore to church on Sundays, along with a crisp, freshly ironed shirt. Nevertheless, when Rose arrived at the Richards home with Georgie in tow, Murial Richards was aghast at the prospect of this filthy Negro boy coming into her house, where he might encounter her own precious daughter Priscilla. Even though Rose apologized profusely, and promised "he a good boy, and he be extra good," a scandalized Richards banished him to the back yard. At home, both Rose and Georgie spoke English perfectly well, but they knew that around white people they needed to "sound Colored" lest they be accused of "being uppity." Rose busied herself cleaning up, hoping to finish early, but it was soon clear this would not be possible. Murial Richards was a haphazard housekeeper during the week, being far too involved in her bridge group to bother herself with such trivialities when Rose would be there on Saturday.

Rose found candy bar wrappers scattered throughout the house, where Priscilla, who went through seven or eight on a slow day, let them fall randomly as she licked her fat little fingers and wandered mindlessly around. Besides cartoons, her chief form of entertainment was reading the comic books strewn carelessly around the house. Her favorite featured a character called *The Candy Kid,* a chubby little girl whose plots centered on her gluttonous consumption of various types of candy—hilarious stuff. Priscilla's foremost goal in life was to emulate *The Candy Kid's* inane adventures. Murial pampered the obese child, ensuring she would never develop the slightest hint of self-discipline, nor be held accountable for any of her bizarre and irresponsible behavior. Certainly, this young paragon of femininity must by no means be defiled by the proximity of brown pigment.

Georgie explored the back yard. Murial Richards had warned him to stay off the swing set, stay out of the playhouse, and refrain from climbing any trees, so this left little to amuse him. He became bored, wandered into the front yard and started down the street, captivated by the grandeur of these white people's houses. As he stood gazing in wonder at what seemed to him to be an enormous home, surrounded by flawless green grass and magnificent old oaks, he was slow to notice the group of three older white boys who encircled him with openly hostile stares.

"You thinkin' about robbin' that house, Nigger? Y'all don't belong here Boy, and you about to find out what happens to Nigger boys who come around here lookin' to rob white folks' houses or mess with white women."

Scrawny, undersized Georgie never had a chance. As one of the three pinned his arms behind him, the others bent down within inches of his face. Their premature pock-marks stood out, and their sour breath fueled his terror, as hot bile erupted and scalded his throat. For a desperate moment he pleaded with the boys, trying to explain why he was there, to tell them he was only looking, that he was innocent of any such motives. "No suh, my mama working over to the Richard house, she the maid. They don't want me in the house, that why I be out here."

How effortlessly the human species devolves into its baser instincts. Is it because when we left our arboreal homes to walk upright, we became dependent on hunting for survival, and developed an insatiable thirst for blood? Could it be we haven't evolved new instincts for the mutual respect and cooperation necessary for life in our new urban and suburban jungles? Or perhaps we simply struggle to reconcile the two. Whatever the reason, those three white boys had become a bestial pack, with cold eyes, flaring nostrils, and contorted, sneering lips drawn back over yellow teeth. For a while they toyed with him, poking here, prodding there—cats playing with a mouse, as their bloodlust grew. First a jab in the narrow chest with an extended finger. A shove on a skinny arm that would knock him to the ground but for the cruel hands gripping him from behind. Now a slap in the face, a punch in the stomach, not too hard at first—then harder and harder, finding new targets as he twisted to escape, while their inchoate anger mushroomed into a vile thirst that could only be quenched by the sight of blood and the impact of fist on flesh. Now he was helpless on the ground and the rib crushing kicks began. If they wore boots rather than sneakers, if a voice from a nearby house failed to ask what was going on, their unsatiated rage might have impelled them until the last breath left his frail body in a final shuddering moan. As it was, when the attack abated, Georgie's lip was split, his nose was broken and bloodied, his left eye was swollen shut, and he would piss blood for the next week. They had ripped his shirt, and the pavement left asphalt stains on his torn trousers. The scornful troika informed him this was what happened to "Nigras" who didn't stay in their own part of town. He should get out of there right now. They chased him, his nose running gore mixed with snot and tears, out of the neighborhood and into the woods, where he was hiding when Mark found him.

As Mark pulled him out on the path, Georgie's panic came flooding back. Rubbery legs that would no longer support him collapsed, and he fell to the ground blubbering and trying for the second time that morning, to explain why he was there.

Anna stepped forward, shoving Mark out of the way. "I know you," kneeling down, looking into his eyes, "yeah, you're Georgie Woods, your mama works with my mother, she helped her find some cheap appliances, she and my mother are friends." Ignoring the others now, "What happened to you Georgie?" With a meaningful glance at Mark, "No one is gonna hurt you now; you're bleeding, are you hurt bad? You remember me?"

"Yes'm, you Miss Anna Belle, yo' mama a nice lady, my mama say she the nicest white lady she know. Yo' mama stay late sometimes, help my mama finish up when she have too much work." His choked words came out in wheezes between wracking sobs. The stream of blood from his nose started up again, as he gasped for breath.

Anna turned to the group, "One of y'all give me your shirt." No one moved, they all just stared. Angry crimson highlights flared in her eyes and her hands gripped the bottom of her T-shirt, "if you won't, I will."

Mark laid a gentle hand on her arm, "You don't need to do that—Stevie, get your shirt off NOW." *Yeah Red, I'm liking you more and more—hurry the hell up and grow up.*

Stevie wanted to protest, but he'd heard this tone from Mark before. He pulled the white T-shirt over his head and handed it to Anna. The boys often went shirtless on hot summer days, so this was no big deal. What he truly objected to was what Anna did next. She used the T-shirt to wipe Georgie's nose and face, and swiped at the blood on his shirt. Then she wadded it up and handed it to him, "Use this when you need it. Keep your head tilted back for a minute and press on your upper lip right below your nose. Like this." She took his finger and showed him how to apply pressure to slow the bleeding. Sometimes it was useful to have a nurse for a mother.

It took a few minutes for the bleeding to stop. Once it did, Anna spoke again, "Can you tell us what happened now? No one here is going to hurt you Georgie, I promise."

The others stood in silence. They rarely thought about racial issues. Once in a while they overheard one of their parent's conversations when the nightly news or morning paper had a report about the progress (in truth, the lack of progress) in school desegregation. In most cases, the talk centered on how they were all for equality, so long as it was separate but equal, and they were smugly convinced this was already the case. The Negroes should stay in their own neighborhoods, attend their own schools, eat at their own restaurants and shop at their own stores. Why did they always make such a fuss? They had the vote and everything. Once when a family from Little Betty's church came to dinner, their teenage daughter related an incident when some Black boys had come RIGHT in the entrance at Northwest Pool, and jumped RIGHT in the water! "Those BLACK Niggers just came right on in! And when THEY got IN, I got OUT! They had to empty every drop of water out of that pool and scrub it down with bleach after they ran those Nigger boys off!"

The pious Christians seated around the table clucked their tongues in sympathy. What was this world coming to? Hadn't Pastor Lewis explained how the Bible said Negroes bore the mark of Cain, and Adam and Eve were white, as were Noah and his wife. So, people with dark skin must have descended from the animals on the ark. Clearly God was white, and he meant for the races to be kept separate.

As a sobbing Georgie related what had happened, the silence from the others continued. Anna shot them another defiant glance, then wrapped her arms around the little boy, "It will be all right Honey, I'll take care of you, and Mark," another meaningful look in his direction, "will make sure those boys don't come anywhere near you." She let him go, but took him by the hand, ignoring the blood stains on her own T-shirt. "What time will your mother be through with her job?"

"My mama be done at two Miss Anna Belle."

Anna checked her watch, it was only ten-forty-five, too early to return him to the Richard's house, but plenty of time to complete their investigation. She would have to make sure Georgie was safe. "It's too early to take you back, would you like to come for a walk with us?"

"Yes'm Miss Anna Belle. I be good."

"Georgie, you don't need to call me Miss, you can call me Anna."

"Yes, Ma'am Mi—uh, I mean Anna."

"You're a good boy Georgie, you didn't do anything wrong. Those boys who hurt you were bad, they deserve to be punished for what they did to you. I'm gonna make sure they are."

"NO MISS ANNA BELLE! You need to just let it go." He struggled for the right words, "Ain't no use trying to do that. White folks don't understand. I be okay now, you fixed me up real good, you a nice lady, just like your mama."

Anna hugged him again, "Okay Georgie, we'll talk about it later, don't you worry." She took his hand as they started down the trail; his small brown hand was lost within hers, but his grip was one of tight desperation for a secure anchor against an insecure world.

As they progressed along the trail, Georgie clung to Anna's hand and stayed close by her side. This was a completely new experience to him, he had never ventured far beyond his East Austin neighborhood, nor made a trip to a remote forest like this. His head swiveled as he tried to take it all in. His left eye had opened to a narrow slit, and he could still see out of the right. So many trees and bushes, and such big ones. He opened up a bit and began peppering Anna with questions—were there bears? What about wolves and snakes? He soon forgot to "talk colored" and sounded like a different person.

Anna smiled inwardly. She first met Georgie when Rose Woods accompanied Carrie to Willie Kochek's to purchase the old washer and dryer. Georgie sat next to Anna in the back. Rose had tried to climb into the back, but Carrie Cook wouldn't hear of it. Rose had spoken with well enunciated English and perfect grammar, each word crisp and melodious, with only a hint of a soft southern accent. That had been about two years ago. As nine-year-old Anna chattered away to the little boy, he hung his head in embarrassment and only said, "Yes'm Miss Anna Belle" when she asked him direct questions.

"Now Georgie, you can talk properly around Mrs. Cook and Anna Belle. Show Anna Belle how well you can speak."

"Yes, Mama." But the shy little boy kept his head bowed and mumbled the same monosyllabic responses to Anna's ongoing stream of chatter. He had never forgotten the incident. It was the first time a white lady had ever entered their house, and to bring her daughter made the incident even more memorable, if unsettling. The white woman and her daughter were friendly and treated him and his mother with respect. He was not accustomed to this in his limited dealings with white people. Anna was being kind now as well. Although four centuries of generational abuse was still very much a part of his emotional inheritance, something in her manner made Georgie instinctively trust Anna.

Now, as they trudged along the trail, there was no confusion or time distortion. Everything looked perfectly normal in the daylight, and before long they came to the rivulet as it splashed across their path on its journey down to Shoal Creek. Much to Georgie's delight, birds chirped all around them, insects buzzed, and in the distance, the hum of traffic up on The Trail was faintly discernible. "Seems pretty normal to me," Mark grumbled, and no one contradicted him.

When they came within a half block of the last crest, Anna stopped them and said she would wait there with Georgie. As they came to the top, the group joined clammy hands, unwilling to risk finding themselves alone again. Anna watched with apprehension as they reached the ridge. The group remained together, holding hands and looking into the valley. Those on the ends were pointing, but no one in the middle was willing to let go. Mark looked down toward Anna and Georgie, and called out for them to join the group. "Y'all better come up here and see this."

Anna led a confused Georgie up the hill, but stopped short of the top. "Someone grab my hand."

The group swung out in a line so she could reach James' hand. Then they climbed the last few feet together. When Anna looked down, the valley had been transformed. Although they had each seen something different during the previous visit, they all agreed that the valley was forested. Now it was transmuted into an image from an apocalyptic nightmare. The trees were shriveled and dead, and the underbrush was reduced to brown rubble—not a leaf remained. From their vantage point they couldn't tell if the forest had burned, or if something even more disquieting had transpired. The entire valley floor was desolate and foreboding; the surrounding hillsides were devoid of vegetation for the first fifty feet, with traces of green gradually appearing and becoming denser as the nascent forest climbed the valley walls.

Mark spoke up above the babble of whispered confusion, "We may not be seeing the boogie men y'all keep going on about, but something ain't right here. Let's take a closer look."

The reluctant group agreed to go so long as they continued to hold hands, and began a cautious descent. As they approached the valley floor, the gradual thinning out of live vegetation took on a menacing aspect. Where trees and bushes had once flourished, only desiccated stumps and withered grasses remained. They felt dry and brittle to the touch, as though some sinister force had sucked the life out of them, leaving only hollowed, sterile husks. When they reached the valley floor, only the parched corpses of vegetation remained. Not a breeze stirred, and the air bore the scent of woody dust. The only resident here was death.

Two brown hands firmly clasped Anna's, and a tearful face was buried in her side. She gently extricated her hand and wrapped her arm around the narrow shoulders. "Shall we take you back to your mama?"

By the time they returned to Maybellene, it was indeed time to take Georgie back. As they got in the car, Betty spoke softly, "We have more room up here, Georgie can sit on my lap," and for the first time in her short life, Little Betty touched brown skin.

Anna told Mark to stop several doors down from the Richards' house. "I'd better take him; his mother knows me and I can tell her what happened to him."

When the three boys once again surrounded the pair, they sensed defenseless prey, and were unprepared for what happened. As the fist met the nose of the largest target, it was as Anna had been taught. You do not tuck your thumb into your fist—that can break it, leave your thumb on the outside. Slide the left foot forward to put your full body weight into the punch. Throw the punch straight from the shoulder with no looping and allow your arm to pronate naturally to add even more force to the blow. The result was most satisfying, the nose erupted in a spray of blood, and the boy hit the pavement hard as his feet flew out from under him. Anna pivoted to face the other two, but Mark was on the way, with a screaming Levi hot on his heels, letting them know in no uncertain terms what their fate would be if they tried to lay a hand on Anna or her friend. The two bullies made tracks, leaving their forgotten buddy bleeding on the street, but he was quickly up and right behind them as the three scrambled away.

Yeah Red, you're something else.

When Murial Richards answered the door, she was aghast. There was that horrible little colored boy, now covered in blood, with one eye swollen shut and his lips split and puffy. He wore a torn shirt stained with blood and grime. Some strange white girl stood next to him and was actually holding his hand! Her T-shirt was streaked with dried blood, and something wet dripped from her left hand. She fixed Muriel with a defiant gaze, almost intimidating; but that was silly, she was just a girl.

Still, those eyes were unnerving...

"Miz Richards, I brought Georgie back, is Mrs. Woods here?"

Rose pushed past Murial Richards. "My baby! What happened to you, Georgie?"

"He's all right now Mrs. Woods. You remember me? I'm Anna Cook. Some boys beat up on Georgie, but I've been taking care of him, he's gonna be just fine. Aren't you Sweetie?"

As his mother wrapped Georgie in an embrace, an enraged Murial Richards demanded to be told what was going on with "you people." She would NOT have this sort of thing in her home. This was what happened when Nigras forgot their place. Of course, the boy had gotten into trouble, that was exactly the sort of thing she would expect. Miss Rose could collect her earnings, and she needn't come back.

Rose gathered herself up to her full five feet, faced Murial Richards and spoke evenly, "You don't need to worry about THAT Mrs. Richards. And you can forget about my pay, Georgie and I will do perfectly well without your precious five dollars." She took Georgie by one hand and Anna by the other, giving it a little squeeze, and marched them away.

As the door slammed behind them, Rose noticed the blood dripping from Anna's hand and turned to her. "Oh Baby, are YOU all right? Can you tell me what happened?"

Anna gave her a condensed version; her friends were waiting, but she would make sure Rose got all the details later on. She gave Georgie a hug and kissed his forehead, "I TOLD you I'd get even with those punks."

"Anna HIT the big one, Mama," exclaimed a suddenly animated Georgie. "You should have seen her—I bet she broke his nose, huh, Miss Anna? I ran into the woods to get away, and she and her friends found me, and Miss Anna took good care of me. Here Miss Anna, you can give that boy his T-shirt back. Tell him I'm sorry I got it all nasty."

"What did I tell you about that MISS Anna stuff? You go on home with your mama now, Georgie. We can talk more later; I need to get home too. I hope he's all right Mrs. Woods, you be sure to tell us if he's not. I cleaned him up the best I could, I'm sorry you didn't get your pay though, that wasn't right."

"Don't you worry your pretty head, Anna Belle, he got cared for by the daughter of the best nurse I know, and that's worth more than some rich lady's money. I'd have paid a lot more than five dollars for you to punch that boy—we're going to laugh about that for a long time! You tell your mama hello for me, and thank her for what you did. I'll call her later, after I clean Georgie up."

The ride home was peppered with speculation about what had happened to the forest. Mark had been that far up the path once (with his now ex-girlfriend; hoping, to no avail, to get lucky—but that part he kept to himself) and he remembered some kind of farm in the valley, with crops laid out in rows, surrounded by dense forest. Weird setup, there was what looked like a monster greenhouse, like an oversized barn, but no farmhouse of any kind.

Maybe it was time to talk to their parents about what was going on, but that might mean they would be restricted, and certainly punished, for the nighttime excursion to the woods. As the old Studie sputtered into the drive at James' house, they had resolved nothing. Anna was deep in thought. Now they could not avoid being found out.

~ ~ ~

Anna's Journal
Log Entry June 14, 1958

What a day! We went back to the woods again, but this time in daylight and Mark (still mega-CUTE but also mega-stupid and <u>WAY</u> too old for me anyway) took us in his old junker 'cause stupid Stevie let him in on our secrets. Anyway, this is a 2 part entry—the part about Georgie and the part about what we saw. So what we saw was that nothing bad happened to us but all the trees and bushes in the valley were dead. That part was pretty scary—when I say dead, I mean dead and rotting and dried out. And it stunk bad, I guess from the plants rotting or something. I can't understand what could cause that, and so fast—I mean we were just there a couple weeks ago and it may have been crazy but there were trees and bushes all over the valley. So that's one part.

The other part is about Georgie Woods—Rose Woods' little boy. When we started into the woods Mark saw him hiding in the bushes. Some kids in that neighborhood had beat him up bad, real bad. His nose was bleeding and probably broken, one of his eyes was all black (I guess Negroes can get black eyes too) and swollen shut and I think he was hurt a lot internally. I took care of him the best I could, and he said he felt good enough to go with us cause he wasn't supposed to go to the house where his mother was working. That poor woman works just as long at the hospital as Mom and still has to clean houses on Saturday or whenever she has a day off. She is a nurse but the hospital will only hire her as a nurse's aide because she got her degree from that Negro college in east Austin. And of course that means she makes even less money than Mom. But anyway, when we got back I went to take him back to where his mother was working, and the boys who beat him up ran up and were gonna beat us both up. There were 3 of them, I didn't know them because I think maybe they are a year ahead of us and go to Lamar Junior High. I guess they thought it would be easy to beat us up, but before they could do anything I punched the biggest one right in his nose and probably broke it cause I got in a really good punch with all my weight behind it. I was getting ready to fight the other two but Mark and Levi came running up and yelling. I don't know what Levi thought he would be able to do, but Mark scared the doo doo out of them and they took off. Know the best thing about punching a boy if you are a girl? You never get in trouble because there is no way in HELL they will ever admit it. HA! Mom said there's this play called "A Streetcar Named Desire." In it this character called Blanche something says "I have always depended on the kindness of strangers." Georgie doesn't get much of that kindness. Poor kid.

But now I'm worried because Mom found out from Rose about us going to the woods. I'm gonna be in so FLACKIN' much trouble!!

Anna Out.

~ ~ ~

Later in the afternoon, the telephone at the Cook home interrupted the abbreviated explanation Anna was giving her mother. She told her about the gang going for a hike, finding Georgie after the boys attacked him, and how she tried to clean him up—then skipped to the part where she delivered him back to his mother and how he should be fine now. She was sorry she got blood all over her T-shirt, but it was an old one and the blood should mostly wash out.

"Oh, HELLO Rose! Yes, Anna was telling me... What? She certainly didn't tell me that. Oh, really? No, I, no please go on..." The one-sided conversation carried on for some time, with a worried Anna trying to figure out what was being said. It ended with, "We would LOVE to come to dinner tomorrow, what can I bring? No, I will not come empty-handed, we can bring the dessert, how would that be? Two, after church? That sounds perfect, Anna Belle and I will see you then."

When she hung up the phone, Carrie walked straight over to Anna and smothered her in a squeeze. "I am SO proud of you, Anna Belle! SO proud." She sniffled, fighting back tears. "How you took care of that poor little boy, and how you stood up to those boys who hurt him, I am just, just, SO PROUD!" This was followed by more sniffling, a rattling, honking nose blow, and wiping of wet eyes. "Now, Young Lady, let's talk about this little excursion into the woods."

CHAPTER 15
THERE'S A STORM A-COMIN'

*"You don't need a weather vane to know
which way this wind is blowing."*
–*Blond Ice*—1948 film noir

A Troubling Forecast

Sunday morning found Rose and Georgie, as always, seated in the fifth-row pew at the Metropolitan African Methodist Episcopalian (AME) Church. The wooden pew was worn to a soft glow from years of uncomplaining use. A small group of 13 founded the church in 1870, and the congregation moved four different times before coming to their current site on East 10th street. This morning Rose and Georgie came to worship in a church that had been serving the African American community for almost 100 years. AME churches are the centers of the Black community in the areas they serve, and Metropolitan AME was no different; it was a place of sanctity and refuge for its members, so it was fitting that Rose offered thanks for Georgie being delivered safely back to her after his brush with death the previous day. She stood up and gave witness for the divine protection afforded to her little son, and thanks for the young girl whom the Lord chose as his vessel. Tears ran down her face, and the congregation met her testimony with Hosannas and Hallelujahs. Each person in attendance understood exactly what it had meant for Georgie to have been attacked in the way he was. They knew it could have ended much differently. After the service, every woman in the building came up to hug Rose and fuss over Georgie.

Once most of the congregation departed, the Reverend Dr. Laws pulled Rose aside and looked at her in earnest. "Sister Woods, you have been touched by the Lord. Big George was lookin' down on you and watchin' out for his boy. You know if you ever need anything, it is the duty of this church to provide. Now I want you to reach into this collection plate, and take back the dollar I saw you put in, and whatever else you need for this week. I'll talk to the ladies, and we'll find you a better place to work than for that Richards lady. You ain't the first housekeeper to have it right up to here (holding his hand above his eyebrows) with that woman."

"Oh NO Reverend Laws, I can manage just fine, really I can, I couldn't take from the collection plate."

The kindly old man reached a hand into the small pile of bills and coins, pulled out several bills, and pressed them into her palm. "You didn't take anything—I did." He glanced around and called out to a woman who had stayed behind to collect hymnals and tidy up. "Sister Greenworth, I think the freezer in the back has a Popsicle with Georgie's name on it, why don't you take him there and see if you can find it. Give him some paper and pencil and ask him if he can draw me a nice picture of the chapel, I want to take Sister Woods into my office for a little chat."

Dr. Laws used the small office for many purposes—writing sermons, conducting the administrative affairs of the church, serving as confessor and counselor, and otherwise attempting to minister to the overwhelming needs of his flock. Once he had Rose seated comfortably on the big, overstuffed couch he had picked up at a garage sale, he pulled his creaky wooden office chair from behind the desk and sat across from her with his face crinkled into a sad smile. "Now Sister Woods, you know how close that boy came to meetin' his maker yesterday. I give praise to Jesus he wasn't ready to call him home; but Sister Woods, God gave us a brain for a reason, and it's time we make some smart decisions about Georgie. If Big George hadn't been taken from us at such an early age, we wouldn't be sittin' here right now. You're one of the best mamas I've ever seen, you've done everything you can for that boy, and he is growin' into a fine young man who will soon be a credit to his daddy. And I'm sure you intend to talk to him one day about how things are; how things are for young Negro men. That is a hard talk to have with a young boy, he's only, what, eight years old? And he already experienced what can happen. He could just as easy be dead, Sister Woods, we both know it. Now we can't protect him from everything, we can't always be there for him, so we got to make sure he understands how to be smarter, how to be more careful, how to act around white folks, and especially around the PO-lice. Sister Woods, you have done all you can, but he needs a man to sit down and talk with him. You know the talk. Colored men been havin' that talk with their boys for generations. You might not think he's ready; he's too young, too innocent, too little, but Sister Woods, the world ain't gonna wait for him to be old enough, the world ain't gonna wait for him to be bigger, or for his mama to be more ready.

There's a storm a-comin', Sister Woods, and we need to be prepared. The winds of freedom are howling and there won't be any turning back, nor any shelter from the gale. Plans are being laid for all manner of protests, and we will need to be ready and do our parts. With the help of the Lord, it will mean a better life for Georgie, but it will also mean even more danger for us all, and for young colored men in particular.

The time for Georgie to have that talk with a grown man is now. What I'm saying, Sister Woods, is I hope you'll trust me enough to let me be that man. If not me, there are plenty of fine men in this congregation, maybe one of the bishops. You tell me who you want it to be, and I'll see to it. It doesn't have to be today, and it doesn't have to be here—might be best to do it in your own home, but it needs to be soon. Now you know I'm right, Sister Woods."

She broke down in tears. The facade of bravery she fought so hard to maintain crumbled at these words she knew to be true. Her fear came rushing out in a torrent of words—it was all her fault, she had waited too long; she had babied Georgie, but she loved him so much, and he was so small, who would want to harm someone so young and innocent? He was only eight years old—barely eight years! Even Jewish boys got to wait until they were thirteen for their people to tell them they had to act like men. Could the Lord ever forgive her? She was a sinner, not worthy of such a fine boy. Sometimes it was just too hard, why was life so hard?

The kindhearted man let her vent for a while, then did everything he could to reassure her, but mixed a potent dose of reality with the assurance. It was NOT her fault, she had nothing to atone for; yesterday was God's way of telling them they needed to take this next step in the boy's life. After their conversation, Rose felt a little better; this church and its congregation provided sanctuary in the truest sense of the word. On Wednesday evening, after Bible Study, Reverend Laws would have the talk with Georgie on the big comfortable couch in his office.

It was time.

An Unlikely Friendship

When Rose and Georgie returned home, the clock on the kitchen showed one PM, just enough time to complete the dinner she had started early that morning before church. Rose rushed around, busying herself with preparing the meal, while Georgie read a book they'd picked up for him last week at the George Washington Carver branch of the Austin Public Library system. All other library branches had remained segregated until 1951, and they still didn't feel comfortable at the main library downtown. Besides, it was a long drive and parking was difficult.

The meal consisted of pan-fried chicken, green beans flavored with bacon fat, sweet corn on the cob, piles of fluffy mashed potatoes with cream gravy, tender homemade biscuits dripping in butter, and a choice of three kinds of homemade jam. There was sweet iced tea, frosty buttermilk, and cherry Kool Aid to drink.

The conversation at the dinner table was animated, with Carrie and Rose chatting about work—it had been so hectic lately with those crazy UT students. Georgie jabbered away guilelessly at Anna, perfectly at ease with her. He wanted to tell her about every aspect of his life—school, Sunday School, the book he was reading, and how his auntie took care of him when Mama was at work. His precociousness charmed Anna, and she took an honest interest in what he was telling her, asking questions and laughing with him.

After they finished, Georgie took Anna by the hand and led her back to his room so he could read to her from his books. Carrie got up to help with the dishes, but Rose shooed her away, those dishes could wait. Besides, they needed to talk, so they adjourned to the living area, not actually a separate room, sipping fresh glasses of cold sweet tea, with condensation from the humid Austin air running down the sides.

Rose started out by thanking Carrie once again. No, this was NOT a small thing. Georgie had been in real danger, in danger of his life. If the other boys had found him hiding in the woods, or if they jumped him again as he returned to the house, he, well, they might have killed him. Carrie had been shocked to see what Georgie's face looked like—one eye was discolored and swollen, his nose had obviously been broken, and his lips were puffy and raw. Anna had described it to her, but she had been certain Anna was exaggerating. Surely, Carrie protested, they were just boys themselves, not capable of murder.

Rose shook her head sadly, "No Carrie, y'all, you, you can't understand the way it is. I don't know how you ever can. No, now don't interrupt, I want to say something, and I need you to hear it. This kind of thing happens to colored people all the time. You—you and Anna, you're the best white folks I ever met. I don't have a single white friend at that hospital other than you. Everyone else treats me like slavery never ended, or even worse, like I don't even exist. Georgie had never played with a white child before in his life. The way he takes to Anna, and the way she looked out for him, is a blessing from the Lord. I'll tell you just one more time—if it hadn't been for Anna yesterday, I would be spending my day today at a funeral parlor. I will never forget that girl, or you for having raised her."

The two women embraced, and tears streamed down Carrie's cheeks. She was overcome with conflicting emotions—overwhelming pride for Anna's actions, mixed with guilt for being blind to the realities of Black life, and despair of knowing what to do.

"Rose, I don't even know how to ask this—how do you, how do you even do it? Aren't you filled with resentment and anger every waking hour of every day? I'm embarrassed to say I never thought of this before, but... I mean— oh, I'm making a mess of this. What I'm trying to say is, first slavery, for so many years, then all the prejudice, segregation, injustice, all of it. How do you live with it, and work for white people, the very group that's responsible? It seems so overwhelming to me when I think about it. I don't understand how you do it."

"I would be lying to say it's easy, Carrie. But at some point, you have to live your life. You can't spend every minute obsessing over it. I'm not saying there aren't those who do, but for me, I have to focus on Georgie, and try to make the best of things. If I just automatically hated every white person, I wouldn't have a friend like you. That hate would eat me up, destroy my soul, and poison Georgie. Change will come, I have to believe that, have to believe that things can be different for Georgie. In the meantime, I endure. There are days I don't think I can get up out of bed—I can't get sick because I can't afford to lose a day's pay, but I endure. Our community here is strong, my church is a refuge, and Georgie is my inspiration to keep going, so I endure. I know you understand because I know your story—I'm one of the few who do."

Carrie held a finger to her lips, "shhhhh."

Rose leaned forward and whispered, "Anna Belle doesn't know? You aren't going to tell her?"

"I intend to—I will—when I think she's ready. Or more accurately, when I can work up the nerve. It's a hard conversation."

"Oh, I understand hard conversations—umm hmm."

They talked quietly for a while. In the Texas of 1958, the gulf between them seemed vast and insurmountable. Yes, tiny bits of progress were made from time to time, but every new victory was met with opposition and indifference to change. After a while, Rose said, "Oh, just listen to us silly women, trying to solve all the problems of the world by ourselves. For me, it's enough you're willing to listen."

"No Rose, it isn't enough, but it's a beginning. Can we meet and talk like this once in a while? I have so much to learn, and it would be instructive for Anna. It would be wrong for me to raise her to be blind to the problems of colored people. The next time dinner will be at my house, and if the neighbors say anything, to hell with 'em! But we need to talk about something else. You mentioned the story Georgie told about what happened while they were in the woods together, and what he overheard the other children talking about. I got a little out of Anna last night, but I'm sure she was holding something back. All she would say is they went for a walk in the woods to kill time before you would be done at the Richard's place, and they saw an area where all the trees had died. Something has been going on with Anna for a few days now. It must have something to do with those woods. I mean, those kids never go there. Trust me, they are not hiking types, especially Betty. And what was Stevie's older brother doing with them? That boy normally wouldn't be caught dead hanging out with his bookworm of a little brother."

"Oh, I'm sorry Carrie, he was babbling nonsense, and I was so worried he was hurt, I didn't pay much attention. He overheard the other children, the younger ones, whispering about something they saw in the woods at night. Whatever it was must have frightened them to death. When they got to the spot where they saw the dead trees, Anna wouldn't let Georgie go at first, and the rest of them held hands when they went. Then they waved for Anna and Georgie to come, said Anna needed to see something, I guess all the dead trees, but she insisted on taking their hands and having Georgie between her and one of the boys. He said they all held hands except for Stevie's brother. He jabbered about a bunch of other things, but none of it made sense—time being messed up, these horrible things they saw when they went at night. Crazy stuff—it kind of reminded me of how some of those students we keep seeing in the ER act, all weird, like they're seeing things that aren't there. Oh, and, now I feel like I'm tattling on your daughter—but the teenage boy, the one with the little brother named Stevie, he took them in his old car. But he said Anna Belle sat in the back seat—he sat in front, on the other little girl's lap, the one he called Little Betty."

Oh my, thought Carrie, eleven years old and riding with teenage boys! Then she snickered to herself, if Betty's mother had seen Georgie sitting on Betty's lap, she would have soiled her white silk panties. But she and Anna would have a long talk when they got home.

They talked a while longer, with conversation flowing easily, mainly about what the children had seen, and those UT students who kept coming into the ER. Underneath her cheerful facade, Carrie was growing concerned. When they called the children back into the living room, Anna asked Rose a strange question. "Mrs. Woods, what grade is Georgie in?"

"He's in the second grade, Honey, or will be when school starts, he should be in the third at his age, but when we lost his Daddy, it set everything back. He's small for his age too. His Daddy was a great big man, everybody at the fire station called him Big George, but I'm afraid Georgie takes after me. I keep hoping he'll take off. I'm well aware the work is too easy for him, but the other boys don't pick on him as much since he's been kept back."

"Mrs. Woods, you need to put him in some kind of special classes. Georgie is smart, way too smart for normal school. He needs to be in an advanced class or special school or something. He's reading books a lot of grownups couldn't read."

Rose beamed for an instant, then looked forlorn. "Honey, there isn't anything like that for little colored boys and girls. I know he's smart, I do what I can for him, and the teachers do their best to help. I try to find advanced workbooks for him and help him pick out the right books. He's bored with his normal school work. I'm afraid it will put him off on school."

"It's not fair! I'll bet if he was white, he'd get plenty of help. It just isn't fair. Why don't they have that for him?"

"Anna! Don't you pester Mrs. Woods now. It may not be fair, but it isn't her fault."

"I KNOW Mom. I'm just saying—it isn't FAIR!

~ ~ ~

Anna's Journal
Log Entry June 15, 1958

Today we had dinner with Mrs. Woods and Georgie. It was to pay me back for helping Georgie I guess, and Mom for being such a good friend to Mrs. Woods. I can guaran-DAMN-tee you that none of the other kid's parents have Negro friends. Their house was even smaller and rattier than ours, but it was neat and clean and I could tell she took pride in it. And Georgie is SMART! His Mom checks out library books for him to read that are really advanced. He gets bored with the books from his school. Boy can I ever relate to that! If it wasn't for the branch library down on The Trail I'd go nuts. I saw their library on the way home and it is so small and shabby looking. I'm gonna find some better books for him at our library. There must be books written by Negroes. I'll get Miss Fischer to help me pick some out – she's really nice. She taught me how to use the card catalog to find books – you can look by title, subject, author – it's really cool. But by now I have the library memorized so I don't need it as much as I used to. It was real nice getting to visit with the Woods (except for Mom finding out about our trips to the valley.) The food was delicious, it was hard to keep from just stuffing myself, but Mom says that's rude so I held back (a little.)

It was like I was afraid of. Mrs. Woods told Mom about our trip to the woods and what Georgie overhead us talking about. I still haven't told her everything, but I had to tell her something. She knows we made the trip at night, but I tried to play it down like nothing really happened – like we were just scared because it was so dark. I did NOT tell her about my dreams. I don't even tell the other kids about those.

–Anna Out

CHAPTER 16
CALORIC INTENSIFICATION

Fire don't care if you believe in science and physics, or God.
Fire gonna burn.

Monday afternoon Jenny was hard at work in the Chem Lab preparing the trays for the chemists. Her work area was at the back of the laboratory, against a solid wall she had always assumed was the back of the building. By three she was almost done, and was thinking about sneaking out for a smoke on her coffee break. She'd been trying to quit, but the tension from her meeting with Johan Arndt was making it difficult.

Over in the EE wing, Jerry scrutinized a blueprint for a new transistor Hal had designed; it was almost ready to be prototyped in the EE lab. They were arguing over whether the positive or negative charge type material held the most promise for the future of transistor technology, when a thunderous explosion shook the building. Within moments, an alarm rang out, and a voice came over the loudspeaker— "There has been a minor accident in the Chemical Laboratory and it resulted in a small fire. Please remain calm and exit the building. Do not panic or run, and be respectful of others as you exit. This is not a drill." The announcement was repeated several times, but once was enough as the engineers all made a rush for the door.

"Minor my ass," Jerry muttered as the crowd of engineers swept them into their wake, all trying to exit the single door. When they entered the corridor, the situation only escalated, with employees from the labs and offices in the EE wing pushing and shoving their way along. The cafeteria was larger, but the Chemical and Agricultural wings were also emptying into it in the panicked rush to the front doors. As the growing mob approached the elevators, the administrative staff from upstairs joined the throng, forcing their way out of the stairwell, onto the floor, and out toward the building exit. The unique V-shape of the building meant the single front exit created a bottleneck and was exacerbating the crowding. Over the shouting and screams, the sonorous thrum of helicopter rotors assaulted Hal's ears. Once out the front doors, he saw a bulky, military style chopper on the roof loading men in dark suits. They recognized the first man to enter the helicopter as Winston Overton Sinclair, the owner of Alpen Labs. Rarely seen, he was referred to in private Alpen employee conversations as "The Gray Man," a reference to both his dress and his demeanor. Today he failed to disappoint, wearing a charcoal gray suit with the faintest of pinstripes, a matching dark gray tie and spotless white shirt. He should have been advertising life insurance.

Sinclair was a reclusive billionaire whose interest in Alpen Labs remained a mystery to the financial world. Traditionally a conservative investor who abhorred risk as much as he did publicity, he preferred to remain in the murky backwaters of the financial ecosphere. Yet he had poured a major portion of his considerable wealth into the creation of Alpen Labs and stepped in as Chairman of the Board, something he had never attempted with his many other holdings.

As the chopper lifted off, Hal recognized it from one of Stevie's models as a Sikorsky CH-37, a hefty cargo carrier, the first helicopter to be powered by two engines. He could see the words U.S. AIR FORCE standing out in distinct contrast to the glossy silver finish.

With choreographed timing, Johan Arndt came out to the front of the building, carrying a large megaphone, and speaking in his strange clipped accent. "Please not alarmed. We experienced little problem in one of Chemical areas. There is some minor damage and small fire, which is well under control. I am happy to tell that no one injured. You will all please to exit in orderly fashion. The Alpen Labs telephone tree will be activated and you will be called when safe to return work, but you not need to report tomorrow. If you are caller, please to stay home this afternoon and wait for contacted with further instruction. Again, no reason for alarmed, please to leave now, be careful driving, and enjoy day off. Thank you for cooperation." But for the heavily accented voice, it could have been a recording. More security guards arrived from the building and formed a semi-circle behind Arndt. With their dark uniforms, badges, and sidearms, they created a grim backdrop and left no doubt it was time to go.

As Jerry looked back at the building, flames raged, with yellow and black smoke billowing up. He scowled, "It sure doesn't look to me like the fire is under control; and what was with the chopper, with 'US AIR FORCE' written on the side? Do the Big Boys rate military transport these days? And did you see Jenny come out? I can't be certain with everybody out at once and in such a panic, but I haven't seen her."

"Come to think of it, I haven't either, but I'm sure she's okay, they said there are no injuries."

"How would they even know with this confusion? But she's a grown girl, we can call her later and check on her."

On the floor at the back of the Chemical Lab, Jenny was anything but okay. When the explosion erupted, the wall behind her blew into the laboratory. It knocked her forward over the table where she was working and smashed her forehead into the surface of the metal table. Her ears rang from the concussion and her thoughts were scrambled. She turned around to see dark gray and yellow smoke pouring through a ragged hole in the wall the size of a small car. Her vision was blurred, but she could see a hallway with doors on either side. Fire raged in the room directly behind the hole and licked at the ceiling of the corridor. At the far end she saw light, and people dashing out of an open door. It looked like they were screaming with panic, but the reverberations in her ears made it impossible to hear. The smoke burned her eyes and her lungs felt scalded when she tried to breathe, forcing her to drop to her knees. Rod lectured her about fire safety often enough that she knew to stay down and crawl away from the flames. She felt blood running down into her eyes from the injury to her head. Grabbing the bottom of her blouse, Jenny lifted it up to wipe at her eyes, getting them clear enough to see where she was going. She looked around anxiously until she found her purse, which she slung across her back. As she started to crawl, she saw a charred metal tube, not any kind of lab equipment she recognized, so she reached for it and put it in her purse. It was burning hot to the touch, forcing her to use the hem of her skirt to pick it up.

The trip to the door seemed to take forever. Glass and chemicals had been strewn everywhere, cutting her hands and knees, and pain seared from those chemicals she couldn't avoid.

~ ~ ~

The lady on the phone, speaking in a hushed whisper, refused to identify herself. There was a huge fire at Alpen Labs, the fire department should come right away, and make sure an ambulance came, there were sure to be injuries. Rod grilled her for details, but she clammed up. If this was a false alarm, as Acting Captain his neck would be on the chopping block, but the woman sounded sincere. Besides, Jenny worked there, so he decided this was not the day to take chances.

Fire Station 16 was well-equipped, boasting two pumpers and one extended hook and ladder, or aerial, truck. Rod yanked down the alarm and shouted, "let's go, everybody, all equipment, fire at

Alpen Labs, on the double!" As the men rushed to don their gear, Rod made a call to the central station—yes, the caller said the fire was massive, and caused by an explosion, so they would need backup.

He hung up, put on his own gear, and took the passenger seat in the lead engine as they rolled out of the station with their sirens wailing and lights flashing. Though Station 16 was the northernmost of the Austin fire stations, it was a long trip out to Alpen Labs. But they made it in record time, with Rod pointing the way through gaps in traffic as his driver swung the bulky truck around like a race car. Still, the winding country roads forced the heavy trucks to lumber along at reduced speeds, and it seemed like an eternity before they pulled into the front entrance to the lab. The guard at the front gate tried to stop them, but when Rod saw the sky ahead filled with plumes of black smoke, he told the driver to ignore the guard and go through. As they did, the guard picked up a telephone connected to the communication system.

They turned into a circular drive at the front of the building. Johan Arndt, flanked by four other guards, confronted them as they pulled up. Arndt's arms hung unbent by his sides, with his hands slightly curved and the palms to the back. It made a peculiar, and oddly unsettling scene.

"Good afternoon, sir, may I ask who called you to come all way out here?"

"Whoever it was, it looks like they were right. How do we get around back to where the fire is? And where are the fire plugs?"

"I am sorry you and your men had to make long trip, but you not needed. We have our own fire service, and they will soon to have everything under control."

"Look mister, I don't know who you are and what kind of fire service you think you have, but this is my jurisdiction. Tell your boys to take their little fire extinguishers and get the hell out of our way, then tell me how we can get around back."

Arndt's smile managed to be both insincere and condescending. "I am afraid I cannot do that, and I must insist you to leave now." As if on cue, the four men behind him drew their sidearms and pointed them at Rod.

Rod was furious, and at 6'4", he was formidable, but the firefighters had no weapons other than hoses, and he was responsible for their safety. He listened in vain for the trucks from the other stations. Given the alarm he had raised, at least two police cars should have accompanied them, but the only sound he heard was the roar of the fire. Then something else. As he listened in astonishment, he heard the wop wop of helicopter rotors and the steady drone of slow flying airplanes.

The two North American B-25's arrived first, they swooped dangerously low, and dropped an orange mist over the building. Close behind, a fleet of five HH-43B Huskie helicopters followed, each bearing the words U.S. Air Force. They hovered over the source of the smoke and dropped a fine spray of water. The yellow-black smoke began to abate at once.

"You see, Mr., uh, Hatcher," said Arndt smoothly, glancing at the nameplate on Rod's shirt, "we do very well by ourselves. Now I must insist you to be on way, we will be need use this drive as we clean up."

The four guards continued to keep their pistols leveled at Rod's chest, joined now by a half dozen more armed guards, some with military style rifles.

"I don't understand what's going on here," Rod said, "we'll go, but I will be back, with the police and a warrant for an arson investigation." He was about to leave, when an exhausted Jenny shouted his name and staggered out of the building. Her head bore a nasty blue lump with blood oozing from it. Multi-colored stains covered her skirt and blouse, and she looked woozy and disoriented. "Jenny" he shouted, and ran toward her. As he did, four pistols turned to follow his path, but Arndt held up a hand, and they were returned to their holsters.

When he reached her, she threw her arms around his neck and collapsed against him as the adrenalin boost that had taken her this far dissipated. She whispered a last, desperate plea in his ear before the world swam away.

"Let's take you home then, we can come back for your car another time," he gathered her up and carried her back towards the truck. He turned to Arndt as they passed him, "Looks like you weren't as much in control as you claim. We'll go, but you and whoever your boss is can expect another visit real soon."

As the convoy of trucks rumbled away from the building, they passed a line of black Ford sedans coming into the facility. Jenny snuggled up against Rod with her head on his chest and her eyes closed, breathing softly. The drive back was more relaxed, Rod told his driver to take it easy, he didn't want to jostle Jenny, and also wanted some time to cool off before reporting this incident to the Austin Fire Chief, Lawrence Crandell. The heavy trucks drove sluggishly on the narrow hill country roads with their blind corners and tight turns. Rod was lost in his own reverie when Jenny began to stir. She had been sleeping with her mouth partly open, and his chest was damp from little rivulets of drool.

Jenny awoke with the strange sensation she was still dreaming. Things within her field of vision drifted in and out of focus. Her eyes played tricks; she thought the red firetruck dashboard was the reddest red she had ever seen, the very essence of redness, color as she had never experienced it before. It was as though she'd been color blind her entire life and was seeing the world in color for the first time. She could taste the redness on her tongue. That was silly, of course, but there it was, as it had always been, the flavor of red. All colors had flavors, just like the sounds coming from the radio had shapes, and the inanimate things around her, the seat, the door, and the dashboard, held life and movement within them. So many layers of reality that had been hidden for all these years.

When objects did focus, their edges were sharply defined, to an otherworldly degree of contrast. The driver had turned on the radio and Pat Boone crooned "April Love." Each note resonated with a clarity that separated it from every other throbbing note, as though the molecular structure of the music was on exhibition. Normally no fan of the syrupy vocalist, now the music lifted her and carried her away. As she gazed around, she could see into Rod's very soul, feel, as though it was her own, the emotional turmoil he held so carefully in check—how silly that was; didn't he realize she shared a oneness with him, shared a oneness with everything around her? Minute, invisible strings, iridescent with every color of the rainbow and humming with flawless resonance, connected it all. Now she understood what religion was about. Not those absurd stories about boats full of animals, stone tablets with ancient laws, or prophets hearing the word of God from angels in caves. What nonsense! Primitive, untutored beings, humans were embryonic strangers in a universe stretching beyond time and space, trying to express the quintessence of life in woefully insufficient languages.

She was euphoric—she understood everything intuitively; she was at peace, at one with the majesty of the universe. She was distraught, despite all this insight, this understanding, this connectedness, she was inadequate to bring this vision to the world; as inadequate as the first shaman who crawled out of a cave in a vain attempt to explain the glory of the heavens; as inadequate as any mystic, oracle, prophet, witch, or holy man with their pitiful parables and potions. Redneck fakirs who pretended to talk in tongues got it, but their exaggerated performances were only a pretense. The language to tell this story did not, could never, exist.

It was clear something was wrong with Jenny. She kept murmuring, seemingly to herself, and gazing around distractedly. When Rod attempted to speak with her, she stared at him with oddly dilated pupils. A soft smile played across her lips, and she reached up to stroke his face with gentle fingers, but otherwise didn't respond. After a few moments, her eyes closed again, and she sank down against his chest. The lump on her head had swollen to the size of a golf ball and turned the color of a glass of young Syrah.

She floated in and out of consciousness all the way to the fire station, but never became fully responsive. Whenever she seemed to be awake, she dwelt in a world of her own. Rod's first aid training was insufficient for anything this severe, he should take her to a hospital at once.

After the trucks pulled into the station, Rod barked orders and the men scurried around, moving the trucks into place and getting out of their emergency gear. He carried Jenny to the red Ford reserved for the station captain and deposited her into the passenger's side of the front seat, asking one of the men to watch her for a few minutes while he made a quick call. Entering the office, he picked up the phone and dialed the number for the central station, asking to be connected to Chief Crandell. After a brief pause and whispered conversation on the other end, the Chief finally answered the phone. The call didn't go the way Rod expected; he started out by giving the Chief a quick summary of what had transpired at the lab, receiving nothing but unhappy sounding grunts in response as he told the story, wrapping up by telling the chief he had an "injured employee" he was taking to the Brackenridge emergency room. He ended by asking when they could go back to the lab with the police and a warrant for an arson investigation. Lawrence Crandell responded abruptly, telling Rod to forget about it and leave it with him. He then asked Rod several uncomfortable questions about Jenny—but there was no way Rod wanted to admit she was his girlfriend. He told the Chief she was obviously in need of medical attention, and he refused to leave her with those hostile security guards who seemed uninterested in her welfare. Crandall fumed over what he termed Rod's "interference" and wanted to send an ambulance to pick her up, but Rod refused to wait, being as evasive as possible about her condition. The call ended badly, with Rod badgering the Chief about why no other stations sent trucks, and why no police were called, and the Chief obviously irate about the situation with Jenny. Rod ended the call by insisting he needed to take Jenny to the hospital, and hung up, figuring it could well be the end of his career.

The trip to the hospital took about ten minutes, the bright red car was equipped with the same engine as police cruisers, along with a cherry top and siren Rod kept going as he tore through traffic. When he arrived, the ER drive was packed with two ambulances, and several cars driven by young men in their early twenties, who panicked when he pulled in with lights flashing and siren blaring. The driver of one car had abandoned it to help a girl of about the same age into the hospital—she was fighting with him and shouting incoherently. An orderly came out in a futile attempt to direct the snarled traffic.

Eventually, a space opened up and Rod pulled behind the last ambulance. He left the car parked there, much to the dismay of the agitated orderly, and carried Jenny into a chaotic lobby where the check-in personnel were outmatched by young men and women crowded around their desk, joined by a maze of others wandering around in confusion, some shouting nonsense, others carrying on loud conversations with no one in particular. Orderlies attempted to navigate through this labyrinth with three stretchers bearing old Black ladies who snored away.

Towering over everyone else, and wearing a bright yellow jumpsuit, Rod stood out even among this bedlam. "I need a stretcher now," he bellowed. This got him plenty of attention, but little help; it had the effect of turning up the flame under an already boiling pot, further exciting the bewildered crowd, rousing one of the Black women, who began adding her two cents worth to the din, and causing a harried woman behind the check-in desk to shout into her phone. At last, a door opened behind the counter and a diminutive Black woman walked calmly around the desk, skillfully wended her way through the mob, and took Rod by the arm.

"Come with me sir," she ordered, as she led him through a door to the back.

This took them to a hallway crowded with gurneys, and lined with beds separated by curtains, as nurses, doctors, and orderlies rushed around. Rod noticed that most of the beds and gurneys were already occupied and these hallways were as chaotic as the lobby. The little woman continued down the hall with Rod in tow, still carrying Jenny, where she hailed a nurse: "Carrie—you got a bed for this one? Her head is in bad shape."

"This way," she led them around a corner to yet another hall, where she found a room with a single bed and one chair. It was austere, but it was private. "Let's put her in here for now. Rose, can you go find a gown and slippers? Once she's settled, I'll find a doc, I don't like the look of her head." Then she turned to Rod, and her eyes narrowed. "Don't I recognize you? Aren't you James Hatcher's father? I'm Carrie Cook, Anna Belle's mother."

"Rod Hatcher, sure I remember you—I really appreciate this Carrie—there was an explosion and fire at Alpen Labs this morning, and this poor woman was injured. She's a bit out of her head from the bump. I haven't been able to get any sense out of her."

He laid Jenny gently on the bed. This had the improbable effect of awakening her; as she looked around, she decided this was more fun than the roller coaster at last year's Texas State Fair. "Yipeeee," she shouted, "no hands." She lifted her arms into the air and began rocking energetically from side to side. Rod was about to stop her when her attention shifted to the hallway, where a young man on a gurney was losing his supper in spectacular fashion. She shrieked out her approval as she clapped her hands enthusiastically, "Whee! More, do it again!"

About this time, Rose reentered the room with a hospital gown, slippers, and extra blankets. "Having fun? Come on Carrie, let's get her into a gown. You can wait in the hall, sir."

The pair went into action with the well-oiled precision of a practiced team. Rose swung Jenny's feet around so she was sitting on the side of the bed, while Carrie corralled the flailing arms.

"Come on, Miss, let's settle down and get you out of these dirty clothes." She unbuttoned the blood-stained blouse while Rose worked on the clasp and zipper of the skirt, managing with some difficulty to pull it down. While Jenny was preoccupied with the obviously fascinating process of having her skirt removed, Carrie pulled off her blouse and bra.

Seeing her unencumbered breasts, Jenny looked up in surprise, and fixed Carrie with an impish grin. She sprang from the bed and began undulating, rotating her hips, thrusting her pelvis forward and back and singing, "Da Da Dum—Ta DA Da Dum—Da Da Dum, Da BUM Bum Bum, Da BOOM, Shakka BOOM, Shakka Boom Boom BOOM." Still singing, she cupped her hands under her breasts, shook them in Carrie's face, laughed riotously, then fell back on the bed, and was instantly asleep.

Carrie looked at Rose and giggled. "Oh my, the stories we'll tell our grandchildren." Choking with laughter, they continued getting Jenny into a proper hospital gown and covering her with a clean sheet and warm blanket. Only then did she open the door and invite a befuddled Rod back into the room. "Wait here with Rose, Mr. Hatcher, I'll go find a doctor."

It took fifteen minutes for Carrie to find an intern not swamped with work. He had been called in to help with the overflow, so Carrie grabbed him before someone else could. In the meantime, Rose had cleaned up Jenny's wound and the scratches on her knees and hands. Thankfully, Jenny continued to sleep, although she moaned and mumbled the whole time.

The young intern didn't look old enough to shave. This stint at Brackenridge was his first rotation following medical school at the Baylor College of Medicine in the burgeoning Texas Medical Center in Houston. He had only been on staff for a few weeks, and this was the first time either Carrie or Rose had met him. He introduced himself as Stephen Coleman, and Carrie struggled to defend him when Rod grumbled that Jenny needed a "real doctor." Rod was technically correct; interns do not earn their MD until they complete at least three years of residency. Never mind that Stephen had finished number one in his class, and a small local hospital like Brackenridge was lucky to have him, some new instinct had awakened in Rod when he saw Jenny injured, helpless, and obviously suffering psychological trauma.

Carrie came to his rescue. "Mr. Hatcher, I can assure you Mr. Coleman is qualified, or he wouldn't be here. If this lady requires a specialist after he makes his examination, one will be called. I understand your concern, but the best thing you can do is cooperate and answer our questions. For now, you need to go to the waiting room until we call." She had given the intern a quick summary of what was going on. He was looking at the head wound, by now deep aubergine and swollen to the size of a small egg, and checking the dilation of Jenny's eyes. He followed this with a standard check-up, paying particular attention to her reflexes, before asking a series of questions Carrie and Rose answered succinctly and professionally. Their attention to detail impressed Coleman, and he thought to himself that the Negro aide was better than most experienced nurses.

"Tell you what, let's get a blood draw to check for drugs. Mark her chart for a urine sample later on when she wakes up. She has quite a bump, but her symptoms indicate a drug reaction rather than a concussion, so it should be safe to let her sleep. I'm going to sedate her, she's sleeping now, but if she behaves anything like the other patients we've been seeing, she won't sleep it off without it. What's your opinion ladies? You've been observing a number of other patients acting oddly, I'll be interested to hear your thoughts in terms of similarities to those others."

Carrie and Rose stared at each other before answering. It was unheard of for a doctor, even the rankest intern, to ask for a nurse's opinion. They were far more accustomed to having orders barked at them and their opinions, if they dared express them, ignored or denigrated. Carrie spoke first, she agreed a bump on the head didn't explain Jenny's bizarre behavior. The other patients they'd been seeing did evidence some differences in their behaviors, but also some striking similarities—dilated pupils, apparent hallucinations, and perception somehow altered, so their responses to external stimuli were abnormal and inappropriate. Rose nodded, adding that patients who had been there a while often exhibited signs of paranoia and talked about someone or something being "out to get them." Some seemed to be reacting to something unseen and trembled from some vaguely perceived terror. Most of them returned to something approaching normal in twelve to twenty-four hours. The more bizarre their behavior had been, the longer it took to recover. Once the hallucinations ended and their pupils returned to normal, they were questioned about the causes and about the experience, but they were oddly uniform in their evasive answers, claiming a total lapse in memory in most cases. There were inconsistencies in their answers however, many mentioned being brought to the hospital by an ambulance or a friend. If they had come by ambulance, they often remembered who made the call. They all insisted they could not understand what brought on the episodes. The tests were coming back with strange chemicals in the blood—nothing the hospital lab had seen before—possibly a drug or a plant allergy. In most instances, the Brackenridge docs recommended referrals for psychiatric evaluation. Carrie spoke up, "As you are aware, psychiatric services are not available here at Brackenridge, so the doctors always make external referrals. We never thought much of it, but we're seeing a few of our first patients relapse. None of them ever received the referral. There are rumors about an investigation going on, all very hush-hush."

"Ladies, let me say how impressed I am with those insights. Either of you," and he looked pointedly at Rose, "can work with me any time. Now, if one of you will fetch the big guy who brought her in, you can help me interview him."

Carrie headed for the waiting room through a hall packed with patients and staff; police had been called in to manage the unruly crowd and attempt to maintain calm. She had seen the situation grow increasingly untenable as the number of patients exploded over the past few weeks, but this was ridiculous. The waiting room was overflowing—for everyone who had a chair, two more were standing, or squatting on the floor. Rod had long since given up his seat to an elderly woman and fidgeted as he leaned against a wall. Carrie gave him a wave from the door— "Rod, come with me now."

He inundated her with questions as they headed back down the hall. She assured him that Jenny was resting comfortably, at least for now, and the doctor wanted to speak with him.

"Hello sir, why don't you take a seat? I would prefer to talk to you in private, but I'm afraid we can't offer any more privacy than this." He indicated the only chair and gestured around the room. "I need any background information you may have. With your job, you've been through this before. We're desperate to figure out what's going on with these people, and so far, no one has admitted to knowing anything. Can you run me through what you know? I understand it started with some kind of accident at her place of work."

"Yeah, sure," and Rod started with the call he received and related everything that transpired. Stephen interrupted a few times to ask about some details—had Rod heard the explosion himself? What color was the smoke, did he smell anything out of the ordinary for a fire of this type, was anyone else acting abnormally? Was Jenny able to walk on her own without hanging on to something, and how far had she come before he saw her? Rod answered these questions perfunctorily, the smoke had yellow mixed in with the normal black and gray—maybe there was an odd smell—no, no one else seemed unduly affected, but Jenny was about to collapse. The young intern busily scribbled notes on the chart. How had she acted on the way to the hospital? How many times was she awake—asleep? Was she at all responsive? Oh, he had noted her dilated pupils—that was great, very observant. Did he notice anything else he hadn't mentioned? Oh, and one more thing, did he know who she was? The driver's license in her purse listed her as Jennifer Weber, and she had been wearing a company badge that said Jenny Weber, Lab Technician. They would call her residence as soon as they had all the information, but was there anything else he could add?

Rod turned red. "Oh, uh, yeah, I do know her, she lives with me. Oh, not with me, I mean, she rents a Granny Flat from me."

"Granny Flat? What's that?"

"That's the local lingo for a garage apartment. That's about it, her family lives in San Antonio. She works out there at Alpen Labs as some sort of Chemical Laboratory assistant, helping the chemists somehow. I can probably get back to you with her family contact information, I think it's back home with the rental agreement. But, uh, we're, ah, friends. I would like to know how she's going to be treated and what's wrong with her. She's never acted like this."

"Does she ever use drugs, prescription or otherwise?"

"No, she's healthy as a horse. Maybe an occasional aspirin for a headache, or, uh, you know... She drinks socially, a few beers, bourbon and coke, or a glass of wine, but never too much. I don't remember ever having seen her completely drunk. A little tipsy, maybe, but no more."

"Has she ever acted like she sees anything that isn't there? Or has she ever mentioned anyone being out to get her?"

"No, she's a perfectly normal, happy girl, very outgoing, can be a bit of a talker, but everyone likes her, she has a great sense of humor."

"Ummm, you say you're friends, so you know her well? Would you say close friends? You would be aware if this was normal behavior for her?"

"Yeah, she's, ah, we're, uh, okay, we've been dating a little, no, I guess a lot, so yeah, we're pretty close." He colored more deeply, glancing at Carrie from the corner of his eye. He was relieved to see no reaction. "I would know, I promise this is not normal for her—

she is NOT a druggie. Isn't it just the bump on the head? It looks bad."

"Did she say anything that seemed normal?"

"Maybe, when she first came out, she reached up and whispered in my ear— 'Get me the hell out of here—NOW. Don't ask questions, just get me and your guys the hell out of here.' Then she passed out, and like I said, she was in and out of consciousness the whole way back, but she didn't make sense again."

"A hematoma wouldn't cause this kind of bizarre behavior. More than likely, she ingested a poison or drug. I'll tell you what Mr. Hatcher, I'm going to schedule one of the other docs to examine her in the morning, then he'll make a referral for a psychiatric work-up, and I would appreciate it if you follow up with her to make sure she goes. Do you think she'll let you do that? We'll keep her here overnight for observation. Even if this is drug induced, that contusion bears watching, and I hardly think we can turn her loose on the world from what these ladies tell me."

"Yeah, I'll make sure she goes, I don't think she'll fight me. If she does, I'll involve her family, or maybe let you do that. Anyway, I think I owe you an apology, I was pretty tough on you when you first came in, but you're okay. I've been through a number of these interviews when fire victims get hurt, and none were as thorough as yours. Let's stay in touch. I know I'm not family, but I'm the closest thing she's got here in town. Carrie, you too, I think we live close together, and our kids are always running around with the same bunch of bra, er friends."

Carrie smiled, "Any father of a friend of Anna Belle's is a friend of mine."

Rod wanted to stay, but Carrie shooed him out and arranged for him to come back the next morning to take Jenny home. Stephen ordered a sedative, and an IV drip to keep Jenny well hydrated. Once the IV was in place, he ordered a blood draw and left orders for a urine test when she awoke. He also wrote an order for a doctor to examine her again in the morning, with a recommendation that she be referred for a psychiatric examination.

Before long, Carrie and Rose were kept busy as the bedlam continued to increase, but they both did their best to monitor Jenny throughout the night. Under the heavy sedation, she snored on in relative calm and gave them no trouble. The two women walked to the parking lot together when their shift was over. They used a side door to avoid being commandeered for extra hours. Normally they would have welcomed the overtime, but exhausted after the chaotic night, they just wanted to go home. Now fast friends, they chatted about the way the hospital was turning into a looney bin. As they approached their cars, Rose frowned uncertainly. "Carrie, do you remember that girl who had been here before? When you asked her about her psychiatric evaluation, she didn't have a clue what you were talking about. And we're having a few others come back from when this mess first started. What do you suppose is going on?"

Carrie yawned, "Humm, it's certainly worth looking into, but that's a battle for another day, it's me to bed before I drop."

CHAPTER 17
THE ILLUSION OF REALITY

"Reality is merely an illusion, albeit a very persistent one."
–Albert Einstein

The following morning Rod was at the hospital emergency room by nine a.m. It was still busy, but quieter than the previous night. The officious lady behind the check-in desk refused to allow Rod to go back, since he was not family. Finally, he pulled out his fire department ID and told her he was making an "official investigation." This did the trick, and with her dour expression unchanged, she called an orderly to take him back to Jenny's room. When he approached the room, a nurse herded him off to a nearby waiting room. After a few minutes, a nurse came and escorted him to Jenny's room, where the doctor, a jovial, stocky man with a British accent, was waiting to speak with him.

"Hello Mate, it seems our friend here has had quite the adventure. The tests aren't showing much out of the ordinary, couple of odd things showed up in her blood last night, but there's bugger all in her pee this morning. That said, I don't think we can attribute her rather odd behavior to a mere bump on the noggin. I understand you're the closest thing she has to family in the area?"

"Hellooo, I'm right here, you can just ask me, you know," called Jenny, waving her hand.

"Yes, my dear, my apologies, but we're still not sure you're, shall we say, all together? Do you mind if this gentleman looks after you for the next day or two? I'm referring you to the State hospital over on Guadalupe, they have the best psychiatric staff in town, and they can do a much better evaluation than we can. I'm afraid we're not staffed for that sort of thing."

"Are you saying I'm nuts? That place is a mental hospital. They told me I was acting crazy yesterday, although I don't remember it, but I was not myself. Something made me behave that way, I am NOT crazy!"

"No, my dear, I'm convinced there is something causing this, you aren't the only one with these symptoms, although your case is unique in some ways. The ER's been looking like a bloody scrum lately, with all these young students, and a few older folks, acting pissed as newts; but none of 'em test for alcohol. We are seeing many of them relapse, and I want to make sure you're properly looked after—the State hospital should contact you within a few days. In the meantime, I'm going to send you some pills to help you get some kip, but only take them at night, and only if you really need them. No work for the rest of the week, I can write you a scrip if you need it, and take it easy. Bed rest is unnecessary; so long as you're not under any strain you should be right as rain. Can I count on you to follow these instructions? No more, ah, dancing or gallivanting around? No alcohol and no sleeping during the day, even if you're feeling knackered."

Jenny struggled a bit with the odd language, figuring out some terms from the context. "OK, got it—I think. The no work part is much appreciated, the no naps, not so much. I am a little woozy from whatever they gave me last night. But Rod will take great care of me," and she batted her eyes in his direction.

"Then I will leave you in his competent care. I understand you're a fireman mate, so you should know the sort of things to look out for. If she seems to relapse or is feeling dickey, and she hasn't received the referral, bring her back in here forthwith."

"Thanks Dr. Smithwick. I'll make her toe the line."

James had been watching for them to return home since his father left early that morning. All Rod had told him was that Jenny had been injured in a fire, he was going to pick her up at the hospital, and James should wait for them. Rod called for James to open the door as he carried her in, then deposited her on the couch, which he'd equipped with two pillows and a blanket before he left. "Jenny's going to stay with us for a few days, she can take my room and I'll sleep out here at night, but she can have the couch during the day. She's going to need her rest, so you'll need to keep it down. You can still go play with your friends; I'm taking a couple of days off, so I can take care of her."

"Is she, uh, are you okay, Miss Weber?"

"What is it going to take to get you to call me Jenny? I'm going to be fine; I just got a little bump on the bean. I'll be back to giving you a hard time before you know it. And don't worry about 'holding it down,' you're way too quiet for a boy your age. This will give us all some time to hang out together, I'm kinda looking forward to it. Tell you what, fetch me a paper and pencil so I can make a list of what I need from my place. Maybe you can go get it for me."

A few minutes later she handed him a short list. His eyes bulged—bras, panties, something called tampons, he didn't even know what half this stuff was. "Uh, Dad, can you go?"

"What's wrong with your legs? I need to talk to Jenny; you go on now."

"But Daaaad."

Suddenly Jenny giggled, "Oh Rod, look, he's embarrassed. I'm sorry Honey, I shouldn't have asked you—Rod, off with you to the uncharted territory of women's underwear and incidentals. Take a bag so you big bad men won't have to look at any of it."

Now even more embarrassed, James asked if he could go to his room and read.

Jenny reached over and ruffled his hair, "You go ahead Handsome, I'll be fine. I need a private talk with your dad, anyway."

James made his escape before Rod could change his mind, but as he closed the door to his room, he was careful to leave it open a crack.

When Rod returned, Jenny scootched over to make room on the couch next to her, "Time for a talk, I have to explain some things, and you need to help me figure out some stuff."

James was sitting next to the door with his ears cocked as he listened to Jenny relate the entire story to Rod, beginning with when she observed the busses of students pulling up behind the lab. She told him everything—the clandestine meetings with Hal and Jerry at The Frisco, the attempt to find the back entrance, how they'd been threatened and pursued, the rumors flying around the lab, her conversations with Barb, and the warning she received from Arndt.

"Hey, Arndt is the asshole who wouldn't let us into the building." Then Rod explained what had transpired before she made it out of the lab, about how the armed guards kept them from doing their job, how the military copters and planes dumped water and chemicals to extinguish the fire, and how vague and unsatisfying the Fire Chief's reaction had been. Then Jenny took over again. She described the explosion, the hallway with the people running out the back, the strange yellow color to the smoke that filled the room, and the thing she picked up.

"Get my purse Rod, I want to show you something."

James sat quietly, taking it in, scarcely breathing, but his mind was racing.

When Rod handed her purse to her, Jenny fumbled through it and pulled out the thing she had picked up. It was a piece of pipe, blackened and charred, one end ruptured, with some residue on it.

"Let me see that." Rod was a trained arson investigator; it was his specialty and the reason he was Assistant Captain instead of just a hose and ladder jockey. He scratched at the residue and sniffed at the pipe, paying particular attention to the end split open like a peeled banana. "This might be from a pipe bomb, but from the way you described the damage, and the amount of smoke I saw, I don't see how it could have been the only source of the fire. We need to have it analyzed, I'll take it in to the station tomorrow and get Captain Schwartzwald to send it downtown to the police bomb squad."

At last, Rod told her about the mayhem he witnessed at the hospital. She said she didn't remember much, certainly not having done some kind of strip tease! She would NEVER do anything like that. Welllll, maybe just for him, but that was IT.

Now James' mouth gaped open and the little soldier was firmly back at attention, as Jenny giggled and rewarded Rod with a playful kiss on the ear. She didn't tell him what she had experienced on the ride back in the fire truck—some nagging something, some primitive instinct for self-preservation, was whispering—*No, this is my secret, can't tell anyone, not anyone. Never know what someone will do, tell no one about this.*

They talked for a while, trying to decide what to do next. Rod would take the length of pipe to his captain; he no longer trusted the Chief. At some point he would need to meet Hal and Jerry, and, then what? Should they contact Carrie Cook? They would take things a step at a time.

The Sound of Beans Spilling

"Sit down for a minute, Anna Belle." Carrie patted the seat next to her on the old couch. "Honey, Rose has been telling me what Georgie said the other day. He heard the little ones, Betty and Levi, talking about another trip you made to the woods, at night. It was a pretty crazy story—frankly. I'm not sure what to believe, but if you and your friends went down there at night, and if something happened, you need to tell me about it—now, Young Lady."

Anna hesitated—*She found out. They always find out. But it's just Mom, Mom should be okay, she needs to know. Why does it feel so wrong, like something bad will happen? Best to play it safe.* "Yeah, sure, it was like this," and she launched into the story. How she refused to believe Stevie—he was always exaggerating and letting his imagination run away with him. So, they went there in the evening just as a gag to show him up. And it <u>was</u> kind of scary being there at night. Some of them thought they saw or heard stuff, but they got back by nine or so, not a big deal, really. She didn't know what Georgie thought he heard, maybe he didn't understand.

At this point a knock interrupted her, it was James, who had come over to tell Anna what he overheard. "Uh, hi Mrs. Cook, is Anna home?"

"Come in James, we're talking, and I think you might be interested in this." She let him in and asked him to sit next to Anna. "James, you remember the little Negro boy you found hiding in the woods Saturday? I work with his mother, and she was telling me what he's been saying about your nighttime trip to the woods. We need to discuss that, and I want to hear your version."

Anna was trying frantically to project her thoughts to James— *Don't tell her ANYTHING, please hear me, please.*

Just as it's said there are no atheists in foxholes, everyone believes in telepathy when they're desperate. However, reality has an exasperating way of intruding on such fantasies. James made the unfortunate assumption that Anna had told her mother everything and spilled his guts. The entire story came out, what they had seen, their terror, the fugue states—everything except the dreams, which they had agreed to keep secret (those were just too personal, they didn't even tell one another.)

"I don't know whether to be angry, incredulous, frightened or concerned—or all of them. Anna Belle, why didn't you tell me this? You know you can be honest with me, I thought you always told me everything."

Anna's lips trembled as she fought back tears. "I'm sorry Mom, I don't understand why I kept everything from you, I don't understand what it was—something about what happened made me afraid to tell any grownups. It was weird."

"Yeah, me too. I haven't told any other grownups, only you. There's more too."

"What more is there, James? You can tell me, nobody's going to be in trouble, you kids know, or you should, that I'm only worried about your safety."

"OK, Mrs. Cook," and he launched into a recitation of the conversation between Rod and Jenny, ending by saying it sounded like what happened to Jenny was something like what happened to them.

"Well, James, it so happens I was the nurse who took care of Jenny. I admit to thinking the same thing." She closed her eyes and sighed. "I'm afraid I'm going to have to involve the other parents, even if it gets some of your friends in trouble. I'll see if I can make them understand, but something's going on. Between the story you just told, what happened to Jenny Weber and all the patients with similar symptoms we've been seeing at the ER, well, we need to figure it out and make sure you kids receive the proper care."

"Mom, just, just, can we not tell Betty's mother yet? She'll go nuts. You know she will—you know what she's like."

"Hmmm, we'll see. She will have to be informed at some point, but perhaps I can talk to the other parents first. Let me tell them. Don't look so worried, James, I'll do everything I can to keep you from getting in too much trouble."

~ ~ ~

"I'd better check in with the lab, Rod. We have a phone tree for emergency situations like this. A friend of mine works in the administration area, I think I'll give her a ring. Do you have a phone directory?"

Rod retrieved the thick Austin phone book and handed it to Jenny. She thumbed through the J's until she found Bertram

Johnson, Barb's husband. It was easy for her to remember because Barb often joked about how they only married because the names fit so well—Barb 'n' Bert. Barbara Johnson was one of those types Jenny found irritating, a woman who defined her identity not as an individual, but as part of a couple. She was always saying things like, "It's off to the lake for Barb 'n' Bert this weekend." It made Jenny want to gag. Barb was okay otherwise, but at times Jenny wanted to take her and shake her.

"Barb, Jenny here. Hi, no, no. I'm not at home, so they can't reach me. I injured my head when the lab blew up, and spent the night at the hospital. No, I'm fine, just got a nasty bump that messed me up. Thing is, the explosion didn't come from inside the Chem Lab, it came from some room behind it. ... Yeah, I didn't either. The explosion blew in the wall, and I was standing right there. It knocked me down onto the table where I was working—what—why not? Sure, well, I'm supposed to take it easy this week and I'm staying with, ah, a friend. Oh, it is? Did they tell you when we'll open again? Two weeks—wow, there must have been considerable damage. It sure looked like it to me—okay, okay. Look, do you know where The Frisco is, on Old Laredo Trail? Let's meet there for breakfast tomorrow morning at 10."

"You are NOT leaving this house—You're supposed to be on total rest!"

"Hang on a minute, Barb. Shush Rod. You can drive me and I'll be fine. An order of Eggs Decorated may be exactly what I need—Sorry Barb, yeah, fine, 10 a.m. it is, and Rod will be with me, he's taking care of me. No, he won't tell anyone, cripes Barb. Okay, okay, we can talk tomorrow, bye." As Barb hung up, Jenny turned to Rod, "Wow, is she ever paranoid! She didn't want me to talk over the phone and refused to say much to me—like she thought someone tapped her phone. I worry about that woman."

CHAPTER 18
FURTHER CONVERGENCE

Three roads converged in a yellow wood
And I, I said, "What the hell? This isn't how it goes."

The next morning James was sleeping in again. When Rod checked on him, it was obvious from the tangled bedclothes he had been tossing and turning. Rod was about to wake him up when Jenny took his arm, "He's a growing boy, Rod. Let him sleep, for goodness' sake."

"He sleeps in all the damn time lately. I never got to sleep in when I was his age, I had a job every summer."

"Oh Rod, I know this is none of my business, but sometimes you can be so hard on him. Eleven is too young to work. Get him to mow the grass once in a while, do dishes, make his bed, that kind of stuff. He has the rest of his life to work. Besides, we need to be going, I should have told Barb we'd meet at nine, I'm starving."

"You're lucky you're so damn cute. Okay, let's go."

Jenny peeked in at James. The covers were wadded up around his feet, and that little soldier was clearly at attention under his thin summer pajamas. *Hmmm, he's starting to get morning wood. I wonder if Rod even notices. He needs to have the birds and bees talk with James—that man can be so dense!*

Moments later, they slid into Jenny's favorite booth at the Frisco. Barb hadn't arrived yet, but Millie was already busying herself bringing menus and coffee without even being asked. "HI Jenny girl. Is this the handsome fireman you been telling me about? He is a big one ain't he?"

"Rod, this is Millie, my favorite waitress and surrogate mother. She watches out for me, everything but my waistline."

"Hi Sugar, nice to meet you. And your waistline is just fine, Honey. Now what I can bring y'all?"

"Coffee is fine for now, Millie; we're waiting on a friend of mine. Oh, I guess it wouldn't hurt if you brought two large OJs. Is it freshly squeezed?"

"Always, we wouldn't serve anything but. Say, what happened to your head? You have a nasty-looking bump."

"You know Alpen Labs where I work? Did you hear about the explosion there Monday? It knocked me down and gave me this little beauty; I spent the night at Brackenridge."

"Oh, my goodness! No, I didn't hear that. Let me fetch the juice and then I want you to tell me all about it."

As Millie bustled off, Jenny wondered why she had not heard about the Alpen Lab fire. *That woman must be oblivious, this story has been all over the local news, and you'd think she would have overheard someone discussing it.* Jenny's reveries were interrupted when she spotted Barb coming in the door. She smiled and waved Barb over to the table.

When Millie returned, she had another coffee, three frosty glasses of freshly squeezed orange juice, and an extra menu.

"Millie, this is my friend, Barb Johnson."

"Oh, hello Barb, I think I seen you in here before. I took the liberty of bringing you juice and coffee, I hope that's all right."

"It's perfect Millie. Yes, I remember you too, you waited on Bert and me once or twice. This is Barb 'n' Bert's favorite restaurant. The juice and coffee are much appreciated. Do y'all know what you want? I don't even need to look at the menu."

Barb ordered the Country Breakfast with two eggs over easy, bacon and two biscuits. True to form, Jenny ordered Eggs Decorated and added a side of crisp bacon.

Rod perused the menu for a few minutes, "Bring me the Beef Enchiladas and a side of hash browns, extra crispy."

"Rod, enchiladas for breakfast?"

"They have the best enchiladas in the world here, Jen. I always order them, morning, noon or night. I added the hash browns to make it a breakfast dish. I'll pass on my usual beer though, and stick to the coffee and juice."

Millie repeated the orders and hustled off, "Holler if y'all need anything else. I still want to hear about the bump on your head."

As Millie headed back for the counter, the conversation turned solemn. Jenny started by telling Barb everything—the wall being blown in, the hidden corridor behind the chemical lab, what she could remember of the trip home, and her night at the hospital. Millie came back, listened, and clucked her tongue as she busied herself around the coffee pots.

About the time Jenny finished her story, Millie showed up with a fully loaded tray she sat down on a folding stand. The plates bubbled with sizzling grease. "Hot plate," she warned as she served each one, holding them with a dishtowel to keep from burning her hands. The oversized plates were filled to the edges. The buttery toast and biscuits, and Rod's order of hash browns had their own plates, so by the time she was done, the table was overflowing with delicious food. Jenny's Eggs Decorated swam in cheese and spicy pinto beans, with four strips of crisp bacon on the side. The more pedestrian Country Breakfast contained two fresh eggs, two hot biscuits, enough hash browns for three people, and four strips of bacon. But the crowning glory was Rod's order of enchiladas, oversized corn tortillas rolled and stuffed full of spiced ground beef, the identical "corn-fed" beef The Frisco served as hamburgers and steaks. Pictures of plump, happy cattle hung in various places around the restaurant as testament to the advantages of allowing livestock to gorge on fattening corn. The enchiladas were drowning in molten chili con carne made from that same corn-fed beef—now laced with jalapeño peppers and chili powder—topped with layers of gooey melted cheese, speckled with onions, and floated in a glorious lake of simmering yellow grease. A hefty dollop of spiced pintos shared the plate, leaving no room for the hash browns, so Rod had two lavish plates deposited in front of him, loaded with enough carbohydrates to clog the most stubborn of arteries, and enough spice to open them right back up again.

Conversation died down as they dug in, with little grunts of satisfaction, and assurances to a beaming Millie that it was all to die for, as she fussed with coffee refills and offers to bring more food if the rapidly disappearing piles on their plates were somehow insufficient.

When Rod announced they had done all the damage they could, Millie began clearing the plates, and Jenny and Barb excused themselves to go to the restroom; an act, in Rod's limited experience, that was impossible for ladies to undertake one at a time.

When they returned, Jenny asked Rod to tell Barb the story from his perspective. He was reluctant to talk about his confrontation with Arndt, but Jenny told him Barb was okay, and he agreed to tell the story, including his frustration with the Fire Chief, and his impressions of what was going on at Brackenridge.

Barb listened spellbound, asking them both questions when something was unclear or seemed of consequence. She was particularly interested in the corridor behind the chemical lab. Like Jenny, she was unaware of the extension to the building. How in the world had they kept it secret, and what was it for? So Arndt was reluctant to let Jenny leave with Rod? She did not like that man.

She shook her head when Rod was finished, trying to make sense of all the threads. "Something is going on for sure. Upstairs has been crazy for the past few weeks; then last week, I think it was Wednesday or Thursday, I thought they'd gone nuts with all the secret meetings and phone calls. I saw some of those guys sweating bullets. Jen, you know what I told you before, about Project Mind Warp being some sort of government deal? That fits right in with those Air Force planes and helicopters, doesn't it? And all the darn secrecy. Remember I told you The Farm is involved? I've been doing as much snooping as I can without getting caught. The Farm is exactly the right name because they have actual farms somewhere, growing something related to project Mind Warp. They are somehow mixed up with the Labbies—our name for people who work in the Chemical Lab, Rod. Jen is a Labbie. They're somehow using something they're growing in chemical experiments. Know anything about THAT, Jen?"

"Hmmm. There are jars of some new chemicals. The glass is dark black so you can't see the ingredients, and they're not marked in chemical symbols like the rest, it looks more like some kind of code, and they're too light to be holding liquids, so they must be powdered. They take those trays to one of the smaller labs; they aren't used in the main lab where I work."

"You can't tell what they contain? How can you do your job?"

"Barb, a trained monkey could do my job. The way they have it organized you can do it by rote. Most of the girls don't even have a background in chemistry. Two or three more semesters and I could have a degree, but I'm very much the exception. I pay attention to the chemical labels. Those in black glass jars frustrate me, but most of the girls are clueless. They just know tube A should fit into slot B. But heaven forbid if they make a mistake, whether or not it was their fault. I pay close attention to the labels, on four or five instances I caught setup errors. They hate it when I call them out on it. I'm damned if I do but double damned if I don't."

"I was thinking Jen, the secret corridor could explain so much. The bigshots disappear for hours at a time. None of the girls have a clue where they go. At the end of the second floor there's a small conference room. It has one of those code-key locks for security. I peeked in once when the board members were going in; the place is awfully barren for a conference room. I saw what looked like a door at the back—a stairwell to a corridor below, if there is one."

"I saw a corridor back there. I was woozy when the wall went down, but I got a look down the hall. It wasn't as long as the Labbie wing. It looked almost like a separate building, maybe half as long, with doors on both sides, and one out the back. That must be where those people on the busses go. Damn—if I'd only had binoculars when we made that trip to look for the back entrance. I was too far away to see clearly, plus I was at the wrong angle. Since the EE and Farm wings are a lot longer, they must hide it unless you're directly behind the building. We need to figure out what's back there."

"Hmmm," Rod mused, "one of the guys at the station is a pilot—Stan Landry—he flew in Korea and he has his own plane. He was pissed off at the treatment we got the other day. How does a flyover sound? I'd better be careful though, I should talk with the captain first."

Before they left, Rod gave Barb his number so she could call Jenny if necessary. Millie hummed around in the background, totaling up their bill, offering more coffee, pie, anything, but they demurred.

After they left, Millie fussed around the booth, mopping up spills and wiping it clean. This was a good thing, because the man from the black Buick sat there.

CHAPTER 19
THE IMPROBABLE INTERSECTION
OF PARALLEL PATHS

In this unbelievable universe in which we live,
there are no absolutes. Even parallel lines,
reaching into infinity, meet somewhere yonder.
–Pearl S. Buck

When they got back home, James had left a note saying, "I'm going over to the Lindquist place to help Stevie build model airplanes. I'll be back before supper."

An empty cereal bowl sat in the sink and Frosted Flakes were scattered across the table. Rod muttered disgustedly, but Jenny smiled, "Boys will be boys. Look on the bright side, we're well-fed, and we have the afternoon to ourselves."

"Are you sure you're up to, uh, it?"

"Well, you heard the doctor, I'm not supposed to sleep during the day, so I'll need SOMETHING to keep me awake." She reached up and wrapped him in an embrace. With the fourteen-inch difference in their heights, he had to bend over, even though she was standing on tiptoe. Just as things started to get interesting, the phone rang.

"Shit! Sorry, but what a time for a phone call. Hold that thought."

"Hello, Rod Hatcher here. Oh, hi Carrie. Yeah, she's doing great, thanks for checking up. Do you want to talk to her? ... Oh, sure, I can talk for a few minutes, go ahead... What? They went to the woods? What woods? Okay, sorry, go ahead." As Carrie spilled out a summarized version of what she had learned from James and Anna, Rod sputtered in anger. What was wrong with those kids, they had no business in the woods at night, especially with the younger children. Carrie tried to calm him, to convince him that the important thing was to ensure their health and safety, and figure out what was going on. They needed to meet and talk, what the children described was chillingly similar to what she was seeing in the emergency room and what Jenny experienced. Finally, he settled down and saw the logic in what she was saying. Could they meet at his place? Jenny needed to take it easy, and he already let her badger him into taking her out one time. Speaking of that, he needed to tell her about what they learned about Jenny's accident. Why didn't he let Jenny explain?

"Hi Carrie, Jenny here. What's going on? Yes, I'm doing pretty well so far—managing not to fall asleep during the day. The lump aches a little, but nothing I can't handle. Thank you again for taking such excellent care of me. And the other lady, what was her name—Rose? Rod said she was super, please thank her for me. But what did you say to set Rod off?"

Carrie summarized what she knew, then asked Jenny if she had any ongoing symptoms. "Yes, I had some funny dreams, but I figured they were from the bump on the head. The doctor mentioned it, how other patients have the same symptoms. He said he would schedule an appointment for me with a shrink. No, I haven't heard a word. Sure, I'll tell you the minute I hear, why? Oh, that is strange. Maybe they're just backed up. Okay, sure, we'll be happy to host a meeting." Before they rang off, Carrie cautioned Jenny to keep Rod calm. He would be angry with James, but she was concerned about the children and it might be bad to stress

James too much. Jenny assured her she could handle Rod, thanked her, and said goodbye.

"Let's talk," she said. "Carrie told me what James and his friends got up to, but said you can give me more details."

They talked for a long time, trying to make sense of what they knew. How could a group of kids walking in the woods have anything to do with any of it—the lab, the fire, what had happened to Jenny, UT students getting high, or whatever it was, the young people who had been coming and going from the back of the lab, or the things Barb had told them? There were so many loose strings, but when you tugged on one, another started to wiggle.

They had agreed to a meeting at Rod's house Friday evening. Carrie had Friday and Saturday off this week, so she would be available. Jenny was to call Hal, Jerry, and the Stieglitz's. They agreed to leave Betty's parents out of it for now, but would need to tell them eventually, something no one was looking forward to. They would invite Barb as well. In the meantime, Rod was going to talk with the station captain. He had a bad feeling about the Chief, but he and Captain Schwartzwald got along well, and Rod felt he could trust him. They needed to discuss the fire at Alpen Labs, it was long overdue. If Jenny felt okay the next day, he would talk with Brad Schwartzwald. They would put off any confrontation with James until after the Friday meeting.

When Rod called Schwartzwald the next morning, he was eager to talk. Once breakfast was over, Jenny settled down with Agatha Christie's latest book, *Ordeal by Innocence,* and he set off for the station.

When Rod pulled up in front of Fire Station 16, he parked along the curb so as not to block the broad driveway that led to the oversized doors. It looked as much like a home as a fire station, with its red brick façade, low gabled roof, oak-shaded lawn, and front-facing windows. The doors were open to allow a breeze on the sweltering day, and the industrial fans rattled away. Rod headed to the Schwartzwald's office, where a window air conditioner provided the only refrigerated cooling in the building. The station was only a year old in 1958. It was built to service the growing North Austin suburbs, and boasted some of the better equipment in the city. Although the station was a few miles east of The Trail, its proximity to Justin Lane made it a straight shot down to The Trail, and even closer to North Lamar. Later on more stations were built, but in 1958 it was well situated to serve the north side of town.

As he walked back to Schwartzwald's office, Rod stopped to say hello to Stan Landry, "Hey, Stan, I have to talk to the captain, but I'd like a word when I'm done."

"Sure, Rod, I ain't going anywhere."

As he entered the office, Captain Schwartzwald, a heavyset man with graying hair, smiled and waved him into a chair, "Come on in, Rod. Thanks for coming in on your day off."

"No problem, Brad, I wanted to talk to you anyway after the lab incident."

"Same here. How's your little girlfriend, what's her name? Jenny? She was injured in the fire?"

"She seems okay now, but what happened to her is a long story, along with everything else."

"Yeah, sure, I got nuthin' but time, start from the beginning."

Rod related the entire sequence of events. He was experienced with making incident reports, so his story was concise, and as complete as he could make it. He included everything Jenny had said about her experience, along with what he and the ER personnel had witnessed, but he focused on their rude treatment at the lab. As he talked, Schwartzwald made a few notes. Rod ended by handing Brad the piece of pipe to examine.

"Here's the piece of pipe Jenny picked up. It looks to me like it could be from a pipe bomb, but I can't understand how it would do so much damage—and remain this intact. That place has all kinds of chemicals though, some may be volatile and were set them off in a chain reaction. What do you think?"

Schwartzwald examined the piece of pipe before speaking. He rubbed a bit of the residue between his fingers, sniffed at it, and sprinkled a little on a white sheet of paper to see it better.

"Yeah, this is a kind of crude accelerant, possibly gunpowder, match heads, maybe some TNT. Those are prone to accidental ignition by friction, but I don't need to tell you—you're the expert. This wouldn't have been enough to do the damage she described. It must have been around other chemicals and set them off. The yellow color in the smoke seems odd. Tell you what, I'll get this analyzed. It may reveal nothing we haven't already guessed, but we'll see. I talked to Crandell, but he's pushing back hard. I can't believe he can sit there and tell me to forget that incident after the way those assholes treated you. I'm not letting this drop, but for now, I think you should. Let me handle it. I can't understand why Crandell won't authorize an arson investigation. If he waits much longer, it will be too late. Leave it with me, I wouldn't want you to get in trouble over this."

This was not what Rod wanted to hear. "Sure, Brad. Just tell me what you find out about the pipe, and if you can get us in there for an arson investigation, I'm your man."

"I know, Rod, you're the best arson investigator in town. Let me work on it."

On his way out, Rod told Stan about his idea for a flyover of the Lab. Stan's eyes lit up and he agreed. "Hell yes, I'm in. Anything to find out what those bastards are up to out there. Just tell me when and I'll make the arrangements."

Rod cautioned him not to tell anyone else, and then, as a second thought, invited him to the Friday meeting.

Chapter 20
The Plan

"The best-laid schemes o' mice an' men
Gang aft agley,"
–Robert Burns — "To a Mouse, on Turning Her Up in Her Nest
With the Plough, November, 1785"

~ ~ ~

Anna's Journal
Log entry Friday, June 20, 1958
    Everybody came over today. We had so much to talk about. We've all turned into spies now, listening to our parents when they talk about everything. They have this big meeting tonight at James' house to figure out what to do next. Our parents know just about everything now, except for Betty's. No one wants to be the one to tell her crazy mother. I feel sorry for Betty, she can be so babyish and acts so spoiled, but her parents are crazy religious and have all kinds of strange ideas. No telling what they'll do to Betty when they find out this stuff. But anyway, here's what we know.

From James—His dad thinks there is something going on out at Alpen Labs (where Stevie's dad works.) They had a big fire and James' dad's fire station had to go and they wouldn't even let them put the fire out! And his "renter" (his dad's GIRLFRIEND named Jenny Weber) got hurt (she works there) and went to the hospital. She was acting weird and seeing things that weren't there (like what they think is happening to us) and Mom and Mrs. Woods took care of her. Miss Weber has been staying with James and his dad since she got hurt (which I bet James just loves cuz she is so pretty) but not in the same bedroom with his dad! She knows Stevie's dad and she's been meeting him and another guy who works at Alpen Labs at The Frisco (so good, but real expensive, it costs 35 cents just for a hamburger!!) to talk about it. They were seeing a busload of UT students come into the lab through a secret (?) entrance and maybe they are the same as the students who were in the hospital when she was. They went out and tried to find the secret entrance and a guy with a gun ran them off before they could find it!

From Stevie—his dad doesn't talk about it much. It was his mom who talked to him about going to the woods at night and what he saw. She was all worried so he didn't really get in much trouble, but she's real worried about him. Mark got in big-time trouble for taking us to the woods last Saturday.

From my Mom: She thinks we were seeing things, what she calls hallucinations (had to look it up), seeing and hearing stuff that isn't really there. Sometimes drugs can do that, like in Alice in Wonderland when she eats the mushrooms. Mom says some mushrooms have a drug like that. But we didn't eat any mushrooms. (I never knew Alice in Wonderland was about drugs!!) Anyway they have had all these people coming into the hospital having hallucinations. Mostly they are UT students, but also some Negroes and Mexicans. Maybe the ones who have been going into the secret entrance at Alpen Labs.

So tonight they're having a big meeting at James' house to talk about all this. James is gonna try to snoop.

Also we are all still having nightmares and losing time like in a trance during the day. I think about this a lot but can't tell my dreams to anyone – we agreed not to tell any grownups about our dreams. I just wish they would stop.

Anna out—end log entry June 20, 1958

~ ~ ~

By 7:30 Friday evening, cars crowded the Hatcher vicinity. The modest brown house was situated on an oversized corner lot at Bentwood and Rift Drive. Rod worked hard to keep the house in tip-top repair. His skills in this area were considerably better than his housekeeping efforts, but Jenny pitched in with the inside duties, so when the guests arrived, it was presentable. The coffee table in the living room held a bowl brimming with hot Ro-Tel cheese dip, flanked by bowls overflowing with Fritos. A pot of coffee was brewing in the kitchen and the fridge held beer and soft drinks. Outside it started raining, with a few large drops splashing onto the pavement. An ominous line of blue-black cumulonimbus clouds hung over the northwest horizon as a cold front converged with the humid gulf flow typical of June weather in Austin. The massive squall line stretched across the entire state, but was especially intense in Austin. Its ragged leading edge roiled like waves crashing on a beach, sending rain, hail, and straight-line winds approaching tornado velocity in its wake. The temperature had reached 101° that day, making conditions ripe for this type of spectacular thunder boomer Austin so often experienced the early summer.

Jenny made the introductions. Rod filled drink orders and encouraged the guests to dig in to the dip before they settled in to talk.

Carrie started by addressing the children's adventures as their parents squirmed around in their chairs, eager to learn the details. Carol Lindquist was in a near state of panic, but Carrie and Hal managed, with some difficulty, to convince her not to interrupt continuously. The other guests listened raptly, leaning in with particular interest when she described what their own children had experienced. As she concluded by describing the second trip and how Anna had defended Georgie Woods, it was clear Hal and Carol struggled with how to react, but Jenny spoke up without hesitation, "Good for her! Carrie, you must be very proud."

Abe chuckled, "I always knew that one was a firecracker. Yes, I agree with Jenny, you should be proud, Carrie—few children are so lacking in prejudice. She may encounter trouble at school because of that, but I suspect she'll be just fine."

Rod furrowed his eyebrows, "I think I knew his father. He was a fireman they called 'Big George,' and he was—he even had a couple inches on me. I have to say, that man was the equal of any three white firefighters I ever met. He died running INTO a burning home to save a small child; he got the little girl out, but died of asphyxiation as a result. Yeah, Carrie, Anna Belle did a great thing if Georgie has even a fraction of his father's courage and integrity. Negroes are the brunt of some nasty racial jokes down at the fire station, but no one ever jokes about Big George Woods."

"Thank you, yes, I am very proud—except for those times when I'd like to wring her little neck. Jenny, take over and tell your part of the story."

"Of course, but first does anyone need a refill on their coffee? Another beer Jerry, Hal, Stan? Is this dip getting cold? Rod or I can heat it up again."

"Go ahead, Jen, I'll take care of the refills," Rod offered, recognizing the gentle prod into action.

Outside, a rumble of thunder announced the arrival of the squall, as the enormous supercell dipped south into Central Texas. The characteristic anvil shape flared with lighting, and its top erupted in an angry blossom of churning clouds. Some ten thousand feet over Austin's northern limits, a drop of rain hurtled skyward, flung by a torrent of wind that formed as the hot humid airflow from the Gulf of Mexico collided with the massive front. The raindrop flew upward, then froze and fell. This cycle repeated several times, with each recurrence adding a layer of ice, until it became too heavy to be lifted, and plummeted to earth as a hailstone. Pounding rain mixed with this pea-sized hail rattled the windows like buckshot and pummeled the roof. The wind raged with savage gusts, and the house trembled before its wrath. The clashes of thunder grew louder and more frequent, accentuated by intense flashes of lightning, whose fiery tongues licked the ground, coming ever closer.

Austin is prone to severe flooding, and as the storm swept across town, Shoal Creek filled with terrifying swiftness, spilling out of its banks in its rush toward the Colorado River. As it passed through Pease Park and streamed around the meandering bend between twelfth and fifteenth streets, the water swelled out over Lamar Avenue, flooded the iconic German bar called The Tavern, a favorite watering hole of UT students, and left a foot of muddy water on the playing field of nearby House Park. Farther upstream the normally placid creek had become a fierce torrent as it churned through the hill country. Its many tributaries overflowed as well, adding to the surge of floodwater coursing along the eleven-mile journey to the river. Murky water swirled through the quarter acre backyard of a home on the east bank of Shoal Creek near Palomino Pathway. It came within inches of flooding the house, the home of one of James and Anna's classmates, and left a water moccasin stranded as an unwelcome guest on the back porch.

Hal peered out the window, trying to see if his precious Edsel was suffering hail damage. As he watched, a bolt of lightning struck a nearby telephone pole, turning night to day in a blinding flash. He could see hail rattling off the roof and windscreen, but fortunately, it was too small to do any damage. Relieved, he returned to his seat and assured the other drivers their cars should be okay. A modicum of calm returned, although the louder thunder crashes caused Carol to cry out with little "eeps."

Rod canvassed the room for drinks, and Jenny started the story from her perspective, speaking loudly to be heard over the storm. She began with when she first started seeing students unloaded behind the lab. Abe and Sophie were confused by what this had to do with the children's experience, but Carrie told them to be patient, and when Jenny described her symptoms, they understood. Carrie jumped in with a more detailed description of Jenny's behavior in the hospital, (omitting her little dance episode), and finished by describing the overflow of UT students, Black, and Hispanic patients in recent weeks, all exhibiting similar symptoms. She asked if Jenny had heard from her referral, and frowned at the negative answer. "I suspect those referrals are going straight into the trash."

Then it was Rod's turn. He hated speaking in front of a crowd, even if it was a "crowd" of only a few, and they were all friends. He soldiered on nervously, describing the call to the fire station and their reception at Alpen Labs, along with the armed guards and military aircraft, and the apparent stonewalling by the Austin Fire Chief when he and Captain Schwartzwald tried to follow up, concluding by telling them about the overflight he and Stan would make the next day.

"Wow, I think I will have another beer," Jerry said in amazement.

"I believe I may need to graduate from root to real beer myself," said Abe, shaking his head.

"The question is—what we do next? There wouldn't be a third seat in that plane tomorrow would there?"

"HAL, I don't want you going up in any airplane."

Stan smiled, "Don't worry Carol, my plane is too small, the back seat will be tight enough for Rod. Sorry Hal."

Carrie interjected, "I see three related sets of events here. The first is the adventure our little brats went on, and what they experienced. The second is whatever is going on at the lab, and the third is what's been going on at the Brackenridge ER. Why don't we make a plan to address each one? I'm sure everyone's highest priority is the children. I'm open to ideas, but I want to take them, or some of them, back to this place in the woods and see it for ourselves. Is tomorrow too soon to make that happen?"

Everyone agreed, but Carrie pushed back when Jenny wanted to go. "No young lady, you are in no shape to go traipsing through the woods. Why don't you and your friend Barb put your heads together and figure out how to get more inside information about the lab. Otherwise, rest and man the phones here." After some discussion, they agreed Carrie, Hal, and Abe would gather their children and everyone would meet at The Frisco at 10 the next morning. Carol insisted she was not "the hiking type," so Hal would take Stevie. Since it would be Saturday, everyone would be available, except for Sophie, who would miss the trip in order to take care of her pharmacy duties. Abe had a UT student who filled in as soda jerk when he was unavailable. They deferred telling Betty's parents for now, and would make that decision after tomorrow's trip to the woods.

Carrie said she would follow up on the missing referrals for psychological evaluations. Rose was friends with several Black filing clerks and could do some clandestine digging.

Chapter 21
Back in the Peanut Gallery

"It was but imagination, yet imagination had all the terrors of reality; nay, it was worse, for the reality would have come and gone, and there an end, but in imagination it was always coming, and never went away."
Charles Dickens, ***The Old Curiosity Shop***

The children's distressing dreams persisted for the entire week. They approached bedtime with dread, but none of them could stay awake—stupor came early, and they struggled to awaken before noon. The most difficult thing was simply pretending everything was normal.

James spent as much time as possible out of the house during the long days. Somehow, seeing Jenny lounging about was triggering the red mist to rise in his chest until his vision was clouded with red fog—redness he could taste and smell, and red heat that centered in his groin. Most days she wore form-fitting Bermuda shorts, and halter tops that exposed her midriff. Even more disconcerting was the day she wore nothing but one of Rod's shirts, with the sleeves rolled up and the top button undone. On her tiny 5'2" frame it came to her knees, but the effect on James' little soldier was distressingly obvious, at least to him. That day he could feel the red mist searing into his loins, hear the malevolent chorus, smell the stench of rotten breath, and taste repellent filth on his tongue. Equally upsetting was Jenny's implied intimacy with Rod—casually wearing his shirt, with no thought of asking permission.

Still rising late each morning, James would grab something quick to eat and head out. One day to Stevie's to build model airplanes, one day to Anna's for basketball—Levi came that day as well—and back to Anna's for two more days of basketball, baseball, splits, and the paper football game that was all the rage. James was convinced he had brought the game to Austin after accompanying Rod and Jenny on a trip to visit her sister in San Antonio, where her children, who referred to Jenny as "Tia Jenny," introduced him to the game.

On this trip, he learned Jenny's mother was Mexican, when she served an enormous platter of homemade tamales for lunch. It wasn't something Jenny talked about, and she seemed a little ill at ease, watching Rod carefully to gauge his reaction. The only reaction James noticed was that his father downed half of that tray of tamales, raving about how delicious these "authentic" tamales were. The firemen made frequent trips into East Austin for tamales from a small taqueria famous city-wide, but Rod said these were even better.

That night the plumbing in Jenny's place needed some urgent repairs.

Friday morning, they gathered excitedly at Levi's house. The previous evening Abe brought home the latest toy he would feature at the drugstore—called a "Hula Hoop." The children had heard rumors of this amazing invention and couldn't wait to try it. They picked it up after only a few tries, except Stevie, who struggled to the limits of the gang's collective patience before he managed to keep the thing up for five rotations. They declared that to be success and continued taking turns. Levi could have kept the hoop rotating all day, and he dazzled the rest of them when he did several fancy tricks he choreographed into a sort of dance. This intrigued Betty, who talked him into hauling out his portable phonograph, so he could teach it to her and set it to music. She ran home and borrowed "Round and Round" by Pat Boone from her mother, insisting this song had the perfect lyrics for their dance. Anna rolled her eyes at this idea and said Levi's suggestion, "All Shook Up" by Elvis Presley, was the obvious choice and a "HELL" of a lot better song. Betty countered, hesitantly, that her mother thought anything by Elvis was immoral, and he was obviously the devil's handiwork.

"BULL SNORT," Anna gruffed, "if Elvis is the work of the devil, then that ol' Satan does DAMN fine work!"

Stevie decided this the funniest thing he had ever heard, collapsing in gales of laughter, and soon was joined by Levi, who whooped uproariously. James snorted and sputtered in his effort not to laugh.

Red-faced, and on the verge of tears, Betty said, "Well, I didn't say I believed it. Go ahead and put on Elvis. 'All Shook Up' has better rhythm, anyway."

The Devil Made Her Do It

Earlier in the week, at the insistence of her mother, Betty had begun attending Vacation Bible School, held at the North Austin Baptist Church. The standard Dupree regime of Sunday School, followed by Sunday services, Sunday evening services, Baptist Youth Fellowship, and further augmented by Wednesday night church services, was obviously insufficient to Little Betty's spiritual development.

Vacation Bible School lasted from nine to three-thirty and consisted of an hour of Bible study, a morning snack, an hour of Christian games, a short lunch break, a children's movie deemed appropriate by the church morality committee (a woefully short list), and ended with Bible story hour, all interspersed by passionate prayers, entreating the Lord to forgive these wicked little children who were born in sin and iniquity and desperately needed his guidance to cast-off their depravity and purify themselves. North Austin Baptist was affiliated with the Southern Baptist Convention, a Bible-believin' denomination that was convinced it was their way or the highway to hell.

Following her latest weekend adventure, Betty asked a series of questions during Bible study:

"Is God white?"

"Yes Dear, he made us in his image."

"And so, Jesus is white?"

"Yes, of course Betty, after all he is the son of God."

"What about Adam and Eve, and Noah and his wife?"

"Since all God's children were made in his image, they must have been white."

"Then where did Negroes come from? Aren't they God's children?"

The flustered teacher answered with some nonsense about the Mark of Cain, the Lost Tribes of Israel, and Ham, the son of Noah who was the Father of Canaan and cursed into slavery. Betty found the stories confusing and contradictory, and they never provided a satisfactory answer to her simple question.

"Then... is it wrong to play with Negroes or have Negro friends?"

The teacher was clear on this point; the answer was an unqualified yes. Little white girls had no business hanging around with Negroes, and in a few years she would understand why.

Upon arriving home that afternoon, Betty announced she wanted to quit Vacation Bible School.

When she tried to explain to her horrified mother, she started with the story of Noah's son, Ham.

Penelope Dupree became confused and started babbling about how ham was a Jewish thing, there were all these things the Jews weren't allowed to eat as punishment for having killed Jesus, and they weren't allowed to go to church on Sundays either. Catholics weren't allowed to eat meat on Fridays because they believed the Pope was the fourth member of the trinity, and worshiped Mary instead of Jesus. The members of all the other Protestant denominations were going to hell because they didn't baptize right. If Betty didn't go to Vacation Bible School, she would never learn these things, (even though her teacher kept telling her she would, as if by magic, "understand in a few more years") and Penelope didn't want to hear another word about it.

Betty gave up and went to her room for a think. It was a think that began to question everything her parents had ever taught her, and the whole religion schtick in general.

Anna Agonistes

Anna's dreams continued in the same vein as before, becoming ever more unnerving. They always began with images of the Wrong Thing. This was followed by disturbing images of Betty in the bath, or Betty standing naked in the hallway. Betty would cry and wrap her in a hug, but now she could not extricate herself. Sometimes Betty changed to James, and James was naked as well, but with Betty's body. One particularly troubling night James morphed into Mark, still nude, but with his own body from the waist up, and Betty's from the waist down. Anna wanted to scream and put them out of her mind, wanted to scrub her brain clean of all the wrongness, but the dreams persisted and seemed to last all night.

In the mornings she would awaken with a jerk, and kept finding her hand "down there." Her sheet and blanket would be in a tangle from her thrashing about, and her pajamas a wrinkled mess. The more she tried to put her dreams out of her thoughts, the more they haunted her consciousness. She would walk into a room and the glow from that night in the woods would wash over her, drowning her in its light. James' visits, and the visit to Levi's house provided welcome respites, times she could just be a child for a few brief hours. The period from supper to bedtime was pure agony. Her attempts to delay the inevitable by staying up with a book turned counter-productive and sleep would overtake her. It seemed she slept an increasing number of hours, falling off around eight or nine and not awakening until noon, or even later, with the extended hours of sleep bringing no real rest. Even the vermillion sunset hidden within her eyes clouded over. She was aware of her mother keeping a worried eye on her and fought to convey an impression of normalcy. That was the hardest of all.

Agony in Amber

Levi dreamed in slow-motion, trapped in the tread of the giant shoe. He sensed the way out, but moved with painful slowness. He could never escape before the enormous golem took another step and trapped him again. Sometimes the monster ant would appear, moving at the same glue-like cadence, and it became a chase through thick resin slowly hardening to amber. This sequence would repeat over and over throughout the night, with Levi's thoughts tortured by the desperate knowledge that if he could only move at normal speed, he could easily escape. In the morning, he would remember the dreams, with the sense of desperation still haunting his thoughts. The daylight hours seemed normal, but then he would look at a clock and realize he had been frozen in place. Time seemed to move at the normal pace, but he would be out of sync for minutes or even hours. He might head into the kitchen at noon, only to realize it was twelve-thirty when he arrived, with no idea of why it had taken so long. It gave him a sense of hopelessness that only increased his stupor. Like the others, he only found relief when they played together, and he could take his mind off the persistent dreams and preternatural episodes.

The children all experienced these sorts of weird fugue states that invaded their waking hours. Jenny was suffering similar spates of amnesia. She would find herself in a room she did not remember entering, fifteen minutes to an hour after her last conscious memory. The losses of time were disconcerting, but she felt oddly calm in their aftermath. She continued to keep these to herself, she could discuss them with the therapist once her psychological referral came through—no sense in worrying anyone else.

CHAPTER 22
WE ALL WENT DOWN TO THE WOODS AGAIN

"It's like Dejá-vù all over again."
–Yogi Berra

Saturday morning when they met at The Frisco, Rod reported that the previous evening's storm had caused some minor damage to Stan's plane, so it would be a few days before they could do a flyover of the lab. The adults took a booth to themselves and let the children sit in the family booth at the back. Sophie had opted out, so the party included Carrie, Rod, Hal, Jerry, and Abe. They ate quickly, the adults musing about what they might find, and the children whispering among themselves, still concerned they were going to be in trouble. They had not invited Betty and Mark—only Anna, James, Levi, and Stevie were there.

Hal chauffeured Jerry, Anna, and Stevie, and the rest piled into Abe's 1956 Lincoln Capri, which rivaled the new Edsel in heft, volume of chrome trim, and even design oddities, with its forward canted headlights, and sloping rear fenders foreshadowing the huge fins that would come into style the following year.

Jerry brought Hal a gift, a decent pair of hiking boots from the Army Surplus store up on The Trail, which Hal exchanged for the Florsheims he had worn once again. The others wore boots or sneakers, and long pants to guard against the spikey underbrush. Rod commissioned James to lead the way, and they started off along a path that was still muddy from the previous night's thunderstorm. The hike began without incident, and they progressed resolutely. Abe proved to be a tough old goat and kept pace as they wound their way up and over the first hill and turned down the rocky path to the creek. They encountered their first problem here; the flood had transformed the narrow rivulet into a rushing stream and washed out a sizable chunk of the path.

Jerry grimaced, "This looks like the end of the trail, Podnas."

The other adults agreed, but then Levi spoke up. "I know how to get there. When I escaped from the giant, I found a different trail that cut across. If we follow the creek, we can cross farther downstream and take the other trail."

"Son, are you sure? You know I don't believe the giant was real. Why should we believe this other path is real?"

"It is there, Uncle Abe, really... Let me try, if I can't find it soon, we can go back. The crossing shouldn't be far."

"What have we got to lose?" asked Carrie. "These kids are a lot smarter than we give them credit for. Levi, do you think we can find it in, let's say, fifteen minutes?"

"Yes, ma'am," he answered, and set off before anyone else could object. He followed the creek bank downstream, and just as Carrie's watch ticked off the fifteenth minute, he pointed, "Look, we can cross there." He was pointing at a spot where debris from the flood formed a natural dam and blocked the flow, with only a shallow trickle remaining. "Do you think you can make it Mrs. Cook?"

"Just watch me—lead the way, Levi!"

On the other side, the trail paralleled the original. This trail was rougher, so they took the first junction leading up to the primary trail, and continued toward the peak.

As they crested the top, the children were visibly nervous, each taking the hand of their parent and holding on to that mooring against their swelling fear. James pointed to the valley, "That's the place," he murmured.

The valley that spread out beneath them was long and broad. It had changed even more. Several yellow bulldozers sat on the distant side of the valley, where they had been grading the dead vegetation smooth, as though to cover it up. These appeared to be still, but it was difficult to tell from so far away. Anna indicated the trail leading to the valley, "We went down here, it goes to the bottom."

Rod looked at the group, "That's why we're here, let's go." The trail down was narrow, rocky and steep, so their progress was slow, but they made it down safely. At the bottom the ground was littered with dead vegetation and fallen trees, as though some unseen killer had swept through the valley.

"See," Stevie insisted, "like I told you, the flying saucer did this."

"Something did," his father replied as he stuffed his pockets with samples of dead plants and bits of dead trees, "I'm thinking poison. This doesn't appear to be due to fire, I wonder if it's safe for us to be here."

"You're right about this not being due to fire," Rod agreed, "there isn't a trace of ash or burned vegetation. I've seen enough forest fires to know this is something very different. I'd feel a lot better if it was fire."

"I think Hal is right, we need to get these kids out of here."

"Mom, I'm not afraid, let's keep going."

"No Anna Belle, the men can go on if they want, but I'm taking you kids back."

"I agree," said Abe, "I'll go with Carrie and the children, the rest of you can make your own decisions."

"I'm going to investigate what those bulldozers are doing. James, you go back with the rest of your friends. Who wants to come with me?"

"I'm going with Rod; Hal, are you with me?"

"You go on with him, Jerry, I'd better take Stevie and help the others with the kids. Call me tonight and tell me what you found."

The group with the children clambered back up the narrow path to the main trail. As they climbed, they noticed a gradual demarcation between the area of dead vegetation and the point where it returned to normal. Hal stopped to gather samples at various points along the way. At the top, they headed down the trail, once again detouring and following Levi's directions in order to cross the creek below the dam formed by the debris. However, when they reached the creek, the debris damming the flow had washed away, and the creek was roaring along again.

Carrie surveyed the white-capping water in despair, "Well, we certainly can't cross here, what do we do now?"

"Head downstream," said Abe, "eventually we'll find a place where we can cross."

Back upstream, a frothing brown torrent spilled over boulders and splashed through vegetation that should have been high and dry. Foam whipped its surface, making the depth impossible to judge.

"It makes no sense to head back upstream," agreed Hal, "let's go."

They shouted to be heard over the roaring cascade, but turned their heads when they heard loud noises far behind them, back toward the valley.

"Were those gunshots?" asked an incredulous Carrie.

"That or a decent imitation," Abe answered, "I hope Rod and Jerry are all right."

"Maybe I'd better go back."

"Don't be foolish, Hal. Exactly what would you do? Besides, Carrie and I will need your help if we ever find a place where we have the remotest chance of getting these kids across."

They started downstream again, now arguing whether they had heard one, two or three shots, as their worry increased. Carrie wrapped an arm around James and whispered, "Don't worry Sweetie, your dad is tough and smart, he'll be okay."

Anna took his hand and squeezed, "Yeah, he'll be just fine, you'll see."

James colored and lowered his gaze, but returned the squeeze and whispered, "Thanks, Anna."

After about another mile, Stevie started complaining of being tired, so Hal lifted him up on his shoulders. It had been a long time since he'd tried this, and it was far more difficult than he remembered. Stevie now weighed in at a solid seventy-four pounds, well above average for his age and height, and Hal grunted as he stooped while Stevie climbed on. Abe and Carrie had been soldiering on without complaint, as had James and Anna. James was dragging, and increasingly worried about Rod, but he refused to complain in the face of Anna's determination. Levi bounded along, his usual energetic self. They slogged on, covering another mile before coming to a spot where a pronounced outcropping caused the creek to divert into two streams, each less violent than before.

"This may be our best shot," said Carrie, "the slope is less severe here, and the water looks shallow enough to wade across. Shall we risk it?"

"I'm the tallest," said Hal, "let me try it, and if I make it, I'll come back and help the rest of you." The current was stronger than it looked, and the water hit him in mid-thigh at the deepest point, causing the six-foot one-inch Hal to struggle to maintain his footing, but he faltered across. "We can do it, but you're going to need my help, let me catch my breath and I'll come back." On the return trip, he tried a slightly different spot and found it to be marginally easier, so the apprehensive group agreed to try it.

Abe offered an idea from a story about a group of Jews who escaped from the Nazis. "They linked arms," and he demonstrated with Levi, "when they had to cross the Rhine into France. Hal, you go first, then Levi, then me, Stevie would be next, then Carrie, no,

James is a little taller than Carrie, so he would be next, then Anna, then Carrie. Are you game? Do we try it?"

"You know, that might work," said Carrie. "Do you kids think you're strong enough to hang on that way? You'd just have to keep your arms bent and link elbows."

"I can do it, and I'm the smallest—Stevie, do you think you can? I dare ya'. This is your chance to make up for the bridge, ah, adventure."

Stevie said if Levi could do it, he could do it. Anna said she could do anything this bunch of wimps could do, drawing a disapproving frown from Carrie.

They lined up and linked arms, practicing pulling without letting go. James said it was like Red Rover.

They started off, finding it easiest to keep their backs to the current. It was slow going, and when they got to the deepest parts, Hal and Abe had to lift Levi. Abe was lifting Stevie with his other arm, while James gamely supported Stevie's left arm and provided Anna a little support when the swirling water hit her waist high. Anna gritted her teeth and hung on doggedly, as she fought for traction on the rocky bottom. In this way, they gained the far bank, and sprawled out, exhausted.

Carrie's smile was rueful, "All we need to do now is make it across the other branch, then walk, oh, maybe two miles back to the car."

After resting for about five minutes, they stood up and took stock. They were a bedraggled-looking bunch, with wet clothes, shoes that squished when they walked, and hair hanging limp from the spray. James and Stevie could not see out of their water and mud-stained glasses, so Hal wiped them on one of the few dry spots on his shirt. Already exhausted, they started off toward the other branch, afraid of what they would find. What if it were deeper, or the water flowed even more wildly?

When they got there, it proved impossible to cross, and they had to head farther downstream. Levi, ever indefatigable, forged ahead, finally returning to report that he found a navigable crossing a little farther on where the terrain flattened out and the current diminished. The spot was still deep, but had almost no current, and they crossed relatively easily. "Good boy, Levi, good boy," said Abe.

"I'm not a DOG, Uncle Abe," said Levi, stealing one of Abe's own corny lines.

The soggy group hiked the remaining two miles. Stevie was stumbling in exhaustion by the time they made it, while Levi was still trotting around as though he was just starting out.

"Oh great," said Hal, "I just realized those guys don't have a car, so one of us will have to wait for them."

CHAPTER 23
SHOWDOWN IN THE VALLEY

"The marvelous richness of human experience would lose something of rewarding joy if there were no limitations to overcome. The hilltop hour would not be half so wonderful if there were no dark valleys to traverse."
Helen Keller

Escape from Desolation

After watching to make sure the rest made it back up, Rod and Jerry continued toward the bulldozers, wending their way through the rotted flora. They had entered a scene from an apocalyptic movie—nothing grew, nothing remained alive, the insects had deserted the landscape, and not even buzzards circled overhead. Under their feet, the ground was thick with the detritus of putrefied vegetation. The unearthly surroundings dampened their spirits, and they walked without talking until they neared the bulldozers. The heavy machines appeared to be mired in muck, but the heavy rain from the night before had not erased what they had been doing. The ground was scraped clear and the dead vegetation plowed into grotesque piles—mute sentries keeping vigil over the devastation. Rod called out to see if anyone was at the site, but they heard no answer. As the two men stood listening for a reply, a loud crack shattered the stillness.

"Did you hear a gunshot?"

"Get down Jerry. I can't tell where it came from or if it was meant for us."

As they crouched behind what remained of two tree stumps, a second shot rang out.

"Oh, I'm pretty sure that one was."

They could not pinpoint the source, or be certain whether the stumps hid them from the shooter's view. They scanned the surrounding hillsides in desperation, and when a third shot resounded, Rod saw a muzzle flash on the hill across from them, about halfway up. Rod pointed to the spot, "He's up there. It's a long shot. If we move fast and keep ducking behind these stumps, I think we can get out of here. Keep zigzagging and don't follow the same path I do, let's give him two targets and make them as hard to hit as possible."

Jerry's reply was less than enthusiastic, but he agreed and started along with Rod. They hunched down, two Quasimodos as they sprinted from stump to stump, always toward the trail back up the hill, pausing to hide at each stump in their path. They heard no more shots, and Rod guessed the shooter only wanted to frighten them away. Jerry hoped he was right, but wasn't about to test the theory by slowing their retreat. Once they reached the path leading up the hillside, there was more cover, but they didn't slow down. At the top, Jerry was winded, but kept on booking it until they were hidden from the gunman's view. When they stopped to catch their breath, their expletive-laced conversation centered on whether they were actual targets or if the shots had only been fired as a warning. Jerry had done a stint in the army in Korea, and remembered the sound of bullets whistling above his foxhole. He heard nothing like it today, but that might simply mean the shooters were lousy shots, or maybe they only had handguns and the distance had been outside their range. Rod was a frequent hunter and said they didn't sound like small caliber pop-guns to him. With most of the vegetation gone, they had never been well hidden, and he suspected the shots weren't actually aimed at them. Whatever the case, they were not welcome in this valley.

They continued talking as they headed back, becoming so absorbed in their conversation they missed the side trail that detoured around the washed-out section. When they reached it, the water still churned far out of the banks. Looking around, Rod noticed the hillside above them flattened out after a few hundred yards. "Let's try upstream, it should be calmer up where the ground is less steep."

Jerry agreed, and they climbed until they reached a sort of plateau. The creek was still far out over its banks, but was shallower and the current had slowed. They waded across with no drama, then climbed back down to rejoin the trail. Once they emerged from the forest, they found the others discussing who would stay behind to wait for them.

James ran up to Rod, "Dad, are you okay? We heard gunshots. Were those gunshots?"

"We're both fine, but it seems a gentleman there was less than thrilled to have us as guests and most emphatically invited us to leave."

"They shot at you!?" Carrie exclaimed.

"Well, at any rate, they shot," said Jerry, "we're not sure whether they shot AT us or merely tried to warn us away. Either way, we didn't stick around to find out."

"I heard three distinct shots," Abe said.

"Exactly, and once we started skedaddling, they quit firing. They, he, whoever it was, was perched up on the hillside above the dozers. Jerry and I ducked down behind a couple of tree stumps after the first shot, and then took off after we heard the next two. We ran from one stump to another until we got back to the trail. But they never shot again."

"We got close enough to see the bulldozers mired in the mud. They had scraped the ground clear of any dead vegetation and piled it up like they plan to burn it or cart it off somehow. Down there, I'd guess they'll have to burn it. Say Hal, you don't suppose this was the farm the agricultural engineers at the lab are supposed to have?"

"That seems a little farfetched, but there must be something that ties all these weird things together. It makes more sense than a flying saucer landing strip," he answered, fixing Stevie with a stern scowl.

Frisco Finis

Too impatient to sit around and wait, Jenny arranged to meet Barb at The Frisco. Barb reported that she had been called in to the lab to help with clean-up and filing, and she had something important to show Jenny, but didn't want to talk about it on the phone.

Barb was carrying a fat file in a large brown envelope when she slid into the booth. Both ladies had already eaten, so they limited their order to pie and coffee. When Millie brought it to the table, the thick wedges of pie, always eye-boggling, were especially generous. By then Barb had the papers spread out on the table, including the newspaper clipping of the UT student who had committed suicide the previous week. Jenny gawked. "She looks familiar... is she... she IS, she's one of those kids who's been coming to the lab, isn't she?"

"Bingo! This is why they've been in such a lather Upstairs. I think her suicide had to do to with something they did to her. They've been melting down the phone lines between the lab and the UT Psychology Department. Most of these papers are notes from phone calls and follow-up meetings. They've also been making calls out to Bergstrom. We already knew the project—Mind Warp—had received funding from the military, and it looks like UT is also involved somehow."

"When I was in the hospital, it was full of UT students who were off their heads. I was off my own head at the time, but the nurse, Carrie Cook, told us they've been overrun lately with students who were apparently hallucinating, and a few Negroes and Mexicans with similar symptoms. She's going to try to get a list of names. Do you have anything we can compare it to?"

"Yes, several files, starting with that poor dead girl."

Over at the coffee service area, Millie was listening intently and interrupted, visibly agitated by the second mention of the dead coed. "Jenny, I think I have to tell you something. Oh, you're gonna hate me, I'm so sorry, I never knew it was anything this serious."

"Millie, what in the world are you talking about?"

Millie slid into the booth next to Jenny, with tears welling up in her eyes. "Honey, I been spyin' on you. Those people out at that Alpen Lab, they've been paying me to tell 'em what you talk about. A man comes in here right after you leave, every time. He's sitting out there in the parking lot now—drives a big black Buick. He's creepy, I get chills up my spine every time. Now let me finish. I tell him what you say, and he goes and makes a phone call up at the front. I don't know who he's calling, but it has something to do with that place. Then, before he leaves, he slips me an envelope with two hundred-dollar bills in it. Two hundred dollars—do you realize what that much money means to somebody like me? And it ain't just the money. The first time he come in, he like, threatened me. Not direct, but I could tell. He asked about my daughter in Dallas, knew her address, knew the names of my grandkids. Sweetie, I might have passed if it was only the money, but when he started talking about those babies..." and she started crying, sobbing and begging forgiveness, saying she did not understand it was so perilous, or that people died, like the poor little girl in the picture.

Jenny slid over and hugged the old woman, "I would have done the same thing Millie. I'm not mad, not at you, just those bastards at the lab. This explains so much. It's been like they knew our every move and what we were doing, they've always been a step ahead of us, and this is why."

Barb's voice quavered, "But what are we gonna do now, how can we protect Millie's family, and ourselves? What happens when they realize she told us she's been spying on us? My God, they already know we're up to something. Or at least they know you are."

"Let me think. Maybe we can buy some time, but you're going to have to be brave, Millie, and a good liar. Barb, we came in separately, so whoever he is, he won't realize we were here together. Before I leave, go sit in a booth on the other side. Order coffee and wait until he comes in and has left again before you go. Millie, tell the man I came in alone, and was waiting on someone who didn't show. Tell him I was worried and said those men and I are dropping the whole investigation. I decided whatever we thought was going on was my silly imagination, and it was none of our business. Make it sound convincing. Can you do that, Millie?"

"I'll try, what choice do I have?"

Barb, do you have time to copy the names? And go through the notes and make a few notes of your own on anything that sounds important? Do you need my help?"

"No, it's already done. I made a list of the names. We have one of those fancy new Xerox machines and I snuck some copies of the call notes, so they should be everything we want."

That afternoon when Rod returned and Jenny told him how Millie had been tipping off the man from the black Buick, he was furious, first at Millie, but when he understood she'd been doing it under threat, his anger turned to the lab. When she told him about the ruse they'd used to buy some time, he looked at her in admiration. "Beautiful, smart, and devious, what a combination."

Of course, James was taking it all in. He had gone to the bathroom for a shower, but dawdled long enough to hear their conversion through a crack in the door. Once Rod launched into the story of what had gone on in the woods, James started the water running, he already knew this story.

Jenny was horrified. "They SHOT at you? Those bastards SHOT at you? It must be that same group of paramilitary assholes I ran into with Hal and Jerry. Rod, this is scaring me, what do we do next?"

His only answer was to cup his hands under her bottom and lift her up into a kiss. In the bathroom, James heard the word 'shot' and peeked out the door again. His unbelieving eyes focused on his dad's embrace of Jenny's hind end, with her Bermuda shorts riding up to bathing suit length, and her legs wrapped as tightly around his waist as her arms were around his neck.

As if on command, that pesky little soldier snapped to attention. Before he even realized what he was doing, James was unconsciously rubbing the little guy, breathing hard, each breath a gasp of ecstasy. Then, when awareness snapped in, he was repulsed. This was his father and Jenny. And he was—what _was_ this thing he had been doing? Why did it feel so FLACKING (borrowing from Anna now) good? The red mist rose in him as he let go and stared at his erection, trying to will it away; but it just stayed there, gazing up at him with its single, unblinking little eye.

CHAPTER 24
FEATHER IN A STORM

"The willow which bends to the tempest, often escapes better than the oak which resists it; and so in great calamities, it sometimes happens that light and frivolous spirits recover their elasticity and presence of mind sooner than those of a loftier character."
–Albert Schweitzer

When the sun rose over Mueller airport on Tuesday morning, it glinted off the chrome yellow surface of Stan Landry's 1939 Piper Cub J3C-65, as he ticked off his twenty-three-item pre-flight checklist. Stan had arrived early to check her out and was waiting on Rod to join him. The Cub, with a range of two hundred twenty miles at the cruising speed of seventy-five mph, was more than adequate for their planned overflight of the Alpen Lab facility. Piper Cubs were among the most popular civilian aircraft due to their modest cost, respectable low speed handling capabilities and war-proven reliability. Stan was fanatical in his maintenance and care of the old girl and welcomed any opportunity to show her off.

Rod had stopped by to pick up the 35mm Hasselblad C with its 350mm Zeiss telephoto lens from a frowning Hal, who had reluctantly agreed that his new camera, Hasselblad's latest and greatest, would be perfect for the aerial photos they wanted. After twenty minutes of detailed instructions regarding shutter speed, exposure, f-stops, and the details of the new Compur Shutter design, an exasperated Rod said "Just set the damn thing and tell me which buttons to push."

Realizing Rod was not going to master the intricacies in the short time available, Hal set the aperture to f/8 and the shutter speed to 1/250, muttered something about a Brownie, and made one last plea.

"OK, but look here, if it's clear and bright can you just change the shutter speed to 1/500? Like this—see 1/500, 1/250—back and forth. If it stays overcast 1/250, if the sun is out, 1/500. Okay?"

"Sure Hal, that seems simple enough."

"Tell your buddy to stay as low and slow as possible."

"Should be no problem, he says his airplane is good at slow speeds."

As he prepared to leave, Carol interrupted, "Can I tempt you to stay to breakfast, Rod? I've made some scrambled eggs." She indicated a bowl full of what Rod had assumed were either raisins or dead flies.

"Oh, uh, I'd love to, but I'm late already and I don't want Stan to give up on me and leave."

"Are you sure I can't join you?" Hal was eyeing the "breakfast" with a look that managed to combine panic with disgust.

"Sorry Hal, much as I'd like to have you along to operate this thing, Stan says there will barely be enough room for me."

Rod had laid the book of Key Maps on the front seat, and when he pulled into the airport parking, he grabbed it to help Stan plan the flight.

The flight plan Stan filed took them north above IH35 to FM183, where they would swing west, following 183 on essentially the same route Jenny had mapped out on their trip two weeks ago, turning south off 183 above Whitetail Crossing toward the area where they would find the back entrance to the lab.

Rod felt like he was climbing into a sardine can as Stan helped him into the rear seat. Once Rod was seated and belted in, Stan performed the "Cub Dance" necessary to shoehorn himself into the tight front seat. It was not only possible but also necessary, due to weight distribution, to fly Cubs from the back seat for solo flights, so the front seat wasn't designed for comfort. Stan fired up the four-cylinder engine with its exposed pistons by manually turning the propeller before getting in, and the roar made it necessary for them to shout to be heard. The Piper Cub is a "tail dragger," meaning it has two oversized pneumatic tires up front and a smaller wheel in back, which causes the airplane to sit at an extreme angle with the nose pointed upward. This makes it impossible for the pilot to view the runway. To see where he was going, Stan had to weave back and forth as he taxied along slowly, a maneuver that continued to undermine Rod's waning enthusiasm.

"When are you going to close the door?"

"I'm leaving it open so you can get good pictures, just make sure the camera's strapped around your neck and your seat belt is tight, you'll be fine and have a great view."

Rod's only response was a quiet, "oh shit."

"Oh, and help me avoid any other planes; we should have the runway to ourselves, but I don't have any way of communicating with the tower, and there's always an outside chance of other traffic.

From then on, Rod's head was on a swivel as he looked around, fearing the worst and knowing Stan's field of vision was limited. This didn't jibe with his expectation that a calm, confident voice from the tower would direct their every move.

Stan made a one hundred eighty degree turn into the wind as he entered the runway and prepared for take-off. He mashed hard on the brakes and took the engine up to seventeen hundred rpm, at which point he waited for the oil pressure to build to his comfort level, as the little Cub rattled and vibrated even more violently than before. Once he was satisfied with the oil pressure and temperature, he eased off the brake and pushed the control stick forward, the exact opposite of the norm, but necessary because of the upward pitch. This caused the nose to drop and gave Stan a forward view as they taxied, until they reached sixty miles per hour, when the lift from the wings started to take them up, climbing at a leisurely one to two hundred feet per minute. Stan continued to circle the airport until they reached the cruising altitude of eight hundred feet, then leveled out, and executed a sweeping turn toward IH35 as he accelerated to the seventy-five mile per hour cruising speed.

Rod finally began to relax as he either became accustomed to the experience or resigned himself to death—he wasn't sure which.

The little Cub quickly covered the distance to FM 183. Then Rod tightened his death grip on the seatbelt as what he was coming to think of as his flying coffin canted left, and they were buzzing along above 183 for another six or seven miles before Stan turned left again, dropped the nose and slowed down. He leveled off at one hundred feet, leaving Rod's stomach well behind, and continued at a reduced speed of fifty miles per hour, as they both watched for their destination.

When the building appeared in the distance, Stan dove to fifty feet, barely skimming the treetops, and followed the contours of the hilly country until they were headed straight toward the back of the complex. Rod released his grip on the bottom of his seat belts, the only handles available, and fumbled around with the camera until he got it more or less into position. The morning was bright and sunny, so he set the shutter speed to 1/500. The expensive camera felt heavy and solid in his hands and helped to calm his jitters as he removed the lens cap and turned toward the open door.

Stan dropped even lower as they approached, and reduced the speed to forty miles per hour, barely above the stall speed of thirty-seven. They floated serenely over the back-entrance gate to the amazement of the guard, who stared up at them with his jaw agape.

As they had surmised, the Agricultural and Electrical Engineering wings vee'd out from the center of the building and extended far to the sides and back. The second story stretched above about half of the vee, forming a cover over much of the Chemical Engineering wing that extended from the center. This third wing comprised two sections, the first the same width as the outer wings, but the second was much broader, so the two formed a short 'T' with a fat crossbar. The explosion had reduced this second section to rubble, and it was now under construction. Stan swung the little plane around so that Rod had an unobstructed view to take pictures, allowing him to snap off several. As they cleared the complex, Rod shouted at Stan to fly over from the front.

Stan soared back to one hundred feet and made a wide circle out and around. As he turned back towards the building, two helicopters entered his airspace at high speed, swooping down toward them and rocking the little Piper Cub violently in their prop-wash. The wings shuddered and dipped, and the light plane bucked as the wind currents battered it, shaking the little plane like a feather in a storm.

CHAPTER 25
SHOOTING THE MESSENGER

Accomplished messengers may need to talk and
dodge bullets at the same time.

The responsibility to talk with Betty's parents fell on Carrie's unhappy shoulders. Betty's mother, Penelope, was rumored to flit back and forth across the narrow borders of sanity, while her father, Arthur, was a bitter, taciturn man with a nasty mean streak. Both of them were bible-believin' Baptists of the "hard-shell" variety. The only soft spot she could hope to exploit was Penelope's obsession with Betty. Carrie decided it was better to navigate the bizarre labyrinth of Penelope's belief system than risk actual physical injury from her explosive husband. She waited until the next Tuesday, when her afternoon was free and she could tell the story slowly and carefully.

"Penelope, Carrie Cook here. Is there any chance you can drop by for coffee and cake this afternoon? I have something rather important to discuss with you concerning Betty's well-being. Now don't worry, she's done nothing wrong, but this is something I feel we should talk about in person... About two, then? I'll look forward to it."

By the time Penelope arrived, she had worked herself into a frenzy. Carrie had years of experience dealing with hysterical patients and their families, but this was beyond the pale. Penelope shot past the driveway in her tiny Nash Metropolitan, slammed on the brakes and immediately began backing up, causing the Chevy coming behind her to swerve into the oncoming lane that, mercifully, was open. She then mashed the gas and pulled into the drive with a short chirp of the tires, all the anemic 1200 cc engine could manage. As she threw the door open and struggled to pull herself from the tight accommodations, the car bucked forward because she had neglected to switch off the key. This caused her to spill out on the drive face first as her elaborately flowered dress flew over her head, revealing a more than ample rear end, ensconced in a heavy white girdle whose garters attached to old-fashioned seamed nylons, now rent with gaping runners. She yanked at her dress, first on one side, then another, all the while twisting her head from side to side to see if anyone had witnessed this decidedly unchristian display of stout white rump.

Carrie rushed out to help the flustered woman to her feet, who wobbled along on high heels that insisted on catching every crack in the driveway, then sank into the lawn as they slogged along to the front door. By the time Carrie had her in and seated, Penelope's face was red, her unblinking eyes bulged, and she was breathing in great ragged huffs. Her hair seemed to have a life of its own, somehow working its way out of her severe bun in frazzled strands and random wisps that she pulled at sporadically.

Desperate to instill calm before broaching the subject of the children's activities, Carrie bustled around, bringing her frenetic guest a tall glass of frosty sweet tea and a thick slice of chocolate cake. In the meantime, Penelope began complaining about the lack of air conditioning in the little house. Carrie apologized and turned on the attic fan, which started up with a loud "whump" when it kicked in, and created a small gale as it sucked in torrents of air. She had to shout to be heard over the racket, telling Penelope she would cut it off when things cooled down.

Finally, Carrie decided the situation was as good as it was going to get, and launched into a carefully redacted version of the children's nighttime adventure. Penelope was horrified to learn that her little Betty had been so influenced by Anna and those other evil children, who were obviously under the spell of Satan. She would have expected it from that little Jew-Boy, but not from the others. Clearly, the hand of Satan was at work in the visions those children saw; this was exactly what happens when you don't cloak yourself in the armor of God.

With little success, Carrie struggled to dissuade her from going down this rathole of illogic, pointing out the high number of UT students coming to the ER with the similar symptoms, most likely from exposure to some kind of poison or drug. Most likely the children had unknowingly come into contact with the same thing.

Of course! Penelope had always known the University was the devil's playground with all its commie professors and ungodly teachings. Logic was simply not going to penetrate the layers of absurdities set like sediment in her irrational mind. In the past, Carrie had seen patients or their families who simply refused to accept what they were being told, as often as not for religious reasons—Jehovah's Witnesses who refused transfusions, Christian Scientists who insisted their family members be released from the ER so they could take them to one of their nursing centers for treatment by prayer. In these cases, the families believed nothing she said, or the doctors recommended, and ultimately the patients had to be released.

Just as Carrie had resigned herself to her guest's intractability, she heard something that presented a tiny opening, a sliver of light through a gap in the dark curtain of Penelope's bizarre belief system. "You can't tell this to Arthur, please promise me you won't never tell him." Her voice held a note of panic that differed from her previous hysterical tone, but also a clarity that was missing from her incoherent ramblings, a quality that signaled the faintest possible intrusion of sanity.

Carrie summoned her best calm, clinical voice, the one she used for dealing with terrified families, forcing down her frustration at

Penelope's obstinacy. "If you don't want me to tell Arthur, of course I won't, but do you mind telling my why? Are you somehow afraid of his reaction?"

"Oh, I can't tell him nothing like this."

"I see. He would be angry?"

"Of course, he would be mad. It is the job of a good wife and mother to raise godly children and protect them from the devil. I failed in my duty and deserve to be punished. I know it's sinful not to own up to it, not to subjugate myself to my husband as head of our Christian family, and endure whatever punishment he thinks is right. But Arthur's is just so harsh. I'm such a sinner, too weak to do what the Lord instructs women to do. I'll pray for forgiveness, truly, I will, with all humble sincerity. Just, please don't tell him Miz Cook. His punishments hurt so bad and I don't think I can take it. I'm such a frail woman and sinful wife." She turned her eyes to the ceiling and burst into tears, wailing and calling out to God for forgiveness, getting down, almost falling, on her knees with her arms raised, as she babbled nonsensical prayers, entreating Jesus to save her, to forgive her, to make her a better woman and wife. She would find the courage somewhere, somehow, to tell her husband, as an obedient wife must, but at a time of her own choosing, when the Lord spoke to her and told her it was the time.

Carrie listened in helpless revulsion. This poor woman was, in her own wretched way, admitting to abuse—a kind of abuse that her church and friends would sanction. Abuse from which there would be no escape, no SafePlace, not in 1958, when a good spanking or the occasional black eye was just what a wife needed if she stepped out of line.

Carrie spoke with measured deliberation, "Penelope, look at me, try to calm down, look at me Penelope. If you ever, EVER, feel threatened, you or Betty, or both of you, CALL ME, or just come here if you're afraid to call. Do you understand me, Penelope? Can you nod your head? Good, now listen to me carefully. What's 'gotten into' Betty is not Satan; it is a kind of poison or drug. Now we don't fully understand how or why, but we will find out. You need to be brave and think about what is best for your little girl. If you think the devil had a hand in this, fine, but doesn't the Bible say the Lord helps those who help themselves? Now you need to help Betty, to help us help Betty and the other children. Will you be able to do that, Penelope? I will assist you in any way I can. I'm sure the other mothers will as well. But this is serious, and it doesn't seem to be going away. Why don't you sit back down in the chair and finish your cake? I can get you more sweet tea, or coffee if you prefer. Maybe you have some questions you'd like to ask me; I'm a nurse and I've been dealing with those UT students for some time now. I don't want you to leave without fully understanding this, and without being quite so upset. Concern is normal and completely warranted, but for the sake of our children we need to stay calm and address this carefully and logically, as a MEDICAL issue. Can you do that?"

It was obvious the woman was fighting for control. Carrie stepped over and placed a comforting hand on her shoulder, squeezing gently. The wave of relief that washed over her was palpable, you could see it in the expression in her eyes as she breathed deeply, rubbing at them to stem the flow of tears as the guilt born of years of cult-like conditioning was, at least temporarily, assuaged. Penelope rose unsteadily and wrapped Carrie in an impulsive embrace, tears starting up anew, but this time tears of release. Her body shook with the birth of a new promise, of the possibility of escape from the despair that she had lived with for many years. Carrie continued to speak calmly, soothingly, and progressively drew the woman into a more rational conversation, explaining how drugs can affect the mind, highlighting parallels between the behavior of her patients and that of the children. She assured her that Betty was an exceptionally bright little girl with tremendous potential, who only needed nurturing and the chance to succeed. When Penelope realized she wasn't alone, and the overwhelming sense of guilt she'd been living with might be unwarranted, it was a window opening into a dark room—far too much to process in a short time, but along with her concern, she felt a faint flicker of hope.

"I have to get home to my baby. I want to hug her and love her and tell her she is all right and I will always make sure of it. She was afraid to come to me and that ain't right. I been doing wrong by her, making her feel like I been feeling all these long years. I been making her fear my fear, suffer my guilt, bear my burdens. I got to make it up to her, be a stronger woman and a better mama. I wanted to keep her a baby forever, but that ain't the way to keep her safe. It's on me, it's all on me now."

"Oh Penelope, children are so resilient, it will surprise you how fast she will bounce back once we get this resolved. Listen, we girls stick together, right? Don't take everything on yourself, we'll figure this out together. Okay?"

Suddenly formal, almost subservient, "Thank you, Mrs. Cook. I will help in any way I can, and not only with Betty—with your Anna Belle, and the other children too. I must go now, but, well, I do appreciate it, appreciate what you've did and what you've said. You know I'm not an educated woman, though I pretend so. I met my Arthur through the church; it was my Daddy and Mama who set it all up like one a' those arranged marriages. I mean, I got to meet him and all, and we courted proper like, but I had no experience of men, and him, none of women. He turned out to be a right stern man who don't brook no foolishness nor no straying from how he sees the path of God to be. He believes in the rod all right, but only for me, never for Betty, thanks the Lord. I fear the day she starts to be a woman, a day that is coming all too soon now, for her womanliness will have some type of effect on him and I don't like to think what it might be.

You will be welcome in my home, only please not when Arthur is at home. And mad as I am at Anna Belle for pretending to be you on the phone, she has been a good friend to my Betty, and she is welcome too. You know, it is kind of funny when you think about it. You should have heard her. She fooled me good." With this last, she seemed to soften and relax a bit, suppressing a little titter, and smiling at the memory of how the voice on the phone had sounded exactly like the woman sitting across from her.

~ ~ ~

Thursday, July 1st
Dear Diary,
    This has been a strange day, and real confusing. Anna's mother called Mommy this morning and asked her to come over for coffee and cake because she had something important to talk to her about and it was about me. I had to stay home and babysit Terry like I do (for free!!!) whenever she has something to do. I was scared to death cause I knew it was about everything that happened in the woods, both trips and I was gonna be in so much trouble!!!!!!
    When she got home I could tell she had been crying and her dress was dirty and her stockings were torn (she wears the stupid old timey ones with stripes in the back.) But Dear Diary, she was NOT mad!!!!! And she was so nice to me!!!!! Anna's mother had told her a lot too, I think almost everything, I was scared to say much cause I didn't know how much. But Dear Diary she just said Anna's mother and the other mothers were gonna get help for us and it would be ok. And she would NOT tell Daddy!!!!!! And she didn't say the kind of stuff she usually does when I've been bad about how Satan makes us do bad things and all. She said they would find out what happened to us and help us get better. That's what's confusing. She didn't say anything about praying to drive out the Devil, and she acted

like she thinks I'm sick or something. I'm not sick Dear Diary, just really really scared. And she said I don't have to go back to Bible School and I can go play with the other kids whenever I want!!!!! Whatever Anna's Mommy said to her must have been something good!!!! She even said I can play with Levi even though he's Jewish (I looked it up, I'm so embarrassed <- looked that up too and I will start looking up words I can't spell. JewASH is NOT a word and you don't say A Jewish, you say A Jew. I have to know this so I can be MRS. LEVI STIEGLITZ!!!!!)

Thank you for always listening to me Dear Diary. Mommy says now I can talk to her and I won't get in trouble even if she thinks I'm wrong.

But I will always tell you things first Dear Diary.

Good night from Mrs. Levi Stieglitz

CHAPTER 26
DRAGONFLIES ON THE HUNT

When they hunt, dragonflies predict
the movements of their prey in advance

Rod was thrown toward the open door and hung by the narrow seatbelt, staring wide-eyed at the tree tops rushing by below as the camera on its strap swung like a demented pendulum. He swallowed the bitterness that rose in his throat and struggled back upright, pulling the camera in with him.

"Time to go," yelled Stan, "what the hell?" He wrestled with the controls and dove to pick up airspeed, bare inches from the top of the building, then plunged even lower, crossing the rear parking lot only a few feet off the ground, before pulling up to clear the fence and head south at treetop level. Like hungry dragonflies on the hunt, the helicopters turned and gave chase. Through the bubble-like front cockpits Rod could see uniformed men with heavy rifles, and he was certain he saw an Air Force logo on the side of one of the Bell 47J Rangers. He swung the camera up quickly and snapped off several shots, fighting to hang on as the Cub trembled and pitched.

Stan flew at treetop level. He knew they outclassed him in speed and rate of climb, but hoped that the Cub's low altitude maneuverability would give them some slight advantage. The chopper pilots were first-rate, but more conservative, choosing to stay at a higher altitude and hang back. As they gained confidence and closed the gap, Stan turned sharply and pushed the nose down into a steep dive where the ground dropped away into a little canyon. They picked up considerable speed this way and popped up the other side at his maximum air speed of eighty-five miles per hour, still slower than the one hundred and five mph top speed of the Rangers, but faster than the Air Force jockeys were willing to risk at treetop level. The copters dropped back again, and seemed content to follow along at a safe height, maintaining a steady distance behind them. They stayed this way for several miles as they pushed deeper into the hill country, two menacing escorts Stan was helpless to evade as he flew at top speed, up and down the rolling hills, so low the tires brushed the taller treetops. At this altitude, with Stan pushing the little Cub to its maximum speed, it was a terrifying ride, and Rod clung even more tightly to his seatbelt.

Suddenly there was a loud pop and the little Cub canted sideways as Stan fought for control. "Lean out and see if you can tell what did that Rod. I can't tell if they shot us or it was something else."

Not for the first or last time that day, Rod's response was a quiet, "Oh shit." He wrapped the seatbelt around his left hand and leaned as far out the open door as his churning stomach would allow. "Goddamn it, Stan, we blew a fucking tire. I can see some small limbs caught in the axle—you must have hit a sharp branch or something. Are we gonna die?"

"No Rod, at least not today. This is actually good news; it means they didn't shoot us. The landing won't be the smoothest, but I can try to ride on the good tire for as far as possible, just make sure that seat belt is secure. For now, I'm more worried about our escorts."

Then, as if on cue, the helicopters peeled off to the east and faded into the distance.

"OK, genius, now that you got us attacked by Air Force choppers, how do you propose we find our way back to the airport?"

"Stan, I am so sorry. Those fuckers were deadly, I had no idea. How the hell did they know we would be there? They must have come across town from Bergstrom."

"Only one answer to that—the flight plan I filed. I don't get it though, that area isn't restricted airspace, at least not officially. But it set off an alarm somewhere. If those guys took off when I filed the flight plan, they could have arrived when they did. The flight plan goes to the FAA. This is dead serious Rod, with emphasis on the word dead. We only have two options—find our way back, or find a place to land and get our bearings; and this country is too rugged for option number two, especially with a blown tire."

"Okay Stan. Since we left the lab, what direction have we been flying?"

"Almost straight south, maybe a little west of south."

"Then we need to go east. Once we can see where we are, it should be easy to find our way back. What will happen since we deviated from the flight plan?"

"We stay low and slow, and return to the original route as soon as we can. We'll probably be safe—or we would be under normal circumstances; today we may find the US Air Force waiting for us back at Mueller." He grimaced, took the bright yellow plane up to one hundred feet and banked to the east.

As residential streets appeared in the distance, Rod glanced down and saw an extensive valley with no greenery. "Hey, I think this is where we came on Saturday. Can you make a slow pass down along this valley?"

Stan dropped back to treetop level and nosed down into the gorge. The bulldozers had continued their progression since the Saturday excursion. Over half the valley was stripped bare, and they could detect three bulldozers hard at work. Rod snapped several more pictures before panic took over and he told Stan to get out of there. As they gained altitude again, Rod snapped one last photo. It would show the faint impression of a half circle, neatly circumscribing the portion of the basin where the valley had not yet been plowed.

From there, it was easy for Rod to direct Stan back to IH35. At this point they were close to the airport and upon arrival, Stan slowed the plane to a near stall, before tilting slightly to the left and riding the remaining tire like a unicycle, until the other wheel finally dropped. There was an immediate pull to the right, and the Cub swung around slowly as the damaged tire tore itself to bits before they finally stopped. Together, they lifted the right wing to take the pressure off the damaged wheel, and pushed the Cub back into the hanger. Rod was stiff and rubbing his rear end. Stan smiled and told him he had "Cub Butt," a typical result of the vibration for which these little airplanes were notorious.

"I'll say one thing my friend, you're a hell of a pilot. You saved our bacon back there. Not a ride I'd sign up for again, but you made monkeys out of those Air Force chopper pilots, and I won't ever forget that landing."

"I'm guessing they did exactly what they came to do. Ran us off and scared us enough that we're unlikely to make any return trips. If they had wanted us on the ground, we'd have been there. This way no one will believe us."

Rod smiled through gritted teeth, "Until I get these pictures developed. Tell me the damages on the wheel and tire and I'll cover it, you've contributed enough for one day."

The flight services office was in a squat gray building next to the terminal. Rod insisted on accompanying Stan for moral support, since they did not know what to expect. Behind a narrow counter, a mouse of a woman frowned as she methodically closed out the plan with Stan. She didn't mention the detour or any communication from Bergstrom. When she pushed the form across the counter for Stan's signature, he scribbled his name, then jerked his head toward the door and hustled out of there with Rod close behind.

As they returned to their cars, the two men agreed that their next step should be to report the experience to Captain Schwartzwald while they waited on the pictures to be developed. They were both back on shift the next day and their first order of business would be to sit down with Captain Schwartzwald.

On his way home, Rod stopped by Stieglitz Drugs, where Abe helped him unload the film and send it off for processing. "I'll put a rush on this Rod, they should be back by Friday. It's a good thing it was sunny, the faster shutter speed should eliminate any blur in the pictures. Let's plan another meeting Friday night. I'm more worried than ever about Levi, he's still yelling out in his sleep, and sometimes during the day he zones out—as if he's in a trance. How is James doing?"

"About the same. Jenny's around him more than I am these days, and she's been after me to have a talk when he's not there. What does Sophie think about this?"

"She's quite concerned. She wants to talk about getting professional help, and not only for Levi, for all the children."

"I don't know Abe, my instinct says those kids are just spoiled and need to toughen up, but I have a feeling I'm gonna be outvoted. Even though we're not married, Jenny acts like it and gets two votes to my one on pretty near everything."

"Stay single then. Sophie gets three."

The Ladies Auxiliary—Hospital Chapter

Later that evening, Carrie and Rose huddled together during their supper break. Carrie had finished updating Rose on everything that had been happening, when Rose opened the oversized purse she was carrying, and showed Carrie that it was crammed full of wrinkled papers.

"These are some of the referrals that have been getting 'lost.' I told you I have a couple of friends who are filing clerks here. I won't tell you her name, but one of them dug these out of the trash. Someone has been pulling them from the files before they can be processed, so none of these referrals were ever made. The good news is they contain all the information about the patients, and the name of the doctor who should be receiving the referrals. She also found out they keep a log of the patients who have been hallucinating. She sneaked it from the files and typed up a copy. There wasn't time to cross-reference it to these referral forms, but I think that would be a good thing to do, it will tell us if she found all the forms or if some had already gone into the trash. And guess what else? One of those forms is for your friend Jenny."

"Rose, you're fantastic. I'm uncertain what we'll do with these, but at a minimum we can get help for Jenny. Maybe for all these people, but we need to be careful. Something truly scary is going on with this. Hmmm, I wonder what happens when these people call in to check on their referrals? Surely some of them must wonder why they've never heard anything."

"That's my next surprise. A friend who works the switchboard told me they have orders to route any call regarding these referrals to a particular number—she thinks it's for one of the hospital administrators, but she isn't sure which one—it isn't in the directory. Here's the worst part. She listened in on a few of the calls. The people are being told their appointments are canceled because their case is so mild they took it off the list."

"Wow. That borders on medical malfeasance. Tell you what Rose, our little group needs to have another meeting, and I'd like you to come, oh, unless you don't want to be involved. I don't want to put you at risk."

"If your white friends won't mess in their panties, I would love to come. Something else, may I ask my sister Dora to come with me? She works at UT and hears things about the students we see as patients. Only—any chance Anna could watch Georgie? If Dora comes, I'll need a sitter. I'll be happy to pay Anna."

"I'll check with her, but I think I can guarantee you she will be delighted to see Georgie. She found a special book at the library for him she wants to give him personally. And forget about paying her, this will be more like play than work."

Trust is an overrated virtue

Schwartzwald was not happy. He scowled at Rod as he and Stan related their story. "I told you to leave this alone, Rod, and now you went and involved Stan? How fucking stupid can you be? I told you I would handle this, and now the goddamn Air Force is involved? Jesus Christ, Rod." He sputtered on for a while, venting his anger in a flood of profanity while Rod glared back at him.

When Schwartzwald finished, Rod spoke evenly, "Look Brad, this involves my son and my girlfriend. If you think I'm going to let it go, you're sadly mistaken. If you want my resignation, you can have it, but this is on me, Stan was only trying to do me a favor."

"Rod, you just don't get it. This is way above both our heads. Didn't those Air Force helicopters and planes give you a hint the first time you were there? Think about it. How did they know you would be there yesterday? I'm trying to tamp this thing down, and here you go like a bull in a china shop, stirring everything up again, muddying the waters, letting all the cows out of the barn and, and..." At this point he ran out of metaphors to mix and sat there staring at Rod. After a long pause, he spoke more calmly, "Okay, fair enough, I understand you're concerned about your family and those other kids. But let's work together, capish? Together. Got it?"

"Okay Brad, but it has to cut both ways. What are you not telling me? For instance, what happened with the pipe you sent to be analyzed?"

"Okay, but first—Stan, this is your chance to walk away and limit your exposure to any fallout. If you want to hear what I'm about to tell Rod, you're in, head and shoulders. I'm warning you, yesterday you found out how risky this is. Do you need some time to think about it?"

"A team of wild horses couldn't drag me away, Brad. I don't take kindly to almost being blown out of the sky. I went through a lot worse in Korea, and besides, this oversized dope needs me to watch his back. No telling what kind of shit he'd fall into on his own."

Brad cracked a grudging smile. "And you're gonna jump in the crapper with him—so be it. First, the laboratory results. I didn't dare go through normal channels with this, but I've been around this city for a while. I got the piece of pipe to a friend in the police lab. I had to do it on the QT, no paperwork, no trail of evidence, no written report, and he shit-canned the thing when he finished. I don't want to know where and neither do you. It was like we suspected Rod, the accelerant was from match heads mixed with TNT, a combustible combination. Easy to set off accidentally. The debris he found on the outside was interesting. There wasn't much, so the results are questionable, but it may have originated from mushrooms and molds. Let me see, I wrote it down." He fumbled through his desk drawer and withdrew a small scrap of paper he had hidden. "Yeah, here it is, possibly a mixture of a thing called psil-o-cy-bin and, uh, ergot, or chemicals similar to those, like it had been altered somehow. But here's the deal, those things are holo, no, halo, hallucinogenic, yeah, hallucinogenic, they can cause hallucinations, cause people who ingest them to see and hear things that aren't real. Sound familiar?"

"Brad, you need to get this to the Chief."

"I agree Rod, but when I tried to bring this up to him after the call out to the fire at Alpen Labs, he shut me down hard. When my friends in the police try to find out what's going on they get the same story. At this point, I'm not sure who to trust. Stan, how could the Air Force have known you would fly over Alpen Labs yesterday?"

"The most obvious would be through the flight plan I filed. They go to the FAA. Right before we took off, I dropped it at the Flight Services building at the airport. That would have given them just enough time to make it there from Bergstrom flying the choppers on a straight line at top speed. They'll do about a hundred five miles an hour wide open. There are only two other possibilities I can think of—one is radar, if they picked us up on radar, for the choppers to arrive so quickly they would have to have been close by. The last is if they were patrolling the area and spotted us. My bet is still on the flight plan, and that's the scariest answer of the three."

"Yeah, that would mean they specifically targeted you, and know who you are. Look you two, I don't have any real answers, and I can't tell you what to do next, just be damn careful and keep me in the loop. I'll do what little is in my power to help, I don't take kindly to my men being attacked, or their families put at risk.

"I know I'm a pain in the ass, Brad, but thanks for your help and understanding."

Brad dismissed this with a wave of his hand, "But from now on, assume you're being watched and your phone and the phones here at the station are tapped. If you need to talk to me about anything, do it here. The last thing I want to do is get you or Stan in trouble over this."

CHAPTER 27
WHAT TO DO NEXT?

"You've got to be very careful if you don't know where you are going, because you might not get there."
–Yogi Berra

The fourth of July weekend was quiet. Except for Carrie and Rose, who worked the graveyard shift at the ER to earn the much-needed holiday bonus, the families each had their own planned activities, with barbecues, picnics, and fireworks over the long weekend, so they didn't meet again until the following Friday. The nervous group decided to meet at the Lindquist home to make it tougher for any spies who might be following their movements. They delivered the invitations among the group by word of mouth, with no telephone communications. The additional space provided by the Lindquist's "Live 'n' Dine" combination living/dining room (a Big Pete Peterson EX-clusive) would be welcome, as the group had continued to add members. Penelope Dupree would be there (minus Arthur, who thought she was attending Bible study with a group of wives from the church), as would Rose Woods and her sister Dora Ham, Millie Holubec, and Barb Johnson. Carrie would also bring the young intern, Stephen Coleman, who had treated Jenny in the ER. The ladies, aware of Carol Lindquist's reputation for culinary calamities, had volunteered to bring covered dishes, now spread out on the dining room table at the 'Dine' section of the Live 'n' Dine.

The ever-efficient Hal had even created an agenda to ensure they covered the many items they wanted to discuss:

Agenda
1. Overview of new information
   • Carrie Cook and Rose Woods - ER Patient Referrals
   • Jenny Weber and Barb Johnson - Lab call notes, meeting notes, list of test subjects
   • Rod Hatcher and Jerry Peterson - trip to the valley
   • Rod Hatcher - lab test on pipe bomb; flyover and photos
2. What to do about the children? Psychiatric help - when and how.
3. Safe haven for Millie's daughter
4. What to do next?

Carrie introduced Rose to the group, some of whom squirmed uncomfortably in the presence of Rose and her sister Dora. The introductions were formal and stilted, the smiles slightly contrived. It was obvious Penelope wanted to hide her unease at her proximity to the Black ladies and appear to be as relaxed as Carrie, who also introduced Stephen Coleman. Rod remembered him, but Jenny did not. Finally, Jenny introduced Millie.

Rose had asked to bring Georgie, and Carrie had Anna in tow to help watch him. Anna had a surprise for Georgie; after doing some research and a few conversations with the librarian at the local branch, she checked out *Notes of a Native Son* by James Baldwin, and presented it to Georgie with the admonition that he needed to finish it before it was overdue. He was thrilled, and for the rest of the evening, clutched it as tightly as Anna's hand. Carol trotted Stevie out to meet the guests as well, and after brief introductions the three children retired to Stevie's room to entertain themselves, where they cracked the door and sat with their ears strained for any snippets of conversation they could hear.

The evening began with a trip to the buffet, where Carol encouraged everyone to try a glass of something she called Sangria, a popular new wine cocktail made with red wine, fruit juices, various liqueurs, sugar, and ginger ale or carbonated water. When she made the drink, Carol realized there was no ginger ale and substituted Stevie's Dr Pepper. The recipes she found also called for various liqueurs, which she assumed was a fancy French word for liquor, and used an ample measure of Hal's Wild Turkey bourbon. For the crowning touch, she doubled up on the sugar to give the drink her own unique stamp. The result was a gag-inducing assault on the taste buds that brought tears to the eye. Fortunately, there was beer for the men, and the ubiquitous sweet tea to wash down the flavor of the single glass of "Sangria" each lady choked down out of politeness. Hal was painfully aware of Carol's kitchen challenges, and he'd volunteered to fix hamburgers and hot dogs on his new outdoor grill. The other ladies brought the side dishes, green bean casserole, potato salad, Jell-O Salad and baked beans, so the meal was not a total disaster. Carol permitted the children to take a plate with a hot dog and some chips back to Stevie's room, a rare treat for Stevie, who was normally not allowed to take food into his room.

After everyone had finished their meal, Stephen Coleman insisted on helping the women clear the table while the men relaxed, and Carrie spread out the list of ER patient names along with the wrinkled referral documents. The HIPPAA Act did not exist in 1958, so while the ethics of disclosing patient names and addresses may have been questionable, it was not illegal. Carrie figured the real ethical lapse had been the way the hospital administration ignored these referrals.

"We can thank Rose for gathering these referrals for us. They were being pulled from the files and dumped into the trash. You can see here that they tossed Jenny's referral along with the others. When Jenny and Barb go over the listing of test subjects at Alpen Labs, I want to cross-reference them to these. I suspect the two lists will have a number of names in common. The question is, what do we do with them? I asked Stephen to come to weigh in on this, and also to get his advice when we discuss what we should do about the children."

"I can tell you what to do with my referral, let me call the doctor they referred me to. I want my damn referral."

"Is that a smart thing to do, Stephen? Will anything come back on you if Jenny calls the clinic?"

"It is certainly her right. There may be repercussions for those of us from the hospital, including Dr. Smithwick and the filing clerks who dug these out of the trash. We'll have the same exposure for the remaining referrals. Jenny, do you mind holding off a bit? I had a talk with Dr. Smithwick, and he may have a better alternative. We can discuss it when we talk about counseling for the children. He's recently been named head of the ER, by the way. I doubt you were aware of that Carrie, or you, Rose."

"OK, I'll wait to hear what he said. He's certainly in a better position than we are to know the right thing to do, and the last thing I want is to get any of you in trouble."

"Thanks Jenny. Excellent idea Stephen. We'll wait until we've heard his feedback, but I feel strongly that we need to ensure these people receive the proper psychiatric care."

"I agree Carrie. They've been taking, or somehow exposed to, some manner of drug, and from all you told me, I'm afraid your children may have as well, although I don't have a clue as to how."

"We should compare these names with Jenny and Barb's list. I guess you're up Jenny."

Jenny unconsciously rubbed the lump on her forehead as she began. "I think Alpen Labs holds the key to this entire mystery. It started with UT Students and minorities coming in a secret rear entrance. They always show up around lunchtime, in yellow school busses. Twenty to thirty get off and the guards lead them to what has to be a back entrance. I had a bird's-eye view when the explosion blew me on the floor of the chemistry lab. When Hal, Jerry, and I tried to find the back entrance, we were met with armed guards and followed much of the way home. And I think you all heard about Rod's adventure trying to get an aerial view. If we can tie a few names Barb found to the referral list from the ER, we'll have what we need. Barb, why don't you show us what you dug up?"

"I found a great deal; I've been trying to get it organized and make sense out of it. First, I made a list of the test subjects with their names and addresses. Then I have all these call notes. When they make important telephone calls, they take notes and the secretaries type them up. For a company that is so security obsessed, they can be incredibly stupid. After the fire, they called me in to help with clean-up and re-filing. They consider it grunt work, so I'm left alone most of the time. I made copies of things that look the most suspicious. First are the calls to Bergstrom Air Base, most are to a Colonel McIntyre, but a few went to various majors. The notes seem coded and center on test results. Here's a good example:

'Test AL580417f
Subject: Bethany Larson. 19 yrs., female, 5'4", 122 pounds, Caucasian.
Delivery Method: injection.
Formula: AL87. 5 cc's, class I, 5-HT$_{2A}$receptor, V-ergot, 65%; NMDA receptor, Salvia divinorum sourced, 30%, DXM 5%.
Subject reaction.
Initial: euphoria, 78-minute duration, reported as pleasant, visual perception—enhanced, aural sensation—mild, pleasant, flavor—none reported, touch—none reported, olfactory—mildly unpleasant.
Sensory confusion ("tasting" colors, "seeing" sounds, "feeling" images, hearing things.)
Midline: tranquil composure, 34 minutes, devolving into confusion, some minor nausea, mild headache lasting 67 minutes.
Day two: residual confusion and some memory loss.
Subject released: 58/04/18, 17:00.'

I found a couple dozen, in that format, but with different formulas and some interesting subject reactions. They seem focused on the reactions, like they're trying to link the components to specific types of reactions, and also as though they're trying to get consistent results from what they term different delivery methods. Those are injection, oral, waterborne, and airborne. They get excited when they get strong reactions from the airborne method. On those they make notes on formula, dry air density, molar mass, distance from source, humidity, air currents, different criteria to derive something they call formula mix. They end up with things that look like complex algebraic formulas. Then they flag them to be delivered, I assume to Bergstrom. Some go out to UT also, to some Psychology professor. Oh, and guess what else? They're keeping track of which of them end up visiting Carrie and her friends in the ER! You thought those referrals were only going into the trash? Well, somehow they're being reported to the lab."

She stopped to take a deep breath and organize her thoughts. "I also found some notes from their internal meetings, like super-secret board meetings. They track their progress and results in a weekly status meeting. They're documenting something they call Project Mind Warp Metrics—number of tests administered broken down by method of delivery. And one last thing, this may be the most interesting of all." She opened the folder and removed the newspaper clipping of the coed who died from jumping off the tower. "They have several copies, and had several impromptu meetings the morning it came out. They burned up the phone lines with calls to UT and Bergstrom, but didn't make a single note. She was also one of the Alpen Lab subjects and on the list of subjects who visited the ER."

The group sat in stunned silence. Anna had clapped her hand over Stevie's mouth to keep him from squealing. She put a finger to her lips and whispered "shhhhh."

Stephen Coleman broke the extended silence, "I don't understand this code, but they are playing around with hallucinogenic substances. The question is—why? Let me see that list of patients who we treated. Carrie, Rose, look at these with me, do you recognize any or remember them?"

"I'm not sure Stephen, things have been so crazy. Umm, I remember this girl, this one, and this guy. Rose, do you see any?"

"Yes, you're right about the first girl, Sally Jenkins, I sure remember her, she was one of the first I saw, and she was shaking with fear, we had to pump her full of sedatives to calm her down. I think there are maybe a couple others, this boy here. And this, this was an old Negro lady. She was hearing voices, and was trying to reply, shouting nonsense. She didn't receive the same treatment as the little white girl. They just stuck her on a gurney and waited for her to calm down. It took several hours and there was no referral for her. I spoke to her before she left. She said she was getting paid to take part in testing out at some new company, it had to be Alpen Labs. I wish I had asked her how she got involved, she said it was a lot of money, and they put her in a funny smelling room while they asked her questions. But then things got crazy again, and I had to go deal with other patients. By the time I got another break, they had released her. I never made the connection between the test and her symptoms, because they didn't give her any pills or injections. I'll bet that was one of those airborne tests."

Jenny gasped, "Oh my god, Rose, that must be what happened to me in the explosion, I breathed in the gases from an airborne test. That has to be it."

Hal stood, "You're next Rod, let's hear about your flight last week, but first, who needs another drink? I sure do."

Back in "Stevie's Place," Anna and Stevie were arguing in hushed tones, debating whether airborne poisons or drugs could have floated as far as the valley. Stevie was not buying the drug story at all, and while Anna thought it answered everything, she doubted drugs could have blown that far on the wind without affecting everything and everyone in their path. Georgie loyally stuck up for Anna in whatever she said. That kid would have walked off a cliff for her.

Once the group was fortified with fresh beers and sweet tea, Rod launched into an account of their run-in with the gunmen. The discussion around the gunshots was animated. The group offered various opinions, but reached no consensus whether they were the actual target, or if the shots were merely meant as a warning. Rod was certain the range and their exposure were such that a competent gunman could have hit them easily, and surmised that they were only warning shots. In any case, they had certainly worked.

At this point Hal had a surprise for the group, despite the difficulty making it back to the cars, he hung on to a few samples of the dead vegetation, and persuaded a chemist friend at the lab to have them secretly analyzed for traces of known herbicides or similar poisons. Strangely, the results came back negative, in fact, the samples were completely sterile. His friend couldn't explain the result, it was as though all evidence of whatever caused the die-off had been neatly erased.

Rod moved on to the fly-over of the lab. He felt certain that if whoever was flying those helicopters had wanted to do more than chase them away, they would be dead. Regardless, the message delivered from both trips was emphatic—stay the hell away.

"The good news is, thanks to Hal's fancy new camera, I got a whole roll of photos. Abe, did they come back yet?"

"They did, and for an amateur hanging out of an airplane bucking like a rodeo bull, you didn't do a half bad job."

Abe laid them out on the table for everyone to see. He had them blown up into 8x10's, and the 1/500 shutter speed had done a decent job of producing sharp photos with only minor blurring. The extension to the chemical wing was the focal point of a flurry of repair activity to what appeared to be considerable damage. In one picture, the rear door was clearly visible. The road to back was also obvious from the photos; there was no washout or road work going on, only a twisting road with guard shacks and heavy gates about a mile from the building. Hal, Jenny, and Jerry examined the pictures. The extension would have been invisible except from directly behind the building, and the two outer wings had no view of it. The second story extended above it, so it was only visible in those photos taken during the approach to the back.

"Talk about well hidden! If that wall hadn't blown in, we'd never have guessed the extension was there. But what are those?"

"These are from when we flew into the valley, Jen. See how much farther the bulldozing had progressed since our trip? This was only three days later; they must have been busy. But look at this, what's making this shape? It looks like half of a giant circle."

Roughly half the valley floor had been bulldozed clean of any dead vegetation. The other half was still littered with dead plants and trees, but there was something else, the clear arc of a giant half circle. It would not have been obvious on foot, but from above it stood out as though a massive branding iron had seared the land.

They were interrupted when Stevie came charging into the room. "I wanna see, that circle is from the flying saucer, I TOLD you there was a saucer. That must be where it came down. It was big and round like that."

"I'm sorry Mr. and Mrs. Lindquist, he got away from me."

"He's not your responsibility, Anna Belle. Stevie, back to your room, I can assure you this is NOT from a spaceship."

"I wouldn't be so sure of that," mused Jerry, ever willing to believe whatever farfetched stories he heard. In today's world, he'd be certain that wearing a face mask would increase his chances of getting some sort of virus.

"See, he believes me!"

"Back to your room now, Young Man, march! Rod, you did a good job on those photos, I guess Hal's expensive new toy is good for something."

"It was a combination of good instruction, luck, and a skilled pilot. My buddy Stan and I have a new agreement, I'll never ask him to take me up again, and he will never offer. One last thing, I took the piece of pipe Jenny retrieved from the explosion to my captain, and he had it analyzed on the QT. It was a pipe bomb, but not powerful enough to cause that extensive an explosion. Either it set off some other chemicals, or there was more than one bomb. There are enough chemicals around that place for a chain reaction to have been possible. But what's interesting about it was what they found on the outside of the pipe." He fished the scrap of paper Brad Schwartzwald had given him out of his pocket, "There were traces of this stuff on the pipe." He handed the paper to Stephen Coleman, "I won't even try to pronounce it, or what it does."

Coleman examined the paper and whistled, "Psilocybin and ergot, or derivatives of the active chemicals. These are potent hallucinogens that could produce the reactions we've been having in the ER, as well as those your children experienced. In its natural form, psilocybin comes from a variety of mushroom. Shamen from cultures all over the world have used it in religious ceremonies for thousands of years. The other stuff, ergot, comes from a fungus, and in recent years is being used to synthesize lysergic-acid-diethylamide, or LSD, LSD-25 to be precise. It was first discovered by a chemist working for the Sandoz pharmaceutical company in Switzerland."

"Yes," Sophie added, "by a man named Albert Hoffman, I'm familiar with some of his research. You're right, Stephen, these are powerful drugs, nothing to experiment with outside of a carefully controlled environment. But, airborne administration? Aren't they usually administered orally?"

"Yes, but much of the interest and research is comparatively recent. I'm far from an expert on the subject, but I wouldn't have expected to find them together, they have quite different effects, LSD affects perception, and can produce feelings of euphoria, but it is less likely to cause hallucinations. Psilocybin works more slowly, the effect is more introspective, and it's more likely to produce hallucinations. In many ways, they're exact opposites, in others they might complement each other. Used together, I can't guess what might happen."

The obvious concern in her eyes exposed Carrie's façade of clinical detachment. "Can we talk about our little brats now? I don't understand how or why, but those kids are describing, and exhibiting, the same symptoms as the emergency room patients. Stephen, what you told us makes me even more concerned. When can you talk to Dr. Smithwick? Can we can get the kids into counseling without risking our jobs? With an independent psychiatrist? Maybe someone experienced in treating drug addiction?"

"Tomorrow and yes. Yeah. I'm thinking of a lady I met in med school, Dr. Christine Ardbeck, a psychiatrist who specializes in addiction in young people. When I talk with Smithwick, I'll pick his brain, too. He knows Dr. Ardbeck, and may be willing to set up an introduction when he sees the lab results. I realize you're anxious about the children, so I'll make it a priority. How many children are involved?"

Carrie frowned, "There are five, plus Jenny, of course. Is, ah, is she, will she be very expensive?"

"We'll work something out. Given the circumstances, group counseling may be best, and it would help hold the cost down."

"I mean, you know, whatever it takes, but that would help. Are we all onboard with this? Does anyone object?"

"You can count on the Stieglitz gang."

"Hal, we're okay with this aren't we? I think Stevie needs it."

"Okay then, Stephen, see what you and Dr. Smithwick can arrange. You can tell me and I'll coordinate with the others."

Hal stood up, clearly accustomed to being in charge. Jenny shot Carrie a quick glance and raised her eyebrow with a wry smile— *Don't fight it, let the big man think he's in charge.*

Hal proceeded to waste another 20 minutes going over what had already been discussed and assigned tasks. Carol interrupted to ask why they didn't just turn it over to the police.

Rod spoke up. "Carol, I would love to, but Captain Schwartzwald is getting pushback from the highest levels of the fire and police departments. We're afraid that would just make things worse. Schwartzwald has his ear to the ground and the minute he feels confident, we will involve them, but we just can't for now."

The conversation became animated. The parents were focused on getting help for their children; Jenny and Jerry wanted to do more sleuthing. Millie and Penelope were struggling to absorb it all, and in Stevie's room, Anna was furiously scribbling notes.

The evening ended with tasks assigned as Hal had outlined. Before everyone left, the ladies, and Stephen Coleman, who hung a little closer to Carrie than was absolutely necessary, helped Carol with clean-up duties, while the men relaxed, smoked and enjoyed that one last beer for the road. Penelope took Carrie aside and asked if they could talk in the next few days. They made plans to meet at Carrie's house the next week. Everyone exited in that way so many parties end, with multiple goodbyes, last-minute conversations, promises to get together soon, and, in this case, many kind, insincere compliments to Carol on the Sangria— "Oh yes, it was wonderful, you must give me the recipe!"

Anna's Journal
Log entry Friday, July 11, 1958

HOLY FLACK! All the parents know everything now—even Little Betty's crazy mother (She wasn't acting crazy tonight just real quiet. I guess she really is worried about Betty and had all the crazy scared out of her!) I have pages of notes so I can tell the others who weren't at the meeting. I'm so glad they wanted me there to watch Georgie, and glad Stevie's room is right across the hall from the living room at his house. We could hear perfectly! There was a bunch of stuff I didn't understand, like the names of drugs, but that's what libraries are for—right? I didn't realize how much our parents had been doing or what all is involved in this. They said Alpen Labs, The University of Texas (UT—HOOK 'EM!!), the hospital where Mom works and the Air Force. The GWARD DHARMED FLACKIN' AIR FORCE!!! Wow.

    Anna Logging Out. July 11, 1958

    P.S. I think Mom is "sweet" on that Stephen Coleman! He IS a HUNK! They thought I was asleep on the way home, but I'm pretty sure I saw them holding hands! It would be so great if Mom found someone. I think he must be around five years younger than she is, so she is robbing the cradle (ha, ha.) Hey, that's about the same as the difference in my age and Mark's! Hmmmm.

Mark Lindquist didn't make the party that night. He was parked in the back row of the Chief Drive-in with Becky Arndt, where the poodle embroidered on her skirt was watching him dig through the tissue paper stuffed into her bra in a quest to find out what was underneath. That his hand was under her bra didn't bother her nearly so much as his discovering the secret to the impressive contours of her blouse. Her girlfriends considered Mark to be a real catch, and she had miscalculated, wanting to appear as attractive as possible, but thinking that things would move a bit more slowly. She'd spent the better part of an hour getting the effect exactly right. She discovered it worked best if she took off her bra and positioned the tissues carefully before putting it back on, to create the pointed, slightly upturned look so popular in the 50s (a look destined to disappoint many young lads once they discovered how most breasts sag a little and tend to be considerably less pointed.) When Mark's wayward hand at last reached its target, she sniffled, unsure of what to say.

"I, I'm sorry Marky, I just wanted you to like me, I know how boys like big ones."

Mark struggled for words. To buy time, he kissed away the tear that was wending its way down her cheek. It was salty—that was a surprise. Of course, he knew tears were salty, but from a girl— weren't they supposed to be sweet, like sugar and spice?

That additional second or two was enough time for him to think of exactly the wrong thing to say, "Uh, it's okay Baby, really it is. I like small ones."

"YOU THINK THEY'RE SMALL!" She erupted in tears as her fragile ego shattered into tiny tinkling bits. She yanked his hand out of her blouse—he hated her, he thought she was ugly, ugly and flat-chested and fat. He only took her out because he thought she had such big boobs. She let him cop a feel and then he said such mean things. She choked out the words, bawling the entire time.

Mark continued his masterful management of the situation, lifting his shirt to wipe her runny nose, "No Baby, No. I only meant small-ER. Don't cry—for God's sake Becky. Look here, you have snot running all over your face, hold still so I don't pop that pimple."

"YOU THINK I'M AN UGLY OLD PIMPLY OLD FLAT-CHESTED SNOT-FACE!"

And so it went.

These two were not exactly candidates for the HI-Q Gang. After a good half hour of groveling and pleading, Mark was finally successful in stemming the waterworks, and since Becky insisted on re-buttoning her blouse, he suggested they go to The Holiday House on The Trail for a coke and to see who was hanging out there. The Holiday House was a favorite of the local teens, it offered drive-in curb service or inside seating, with a menu featuring "flame-kissed" hamburgers as its specialty. Couples on their way home from dates would pack the place on Friday and Saturday nights.

Mark pulled into the lot, mashed the gas to the floorboard, then let up. Maybellene responded with a resounding backfire. Becky's eyes glowed with pride, he was HER boyfriend, and he was SO COOL! As Mark circled the lot to check out who was there, she basked in the envious stares of those girls with less glamorous boyfriends.

Mark found a parking space and turned the conversation away from Becky's rather average breasts. "So, uh, how long have y'all lived here?"

"Just a few years, my dad is the head of security at Alpen Labs."

"Alpen Labs? My dad works at that place. He's a senior engineer out there. Say, uh, has he maybe said anything about what's going on there?"

"No, he said there had been a fire, and they had to shut down for a while, that was all. He still had to work every day though, and sometimes all weekend."

"What did he say about the fire?"

"Nothing. He got real mad when I asked him about it. He's so mean, Mark. He wasn't always, but he completely changed when he took this new job. I wish my mom would divorce him, but she never will. He's cruel to her, and he's mean to me. He just works all the time. Mom likes it cuz we can have a fancy house in the hills, and she gets to socialize with all these important rich people because he's this hot-shot out at the lab. Wanna know something? I wish he'd burned up in that fire."

"Jeezus—that's terrible. Hey Becky, can you keep a secret? You can never tell anyone else. You know I really like you, don't you? I didn't mean to start a fight tonight, you know I think, I think of you as, you know, my girl."

"Oh Marky, truly? I DO want to be your girl. That makes me so happy. I can keep any secret you want, as long as I'm your only girl and you're my boyfriend. You can tell me anything Marky."

Mark hated being called "Marky," but had just learned the first of a lifelong series of tough lessons regarding the opposite sex, so he put up with it. He told her about the testing at the lab, how her father had turned away the fire department, about the Air Force arriving to extinguish the blaze, how Stevie and his friends suffered hallucinations, what they found when they returned to the valley, and their suspicions about it being associated with the lab.

Becky's eyes grew as she listened. "Marky, you remember how I said my dad has all these important friends? Well, some of them are officers from the Air Force, and some are from UT, and some from the government—senators or something. He's always going to parties or meetings with them. He'll tell Mom that Senator so and so is gonna be there, or Colonel something, or Professor blah blah, and she goes into a tizzy, putting on fancy dresses and jewelry. He makes sure I hear cuz he thinks it impresses me. Real casual, like he didn't really mean for me to hear, but I know he does. Big shots from the lab go too. He always mentions them by their last name, like they're his buddies. He loves it when he can say, 'oh, and Sinclair is going to be there,' Sinclair is the guy who owns the lab, he's supposedly this bigwig, important guy."

"Holy crap. Hey Baby, can you get me a list of some of those names? I know this is asking you to spy on your dad, but it would be real helpful to find out if what we suspect is true."

"I'll do anything for my Marky. The next time we go to the drive-in, maybe I'll show you how much..."

CHAPTER 28
TURNING THE WHEELS

Think about a wheel. Make a mark on it. The mark returns to the same position with each rotation, yet somehow moves forward. So it is, with wheels, clocks, planets, and lives.

~ ~ ~

Saturday morning was quieter in the Brackenridge ER, so Stephen Coleman used the opportunity to meet with Dr. Smithwick in his office. Smithwick was incensed when he heard the referrals were being discarded.

"What the bloody hell are those wankers playing at? You mean to tell me we're sending patients home with no follow-up?"

"Yes sir, Dr. Smithwick. On top of that, one of those patients was the UT coed who jumped off the tower."

"Are you taking the piss out of me? That girl was in here and her referral was shit-binned? What a bloody cock-up! Do you realize the exposure to the hospital for that sort of thing? Thank you for bringing this to my attention, Stephen."

"No problem, Dr. Smithwick, and there's a good deal more."

"Crikey, precisely what I needed on a Saturday morning. And call me George, Mate; you can drop the Dr. Smithwick and the sirs, let's hear the rest of it."

Coleman summarized what he knew, focusing on how to get help for Jenny and the children.

"Let me make some calls, Stephen. This situation sounds bloody serious. Until we're certain what gormless prat is behind this, I'll need to tread carefully. Pop by at the end of shift, and I'll have a name or two to get counseling for those children. Are they exhibiting any physiological symptoms? Or does it all seem to be psychological? I'm happy to examine them on the QT if their parents have any concerns, or I can refer them to a pediatrician."

"They're fine physically. The only one with any kind of injury is the young lady we treated here, Jenny Weber. Thank you, Dr.—uh, George, I'll drop by at three when my shift ends."

"Thank YOU, Stephen. Ta."

Kids' Connivance

Saturday afternoon it was Anna's turn to dry. With only the two of them, lunch clean-up was a snap. She offered to do everything, but Carrie wanted a little rare mother-daughter time, so they were standing together at the sink as Carrie soaped the dishes while Anna rinsed and dried. They had not eaten lunch until almost two, both having slept in since Carrie was once again on the three to midnight shift at the hospital. Carrie was telling Anna that she was hoping the children would be able to "talk with" a counselor next week. That nice Stephen Coleman was looking into it and she was hoping to catch him during shift turnover. She was planning to leave a few minutes early, and, oh my, look at the time, she'd better get a move on.

"I hate leaving you so much, Anna Belle, are you sure you'll be all right? No running off to the woods?"

"I'll be fine, Mom. How about if I make a meatloaf you can heat up when you get home?"

"What did I ever do to deserve a daughter like you?"

"Only just about everything! Working so hard and raising me after Daddy died. I'm the one who's lucky. You go on to work and don't worry about a thing."

Carrie gulped and smiled. Anna had always been told her father died in Korea, and Carrie went by Mrs. Cook. Few of her friends who knew the true story were still around, and in 1947 when Anna was born, there was little sympathy or support for unwed mothers. Still, she felt constant guilt, and was determined to tell Anna the truth when "the time was right." That wretched time never seemed to be right, though.

As Carrie was pulling away, Anna picked up the phone and began calling the other children, and presently the driveway was full of bicycles and one ratty old Studebaker.

As they gathered in the living room, Anna updated them on what was said at Friday night's meeting, checking her notes to ensure she didn't forget anything. They peppered her with questions as she went over what she'd learned.

"We have to see a shrink over at the crazy house?"

"State Hospital, Levi, but yes, Mom called it a counselor, but she was trying to keep from upsetting me. She'll find out who it is tonight—I guess a psychologist or psychiatrist."

"What did my mom say?"

"Nothing bad, she wasn't all religious—she didn't actually talk much at all."

"Honest? She didn't talk about praying away Satan or anything? Something's up with her."

"All that's up is that she's worried about you, Betty. Our parents are real worried, they think we're gonna turn into druggies or something. They don't think what happened to us is real, they think we were exposed to drugs that go through the air."

"The word is airborne," said Stevie, "but drugs couldn't travel through the air all the way from the lab to the woods where we were, and tell 'em about the circle on the ground—that's from the saucer, but none of them would believe it, 'cept for my dad's friend Jerry. I'm sure he believed it."

"There's no gahdamned flying saucer Buttface. Shut up and let Red finish, then I have something to tell."

Anna grinned up at Mark, "Buttface—I like it." She continued telling them everything else she and Stevie overheard. There were several new details—the pictures Rod had taken, the list of experiment subjects and how they matched the ER patients. They argued about whether what happened to them could be from a drug, and how drugs could have traveled so far, then been gone the next time they went to the woods. Anna had done some research at the library about the use of mustard gas in World War I. Most airborne gasses, like mustard gas, could not travel that far, and tended to settle in low areas, so they should have been safe up on the hill. But who knew for sure? Maybe they had figured out a way to send it farther. And maybe their stuff was lighter or something.

None of them believed, not with certainty, that what they experienced was caused by drugs or plants. It felt real, it just felt real.

"OK, you all know better than your parents. A flying saucer full of little green men came down and, what? Turned into all the stuff you claim you saw? A giant, a half-man-half-woman, a red-mist creature, a fairy princess that turns into a witch? Yeah, just because there's a ring on the ground where they're working with bulldozers. So, guess what—I have some news of my own. The girl I'm dating, some of you might know her, Becky Arndt—her father is the head of security at the lab. He's the guy who wouldn't let the fire department put out the fire there. When I was telling her, she told me he and her mother are always hobnobbing with Air Force Officers, UT Professors, all the people who are supposed to be in on this drug project. And also—get this—a bunch of important politicians, like senators and all."

"Are you out of your GWARD DHARM FLACKING MIND? Her daddy is the head of security at the lab and you told her our secrets? Do you have even the tiniest clue how much trouble you could get our folks into? You may have gotten the tall in your family, but you sure as HELL didn't end up with the brains!"

"Whoa, Red. Becky won't tell anybody—she hates her old man. She wishes he had died in the fire. She's making us a list of the people her dad meets with. You'll see." *This one may be a little too hot to handle, but in a few years, she is gonna be FUN!*

Anna scowled at him, her eyes flaring as red as her temper. "You'd better be right. I know a few things about that girl—she's not, ah, shall we say—everything she appears to be. I overheard some high school girls talking about her at the library. Girls who are in her gym class—who see her in the shower. Get my drift?"

Mark got her drift and struggled for something to say, eager to change the subject. "Yeah, well, I guess I know more about her than those girls. You shouldn't believe everything you hear, Red."

Stevie, Betty, and Levi, were totally lost. James was wearing an unsure grin, thinking he might understand, but he was far from certain.

Stevie's falsetto filled the room and may have been responsible for the cracks in several glasses in the kitchen cabinets. "What does the shower have to do with who her daddy meets with?"

Mark flicked Stevie painfully on the ear, triggering an eruption of sound that topped out well above the upper bar in a treble clef. A block away, Mr. and Mrs. Fleabert Muttowski yelped and hid under the bed.

Anna grimaced, subconsciously sympathizing with the Muttowski's, "All right, let's leave it. The question is, what are WE gonna do? Do any of you think getting our heads shrunk is going to make this go away? Do any of you honestly think it's nothing but a bunch of hallucinations?"

Almost as one, four heads slowly shook back and forth. "So, what do we do?"

There was a long pause. When the silence was broken, it was by the last one Anna expected.

"We go back," said Betty firmly, "you know I don't want to; I never wanted to go in the first place, but these dreams aren't going away, and I still feel—something's coming—or maybe it's already here."

"You went back twice, and there was no flying saucer, no little green men, no monsters, or fairies or giants. Nothing but dead plants. What do you think you're gonna find that's any different?"

"We go at night, but when we get to the top, we hang on to each other."

"Like when we crossed the creek," said Levi, "You weren't there Betty, but when we had to wade across the creek, we all linked arms—my Uncle Levi showed us how. That's what we do. Then whatever happens, it happens to all of us, all at once, all the same."

"We are gonna be in so FLACKIN' much trouble! Mark—not a GWARD DHARMED word about this. Not to your mommy or daddy and not to your dopey girlfriend. You can come, and you can bring that Becky girl, but not—a—word."

Mark grinned, somehow the madder she got, the more he liked it. *Hurry the hell up and grow up Red.* "Okay Freckles, I won't tell anyone, except—how can I bring Becky if I don't tell her?"

Stamping her foot now, "You know what I mean. The trouble is—when can we do it? My mom works nights, so it won't be a problem for me, but your parents are watching you like hawks. We're gonna need a HELL of a good story."

Mark smirked, "I think it's about time I took my dear little brother and his nice little friends to a movie at The Trail Drive-in. They only charge a buck a carload, and that new comedy with Andy Griffith, *No Time for Sergeants,* is playing there in a couple weeks—that will make a perfect excuse. Mom and Dad are always on my case to do more with Stevie, so I'll volunteer to take him and his friends to a movie. That way you'll have time to go to the shrink first and come to your senses."

Chapter 29
A Trap Well-Laid

"Keep fighting for freedom and justice ... but don't forget to have fun doin' it. Let your laughter ring forth. Be outrageous. Ridicule the fraidy-cat, rejoice in the oddities that freedom can produce. And when you get through kickin' ass and celebratin' the sheer joy of a good fight, be sure to tell those who come after how much fun it was."
–Molly Ivins, 1944–2007

It doesn't matter much whether your story is on the front page, so long as it's not in the obits or the funnies.

The Two J's meet (Sunday)
Agent J was impatient. Agent J was mad. Agent J was not to be messed with when she was either of those things. When Jerry joined her at The Frisco on Sunday morning, she was ready to get cracking.

"OK, Jerry, here's what we know—Alpen Labs seems to be at the center of this thing, it connects to UT, Bergstrom, Breckenridge Hospital, and possibly that valley. All the people and children in our little group are involved in various ways. We're doing a fair job of following up on the lab and the hospital, and gathering documentation. We have pictures documenting the Air Force involvement, the die-off in the valley and the damages to the lab.

There are two things no one is following up on—UT and Bergstrom. Bergstrom, we shouldn't touch, at least not now. UT though, Rose's sister, Dora, works there. Friday night she mentioned a kind of muckraking independent newspaper called *The Texas Sentinel* published somewhere around the Drag. She said they've been running some articles about the coed who jumped off the tower—who had been a subject at the lab and showed up at the ER. I'll bet the reporter who's running that series would love this information."

"We'll need to be careful; this could blow the whole thing up and there are some scary organizations behind this. We can't give the reporter any of our names. Reporters always claim they keep their sources confidential, but we don't really know who to trust. If the military truly is part of this, they can put extreme pressure on a small publication. How's this, everything by phone, from a different phone booth each time. Send a letter with enough documentation to gain their trust, but no return address, different mail boxes, or at least move it around."

"I like the way your mind works, Agent J2, but maybe I can shortcut all that. Tell you what, I'll drop by the University this afternoon and find out who has the byline on that series of articles. Then I'll call him to start the conversation."

"Are you sure you're ready for this?"

"I'm sick and tired of screwing around. Those assholes at the lab are messing with people's lives—naïve students and people who are poor and desperate. Well, this gal is neither, and this gal is mad. You can beg off if you want, Jerry, I won't think any less of you— give it some thought. You have a family; your job is important to you. I can keep you completely out of it if you prefer. Of course, I won't say a word about the kids. I'm afraid Arndt will guess much of it, but they can't prove anything, and I'll do my damnedest to keep it that way."

"No, I'm still in Jenny. I'll tell you if I get too spooked, but I'm with you on this—I'm tired of being shot at, being threatened and chased off public roads, all of it. I'm familiar with *The Sentinel*, they go after politicians no one else will touch and expose covert corruption. They do solid research and they're fearless. I think this is a fantastic idea."

Millie was not there that morning, nor was the black Buick parked in the lot. Nevertheless, Jenny took a circuitous route to "The Drag," UT students' name for the section of Guadalupe Street that borders the University of Texas campus. At one point she kept circling the same block, all the while checking the rear-view mirror; then continued when she was sure no one was following her.

The section of campus fronted by Guadalupe was lovely in those days, with the Spanish architecture of the administration building superimposed in front of the iconic tower rising behind it, all surrounded by broad grassy malls where venerable old oaks shaded the grounds—oaks with massive trunks, fat from centuries of patient waiting as growth rings were added year-on-year, and the lush canopy of leaves was renewed and expanded, weighing down the spreading branches until they bent to the ground, graceful and serene. On many a fall or spring day you would find professors holding class in the sun-dappled shelter of those welcoming trees, as students lounged in the grass under the streamers of Spanish moss draped from the cathedral of branches arching above. The stuff of dreams was fashioned here for those fortunate enough to attend and endowed with enough imagination to grasp the promise of their visions. Jenny's heart always quickened when she contemplated a return to finish her degree.

Someday...

The Texas Sentinel was sold on street corners in metal boxes for a dime a copy—she picked one up and saw that the latest in the series of articles about the UT coed who committed suicide was headlined under the byline reading Molly Dugger. The article was mostly conjecture, but was a masterwork of insight, and included some interesting background. The girl's name had been Sharon Tisdale, and according to the article, she had been a normal, happy young girl until she volunteered as a test subject in an experiment for one of her Psychology professors. The assignment had been hard for her to pass up; it counted the same as a grade of A on the class mid-term exam and also paid a generous stipend. Initially, she had been bragging about it around her dorm, but had gone quiet after a few weeks. When her roommate asked her about it, Sharon told her she was not allowed to talk about it. The roommate said she had exhibited odd behavior, whimpering in her sleep, and seeming to lose focus, almost as though she were in a trance. She was no longer her cheerful, easy-going self. Still, the suicide was a surprise, as it had been a surprise to learn that Sharon's date had taken her to the Student Health Center one evening, and they had transferred her to the emergency room at Breckenridge Hospital.

After reading the article and perusing a few more dealing with the sordid underbelly of Texas politics, Jenny found the number for the paper on the back page. She crossed the street and climbed the stairs into the Student Union where there were several pay phones. She waited for one in a private area to become available, then dialed the number.

A callow sounding man answered, and when she asked to speak with Molly Dugger, he replied in a voice that still occupied the treble end of the scale, saying, yeah, she was around somewhere, and yelled "Hey Molly, call for you."

She heard footsteps, and a husky female voice said, "You got Molly and it's your dime, lay it on me."

"Hello, Miss Dugger? My name is Jenny Weber, I have some information about the young girl you've been writing about, some real bombshells."

"Don't call me Miss Dugger, name's Molly. Meet me at Dirty's in 10 minutes."

"What's that?" Jenny was taken aback by the directness.

"You don't know Dirty's? It's at 28th and Guadalupe, a local burger joint. Where are you now?"

"I'm calling from the Student Union."

"Okay, you're close by, do you have wheels?"

"Yes, I'm parked nearby."

"Great, head north on Guadalupe, you'll see it on the left, the sign says Martin's Kumback Place. I'm six one, so I'm easy to spot. See you there in about 10 minutes. Bring whatever you have."

~ ~ ~

Molly's large hand engulfed Jenny's in a crushing grip. She wore blue jeans, an untucked men's shirt and low-heeled western boots. Looming over the other customers with her unruly red hair, Molly was an imposing figure, but her smile was as expansive as the Texas prairies her twang invoked. They grabbed a relatively (relatively being a relative term in this case) quiet table among the throng of students downing greasy hamburgers and fries.

"All right—shoot—tell me what you have," she said after ordering a double cheeseburger, fries, and a chocolate shake. Jenny had passed on the fries, and ordered only a single burger and unsweetened tea, blasphemy in this place.

Between juice inducing bites, Jenny told the story from the beginning. Molly scribbled notes on a Big Chief tablet, interrupting to ask details and honing in on those areas she thought warranted follow-up. "This is pure dynamite Jenny, tell me, what made you come to me?"

"A lady in our—I don't know what to call it—group—conspiracy—club? Whatever it is, one of our members, a Negro lady, works at UT cleaning dorms and some other buildings. She was familiar with your paper and had been following your articles, so she suggested I contact you."

"Well God damn me to hell or Waco. So, these papers you mentioned, the referrals from the hospital, the notes from the secretary at the lab, may I see them? Or have copies?"

"Can you take the documents and make copies so we can have them back? I'm out on a limb here Molly, these people are powerful and ruthless. I'm afraid I have to ask you to keep our names strictly confidential. Otherwise, I'll deny every word if anyone asks."

Molly's blue eyes burned into hers, "You can absolutely count on my discretion—I always protect my sources and will go to jail on their behalf; already have on more than one occasion. All we have at *The Sentinel* is our integrity; without it, we're just another grocery store gossip rag."

"Well Dora certainly speaks highly of your paper and its reporting. She said you wrote some scathing articles about the redlining of Negro neighborhoods in Austin and the ongoing impact of Jim Crow laws on the lives of Austin Negroes. For somebody who cleans dorms for a living, that lady is pretty damn smart."

"I took a crapload of heat for those articles! One of the Austin city councilmen tried to sue me for slander. I said, 'Come on big boy, I got $63.50 in my bank account, a half bottle of Jack Daniels in the cupboard and a First Amendment right.' When I published the research I did for those articles, he backed off in a hurry."

Jenny couldn't suppress a laugh, Dugger's humor was infectious. "And obviously more of what some of my friends call 'testicular fortitude' than he'll ever dream of having. Those good ol' boys can't stand it when a member of the 'weaker sex' puts them in their place. I have a feeling we're going to be great friends, Molly."

With tears of laughter in her eyes, she laid out the documents, pointing out her own referral paper from the ER.

Molly stared across the small table with narrowed eyes, "Remember Jenny, lettin' the cat outta the bag is a whole lot easier than puttin' it back in. Do I run with this?"

Jenny inhaled, her heart pounding, "Go for it Molly, just keep me in the loop and let me know what you come up with. Let's blow the lid off this mess!"

Who's Shrinking Whom?

"The dirty little secret of both clinical psychology and biological psychiatry is that they have completely given up on the notion of cure."
–Martin Seligman

We can only understand that which we are first willing to believe.

Carol Lindquist had volunteered to drop the children at Dr. Christine Ardbeck's office and pick them up after the two-hour session.

Dr. Ardbeck had firmly rejected the idea of letting the parents attend, as their presence would inhibit the children. If she felt individual sessions were in order for any of the children, she would make that determination and schedule those individually with the parents. This introductory session would be longer than the standard 50-minute visits for individuals. After talking to Dr. Smithwick, she had been horrified at the hospital's actions and agreed to do the sessions in secret and on a pro bono basis. She would see Jenny separately.

As usual, Carol Lindquist was running behind—her hair was frizzed out and needed a good combing, she had buttoned her blouse into the wrong holes, and her slip hung below the hem of her dress; the haphazard smear of lipstick she'd hastily applied missed its mark in places and her coke-bottle glasses hung crookedly across her nose. While working in her "art studio," actually a corner of the master bedroom, she had forgotten the time as she had been painting away on her latest paint by numbers magnum opus. Her masterworks hung throughout the house, testament to the fact that she <u>could</u> follow simple directions, a truth not in evidence in her culinary endeavors. As she pulled into Anna's drive, she was pounding on the horn button of her black 1950 Hudson Hornet, sending a series of bleating honks into the summer morning calm.

Anna was ready, she was wearing the green dress her mother had insisted on laying out for her, and her braids were secured with the green bows Carrie had substituted for the rubber bands Anna preferred. She donned the same worn sneakers she wore with blue jean shorts and T-shirts every other day—Carrie had neglected to give her any instructions regarding footwear, and she was out the door before Carrie had the chance to say anything about them. The forest green outfit was the perfect color to complement her red hair and light, freckled complexion, so she looked unusually pretty, despite all her best efforts to the contrary.

Dr. Ardbeck had established her private practice in a small, slightly shabby office on the south end of The Trail, so Carol aimed the old Hudson down The Trail and proceeded to treat the speed limit signs and stop lights as mere suggestions. This lily-white area of town was only sporadically patrolled, so she completed the journey without being stopped, and jounced into the parking lot on the stroke of 10.

Dr. Ardbeck herself greeted the group as they entered the tiny reception area. The office building was an old farmhouse she had remodeled. Her office was in what had been the larger of two bedrooms, and she held group therapy sessions like this in the old living room. Her chair faced a couch, two smaller chairs, and a beanbag chair arranged in a half-circle. Betty seated herself on the side of the couch closest to the bean bag where Levi had flopped down. Anna sprawled on the opposite end in distinctly unladylike fashion, while James and Stevie sat self-consciously in the remaining chairs.

~ ~ ~

Tuesday July fifteen, 1958
Dear Diary,

 Today we all went to the psychiatrist <- looked it up. Her name is Dr. Ardbeck and she was real nice. She promised us she wouldn't tell our parents about anything we said without our permission. Mommy knows I went but not Daddy he would be mad. So anyways first she asked us how we were feeling, like dizzy or headaches or trouble seeing or hearing or sick or anything. We all said no, only nightmares and real tired sometimes and loosing time what she called "episodes". Then she asked how we felt emotionally <- also looked up. We all said still scared. James said mad sometimes, but mostly scared. She said it's ok to be scared, some things scare her too but I don't think she was ever scared like we were.

 Then she had us tell our stories and that took most of the time even though we tried to go fast. When we were done Anna said "well, do you believe us" and she said "I believe you believe what you're saying". Then she said we should come twice a week for a while, but she has to ask our parents. And she said it might help to talk about how we are feeling.

She said it can be to our parents or to each other or in a diary like YOU Dear Diary. She said also write it down then the next day read it and see if you still think it is right. And write every day. She said we can bring what we wrote to our sessions if we want to but we don't have to. I don't think I will.

We didn't tell her about our plans to go back again at night. That scares me but I think we have to do it. More like I KNOW we have to do it. I don't know how I know but I do.

So anyways I'm still scared all the time. I still have bad nightmares where I see the Fairywitch (what I will call her.) And I still loose time sometimes during the day. The others said they loose time too. Dr. Ardbeck calls them "episodes" but loosing time seems like the right word to me. Tomorrow I'll tell you if what I wrote is still right.

Good night Dear Diary,

Betty

~ ~ ~

Anna's Journal

Log entry, Tuesday, July 15th

I'm officially sick and tired of telling our stories to grownups.

We had to go talk to the counselor today after the car ride from HELL. I had to wear a dress with petticoats and everything and it wasn't even school. ICK! The psychiatrist was nice and all, but after we told our stories I asked her if she believed us and she said she believed WE believed what we were saying. So – NO!!! She's just like all the other grownups, she wants it to be some drug that magically flies through the air. So how did it get from the lab to those woods? Why did we all see different stuff? Why wasn't it there in daytime? What happened to all the trees? It's a mystery and I'm not Nancy DAMN Drew.

So anyway we're supposed to write down how we're feeling. Here goes.

I'm scared, ok? Still scared. Still having nightmares and all. Still losing time. And writing this down didn't make me feel any DAMN better.

So what happened to us, what we saw, what I saw, it was almost like something got inside our minds and exploited our greatest fears. My dreams are so wrong, it's like I can't decide whether I like girls or boys or both. That's so wrong. I don't THINK I'm homosexual, but I keep seeing Betty naked in my dreams and then I wake up and I'm - you know. But I also see James and Mark naked, except with girl parts. Maybe I just don't know enough about what boy parts look like to dream about them. I kinda know, but I've never actually seen any, you know, of their THINGS. (Penis Anna, say the damn word, you've never seen a flackin' PENIS!!) But the WRONG THING, it's like a mix of boy and girl but so ugly and WRONG - that's the only word for it. Like distorted or something. I'm so confused. I can talk to Mom about a lot, but not this. Never this.

We have to go back at night. We all know it. Knowing we know is making me even more scared. I just want to get it over with.

Anna out.

~ ~ ~

James Hatcher—my notes, second session—July 17

1. I'm still scared. I can forget for a little while if I'm playing or watching T V or reading but then it comes back.

2. I still get mad for no reason. I hate it.

3. Sometimes I forget where I am or how I got there.

4. I still have really bad dreams. It's like it happens all over again. I hate going to sleep but I keep falling asleep really early and sleeping really long. That makes it worse.

We had the second session with Dr. Ardbeck today. I don't think they help and I don't think writing this stuff down helps. Being with my friends is the only thing that helps because they understand. Everyone else thinks we're imagining things. Well, we're not.

P.S. So when Anna sat down she just kinda flopped and her dress and petticoats flew up, just for a second, but anyway, she wears white panties, or she did today (but not the see through kind.) I got a boner anyway. These days I get a boner even thinking about getting a boner. I hate it.

~ ~ ~

Levi's Journal Entries—July 22
We had psychiatric session number 3 yesterday. These are my notes for next time.
Here is how I am feeling today.

Once Uncle Abe told me about Dachau and how it made him feel when he was taken there and went through the gate. These words over the gate said "Arbeit macht frei." It means work makes you free. But he said when you went through that gate and saw those words it just made you give up. He thought it was like in a story called The Divine Comedy where there are these gates to hell. Over them it said "Abandon hope all ye who enter here." He told me that's how it made him feel. Uncle Abe was lucky, the war was almost over and he was rescued (but his parents were old and they died.) It's where he met Aunt Sophie and she says the same thing about it.

Well that's how I feel. I feel scared all the time. At first I thought I'd just get over it, but that golem thing doesn't go away. I have nightmares where I see it and I'm not stupid, I know I'm short and it's huge so that's how I feel about everything only worse. I hope it IS just drugs (but I don't really believe it is) and it will wear off (but I don't think it will.) Writing down how I feel and going to these sessions is not making me feel any better either.

I think I have abandoned hope.

~ ~ ~

Stevie Lindquist, July 24
How I feel.
How I feel is scared. I wanted to talk to the space men but it hurt when they tried to talk to me because it was too loud. And the noise is not loud

now but it never really goes away. Like they keep trying to talk to me but if I try to listen it never makes words I can understand. It's just this noise in my head. I'm always scared it will get worse. Writing how I feel makes it worse. Talking about it to Dr. Ardbeck makes it worse. I hear it when I sleep. I have black outs. It only helps to be with my friends. I wish there was a pill I could take to make it go away.

Nightwalk

Everyone says to face your fears. Have you ever considered that you might not like what you see?

Carol thought it was sweet of Mark to take Stevie and his friends to the drive-in movie. He was always so mean to Stevie. She guessed it was just the way boys were, but it frustrated her that she could no longer control Mark. Once he hit 14, his obstinate brattiness turned into arrogance and outright defiance. Hal could control him sometimes, but mostly didn't bother to make the effort. She rationalized that it was part of growing up—perhaps this was a new phase where he would act more adult and be kinder to Stevie. She hummed around the kitchen, making sandwiches for the children. She made Stevie's favorite: peanut butter, honey, and banana slices on white bread with the crust cut off. Mark got bologna slathered with mayonnaise, and she made extras for the other children, throwing in a few pickle and cheese sandwiches like the ones she saw in *Good Housekeeping*. Only she didn't have any bread and butter pickles, so she cut some dill pickles in half. Nor did she have any cheese slices, so she used some Cheez Whiz she found in the pantry. With her thick glasses covered in paint smudges, she hadn't noticed the green spots on the cheese, and troweled it on so the children would have plenty, then added a thick layer of mayonnaise for good measure. She threw in a big bag of long forgotten potato chips from the dark recesses of the pantry, then packed these treats in a picnic basket with some paper towels. But it seemed like she had forgotten something, what? Oh, she knew, popcorn! She rummaged around but couldn't find any popcorn, so she grabbed a couple cans of creamed corn from the pantry near the Cheez Whiz, put it in a pan with some butter and cranked up the burner. As she waited for it to pop, she began singing "Blue Moon," imagining herself in a smoky nightclub, wearing a slinky, low-cut dress slit high up the sides, lounging on top of the piano, and singing in a sultry voice to an adoring crowd. As she came back for the third encore, she smelled something rather odd. She blinked to clear her eyes and noticed a column of black smoke pouring from under the cover on the pan of corn, as the liquids boiled dry and scorched, while the corn itself burned down to little black nuggets. She quickly turned off the fire and yanked the pan off the burner. Oh well, she would give the boys some money for popcorn at the movies, and she would add a little fresh butter to this corn, then she and Hal could eat it with their dinner.

At 7:20, Mark emerged from the bathroom after completing a 45-minute shower, shaving some imaginary whiskers, rubbing his underarms with cream deodorant and splashing Old Spice all over his face, torso and between his legs. Stevie was dancing around desperately in the hall. Once Mark came out, Stevie ran in, yanked down his pants and sprayed pee everywhere except the designated target area. Dressing went more smoothly; soon they both finished getting ready and headed out.

The first stop (after dumping the contents of the picnic basket into a garbage bin) was to pick up Becky at her house up on Balcones Overlook. This route made no logistical sense, but Stevie's bratty friends could wait. He had relegated Stevie to the back seat, so Becky had plenty of room, but she slid across to sit next to Mark, and rested her left hand casually between his thighs.

The drive then became a carefully choreographed sequence—put his arm around Becky, remove it to shift gears, put it back around her shoulders, remove it the next time he needed to shift—and so on. He headed up Koenig Lane to Bentwood Acres where he picked up Anna and James, telling them to climb in the back with Stevie. Since Levi and Betty both lived on the west side of the Trail, he picked them up last and, being the smallest, ordered them to sit in front. Nonetheless, accommodations in the front seat were constricted. This delighted Betty, who got in last and squeezed up against Levi. Noting Becky's example, she guilelessly stuck her hand between Levi's legs, causing him to freeze in horror and remain that way until they reached their destination.

By the time they pulled up at the trail into the woods, the sun's rays were slanted and flecked thick with gold. The days were getting slightly shorter now, but sundown still didn't start until around 8:30. This was a relief to the children as they scrambled out. Mark's slower exit involved some surreptitious rearrangement of his crotch.

The shadows stretched long, and a chorus of cicadas trilled rapidly, testament to the heat of the July night. Mark led the way, holding Becky close beside him.

"We need to stay close, let's hold hands," said Anna, taking James' hand in her left and Stevie's in her right. Betty happily grabbed Levi's hand. He had not quite recovered from the trauma of the ride over, but reluctantly allowed Betty to hold his hand. She sure could squeeze hard for such a little girl. He gazed longingly at how Anna had interlaced her fingers with James', but, ironically, James did not seem especially thrilled with the arrangement, as he directed several wistful glances in Betty and Levi's direction.

The walk was uneventful, without the time distortion or confusion of their first trip. As night fell, the branches overhead took on a slightly ethereal aspect, but the waxing moon provided some illumination, rendering the branches less frightening and unfamiliar than they had been on the first trip. The sounds and smells drifting through the humid breeze were normal, though with a definite overtone of Old Spice. When they came to the Shoal Creek tributary, the flow had returned to normal, as it burbled across their path, narrow, and only a few inches deep.

Heading up the last hill, they heard a muted humming, similar to what they'd experienced on their first trip, but not as loud. "Do y'all hear something?" said Becky, and five heads nodded as one, Mark simply grunted.

When they approached the summit, Anna said, "Link arms now, like I showed you. Mark, you and Becky take the ends—go Mark, Stevie, then me, Levi, James, Betty and then Becky on the end. Then we go up together."

No one argued. Mark muttered something about Red being the boss, but lined up as she instructed and led the way to the top, where the flat, broad hilltop provided an expansive view of the valley. In the moonlight, they could see part of the way into the valley, but the bottom was obscured in shadow and a dull gray mist. As they watched, the mist began to take on luminescence. It crept higher, sending smokey tendrils up the sides of the valley as it rose. An irrational fear consumed the small group, purging the oxygen from their breath and rendering them immobile. The humming took on a metallic quality, rising and falling, with the mist pulsating in time, as memories of the first trip came trickling back. Not yet a flood; a few nagging images playing around the periphery of their perception—remembered sounds blended with the rhythmic hum, and a sour stench intermingled with the sweetness of the night air. To Mark and Becky, it was the frigid touch of existential dread from something unseen, but they all stood motionless as the mist continued its inexorable journey up the valley walls.

Anna was desperately fighting a slow surge of fear that threatened to consume her consciousness, pushing back with her mind, struggling for the strength to resist. Something was flowing through her, as if the linking of their arms was serving as a conduit for their thoughts and fears. She felt dread, anger, and confusion. Images of the Wrong Thing flickered through her mind. With effort, she found her voice, "Fight it, fight it together, we can do it if we all concentrate together. Focus your thoughts on beating it back."

The moon had crested the distant hills and hung there, bloated and glowing, swollen by the layers of atmosphere filtering its shimmering, gold-orange luminosity. Anna stared up into its face like a wild thing, her eyes reflecting the moon's radiance as their natural crimson undertones blazed scarlet and inflamed. Then she turned her gaze back down. She could feel an electric current of strength coursing into her through her linked arms and out from her eyes, as though she was projecting all their energy onto that profane grayness. The others followed her example. Stevie's mouth opened into a pink ring, with a piercing, wraithlike wail shattering the silence of the night. Levi's eyes focused into hellish black flames. James wore an angry sneer beneath narrowed eyes, and Betty—Betty's face contorted into blasphemous madness, as she directed her anger and confusion down into the smokey mist.

There was a sudden tortured noise, like metal on metal, the sound of a junked car in a crusher, followed by a reverberating crash. The mist vanished, blown out like a candle, and the valley floor was no longer obscured. It was visible now, plowed smooth of any remaining dead vegetation, with a large ring-shaped depression around the perimeter showing clearly in the moonlight. Anna felt her feet hit the ground hard, and she almost fell. It was as though the group had risen into the air and fallen back. They panted, trying to suck in enough oxygen from the humid air to overcome their exhaustion. Anna realized she had been suffering a splitting headache that was finally dissipating.

They looked at one another for a moment before reacting. Mark turned to Stevie and lifted him up in a hug, "I'll never doubt you again, Twerp." Then he put Stevie down and wrapped his arms around an astonished Anna and spun her around, "And you— you're something else, Red."

"Th, thanks? Now can we get the HELL out of here?"

Walking back, they continued to hold hands and whispered, as though they might be overheard. They had all felt it. Sensed that— power. Becky was crying into Mark's shoulder, still shaking with fright. Betty squeezed Levi's hand harder than ever, but now he welcomed the human contact.

They all did.

~ ~ ~

Friday, July 25th
Dear Diary,
Well we went back there tonight. But we all linked up by holding elbows like in Red Rover and it worked. At first I was so scared, I could see that fog stuff but then Anna said to fight. Like with our minds to think hard at it. So I did. We all did and it was like we could all feel each other thinking or something. Anyhow it worked and the stuff went away—poof! And there was a noise like metal scraping and a crash. Then it was just the valley floor again. And Anna said we fell down, but I think we were just up on our toes, like in ballet when we are en pointe. Dear Diary, tonight we, won I guess. But it doesn't feel like it's over—we all said that. We're gonna talk about it more next week.

And Dear Diary, I got to hold hands with Levi ALL NIGHT!!!! I love him so much (not Like— LOVE)!!! I wish he loved me back. On the way home though he kept holding my hand even in the car, especially when I tried to do like Becky, so maybe he likes me a little. Or maybe he was just scared. I don't know but it was so <u>wonderful</u>.

Good Night, I'm real tired,

MRS. LEVI STIEGLITZ!!!! BETTY LOU STIEGLITZ!!!

~ ~ ~

Anna's Journal
Log Entry—Friday, July 25, 1958

We did it. We went back and we triumphed over whatever the HELL it is. At least I think we did, but only for now. I think it means if we stick together maybe we can figure out what is going on and keep it from hurting us. It was like we were able to combine our resistance or something.

Mark picked me up and swung me around and hugged me! He is really cute (MEGA-cute!) but <u>WAY</u> too old for me and also kinda dumb. And anyway, it didn't mean anything, he was just happy I got everyone to stop it from coming and besides, his stupid slut girlfriend was climbing all over him all night, she calls him Marky—yuck. But it sure was F—U—N! And at least now he believes us.

But we don't know what to do next. We will talk more about it Monday.

Anna out.

~ ~ ~

That night, the children slept peacefully for the first time since their initial trip to the forest. As Morpheus overtook them, they were visited with bizarre, yet comforting, dreams.

Anna stood in a shining room with a round platform in the middle. On it sat a gleaming object made of polished brass—it looked a little like an orrery, one of those solar system models, with a central shaft from which rotating bars hold globes representing the planets. Except in her dream the globes floated without restraint, having no apparent attachment to the center shaft, which itself terminated in a radiant crystalline sphere at the top. At first the room was tilting, causing her to fight for equilibrium. Anna began manipulating the movement of the orrery with her mind, taking control, causing the globes to spin faster and slower, to change direction and plane of orbit. The room moved as she did this, canting left or right, up or down, and at one point, rotating in giddy gyration, as she slowly brought it into balance. The dream wasn't frightening, it was soothing and gave her an enigmatic sense of power. She awoke feeling rested, with her hands tucked up under her pillow, and without the nagging sense of disquiet that had been clouding her every waking moment.

In Stevie's dream, he was floating in an endless sea, rocking with gentle undulations. The sky was the same color blue as the sea; it was impossible to make out the horizon, and there was, blessedly, total silence. He awoke early, with a welcome sense of relief, and went for hours at a time without hearing those distressing voices.

Levi stood in a translucent place, high above the earth. The ebony void surrounding him was teeming with stars and planets. When he looked down, he saw the earth suspended far below him among the cosmos—an effervescent bubble glazed with the cobalt, viridian, and turquoise of its oceans, the jade hues of its forests, and the beige, sienna, and russet tones of its plains and deserts—an opalescent gem set against black infinity. He was as a god looking down on all of creation and within it, saw the insignificance of our tiny world and of humankind itself.

James was reclining serenely, dreaming in his dream, at rest, free of the crimson rage that so often crept in, unannounced, with padded footsteps. His awakening was untroubled; his penis lay flaccid and untouched.

Little Betty was staring into a mirror. She watched as the ravages of age crept across her reflection, but each new line, each sagging bit of flesh or sallowing of skin tone brought with it a sense of contentment, and appreciation for a different form of beauty. With that perception, her insecurities waned, replaced by an embryonic embrace of life's measured unfolding.

~ ~ ~

Anna's Journal
Log Entry, Saturday, July 26th
So, I've been thinking about this a lot. First I had that really weird dream. I don't understand any of it except it made me be less afraid. I felt more normal today, whatever normal means. I was actually rested when I woke up this morning and my hands were where they were SUPPOSED to be!

I feel other things too though. I <u>know</u> I have to be the one in charge. I guess I already am, kinda, but now I feel a kind of responsibility. I'm not sure I like that much. I mean, I don't even know what I'm responsible FOR. Something is out there in that DAMN valley and I know it isn't gonna go away and I know it's bad (we all do.) When we met today we all said we have to do something—we just don't know what something is. But for now (and only for now I bet) things are better.

End Log Entry - July 26th

~ ~ ~

Saturday, July 26th
Dear Diary,
It's better now. Last night I had a different kind of dream, like it's ok to get old and how old isn't ugly, it's just a different kind of beautiful. Like when

you get wrinkled and all you EARNED those wrinkles and you should be proud of them. And it's normal and natural and not to be afraid. But Dear Diary, I AM still afraid. Somehow I know this won't last, but at least it's better for now. I haven't lost any time since we went back so that's good. I don't know what we'll do now, I need to talk to Anna about it but I know there's still something we need to do. Whatever was there the other night proved there's something there and it isn't gone. We beat it one time but I don't think we made it go away. Anyways our parents are off our backs now. We've convinced them that Dr. Ardbeck has cured us, so they aren't so worried anymore.

We talked about it this afternoon and two things. We all slept better with no nightmares and felt better. BUT like me, everybody doesn't think it's over but we don't know what to do. Anna said we all know we have to go back to that (bad word) valley and do something. We will have to figure that out.

Mrs. Levi Stieglitz (SOMEDAY!)

CHAPTER 30
STIR CAREFULLY

"Only the spoon knows what is stirring in the pot."
–Sicilian Proverb

When Hal rolled up to the gate at the lab Monday morning, the guard made no pretense of not recognizing him, but waved him in with a curt "Good morning, Mr. Lindquist, have a nice day." The last two words hung in the air, an ominous warning that this day might be anything but nice. By lunchtime, however, nothing untoward had happened. When Hal and Jerry huddled over some blueprints around 10:00 a.m. they had whispered furtively, but neither had noticed anything. Lunchtime found Hal scarfing down a double order of lasagna. For breakfast that morning, Carol discovered an old quart of milk, now sour and full of lumps, hidden behind the leftovers stacked in the fridge. Funny how there were always so many leftovers. It was a running joke for their housekeeper, Esmeralda Lopez, to ask, "Mrs. Lindquist, do you want me to throw this away, or wrap it up and throw it away later?"

The soured milk gave Carol an inspiration, she would make those sour dough pancakes she read about in *Good Housekeeping*. The milk was good and sour, so that should work perfectly. The article had mentioned that adding some fruit to the batter would make for a special treat. She dug through the pantry and found an old package of raisins and a jar of dried prunes which she added, humming away happily at the thought of the creative breakfast she would serve her family. Seeing (and smelling) the rancid, half-cooked pancakes, Hal suddenly remembered an early meeting, and told Carol to wrap up a couple for him to eat on the way to work. He did that frequently. Carol wished he had more time to eat breakfast with her, but she understood—he had a very important job after all.

At lunch Hal was scraping up the last of his lasagna when a small brown envelope landed next to his plate. He looked up to see a clearly nervous Barb hurrying away. He slid his plate on top of it and otherwise left it untouched until they got up to leave, when he covered it with a napkin, pretended to wipe his chin and slid it furtively into his coat pocket. Jerry rolled his eyes at the clumsy effort, but said nothing. Leaving the lunchroom, they saw Jenny walking out, she glanced back at them and wiggled a similar envelope she was holding.

Back in the lab, they found a private corner. "Do you think this is my pink slip?"

"Naw, they'd call you in and Barbara wouldn't be delivering it. Open it and end the suspense."

Hal opened the envelope quickly, it held only a small slip of paper with "o D 3 : S 5" written on it in shaky hand. "What the hell does that mean?"

"Looks like a code or cipher," said Jerry, slipping smoothly into amateur detective mode. He began transcribing the characters in different sequences and muttering to himself. He separated the numbers from the letters and frowned at the colon. Then he smiled—5:30, this designates a time. DS or SD? "

"SD—Stieglitz Drugs," said Hal triumphantly. "She wrote everything backwards—she wants us to meet her at Stieglitz Drugs at 5:30."

"Brilliant deduction, Sherlock. I guess it couldn't hurt to go there and see. Looks like Jenny is back and got one too. Barb must have some new information."

Stieglitz Drugs was crowded with teens huddled together in the booths, where the plaintive strains of the Everly Brothers harmonizing to "Bye Bye Love" competed with the sounds of laughter and raucous conversations. When Hal and Jerry walked in, Abe jerked his head toward the back where Sophie stood behind the pharmacy counter. She opened a side door and led them to a small back office where they found Barb and Jenny standing beside the small desk Sophie used for her bookkeeping. "I'd best keep an eye on those hooligans so Abe doesn't let them tear the place down, but give us an update before you leave."

"Thanks Sophie," Jenny said, "we're afraid to keep meeting at The Frisco. We'll let y'all know what Barb has to report."

Barb had come with another small file containing a sheath of papers. "Someone at the lab has been changing out files. They're trashing the files on the test subjects and replacing them with these, the names are all different, and they indicate the subjects were here to do taste tests on different vegetables and processed foods. Completely innocuous, no mention of drug reactions or chemicals like in the original files. I only had time to copy a few, and frankly, I'm freaking out—this has to be the last, I'm terrified of getting caught. I tried to look up these people and most of them don't exist, at least not in the Austin phone directory. I found a few, but they were common names, Joan Smith, Roger Brown, and one or two others."

Jenny's lips pulled back in a tight grimace, "Barb, do you realize what this means? It's proof they're covering up the drug testing." She took a deep breath, "I have to tell y'all something. A couple weeks ago I met with a reporter for *The Texas Sentinel*, a lady by the name of Molly Dugger. *The Sentinel* is a small paper published down by the University—they do what's called 'muckraking,' going after sensitive stories the mainstream papers won't touch. They've exposed all kinds of dirt on the Texas Legislature and brought down some big-name crooks—politicians and lobbyists. They have a reputation for honesty and integrity. I researched them before I called Molly, and I was impressed. I didn't give her anything, I only let her look, told her the basics of the story, and let her take notes. She's going to follow up on the leads; given the things she's published in the past I'd say she's a hell of an investigative journalist. You should read some of her articles, they can be biting and to the point, but she does it with a sense of humor that leaves you laughing so hard tears run down your face. I think this information is further proof we aren't making this up. With your permission, since y'all are the most vulnerable, I'll give her this and everything else to copy so she can finish her research and publish an article. Oh, I forgot the most important thing—she will not give any of us up, absolutely no names. She told me she'd go to jail before she'd give up her sources—she's done it before, spent a month in the slammer when she exposed Cal Rafer for taking bribes to approve that obscene development in Dallas. So, what do you say? Can I go ahead?"

"You know I'm in," said Jerry.

Barb drew in a lungful of air, "I'll be frank, I'm worried, but what they've been doing is despicable, those poor students, especially the little girl who jumped off the tower. All right, I say go for it, quick, before I change my mind."

Hal looked at the others. He had been about to say "no," but when Barb mentioned the girl who had committed suicide, he thought about the grainy picture he'd seen in the paper, what now seemed like years ago. "Oh, what the hell, what can they prove? If they fire me, or any of us, I say we sue the pants off them. Go for it, Jenny."

"I'll check with Carrie first, and Rose, since the hospital seems deeply involved, but I have a hunch they'll go along after having to deal with those patients first hand."

~ ~ ~

Carrie and Rose quickly approved the idea of Jenny turning over their evidence to Molly and letting the article go forward. In fact, Carrie praised Jenny for her initiative. Rose was acquainted with *The Sentinel*, and after reading a few of Molly's exposes, Carrie called back to say how impressed she was with the quality of the reporting, especially for a "mere" woman.

~ ~ ~

"They call it 'Dirty's, because when it opened in 1926, it actually had dirt floors. I still can't believe you'd never heard of it, it's legendary at UT, right up there with Schultz's. You DO know Schultz's, right?"

"Oh yeah, I celebrated my twenty-first birthday there. In my youthful innocence I made the mistake of eating an order of their enchiladas, washed down with more beers than I could count, all of which came back up in spectacular fashion the next morning, along with a skull-crusher of a hangover."

Molly laughed, "Okay Jen, let's see what you brung me and I'll give you the rundown on what I found out."

Jenny laid out the the new files that replaced the old ones, and pointed out how Barb had cross-referenced a few.

Molly smiled, "A few should be enough; the important thing is to have evidence they're being changed out, and this is perfect—we can show the original right next to the modified version. So, you say I can take all these files with me?"

"Yes, and you already have the others. You can take them and copy them or keep them until you publish, but we would like to ᵊm back eventually."

roblem, Jen, we'll make copies of everything and return let me tell you what I found out."

Molly had ordered a new menu item, a chicken fried steak sandwich that hung well out of the bun, along with a family-sized basket of fried onion rings. Even though it was barely noon, two Lone Star "Long Necks," sat in front of her, with melting ice sending rivulets of water down their sides. Jenny ordered a "Sissy Burger" and unsweetened ice tea, but this time broke down and included a side of crispy fries that glistened with hot grease.

In between crunchy bites of her sandwich and slugs of beer, Molly summarized her findings. Each bite produced a deluge of juice and mayonnaise that she wiped at as she spoke, making it a little difficult for Jenny to concentrate on what she was saying. She'd interviewed, or attempted to interview, almost everyone involved. No one at Bergstrom would talk, they called the story "absurd," and assured Molly none of their aircraft had anything to do with extinguishing the fire at Alpen Labs, nor had any helicopters been dispatched there on any other occasion. When she called Alpen Labs, she was given the run-around with an obviously concocted story of how the testing was taste-testing of processed food products and had nothing to do with drugs. The fire was due to an employee who violated the no-smoking policy. It was quickly extinguished with on-site fire extinguishers, and that was why the fire department was not needed. The hospital's response was equally farfetched, just nonsense about student hi-jinks, and as for the minorities, "Well, you know what THOSE people are like." The reply from Bergstrom was curt, a categorical denial, as was the one from UT. The students themselves were much less reticent and provided a number of details about their experiences, but had disturbing lapses in memory. The minorities were afraid to respond, having been forced to sign what would be a non-disclosure agreement today.

When they'd finished eating, Molly gathered up the papers, and ordered a couple more Lone Stars in a paper bag "for the road." before fixing Jenny with a searching blue-eyed gaze and asking last time if she had permission to publish the information.

"Miss Dugger, I'll come looking for you if you don't. Please be sure to stay in touch with me. When do you think you'll publish the article?"

Molly smiled conspiratorially, "Okay, but keep this under yer Stetson. We're doing this as a special edition—only this story, nothing else. Look for it next Monday, it will be a push, all-hands-on-deck this weekend, but we hope to have it on the stands then, August 4th. And hang on, we think this will be the biggest expose ' we've ever done. I sincerely hope they don't guess who any of your group are, but prepare for some heavy pressure. Just play innocent. If any of y'all get fired, or threatened—physically or otherwise—tell me immediately. Sometimes the best defense is an aggressive offense and we'll make more noise than a bull about to donate to the world supply of mountain oysters."

CHAPTER 31
DOVES IN A TEMPEST

"What's past is prologue."
–William Shakespeare, *The Tempest*

Monday

The Sentinel article was published the following Monday as a special edition. It ran a full one hundred twenty-five pages and was a tour de force of journalistic brilliance. The simple title "*Doves in a Tempest*" was emblazoned the full width of the page above Molly Dugger's byline. Her treatment of the story was at once captivating and detailed, and spiced throughout with her acerbic wit. It began with a summary that immediately captured the reader's imagination, included the background, and laid the foundation for the detail that followed. This was followed by an exhaustive chronological rendition of events, and included all the documentation, along with meticulous footnotes. She named names of the villains in the story, and detailed her attempts at interviews, along with those responses she got, providing a fair but cynical interpretation of their excuses, pointing out their fabrications and the inconsistencies in their stories. It was here that her sardonic humor was at its best, calling the story from Alpen Labs "Dumber than a room full of Texas politicians," saying of the response from Bergstrom, "Bless their little hearts, that smells like a week-old stringer of catfish," and that the excuse from the Breckenridge Hospital Administration was, "Like some of their incomin' ambulance patients, Dead on Arrival."

~ ~ ~

Dugger pulled her rusty old Chevy pickup into the Hatcher driveway early Monday morning to hand deliver several copies to Jenny, thanking her profusely for the information. She also brought along the documents she had borrowed to write the stories. Jenny invited her to breakfast, but she demurred, saying the phones back at the office were ringing off the wall. After she left, Jenny, Rod, and James each grabbed a copy and started digging through it. True to her promise, Dugger had left out their names, as well as those of Dr. Smithwick and the test subjects. She had incorporated photocopies of documents, but replaced the names with "subject 1, subject 2," and so on. She included the names of those she called "the villains in this story;" the Alpen Lab board members and Johan Arndt, the bogus names she was given when she called the hospital, the Psychology Professors running the experiments, and, thanks to Becky, the names of the Air Force officers Arndt had been hobnobbing with, along with a few actual people in the Breckenridge Hospital administration. She made no mention of the children or what they had experienced; another promise she had made to Jenny.

After they had each perused the article, James begged to be allowed to deliver copies to the other children and their families. Rod found a battered old suitcase that would hold them, and helped James secure it to his bike rack, admonishing him several times to take care, until Jenny spoke up, saying, "Oh for heaven's sake Rod, let the boy go."

Anna's house was only a few blocks away, so he swung by there first. They had just finished breakfast when he knocked. Anna had volunteered to do the breakfast dishes and was elbow-deep in dishwater. Carrie was relaxing on the couch, so she opened the door for the excited James. When he pulled a copy out from the suitcase and showed it to them, Anna threw her arms around his neck and kissed him on the cheek, quickly saying, "Th-That's for Jenny, don't forget to deliver it!" It was a close call as to whose face was the reddest, and she quickly changed the subject, "Bring it over here to the table where we can all look at it."

He stopped next at Stieglitz Drugs where he dropped off a copy to Abe and Sophie, making them promise to show it to Levi as soon as possible.

His final stop was at the Lindquist home. Hal was gone to the office, but Carol cleared off a space on the kitchen table, still cluttered with the remnants of yet another breakfast misadventure, and spread the paper out there. Stevie and Mark ran in from their bedrooms to huddle around it with her. Stevie repeatedly admonished the slow reading Mark to hurry so they could turn to the next page, in a register which ensured that, sadly, they would never own a dog.

James left extra copies with Carrie to take to Dr. Smithwick, Stephen Coleman, Rose and her sister. Jenny kept an extra copy for Millie. Rod would share his copy with Brad Schwartzwald and Stan Landry. When James returned, he quickly pecked Jenny on the cheek, saying "That's from Anna, she made me promise to thank you."

"Oh, for goodness' sake, that's no way to kiss a gal." Jenny laughed, then bent in toward his terrified lips before detouring at the very last second to land a loud red smack square on the end of his nose. "I'm telling you Rod; you need to watch out for this one. He's gonna be competition for you one of these days." James' little soldier snapped to attention and saluted.

Tuesday

For the first day things remained quiet, but Tuesday morning the phone in Dr. Edward Hamm's office jarred him out of his morning revere. Hamm was Dean of Psychology, and on the other end of the line, the University of Texas President, Dr. John Rankle, raged—how in the hell was this allowed to happen? Did Hamm realize the lawsuits they would face?

The article lay open on the Dean's desk. Yes, he had seen it. No, he had not been aware, not at all. Yes, he would launch a full investigation without further delay. No, he did not know how this had happened without his knowledge, but he would find out. And on it went, Rankle shouting into the phone and Hamm groveling and stuttering monosyllabic answers. When Dr. Rankle finished his tirade and banged down the phone, a livid and flustered Hamm called for a staff meeting.

Elsewhere in the Psychology Building, the phone lines burned between professors' offices and Alpen Labs. Following one of these calls, a senior level security guard from Alpen Labs was dispatched with a wad of cash to pick up as many copies of *The Sentinel* as possible, and the one they called The Gray Man picked up his private line and dialed a certain number at Bergstrom Air Force Base.

Wednesday

By Wednesday the essence of the article was being reported in *The Austin-American Statesman's* morning edition, and the UT student newspaper, *The Daily Texan,* ran it in full. By noon KVET radio was carrying the story, and it was the lead on the nightly KTBC television news.

That morning, the speaker above Jenny's workspace came on to announce a meeting in the company cafeteria. All employees were to report there at once, with no exceptions. By the time she made her way into the lunchroom it was standing room only, as she fought to contain the acid rising in her throat. She could see Hal and Jerry standing to the side, as Jerry gave her a worried nod. A board member, a Vice President, stood at a podium at the front by the serving area. "Good morning, everyone. I will come straight to the point. You may hear some disturbing stories about Alpen Labs on the news, or read about them in the paper. Let me assure you that there is absolutely no truth to these tales. Any photocopies of documents that may accompany these articles will have been forged. Please convey this message to your friends and families. This story originated from an absolutely disreputable source; a purveyor of yellow journalism called *The Texas Sentinel*. This newspaper, and I hesitate to credit them with the term, is well known to fabricate salacious stories simply to boost their sales. The woman who authored this article is widely considered to be hysterical and an alcoholic, with no credibility whatsoever. You can be confident Alpen Labs adheres to only the highest ethical standards. We always have and we always will. You can also be confident your jobs are secure, so please ignore any rumors or reports to the contrary, and please discourage your families from spreading any rumors, especially any that might violate the confidentiality agreement you all signed before coming to work at Alpen Labs, as this agreement covers the actions of your families as well as your own. It would be tragic if any of our valued employees faced dismissal or legal consequences as a result of this shabby fabrication of a story. Please put this matter out of your minds as you return to your workplaces, and have a wonderful afternoon. Thank you all.

When lunchtime did roll around, Jenny dug the red scarf out of her supply drawer and wrapped it around her neck. That afternoon Hal and Jerry hurried in to Stieglitz Drugs to find Jenny sitting in a booth. When they sat down, Jerry dropped a nickel in the jukebox, and selected Jerry Lee Lewis rocking out on "Great Balls of Fire," to mask their whispered conversation. "What are you hearing Jenny?".

"First of all—WOW—that little nugget about the confidentiality agreement was delivered in exactly the same tone as the unsubtle warning I got from Arndt back when this all started.

These assholes sure know how to coat their threats with honey. But that's not why I asked you to come here. Do you remember those strange chemicals I told you about? The ones in the opaque jars with weird labels? This morning they were all gone, as if they had never existed. I mean, the fire destroyed most of them, but some survived and they'd been replacing the rest. The cutouts in the sorting trays were changed back to the original configuration. And rumors are flying around about layoffs and budget reductions. We'd been adding staff for several months, and now everyone's walking around on eggshells."

"We've observed changes too, some subtle and some not-so-subtle. There's suddenly renewed emphasis on completing the new chip design early. For a while it seemed like they didn't even care if we finished, but this morning the managers walked around grilling everyone about the progress they're making on their projects. Our manager ordered Jerry and I to draft a schedule by the end of business tomorrow. I asked him if we could expect any more funding cutbacks that would affect our ability to deliver, and he told us not to worry, we will be provided with all the resources we need, and if we need anything more, anything—he said it exactly like that—just to tell him, and he'll make it happen."

"Yeah, Hal's right. I told our manager I've been a little worried about my job with all the cutbacks we'd been having and he told me our jobs, Hal and I both, are considered company-critical and we have nothing to worry about. First thing this morning, I saw Arndt wandering around and caught him staring at us—then he started talking to our boss and arguing with him. Before he walked out, Arndt nodded like he was agreeing to something—that was before they told us our jobs are golden."

"My goodness, things are being shaken up. I can't wait to talk to Barb and get the scoop on what she's hearing Upstairs. Oh, and that reminds me, rumor has it Arndt is in the doghouse for letting this get out. If that Nazi gets shit-canned I'll throw the party. Remind me to buy Mollie Duggar a case of Lone Star and a bottle of JD."

Hal pulled out his wallet and handed Jenny a ten. "My contribution," he said with an uncharacteristically broad smile, "make it two bottles."

Thursday

The *Statesman* was flooded with letters to the editor by Thursday, and the call volume to KVET radio was setting records.

Breckenridge Hospital issued an immediate disclaimer, but nobody was buying it and reporters flooded their lobby. Bergstrom issued a sternly worded denial, then went silent. Dr. Rankle made an unprecedented public announcement, rife with contradictions, in which he concurrently apologized to the parents of the affected students, denied any knowledge of the incidents, denied the incidents themselves, denied any link between the coed who had committed suicide and any University actions, and promised to find any professors involved and hold them accountable. The main mall was crawling with reporters by the next day and journalists begging for interviews accosted the students.

Johan Arndt had dispatched every available security guard to the entrance gate to the lab to ensure that no journalists or curiosity seekers made it in. The optics were terrible, two rows of guards armed with military style rifles barred the entrance and dark clouds formed an ominous backdrop. The next morning the *Statesman* ran the picture above the headline, "What are They Trying to Hide?"

Austin police were dispatched to Breckenridge Hospital to turn away reporters and Nosey Nellies, a seemingly hopeless undertaking.

Bergstrom Air Force base beefed up its usual tight security to include Jeeps with mounted machine guns at all gates.

Mollie Duggar had achieved her fifteen minutes of fame, and her phone rang constantly with requests for interviews, none of which she granted, and job offers, including one from the *New York Times*. She politely refused them all, saying, "Thankee Boys, but I reckon I'll keep on a-ridin' the pony what brung me."

Friday

Edward R. Murrow wore his most stern expression as he introduced the article on the CBS evening news as the lead story, speaking in his unmistakable, carefully measured voice, "Good evening, Ladies and Gentlemen, this is Friday, the 8th of August 1958. Tonight, I'm going to deviate from the national news, and tell you about a small independent newspaper in Austin, Texas, that published an article this week which has shocked that small town, the seat of Texas government. Some very powerful people have encouraged, even threatened us, to ignore this story, but to do so would be a disservice to you, our viewers." He encapsulated the complex story into a neatly digestible, twenty-five-minute summary, uninterrupted by commercials. When he finished, he turned to look straight into the camera as it zoomed in to the tightest shot possible. "Our decision to air this segment was not taken lightly, especially since it raises grave accusations against the United States Air Force. I should tell you we contacted officials at Bergstrom Air Force Base in Austin and they categorically deny any involvement in the reported incidents. However, there is ample documented evidence, including photographs of Air Force helicopters, to support the report's veracity. If this story is true, and based on our independent investigations we believe it is, it is evidence of a rouge element within the U.S. Air Force that has disregarded the safety of young people barely out of high school, and ignored all norms of ethical behavior by our armed forces. Furthermore, it implicates one of our nation's greatest universities, a trusted community hospital, and an independent laboratory that routinely bids for top secret government contracts. We understand the fearless journalist who exposed this story has been receiving anonymous threats, as has the newspaper she works for. Some say the best protection from danger is a bright light. For as long as it is in our power, we here at CBS will continue to shine that light. We owe our viewers nothing less." He closed with his famous tagline, "Good night and good luck."

On the NBC news, John Huntley and David Brinkley enhanced their rather mundane coverage with a conversation in which they discussed whether the story was plausible, and reached no conclusion, but raised numerous questions about the organizations and individuals involved.

ABC was hesitant to lead with a story critical of the U.S. military, so John Charles Daly was instructed to treat the story as more of a curiosity rather than anything truly newsworthy. Instead, they covered the atmospheric nuclear test at Johnston Island, and the underwater transit of the North Pole by the submarine, USS Nautilus. They would come to regret this decision as the story took on national prominence, and they scrambled to catch up.

Chapter 32
End of the Lab?

Nothing is ever truly gone.
Matter is transformed into energy and energy is conserved forever.
I'm every bit as certain of this as was that Heisenberg fella.

Metamorphosis

The impact was felt immediately at Alpen Labs. They were hit by a raft of lawsuits from the families of the students who had been test subjects. Unethical lawyers fell on the Negro and Mexican communities like mosquitos swarming on the evening shore of an East Texas river, writing contracts for legal representation that ensured the bulk of the settlements would find their way into the attorneys' pockets. Eventually a prominent law firm out of New York came in and took over, merging all the lawsuits into one huge class action suit that was eventually settled out of court for $200 million, a massive settlement for the time. It was essentially a buy off to exempt Alpen Labs and Breckenridge Hospital from any culpability. The agreement further stipulated that Alpen Labs would not take part in any kind of drug experimentation and set up periodic audits of Breckenridge's case referral procedures. There was astonishingly little quibbling, Alpen Labs proved to be unexpectedly flush with cash and the settlement was complete within weeks. Those few attorneys who attempted to sue the

Bergstrom Air Force Base or U.S. Air Force on behalf of their clients saw the suits summarily dismissed for lack of evidence.

Alpen Labs was bought out within days of the settlement. The company name was changed to Texas Advanced Electronics and quickly became known as TAE. There was a corresponding shake up in management, with all but four board members dismissed and rewarded with lucrative buy-out packages, along with several five-striped managers. Oddly, the most senior board members were retained, and included Winston Overton Sinclair. Hal was promoted to five stripes, although that system of classification was replaced by more conventional titles, and Jerry was bumped up a peg as well, as the chip design they had been working on became the focus of company activities. Johan Arndt was dismissed, but used his remarkably generous severance to form an independent security firm which was subsequently hired to provide security for TAE, although Arndt stayed strictly behind the scenes.

~ ~ ~

"From the tables down at Schultz's..."
–Alpha Phi Omega, Alpha Rho chapter drinking song

"To Molly!"

"To Molly!"

"To Morry! An' don' forgeh Ashunt J! Heersch tew Ashun J!"

"To Agent J!"

"To Jenny!"

The gathering at Schultz's was boisterous, the mood upbeat. Molly Dugger was toasted over and over, as cold pitchers of Lone Star disappeared and were refilled. Even the teetotal Penelope choked down what may well have been her first beer (and second and third.) Everyone agreed, the children were doing better, and the article had been an unqualified success, with consequences beyond their wildest dreams. When the neon signs lining the walls swayed before her eyes, Carol tugged at Hal's arm.

"Harul' I shink iss timea go hom. I haff planzzz for YOU tonide Harul', an' iffiz a gurl we're gun-na nam her Mor-ry, Mor-ry Jen-di-fer Car-ra-rine." She giggled as she pointed at each lady whose name she was murdering. "An' iffiz a boy we'll nam hum Harul,' Harul' Aberhum Jerul'. Oh, an' Ro-nud-ny, can'd for-geh Ron-dud-ny. Heee can jus' hav' four namzz. Now take me hom Harul'!"

The others agreed, and began peeling off, with promises to stay in touch— "oh yes, we must get together, make a regular thing of it, after all, the children are so close." Hal downed one more longneck for the road, grabbed another to take with him, and they set out.

Rose and Dora had elected to stay home and avoid any embarrassment, but sent their thanks and congratulations. Rod had also sent his regrets, he was on a 48-hour shift at the fire station, but dispatched Jenny in his stead, as though he could have kept her away. She hung around, chatting with Molly and Jerry, and savoring that one last "roadie."

Once the others left, Molly's expression turned grim, "I didn't want to drop this turd in front of all the parents, but I need to talk to y'all about a few things that didn't add up. You asked me to leave the children out of it and I agree, it would have been unethical to expose them, even unnamed, in this explosive an article. But it didn't mean we couldn't investigate a few things. The one thing that stunk like a dead skunk was how they were affected when they made their first hike into the woods. The valley is at least four miles to the south and east of Alpen Labs as the Turkey Buzzard flies. We checked the weather from that evening, and there was a light breeze blowin' from the southeast, a typical gulf flow for Austin that time of year. So any airborne chemicals comin' from the lab would have been blown away from them. Whatever they breathed in had to come from the valley, or somewhere in their immediate vicinity. And the story that the lab had been growin' hallucinogenic plants down there and somehow burned or killed them out is as leaky as a rusty waterin' trough. That kind of plant doesn't release chemicals into the air, not over so great a distance, and not in great enough concentrations to send five kids to dreamland and linger for weeks afterward. When they were tested, their pee was as clear as a cold Lone Star and twice as pure. Everything else makes sense, but that part of the story is one for Perry Mason.

"I'm thinking the same thing. And another thing, Molly, those kids have convinced the psychologist they're magically cured. I've been watching James and I'll bet money he isn't. I'm sure some of his behavior is because he's growing up and becoming a little horn-dog, but he still zones out at times, and keeps running off to clandestine meetings with the other brats. I have no idea how to get to the bottom of what's going on with them, but I'll keep trying to figure it out. As soon as I can swing it, I'm going to reenlist at UT with a concentration on chemistry, and focus on hallucinogenic drugs. Some interesting research is going on these days and I want to get involved; if nothing else, for my own sake."

"Oh, and one more thing, Jenny, and this may be the biggest pile 'a' cow flop of them all. The way the vegetation died off in the valley the kids visited. Our research didn't uncover anything that would cause a die-off like you described. What's worse, we sent a few of our interns out there to investigate, but they couldn't even find it. They swear they went right to the spot based on the photos you gave me, but saw nothing like the photos showed. So a number of questions remain unanswered, and the answers we have seem to raise more questions."

Aftermath

Jenny was laid off, but not before receiving her portion of the legal settlement, a generous one hundred thousand dollars. She also received a severance package far beyond what her employment contract stipulated, bringing her total bank account balance to one hundred twenty-five thousand, a substantial amount of money in those days of five cent Cokes and twenty cent hamburgers, or put another way, enough for sixty-two thousand five hundred gallons of cold Lone Star at Schultz's. She put her feet up for a few days to think things over, then registered at UT on a full-time basis to pursue her degree in chemistry, with the eventual goal of hauling down a PHD.

Repairs to the secret chemical lab were halted, and the structure was torn down, returning the building to its original footprint. The press was invited out to witness the destruction, and Lab executives publicly promised to curtail any chemical experimentation. The company's public persona was transformed, and the negative press was quickly forgotten as nuclear testing continued, the space race intensified, and the Cold War dominated the news.

EPILOGUE

The respite from night terrors was, as they feared, short-lived. It was just long enough for them to convince Dr. Ardbeck that she had cured them, something she was all too willing to believe. Something she wanted, needed to believe—her ego craved it—a victory! That her belief coincided with the parents (oh, they were watching ever so carefully) seeing the evidence of nightmares fade, ensured that they believed this triumph as well. No more moaning or shouting out in the night, no more tangled bedclothes in the morning, no more "episodes" during the day. They also needed to believe; they had been so worried. Raising these gifted children was worry enough as it was. Let them get on with school, it started soon enough.

Jenny was not so sure. The effects of the drugs on her had faded, but the memory had not. Her sessions with Dr. Ardbeck were perfunctory, and she curtailed them after only a few meetings. Ardbeck assured her that her symptoms were quite different and could easily be explained by the lingering effects of a drug overdose. But that last conversation with Molly nagged at her. She was certain this was not over.

Before summer ended, the gang's nightmares had returned. Whatever this really was, it had not finished with these children.

Nor they with it.*

Look for the next volume in the
Doves in a Tempest series:

THE UNDERGROUND WORLD

PART 1
SUMMER'S END

CHAPTER 1
RETROSPECTIVE

August 20th

James awakened late after a fitful sleep. The respite from the night terrors had proved distressingly brief. In this dream the images of Betty and Jenny were joined by the quick flash of white panties when Anna flounced down on the psychiatrist's couch. That little soldier was like a chunk of petrified wood, almost painful in its physical yearning for relief.

The nightmares had begun to return for the others, as well. Slowly at first, but back full-blown all too soon. They remained convinced that whatever happened to them was not simply the result of some kind of airborne drugs, and determined to figure it out. ...

October 31, 1958
Dear Diary,
Tonight was Halloween. I got a whole grocery bag full of candy (a big one)! We went everywhere! The HI-Q gang all went together, even Georgie. He wore a big white sheet and went as a ghost so no one could tell he was a Negro. Anna said "Boy is that costume ironic." I have to ask her what she meant.

Anna said she was too old for Trick or Treat now and was only going to watch out for Georgie, but she ate as much candy as any of us!! She went as some lady named Susan B. Anthony and was made up to look like an old lady in olden days clothes. She said Susan B. Anthony helped win women the right to vote. I thought women could always vote. In our old church none of them ever did but it is a big deal at Metropolitan AME where we go now. I'm learning a lot there and it isn't all religious stuff. It mostly isn't not the really important parts. The services are so much fun, people sing and yell and sometimes they dance in the isles 'cause that church makes people feel good, not all guilty like our old church. I couldn't believe it when Mom said she wanted to start going there.

Oh, and I went as a lady hobo because that was an easy costume and didn't cost much money, we just put patches on some old jeans and James gave me an old shirt and we put some patches on it too. Then Mom smudged my face with mascara to make it look all dirty. James was a fireman, his dad got him a real uniform that fit him he is so tall he could wear one they had at the fire station. Stevie went as a scientist. He wore a white coat and carried something called a slide rule. He already had glasses. Levi went as Elvis. His aunt Sophie found him a wig somewhere and combed it like Elvis and got him a toy guitar. And Dear Diary, he looked DREAMY!

We talked about what we would do next about the flying saucer, which is what we decided to go ahead and call it (Stevie said "I told you so!"). But I'm tired, so I guess I'll have to tell you about that some other time.

Mrs. Levi Stieglitz!!!

About the Author

Bill Schweitzer lives in Austin, Texas with his beautiful wife, little faux beagle Sami (per DNA, 1/2 basset hound and a slew of other breeds, but you'd swear she's a beagle), and Sami's cat. Bill waited 73 years to write his first novel, so you know it's gotta be good.

ϞOTE FROM THE AUTHOR

Word-of-mouth is crucial for any author to succeed. If you enjoyed *Doves in a Tempest*, please leave a review online—anywhere you are able. Even if it's just a sentence or two. It would make all the difference and would be very much appreciated.

Thanks!
Bill Schweitzer

We hope you enjoyed reading this title from:

BLACK ROSE
writing™

www.blackrosewriting.com

Subscribe to our mailing list – *The Rosevine* – and receive **FREE** books, daily deals, and stay current with news about upcoming releases and our hottest authors.
Scan the QR code below to sign up.

Already a subscriber? Please accept a sincere thank you for being a fan of Black Rose Writing authors.

View other Black Rose Writing titles at www.blackrosewriting.com/books and use promo code **PRINT** to receive a **20% discount** when purchasing.

www.ingramcontent.com/pod-product-compliance
Lightning Source LLC
Chambersburg PA
CBHW050140120726
47903CB00002B/427